RAVE REVIEWS FOR JOSEPH T. KLEMPNER

FLAT LAKE IN WINTER

"Joseph T. Klempner brings a fine lyric beauty to his tale of a vicious double murder in the Flat Lake area of upstate New York . . . Klempner knows the ins and outs of homicide investigation."
—*The Atlanta Journal-Constitution*

"Told in extraordinary detail . . . The characters are well-drawn, the story well-told . . . The final chapter brings this complex story to a stunning conclusion."
—*Norfolk Virginian-Pilot*

"Klempner, a criminal defense attorney and former FBI undercover agent, writes so well that even if the story he had to tell weren't so gripping, one would still be swept along by his clear, evocative prose . . . A gem of a novel."
—*Orlando Sentinel*

"A taut, compelling yarn."
—*Omaha* (NE) *World-Herald*

"Joseph Klempner proves adept at weaving a good yarn."
—*Knoxville* (TN) *News-Sentinel*

"The book is interesting not only as a cleverly constructed mystery but as a glimpse into a profession which has been both glamorized and maligned."
—*The Chatham* (NY) *Courier*

"A thoroughly entertaining legal thriller . . . An absorbing story and an engaging cast. And the ending is a smash."
—*Kirkus Reviews*

"Klempner's delicate meditations on legal and moral responsibility, and his riveting depiction of capital case warfare, make this novel stand out."
—*Publishers Weekly*

SHOOT THE MOON

"Suspense and humor are deftly mixed in SHOOT THE MOON."
—*The San Diego Union-Tribune*

"If you are looking for a straight-out, enjoyable story you won't find one better than this . . . A fine, engaging book."
—*Rocky Mountain News*

"A cleverly executed hybrid, this feel-good thriller drops an unlikely hero, an inept but super-straight accountant-on-the-skids, into the thick of the New York City drug culture. . . . Will satisfy thrill seekers, especially those who still believe in happy endings."
—*Publishers Weekly*

"A funny, poignant novel with a menagerie of characters that could have stepped straight from the pages of Jimmy Breslin's *The Gang That Couldn't Shoot Straight*."
—William Heffernan, author of *The Dinosaur Club*

"A gripping, deeply satisfying novel . . . neatly blends suspense, tenderness, romance and humor."
—*Sullivan County Democrat*

FELONY MURDER

"Joe Klempner has made good use of his background both as an investigator and a criminal defense attorney—but it's his skill as a storyteller that makes this a book you can't put down. He's got a winner here."
—Edwin Torres, State Supreme Court Justice and author of *Carlito's Way*

"Klempner is not only a good writer, he teaches you things about the courts and the criminal justice system you'll find nowhere else."
—Robert Leuci, author of *Fence Jumpers*

"A crackling thriller . . . Klempner's fast-paced page-turner is more than entertainment . . . He writes with power, color and compassion."
—William Kunstler and Ronald L. Kuby, Attorneys-at-Law

"Deeply satisfying . . . Klempner, a New York criminal defense attorney, is a writer to watch."
—*Publishers Weekly*

"This tautly woven legal drama features enough action, tension, and romance to appeal to a wide variety of readers."
—*Booklist*

"An enjoyable, deliberately unsteady ride with just enough twists, turns, bumps and potholes to keep the reader interested, focused and clinging to the pages that will reveal the solution at the final destination."
—*New York Law Journal*

"This first novel will provide plenty of fun for conspiracy thriller fans."
—*Ellery Queen* magazine

ST. MARTIN'S PAPERBACKS TITLES
BY JOSEPH T. KLEMPNER

Felony Murder

Shoot the Moon

Flat Lake in Winter

FLAT
LAKE IN
WINTER

JOSEPH T.
KLEMPNER

St. Martin's Paperbacks

NOTE: If you purchased this book without a cover you should be aware that this book is stolen property. It was reported as "unsold and destroyed" to the publisher, and neither the author nor the publisher has received any payment for this "stripped book."

FLAT LAKE IN WINTER

Copyright © 1999 by Joseph T. Klempner.

Cover photograph by Ryan-Beyer/Stone.

All rights reserved. No part of this book may be used or reproduced in any manner whatsoever without written permission except in the case of brief quotations embodied in critical articles or reviews. For information address St. Martin's Press, 175 Fifth Avenue, New York, N.Y. 10010.

Library of Congress Catalog Card Number: 98-40887

ISBN: 0-312-97068-4

Printed in the United States of America

St. Martin's Press hardcover edition / January 1999
St. Martin's Paperbacks edition / May 2000

10 9 8 7 6 5 4 3 2 1

To the David Brucks of the world, the Andrea Lyons, the Judy Clarkes, the Kevin Doyles. They, far more than I, are the ones who continue to fight the battle. They are my heroes.

ACKNOWLEDGMENTS

My heartfelt thanks, as always, to my wife, Sandy; my children, Wendy, Ron, and Tracy; my editor, Ruth Cavin, and her assistant, Marika Rohn; my literary agent, Bob Diforio; and my circle of loyal manuscript readers.

My appreciation to my sister, Tillie Young, for medical assistance, and to Dina Vanides, for legal research.

Beyond that, I am forever in debt to my parents, Fran and Mac, who (though gone nearly twenty-five years now) continue to shape so much of who I am and what I do.

If a man is not truly his self when he acts, shall he be said to be answerable before the Crown?

Or is it not as though someone separate and apart from him has committed the offense?

—*Regina v. Hawkins*

1
THE CALL

SOME MURDER STORIES begin with noisy struggles, with blood-chilling screams in the night, with sirens wailing through city streets. But this story begins in a place called Flat Lake, a tiny smudge on the map in the middle of Ottawa County, buried deep in the heart of New York State's Adirondack Mountains. And because folks up there tend to live somewhat far apart from one another, there *are* no streets to speak of. So there were no noisy struggles heard, no blood-chilling screams in the night to wake neighbors, and no sirens to come wailing.

This story begins with a phone call.

THE CALL CAME into the Flat Lake Police Headquarters at 5:13 the morning of August 31, 1997. The title Flat Lake Police Headquarters was something of a misnomer, actually. What was grandly termed "headquarters" was in reality little more than a telephone—an old-fashioned, black rotary one, at that—sitting atop a worn oak desk that was in turn shared with the Flat Lake Town Supervisor, the Flat Lake Chamber of Commerce, and the Flat Lake Fish and Game Warden.

It being well before nine o'clock (not to mention the Sunday in the middle of Labor Day weekend), there was nobody at headquarters to hear the ringing of the telephone—not the part-time Chief of Police, nor his part-time deputy; not the Town Supervisor; not the head of the local Chamber of Commerce; and certainly not the Fish and Game Warden.

But modern technology had come to Flat Lake earlier that year, discovering it hiding in the woods of northwest Ottawa County. By some feat of electronic wizardry explained only as "call forwarding" by the telephone sales representative, the phone now ceased to ring altogether at headquarters after the first two rings, and began instead to ring at the home of the Duty Officer On Call.

Now there really was no duty officer, not in the sense of it being a real *person*, that is. The duty officer was more like a *concept*, a designation: it was simply whoever's turn it was to be the "call forwardee" when the phone rang at headquarters and there was nobody there to hear it or pick it up. Which was just about all the time.

On this particular Sunday morning, it happened that both the Chief of Police, a round, amiable fellow named Jess Markham, and his deputy were up in Quebec, camping and fishing for great northern pike. While some would wonder about this arrangement in the days and weeks to follow— the notion of the entire police force taking the weekend off—none of the locals was surprised to hear about it. For one thing, the deputy was the chief's wife, Sally; for another, they were both unpaid volunteers; and finally, most towns no longer even *had* police departments, having long since surrendered policing to the county folks. So even if Chief Markham had been around that weekend, it is highly unlikely that he would have played a significant role in the affair: he had virtually no experience with criminal investigations, and had never so much as seen a dead body, or worked a homicide case. Almost all of his duties—and those of his wife—were devoted to ceremonial matters and enforcing the town's 35-miles-an-hour speed limit.

The Town Supervisor, Walter Nash—a seventy-nine-year-old stick of a man who had held the job (also as an unpaid volunteer) for a shade under forty years—was spending the weekend visiting his sister in Tyler Falls, way down in Dutchess County. Something about a big family picnic.

As for the head of the Chamber of Commerce, there was none. Maude Terwilliger had served in that capacity ever since its inception eleven years earlier. But when a bad case of gallstones had forced Maude to retire the winter before, the position (once again a voluntary, unpaid one) had remained vacant. Not that anyone really noticed: truth was, there really wasn't any commerce in Flat Lake, except for a general store, a rod and gun shop, an outboard-engine and snowmobile dealership, a diner, a filling station, and a few women who rented out rooms on a bed-and-breakfast basis.

Thus by a simple process of elimination, Bass McClure, the equally unpaid volunteer Fish and Game Warden, had become the Duty Officer On Call for the weekend.

It should be noted that McClure's given name was not really Bass. He'd been born Brian Carlin McClure fifty-seven years earlier, right there in Flat Lake. Or at least over in Mercy Hospital, which was located in Cedar Falls, the county seat and the only town of consequence for fifty miles no matter which direction you drove. He'd taken up fishing and hunting and trapping as a youngster, pretty much to the exclusion of schoolwork, ignoring warnings from his parents and teachers that he'd never amount to anything but a "mountain man." But in the prosperity of the 1980s, he'd found a living as a guide for hunters and sport fishermen who came up from Albany, or New York City, or even Long Island, in search of largemouth bass in summer, or deer, bear, and moose in winter. People had been calling him Bass for so long that almost nobody remembered his real name any more. His driver's license identified him as Bass M. McClure; even the plate on his old Jeep Renegade read BASS 1. Cost him an extra $18 every two years for that.

As soon as he heard the phone ringing, McClure knew it had to be from headquarters, the way it rang two rings at a time, unlike an ordinary call. *Ring, ring . . . ring, ring . . . ring, ring*—He reached out in the darkness and picked it up after the third pair of rings, at the same time glancing at the red digital display of his clock radio. Five-thirteen. He shut his eyes as soon as he had the receiver in his hand, but he continued to see a red 5:13 burned into his retinas. He wondered if it would turn to 5:14 when it changed on the clock radio, or if it would stay frozen at 5:13.

"McClure," he said into the phone.

For a moment there was silence. Then a boy's voice, or perhaps a young man's. "Hello? Hello?" Urgency was McClure's first impression. Urgency, and confusion.

"Who's this?" McClure asked, coming fully awake.

"This is Jonathan Hamilton."

McClure recognized not only the name, but the voice. He'd known Jonathan almost since the boy'd been born. Knew how, ever since the death of his parents, he'd lived alone with his grandparents on the family estate, up on the north end of the lake. Even knew he'd been named after two uncles, John and Nathan.

"Hello, Jonathan. This is Bass, Bass McClure." He tried to say it in as soothing a voice as he could, sensing right away that there was something the matter, and wanting to calm the youngster.

"Hel—hello, Bass."

"Is something the matter?"

"Y-yes."

"What's the problem, Jonathan?"

"Grandpa Carter," he said. "And Grandma Mary Alice."

"What about them?" McClure found himself talking as he would to a child. Jonathan Hamilton was close to thirty years old, but he was widely known to be slow. At least that was the charitable way of putting it.

"Th-th-they're hurt?"

McClure would remember later that it was a statement, all the way until the very end, when Jonathan's voice had risen, turning it into a question.

"Hurt bad?" McClure asked.

"Bad."

"*Real* bad?"

It took a moment before McClure got a response. When he did, it was an echo of his own words, but without the inflection, and without the question.

"Real bad," Jonathan said.

IN THE INVESTIGATION that followed, Bass McClure would explain that the thought had occurred to him to call Mercy Hospital before heading over to the Hamilton place, and suggest they have an ambulance meet him there. He'd also thought about ringing up the state troopers at the barracks on Route 30. But he'd dismissed both ideas, and decided instead to go himself, without doing anything else other than slipping into his trousers and shoes, and grabbing a windbreaker. As for his car keys, they were already in the ignition of the Renegade. Flat Lake was that kind of place.

When asked why he didn't phone for backup, or at least try to raise somebody on his CB while driving, McClure could only stare back at the investigator.

"Backup? I'm not a cop. I'm a fishin' guide. What do I know about *backup*?"

It is exactly 18.2 miles by road from Bass McClure's home to the Hamilton estate. Most of the trip is by dirt road. Because there had been little in the way of rain over the last several weeks, the road was in pretty good shape, and McClure was able to push the Renegade, covering the distance in just over twenty-five minutes. He would recall later that it was already beginning to get light by the time he turned into the long driveway that led up to the main house. That would have made it right about six o'clock, working from reports of local weather observations obtained from the U.S. Department of Commerce.

McClure had been on the Hamilton estate many times over the years. He'd grown up with Porter Hamilton, who was Jonathan's father. He'd hunted and fished the land with Porter, and had been an occasional house guest of Porter and his wife, before the two of them had been asleep in separate wings of the house one night, when a fire had broken out, sending smoke pouring through the building.

The carbon monoxide that had killed Porter and his wife had landed Jonathan in the hospital for a week, and left its mark on him thereafter, causing him to be even more slow, as McClure put it, than before. Others weren't always so kind; "strange," "different," and "retarded" were some of the adjectives he'd heard used from time to time.

Porter's parents—Jonathan's grandparents—still allowed McClure the run of the property after the accident, but it had been some time since he'd taken them up on the invitation. Now, as he climbed out of the Renegade, he was struck again by the quiet beauty of the place, its stone walls and cedar buildings set back among the huge, old-growth evergreens—majestic spruce, pine, hemlock, and cedar—some of them upward of sixty feet tall.

The first building McClure came to was the gatehouse, a small structure that had never been occupied so far as he knew, and which looked dark and empty from the outside that morning. Continuing past it, he headed up the gentle incline of a pathway. He knew from having taken it numerous times that it was made of flagstone, large slabs that had been hauled in by horse-drawn wagon from a local quarry during the construction of the place, almost a hundred years ago. But the pine needles that covered the stones were by now so deep as to make the underfooting soft, and as he listened to the crunching of his steps McClure had the sensation that he was walking on bare earth, as it might have been centuries ago. This from a man born and raised in Flat Lake, who made his living off the land and knew the woods of Ottawa County as well as anyone.

About a hundred yards up, the pathway forked. To the left would be the modest guest cottage, in which Jonathan made his home; to the right the great house, the largest of the half dozen buildings that dotted the estate. Pausing for a moment at the juncture to silence the crunching noise of his footsteps, McClure looked for some hint, and listened for some sound, that might direct him to wherever the problem lay.

What he heard was a soft moaning sound, a keening that

at first he thought had to be coming from a small animal. In years past, McClure had done some trapping. The sound he heard now reminded him more than anything else of the cry of a coyote with its leg caught in a snare. It was plaintive, but no longer urgent, as though the animal had been like that for some time—past the initial surprise and panic at its capture, it had settled down to a steady crying over the permanence of its predicament.

McClure cocked his head back and forth, the way a deer might do, giving each ear a chance to locate the source of the sound, in order to get a fix on it. It was early enough that the wind wasn't up yet, so there was no creaking of tree trunks or rustling of branches to throw him off. He became aware for the first time of the chirping of birds greeting the new daylight, but their sounds were high-pitched, different enough to filter out without difficulty.

The moaning was definitely coming from his right, the direction of the main house. Walking rapidly—McClure was not a man who ran—he followed the right fork until it brought him out into the clearing that surrounded the house. The light was much better there, without the canopy of overhead branches that had blocked out the sky along the pathway. And there, sitting on the front steps, hunched over with his arms wrapped tightly around his rib cage, rocking forward and back almost imperceptibly, was Jonathan Hamilton. And though Jonathan's mouth was closed and his lips didn't appear to be moving, McClure could tell that the moaning sound was coming from somewhere deep inside him.

Because Jonathan didn't appear to notice McClure—and because McClure didn't want to startle him—McClure spoke as he approached, from about twenty paces away. "Hello, Jonathan," he said.

Jonathan didn't say anything at that point, McClure would later write in his report, but he did look up. His eyes had a "faraway look," according to McClure, and he seemed to be in a state of shock or "unawareness." Unsure that Jonathan had recognized him, McClure identified himself.

"It's me," he said. "Bass."

Still, Jonathan gave no indication of real recognition, and continued to sit—and rock—even when McClure walked right up to him. At that point, McClure could see what looked like blood on Jonathan's forehead.

"What happened?" McClure asked him.

Though Jonathan said nothing, he took his arms from around his upper body and, elbows bent, extended his hands in front of him in such a way that the palms were turned upward, as though to indicate that he didn't know. McClure could see right away that there was blood—or what appeared to be blood—on both hands. Laboratory tests would later confirm that it was indeed human blood, as were stains under the arms of the flannel shirt he had on, apparently left there when Jonathan had wrapped his own arms around his body.

"Stand up," McClure said in a firm voice, trying to bring Jonathan out of his stupor.

Jonathan did as he was told. McClure—himself a shade over six feet tall—was struck by Jonathan's height: he found himself looking up into the other man's eyes, which were a good three or four inches above the level of his own. And, as his report would later indicate, Jonathan was barefoot at the time.

McClure nodded toward the inside of the house. "Show me," he said.

ROUTE 30 IS one of New York State's longest roads, aside from the Thruway system itself. It begins in the south-central crook of the state, where the east branch of the Delaware River has created a trout fisherman's haven on the New York and Pennsylvania line, amid towns given names like Fishs Eddy, Hale Eddy, Long Eddy, and East Branch. From there it meanders northeast, before turning pretty much due north at Margaretville, føllowing the east branch until it becomes the Schoharie, winding its way up past Grand Gorge, Cobbleskill, Schenectady, Johnstown, and Gloversville. As though motivated by thirst, it continues up the west shore of Great Sacandaga Lake, finds Lake Pleasant, Indian Lake, Blue Lake, Long Lake, and Lake Eaton, before entering Ottawa County. As it continues ever northward, it will take the traveler to Tupper Lake, Raquette Pond, the Saranac Lakes, Meacham Lake, the Deer River Flow, and Lake Titus, before crossing the Salmon River at Malone, some 270 miles from where it began. As though bowing to some symmetry in nomenclature, it ends at the Canadian border almost as it began, at a fishing town called Trout River.

Nowhere, however, does Route 30 cut through more spectacular country than it does in Ottawa County, simply because no part of New York—which can be an awesomely beautiful state—is more magnificent than the old-growth forests of Ottawa County, deep in the heart of the Adirondack range. The steep terrain, the harsh climate, and the sheer remoteness of the place have conspired to give it a pristine, almost primitive grace. Crystal-clear streams, lakes, and ponds are framed by ancient, towering conifers with hues that range from pale blue-gray, through ever-darkening shades of green, to almost black. Against them, the delicate lines of white birch offer stark contrast. And with no serious source of air pollution for hundreds of miles to the west, the sky can take on a blue that is nothing short of dazzling.

Amid all this splendor, someone has decided to erect the barracks to house Troop J of the New York State Police, presumably selecting the location on Route 30 not so much for the beauty of the place, but for its proximity to the two main east-west highways that cut through the region, Route 3 to the north, and Route 28 to the south. Yet even the barracks fit into the surrounding landscape, constructed as they are from local stone and timber, and protected by natural stains, with a minimum of glass showing, so as to keep the cold at bay.

The Sunday morning before Labor Day was traditionally

a quiet time at the barracks, and there was every expectation that it would be that way this year. What traffic there was (and there was never very much to speak of) would be spread out over the three-day weekend, with the bulk of it coming on Monday, as vacationers pulled their tents or packed their trailers and headed back downstate. It was the end of summer: already too late for swimming and fishing, but still too early for the turning of leaves. And hunting season was two months away; not even the bow hunters were due for another six weeks.

That particular Sunday morning found three officers at the barracks—two troopers and one investigator (a title the equivalent of that of detective). When the call came in at 0618 military time, one of the troopers, a young man named Edward Manning, was the only one of the three who was awake. He picked up the phone on the second ring.

"Troop J, Manning," he said.

"This is Bass McClure," the voice on the phone said. "I need to speak to the senior investigator on duty."

It turns out Trooper Manning had met McClure, but only once; when the call came in, he couldn't quite place the name. Nonetheless, there was something about McClure's voice that prompted Manning to take the request seriously. It wasn't a sense of urgency, so much, he'd explain later; it was more an air of authority.

"Hold on," Manning said. Then he went into the bunk room and roused the investigator, Deke Stanton.

Deke Stanton's real name was Dwight Kirkbride Stanton. The Dwight Kirkbride portion had given way in high school to D.K.; eventually that had yielded to Deke. At thirty-three Stanton was a rising star in the state police ranks. In a system that prided itself on its paramilitary trappings, he carried himself with the bearing of the former marine he was, from his crew cut to his chiseled facial features, down his lean, athletic build and erect posture, all the way to his spit-shined shoes.

Stanton came to attention as soon as Manning put a hand

on his shoulder and spoke his name. "What's up?" he
asked.

"I've got a fellow named McClure on the horn, sir. Says
he needs to speak with the senior investigator. Sounds important."

"Bass McClure?" Stanton asked. He knew McClure,
having worked a couple of small-time poaching cases with
him. Deer out of season, counterfeit fishing licenses, stuff
like that.

"Yes, sir."

"I'll be right there."

The conversation between Bass McClure and Deke Stanton lasted less than two minutes, from 0620 to 0622. It was
preserved in its entirety by the automatic recording device
that had been installed on the barracks phone, and later
became known as "The Call."

STANTON: Stanton here.
MCCLURE: Mornin, Deke. This is Bass McClure.
           Sorry to bother you so early.
STANTON: That's okay, What do you have?
MCCLURE: Two dead bodies and a mess of blood.

McClure had never been one to waste words. But in this
particular case, his brevity would throw Stanton off for a
moment.

STANTON: What kind of bodies? Deer?
MCCLURE: Ah, no. Human kind.
STANTON: Christ. What's your Ten-twenty?
MCCLURE: Say what?
STANTON: Where are you?
MCCLURE: Up at the old Hamilton estate, north
           end of Flat Lake.
STANTON: Do you have an ID on the DOAs?
MCCLURE: They're the Hamiltons. Were.
STANTON: Christ.

There is a pause in the conversation at this point, as though Stanton is thinking something over. But the pause lasts only four seconds before Stanton continues. It would seem that, even from some fifty-five miles away, he needed no more time than that to decide who the likely killer was.

STANTON: Who did them? The boy?

There is no pause at all before McClure answers him. In spite of the fact that Jonathan Hamilton was twenty-eight years old at the time, there apparently was no doubt in McClure's mind that he was the one to whom Stanton was referring when he used the term "the boy." Nor did there appear to be any hesitancy in McClure's own willingness to conclude that Jonathan had indeed been the one who "did them."

MCCLURE: Seems so.
STANTON: Okay, okay. Don't touch anything. I'm on my [inaudible] way.

WHEN BASS MCCLURE said, "Show me," to Jonathan Hamilton, Jonathan nodded once. Then he turned and walked up the steps leading into the greathouse, with Mc- Clure following him. As they entered the front hallway, McClure switched on the lights. He wasn't looking for any- thing in particular, he would explain later; he was only interested in illuminating the interior so as to avoid bump- ing into things and possibly disturbing or destroying evi- dence. But as soon as the lights were on, he saw what appeared to be bloodstains on the floor. And the stains told him a story that struck him as almost comical in its obvi- ousness. The largest of them were in the shape of bare feet, *large* bare feet. From the direction of the footprints and the way in which they gradually faded, it was clear that the person who had left them had come down the stairs, walked to a small table containing a lamp and a telephone, before continuing to and out the same door through which Jonathan and McClure had just entered. In addition to the footprints, there were numerous drops. The pattern of the drops was different from that of the footprints: they came from the stairs, too, but then led directly to the door, without making a detour for the table.

Upon noticing the stains, McClure grasped Jonathan by the elbow. He did this, he would explain later, not to restrain Jonathan in any way, but simply to steer him clear of the stains, so as to preserve them for future examination. At the same time, he looked down at Jonathan's feet, making a mental note that they were both bare and large. Then, with McClure guiding Jonathan in front of him by applying gentle pressure to his elbow, they climbed the stairs, hugging the wall to avoid both the stains on the steps and the banister, the polished wood of which McClure instinctively knew would be an ideal surface to test for fingerprints.

The top of the stairs held no mystery for McClure. The footprints, increasingly clearer, led to—or, more accurately, led *from*—the second of three doorways off to the left. As they neared the open doorway, McClure felt Jonathan's body gradually stiffen and resist, and McClure complied with what he took to be Jonathan's unstated but clear desire to go no farther by steering him past the doorway, where there were no visible stains, and motioning him to stay there. Then McClure stepped through the doorway and into the room, again flicking on the light switch.

Bass McClure had always thought of himself as a pretty tough guy. In his day he'd pulled bloated bodies out of lakes, and mangled ones out of car wrecks. He'd gutted deer so freshly killed that their entrails steamed when exposed to the cold air. Once he'd come upon the body of a fallen climber and mistook the man for being alive, until he realized that the twitching movements were actually being caused by the infestation of maggots beneath the skin. But nothing McClure had ever seen—nothing—prepared him for the sight that greeted him in the room he had just entered. He gagged audibly and, he would readily admit later, came dangerously close to vomiting.

The two bodies lay on the huge bed at right angles to each other, forming a T. Although the enormous amount of blood obscured most of the individual puncture wounds, McClure could see enough to tell that both victims had had their heads nearly severed. The blood was still shiny and sticky-looking where it had pooled most thickly; elsewhere it appeared dried and almost black. Cluster flies had begun to congregate, and were buzzing loudly as they competed for choice feasting sites.

It was only because McClure already knew that the bodies had to be those of Carter and Mary Alice Hamilton, Jonathan's grandparents, that he was able make a tentative identification and would be able to tell Deke Stanton who they were when he walked Jonathan back downstairs and used the phone on the table to call the state police barracks. By that time, McClure would recall, Jonathan was visibly trembling. McClure took the trembling for shivering, and surmised that Jonathan was cold, either from fear or the early morning chill.

"C'mon, Jonathan," he said. "Let's get some shoes on you, warm you up a bit." And, putting an arm around the young man's shoulders, he led him out of the house and down the path to the guest cottage, where (as McClure knew) Jonathan lived.

McClure would eventually come in for a good bit of criticism for his handling of the situation. Yes, he would admit, he probably shouldn't have used the same phone that Jonathan himself had apparently used earlier that morning. Yes, he shouldn't have used the same pathway from the greathouse to the cottage, knowing that doing so would make it difficult—if not altogether impossible—to distinguish Jonathan's second set of barefoot-prints from those he might have made earlier. And yes, he shouldn't have let Jonathan put shoes and socks on, seeing as the investigators would no doubt be interested in examining the bottoms of Jonathan's feet before they could be wiped clean.

But McClure did all of these things. When asked why, he would later shrug and say, "I'm not a police officer."

And when that explanation didn't seem to satisfy anybody, he would open up a bit, something Bass McClure didn't do very often. "As far as I could see, it was a no-brainer. Everything about the scene had the boy's name written all over it. Way I saw it, in an hour's time, they were going to come lock him up and take him away, put him in a cage for the rest of his life. Figured the least I could do was to make him warm for that hour."

2

TAKIN' NINERS

BEFORE LEAVING THE barracks, Deke Stanton roused Hank
Carlson, the other trooper who'd been asleep when the call
had come in. Leaving Trooper Manning to handle the radio
and phones, Stanton and Carlson suited up, grabbed evidence kits, and jumped into their cruiser. They were on the
road—according to their own log entry—by 0634, just
twelve minutes after the completion of Stanton's conversation with Bass McClure. As they headed north, with Stanton at the wheel, Carlson radioed back to Manning,
instructing him to try to reach their commanding officer,
Captain Roger Duquesne, at home, and apprise him of the
situation, and to call Mercy Hospital and have them send
a bus to the Hamilton place. A "bus" is universal police
jargon for ambulance. Carlson—no doubt at Stanton's direction—also told Manning to notify the Franklin County
Medical Examiner's Office to dispatch an investigator to
the scene and expect two cases sometime around midafternoon. Ottawa County had no medical examiner of its
own: there simply weren't enough suspicious or unexplai-
ned deaths during the course of a year to warrant budgeting
for one.

With Route 30 all but deserted early that Sunday morning, Stanton drove with his headlights on and his roof lights
flashing, but without his siren. He kept the speedometer at
a pretty level 85 on the straightaways, slowing for turns.

He would have gone even faster, he explained later, but was on the lookout for the most common, and most dangerous, road hazard likely to be encountered at that hour: the four-legged variety. Hit a deer while you were doing 90, and your car was history, he knew; hit a moose and you were, too.

Leaving Route 30 for county roads that became progressively less paved, Stanton had to slow down considerably. As he turned onto Flat Lake Road, the asphalt gave way to hard-packed dirt, and for the last few miles he rode his brake with his left foot while working the accelerator with his right. Even so, he wasn't able to make as good time as Bass McClure had earlier that morning: despite an overabundance of horsepower, the low clearance and automatic transmission of the cruiser made it no match for the Renegade.

By the time Stanton and Carlson arrived, it was somewhere around seven-thirty. There would be some disagreement as to the exact time, with Stanton placing it at 0724, while McClure insisted that he'd looked at his watch at one point and noticed it was seven-forty, and the cruiser was still nowhere in sight. That wouldn't be the only point of contention to arise between the two men, who had little in common and had always been a bit wary of each other. Stanton's spit-and-polish military bearing struck McClure as a silly affectation; he saw no reason for a by-the-book approach to every little detail, when common sense and native intuition generally cut to the heart of things much more quickly. Stanton, for his part, regarded McClure as a seat-of-the-pants amateur, with little technical knowledge regarding the preservation of a crime scene. The truth is, that when it came to their criticisms of one another, they were both pretty much on target.

McClure came out of the guest cottage with Jonathan Hamilton, and met Stanton and Carlson on the pathway. As Stanton would learn, this marked at least the second trip Jonathan had been permitted to make on the path since McClure's arrival: first in bare feet, and now in shoes.

"Is he in your custody?" Stanton asked McClure, nodding at Jonathan and dispensing with so much as a greeting.

"Custody?" McClure replied. "It's not like I caught him takin' niners." "Niners," were bass under ten inches, which had to be released.

"Where are the DOAs?" Stanton asked.

McClure pointed in the direction of the path that led to the greathouse. "Main house," he said. "Second floor."

Stanton asked McClure to accompany him, motioning Carlson to stay with Jonathan. "Don't let him out of your sight," he instructed the trooper, "and don't let him touch anything." In his initial report, Stanton would write that the subject (meaning Jonathan) appeared agitated, nervous, and unwilling to make eye contact with any of the other men.

Instead of walking on the flagstones of the pathway, Stanton insisted that he and McClure walk alongside them, in the ivy and pachysandra that bordered them. To McClure, this precaution seemed no better than a tradeoff, risking the contamination of one area for that of another. But he said nothing.

At the greathouse, Stanton took pains to avoid disturbing anything, donning rubber gloves before entering, being careful to avoid stepping on visible bloodstains, and disturbing nothing that might prove to have evidentiary value. When McClure led him to the second-floor doorway, Stanton poked his head in and studied the sight that greeted him. He said nothing, nodding rather nonchalantly. But McClure was certain he saw the investigator swallow hard several times and turn nearly white.

While McClure waited in the hallway, Stanton entered the room and looked about. It was the first of four visits he would make to the crime scene that morning, returning to take blood samples, photographs, and measurements; to dust for latent fingerprints; and to take an inventory of every item in the room. To McClure's way of thinking, all of those things could have been accomplished on a single visit. He suspected that Stanton was having some difficulty remaining in the room, but again he said nothing.

By the time Stanton was finished, an ambulance from Mercy Hospital had arrived. Stanton let the EMTs observe the bodies from the doorway, but wouldn't let them into the room itself until the medical examiner's investigator had arrived, which took another half hour. When she did arrive ("she" being a rather striking redhead who couldn't have been more than twenty-five by McClure's guess), she needed less than ten minutes to do whatever it was she needed to—or perhaps she, too, wanted to be out of the room as soon as possible. She moved the bodies gingerly, bagged the hands with plastic and tape, and took rectal temperatures with separate thermometers. She reported Carter Hamilton's as 92.6°, and Mary Alice Hamilton's as 92.2°. She told Stanton that, given the room temperature and the fact that the bodies were pretty much uncovered, the numbers suggested that the deaths had occurred some six to eight hours earlier, or sometime between one and three in the morning.

"What was the weapon?" Stanton asked her.

"The weapon—or weapons," she said pointedly, "will probably turn out to be some kind of hunting knife or knives. You'll have to wait for the post."

Finally, Stanton let the EMTs come into the room. Although by law they didn't have the authority to pronounce the victims dead, no one raised an objection when they placed them in body bags. There may have been some disagreement about time of occurrence, contamination of evidence, and number of weapons, but nobody had any doubts about the fact that Carter and Mary Alice Hamilton were good and dead.

ONLY AFTER THE bodies had been transported off in the ambulance, and the ME's investigator had driven her own car back down the dirt road, did Deke Stanton turn his attention back to Jonathan Hamilton. Instructing Trooper Carlson to secure the crime scene—including the great-house, the guest cottage, and the pathway that connected them—with yellow plastic tape, he addressed Jonathan for the very first time. By then it had been roughly an hour and a half since Stanton's arrival.

"Come on over here, son," he said.

Jonathan, who had been sitting on a tree stump under Trooper Carlson's watchful gaze until that time, looked up uncertainly.

"Yes, you," Stanton said.

As McClure watched from perhaps ten feet away, Jonathan rose slowly and walked toward Stanton. When he got within arm's length, Stanton stopped him by holding up a hand. To McClure, it seemed as though Stanton, who was about five-ten, was a bit put off by Jonathan's height.

"What happened here, son?" Stanton asked.

Jonathan shrugged and said, "I d-don't know."

The sun was up by this time, and Stanton was wearing aviator-style sunglasses, the kind with mirrored lenses. He kept them on as he spoke. "I think you do," he said. "Your granddaddy and grandma are upstairs in the main house. They say you cut them. All I want to know is why you did it. I know there must have been a good reason."

McClure was surprised at the transparency of Stanton's ploy. If Jonathan had indeed committed the crime—and McClure had little doubt that he had—surely he knew that the victims were in no condition to tell Stanton anything. But then again, maybe nothing was transparent to Jonathan.

When Jonathan said nothing, Stanton repeated himself. "Tell me why you did it," he said.

Both McClure and Stanton would later agree that those were the investigator's words: *"Tell me why you did it."* It was their recollections of Jonathan's response that would differ. McClure would recall that Jonathan replied, "I don't know what happened." Stanton would write in his report that all Jonathan said was, "I don't know."

The two men would also disagree on precisely what happened next. According to Stanton's report, the investigator asked Jonathan if he'd be willing to take a ride with him down to his office to answer a few questions, and Jonathan said he would. As McClure would remember it, Stanton simply took Jonathan by the upper arm, led him down the pathway to the cruiser, and placed him in the backseat. Both men would agree that Jonathan was not handcuffed at that point.

It is unclear exactly what Stanton had in mind next. He'd closed the back door of the cruiser and walked around to the driver's-side door. It appeared to McClure that the investigator was about to get behind the wheel and drive off with Jonathan, leaving Trooper Carlson behind to safeguard the crime scene. But doing so—driving off alone with an unhandcuffed suspect—would have been in direct violation of state police regulations, notwithstanding the fact that the cruiser was outfitted with a wire partition that divided the front seat from the back. And Stanton certainly considered Jonathan to be a suspect, or more precisely *the* suspect, particularly given his later version of Jonathan's statement to the effect that he didn't know why he'd killed his grandparents.

But before Stanton could do whatever it was he was about to do, the relative silence was broken by the sound of sirens approaching in the distance. Within a minute or so, an entourage of four vehicles pulled up the driveway, two with roof lights flashing, one with the wail of its siren winding down. The first three were state police cruisers: two of them similar in appearance to the one in which Stanton and Carlson had arrived, the third one unmarked. The fourth vehicle was a sport-utility model of some sort, either a Ford Explorer or a Toyota 4-Runner.

A beefy, red-faced man in civilian clothes stepped out of the lead car and looked around. After a moment, he spotted Deke Stanton and ambled over to him. McClure could hear Stanton greet him as "Captain" before they huddled; he couldn't pick up their conversation. After a few minutes, they stepped apart, and it became apparent to McClure that the captain (who was most certainly Roger Duquesne, although later reports referred to him only as "the responding supervising officer") had drawn up a plan of sorts. He would lead the way in his cruiser, with Stanton,

Carlson, and the prisoner (McClure distinctly heard him refer to Jonathan Hamilton as "the prisoner") following him in a second car. But rather than driving south back to the Troop J barracks, they would head over to Northeast Regional Headquarters in Saranac Lake, where the facilities were larger, and where the interrogation room was fitted with a recording device and a two-way mirror. The four other investigators, who had arrived in the remaining two cruisers, would stay behind and complete the crime-scene investigation.

As for the remaining car, the sport-utility vehicle, it turned out that it belonged to a newspaper reporter. She'd picked up the radio traffic on her police scanner and had been heading to the scene when the convoy of cruisers had sped past him. She fell in line, matching their speed, figuring correctly that, under the circumstances, they had better things to do than pull her over and ticket her. The name of the reporter was Stefanie Grovesner, and she worked for the *Daily Record*, up in Plattsburgh.

By that afternoon, news of the double murder and the arrest of Jonathan Hamilton would begin to spread across the state and into neighboring Vermont and Canada. By evening, local affiliates would have picked up the story. To most of the viewers who caught it on the ten o'clock news, it was just another grisly crime, made a bit more interesting because of the remote rustic setting, and the fact that the suspect was the grandson of the victims. Only Chuck Scarborough of NBC's *Channel 4 News* down in New York City, would point out the true significance of the story: Because it was a double murder, it meant that the perpetrator would be eligible for the death sentence under New York's recently revived capital-punishment murder statute.

3

DOYLE

THE TOWN OF SARANAC Lake straddles the line between Franklin and Essex Counties, in the northeastern corner of New York State. For the traveler, it is equidistant from the Canadian border to the north, and Burlington, Vermont, across Lake Champlain to the east. For the serious hiker, it affords a stopover between the Adirondack Mountains that stretch to the southwest, and the Alder Brook Range that reaches up toward the northeast. It is surrounded by hundreds of lakes and ponds with names that only hint at their beauty: Placid, Rainbow, Clear, Silver, Wolf, Buck, Loon, and Fern.

According to an entry in Deke Stanton's *Daily Activity Log*, he arrived at State Police Headquarters in Saranac Lake with his "suspect" Jonathan Hamilton at 1225 hours, or twelve twenty-five that Sunday afternoon. There is no mention in the log of Captain Duquesne's having accompanied them, let alone having driven them. From 1245 to 1350, Stanton processed his suspect. "Processed" is a term usually reserved for what an arresting officer does with a prisoner, not a *suspect*: taking fingerprints and photographs, and asking "pedigree" questions—the individual's full name, address, date and place of birth, type of employment, and related information. Processing is an activity that can normally be accomplished in twenty minutes or so.

Although the facilities at Saranac Lake included a state-of-the-art interrogation room, complete with an audio-video recording device hidden behind a two-way mirror, it was not unusual for an investigator to conduct a "pre-interview session" with a subject in a smaller room, without benefit of any recording equipment. In the case of Jonathan Hamilton, Stanton did just that: he sat down and talked with Jonathan for a while in a small room. Because only the two of them were present, no one but Jonathan would ever be able to dispute Stanton's subsequent recollection of what questions were asked during the session, and what answers were given.

According to Stanton's account, Jonathan initially admitted killing his grandparents in a "rage," stabbing first his grandfather, then his grandmother, as the two of them slept together on the bed in their room. Asked why he had killed them, Jonathan replied that his grandparents had been "mean" to him, and had treated him "like a little boy," something that had made him "so frustrated" that he had finally "lost it" and "couldn't take any more of them." As Stanton pressed Jonathan for more details, however, Jonathan "clammed up," at one point saying that "Mr. Bass" had told him he didn't have to answer questions until they gave him a lawyer. This last point would serve to drive a wedge between Stanton and McClure that continues to exist to this very day. Publicly McClure insists that he never gave Jonathan such advice, and speculates that if Jonathan indeed said it, he must have misunderstood McClure, and certainly misquoted him. But there can be little doubt that McClure liked Jonathan and felt sorry for him that morning, and, in the minds of some observers, it doesn't overly strain credulity to believe that Stanton may have been telling the truth here.

In any case, Stanton appears to have concluded processing Jonathan at that point, or shortly thereafter. According to his log, Jonathan was still a suspect, meaning he hadn't yet been formally arrested. Stanton would later contend that Jonathan wasn't even in custody, and was therefore free to leave had he wanted to. But the notion that Stanton would have let Jonathan get up and walk out the door after admitting a double murder is unthinkable. Far more likely is the conclusion that, in Stanton's mind, as long as he didn't formally arrest Jonathan, he could continue to question him without the necessity of giving him his *Miranda* rights.

Later that afternoon, Stanton brought Jonathan to the interview room and seated him at a table in such a way that Jonathan was facing where the interviewer would be sitting, as well as the mirror that concealed the hidden video camera. Stanton then locked the door from the outside (an act that arguably sheds some light on the issue of whether or not Jonathan was free to leave) while he rounded up a video technician and a second investigator, Phillip Manley, to sit in on the interview.

As the tape begins, Jonathan can be seen sitting at the table in what can only be described as a daze. His hair is uncombed and his face unshaven. The wooden chair in which he sits has arms and has been pulled all the way up to the table, the way court officers seat an incarcerated defendant at trial. But Jonathan's hands are visible from time to time, and it is obvious that he isn't handcuffed. On the desk, conspicuously facing the camera, is a large clock. The camera zooms in on the face of the clock, which shows the time to be three-fourteen. The camera pans back, then closes in on Jonathan's face. Other than a smudge of dried blood across his forehead, there is no sign of injury of any sort.

Stanton begins the interview by identifying himself, Investigator Manley, and Jonathan for the record. He gives the date, time, and place. He states that they are there to discuss "an incident" that happened earlier that morning, down at Flat Lake. He then proceeds to administer the *Miranda* rights to Jonathan, advising him that he has a right to remain silent, a right to an attorney, and a right to have an attorney appointed free of charge if he can't afford one. Next he tells Jonathan that anything he says may be used against him in a court of law. After each warning, Stanton asks Jonathan if he understands; Jonathan says the word "yes" four times in response, softly but distinctly. Finally he asks if Jonathan is willing to answer some questions without a lawyer.

Jonathan's response is given so softly that one has to turn the volume all the way up to hear it. Even then, it is almost impossible to make out, and the tape may have to be rewound and played several times for the listener to catch it. It is only when one *knows* the words one is listening for that they become apparent. What Jonathan says is this: "I—I—I still think I want a l-l-lawyer."

Under the law, these are magic words. By invoking his right to counsel, a suspect effectively ends an interrogation. Stanton, quick to recognize that this is what has happened, terminates the interview immediately, at 1521 hours, or 3:21 P.M., seven minutes after it has begun. The tape goes black.

In retrospect, Jonathan's response would seem to raise far more questions than it answers. First, given Jonathan's limited, almost primitive understanding of the questioning process—and his complete lack of familiarity with the legal system, which he had never encountered before—it is highly doubtful that the decision to invoke his right to counsel was his own. During the preliminary questioning regarding the rights, Jonathan replied directly four times, each time in a normal voice, giving no hint that he would suddenly refuse to answer when it comes to substantive questions. Second, there is the little matter of the word *still*: "I *still* think I want a lawyer." Had Jonathan told Stanton earlier that he wanted a lawyer, and had Stanton ignored the request? That is certainly one possibility, though those who knew Jonathan Hamilton best have great difficulty accepting that scenario, given Jonathan's limited resources and his history of compliance. They argue that for Jonathan to have asked for a lawyer at *any* point, someone must have planted the seed in his mind. Had Bass McClure made the suggestion? McClure vehemently denies it.

There remains yet another possibility. As an investigator, Deke Stanton had earned a reputation as something of a bulldog. He was energetic and tenacious, and certainly wasn't above cutting a corner or two in order to get a result. Witness, for example, his apparent readiness to violate regulations by driving off alone with Jonathan from the crime scene earlier that day. Yet Stanton's willingness to terminate the interview the moment Jonathan almost inaudibly asked for a lawyer borders on eagerness.

Could it be that Stanton himself had moments before coached Jonathan into asking for a lawyer? Remember that Stanton already had a confession of sorts from Jonathan, albeit one that wasn't preserved on tape or witnessed by anyone other than Stanton. Was Stanton for some reason afraid that Jonathan would deny the crime on camera, thereby casting doubt on Stanton's account of the earlier statement? And if he *was* afraid, what does that say about the reliability of his account?

FOLLOWING THE TERMINATION of the aborted videotaped interview, the next entry in Deke Stanton's log is at 1530, or 3:30 P.M., and reads simply: "Subject arrested." After that there is a one-hour period, from 1530 to 1630, devoted to "further processing of prisoner." Just what this could have been is unclear. Combined with the earlier "processing of suspect," it means that Stanton had devoted two hours and five minutes to activities that should have taken no more than twenty minutes. In other words, either Stanton was deliberately misrepresenting his entries, or by four-thirty that afternoon, Jonathan Hamilton had become the most thoroughly processed person in New York State.

Even giving Stanton the benefit of the doubt here, once the processing was completed, it was incumbent upon him to take steps to see that his prisoner was brought before a judge or magistrate "without unreasonable delay," according to the New York Criminal Procedure Law. Now the term "without unreasonable delay" is more than a little vague, and that is probably not by accident. The legislature has apparently recognized, and wisely so, that what is reasonable in a major metropolitan city may be totally unfeasible in a sparsely populated upstate region. In New York County, for example, one part of the Criminal Court routinely operates until one A.M. just to conduct initial appearances; on Fridays and Saturdays they work around the clock. For a person arrested in Manhattan, therefore, "reasonable" means within twenty-four hours. For Jonathan Hamilton, who had been arrested either in Flat Lake or Saranac Lake, depending upon how you looked at it, "reasonable" was going to be something altogether different.

The crimes Jonathan was accused of committing had occurred in Flat Lake. But Flat Lake is so small that it doesn't even have a local town or justice court. That means that, in a case involving felony charges such as murder, the initial appearance has to take place in either the nearest town or justice court in the county, or at the Ottawa County Courthouse. In this particular case, those happened to be one and the same. The only problem was that it was Sunday, and the following day was Labor Day, which was a court holiday, meaning there could be no court appearance at all until Tuesday morning.

But surely a system is unfair if it keeps people who have the misfortune to be arrested Saturday or Sunday (or even Friday evening) locked up all weekend without recourse, particularly if their offense is a relatively minor one. So over time, a process has evolved in such situations whereby the arresting officer notifies whatever county or local prosecutor he can find, by the simple device of calling one at home. Failing that, the officer may call a town or village justice, or a county judge, also at home. The officer proceeds to explain the situation, and the prosecutor or justice makes an on-the-spot determination whether to authorize the outright release of the prisoner pending his appearance Monday morning, or sets an amount of bail that has to be posted first. If the prisoner is affluent and fortunate enough to reach a lawyer, then counsel can get in on the act, too.

Occasionally there are situations where the great likelihood is that bail will be prohibitively high, or the prisoner will be held in remand, meaning he won't be entitled to bail at all. Jonathan Hamilton's case certainly fell into that category. But even in such instances, the arresting officer still has an obligation to make the notification. Furthermore, where the crime is a serious felony (and a double murder is that and more), a state police officer is bound by departmental regulations to confer with the county prosecutor as soon as practically possible.

According to Deke Stanton's next log entry, he did precisely that, reaching the Ottawa County District Attorney by telephone at home at ten minutes before five o'clock Sunday afternoon. Stanton's next entry purports to contain the results of that conversation:

1650   Reached D. A. Cavanaugh by phone at his residence. Advised to book prisoner on 2 counts Murder One and lodge at County pending court appearance 0900 9/2/97. Status: Remand.

There seems to be little reason why Stanton should have written those words, were they untrue. Certainly, his actions immediately thereafter are consistent in every way with the entry: He and another investigator drove Jonathan Hamilton, who was by that time in handcuffs, to Cedar Falls, and brought him to Ottawa County Jail. According to the *Sign-In Book*, Jonathan was received at 1817 hours, or 6:17 that evening. His charge was listed as "Murder 1st" and his disposition as "County Ct, 09-02-97, 0900, Part 1."

On the other hand, if you talk to Gil Cavanaugh, he didn't hear about the Flat Lake murders and the arrest of Jonathan Hamilton until sometime Monday afternoon.

FRANCIS GILMORE CAVANAUGH, Jr., is, and has been for close to twenty years, the District Attorney of Ottawa County. Pushing sixty at the time of the Hamilton murders, he is tall, good-looking, and silver-haired. He has a ready smile and a handshake so firm that it borders on the painful.

Only the slightly pronounced veins in his nose give away the fact that, in addition to being a career politician and prosecutor, he is also something of a career drinker. He knows everybody there is to know in the county, and in just about all of upstate New York, for that matter. He plays golf with the state senators, representatives, and judges in the summer, hunts with them in autumn, and skis with them in winter. He trades war stories with the best of them, though he has the reputation of being a better talker than he is a listener. He is known as a good friend to have on your side, and a bad enemy to have against you.

Gil Cavanaugh's insistence that he knew nothing of the charges against Jonathan Hamilton until the day following the arrest takes on special significance in the context of the law. The same statute that brought back the death penalty to New York after a thirty-year moratorium (if that somewhat oxymoronic term can be forgiven) created a Capital Defender's Office. Included in the Capital Defender's mandate was the responsibility to maintain a house staff of attorneys to represent defendants accused of capital crimes; to train a small but select group of lawyers from the private sector, public-defender agencies, and legal-aid offices, so that they, too, would be qualified to accept assignments in capital cases; to provide a resource center to assist in all such defenses; and to assist in the education of those judges throughout the state who would be designated to hear the cases.

One of the points of contention during the debate that restored the death penalty involved the issue of just when in the accusatory process a person charged with capital murder should be provided counsel. Prosecutors argued that the traditional method of assigning a lawyer at the first court appearance was adequate; defense attorneys contended that the early stages of the process were often the most critical, and that the accused should be provided counsel at the earliest possible opportunity. After a good degree of haggling in the legislature, a compromise of sorts was hammered out: The district attorney in whose county the charges are being brought has an affirmative obligation to notify the Capital Defender as soon as he authorizes the filing of first degree murder charges, so that the Capital Defender, acting as a clearing house of sorts, can designate either a member of his staff, or an outside qualified attorney, to immediately begin representing the accused.

The person appointed as New York's first Capital Defender is a man named Kevin Doyle. Doyle is lean, youthful looking, and clear-eyed. He is bright, well spoken, and absolutely indefatigable. He is no stranger to the arena, having spent most of his career representing death-row inmates in Alabama, where the state pays $10 an hour—ditchdiggers' rates—to those lawyers willing to devote their lives to the business of trying to save defendants from the electric chair.

As one of Doyle's first official acts, he sent a letter, by certified mail, to the district attorneys of each of the sixty-two counties in the state, informing them of their statutory obligation to notify him the moment they had authorized the filing of capital charges. The letter included emergency pager numbers, whereby Doyle or a member of his staff could be reached at any time, day or night, no matter where they were, or what the circumstance.

There is some doubt as to whether Gil Cavanaugh (who had personally been one of the sixty-two recipients of Doyle's letter) neglected through oversight to comply with the notification requirement, or deliberately chose to ignore it. But his version, that he was unaware of the case until Monday afternoon, is simply belied by the facts. In any event, he never notified Doyle's office.

It wasn't until late Monday afternoon, a full twenty-four hours after the time of Stanton's log entry regarding his conversation with Cavanaugh, that Doyle, visiting friends on the south shore of Long Island, received a call from a member of his staff, informing him that the networks were airing reports of a double murder in some place called Flat Lake. Mumbling apologies to his hosts, Doyle rushed out to his car, grabbed a handful of road maps, and tore through them until he found the town. Back inside, he spent the next hour on the phone trying to identify and track down the Ottawa County District Attorney. He finally reached Gil Cavanaugh at the clubhouse of the Green Tree Country Club, outside of Cedar Falls.

Doyle got right to the point. "I'm told your office has authorized the filing of a complaint in what could be a capital murder case," he said.

"That's right," Cavanaugh acknowledged. "Just found out about it myself."

"When?" Doyle pressed him.

"When what?"

"When did you find out about it?"

"Just now, just now," Cavanaugh said. "About, ah, a little while ago, more or less."

UP AND RUNNING for less than two years at the time, the Capital Defender's Office occupied temporary space in lower Manhattan, and had a single branch office, in Rochester. Back at the road map, Doyle estimated that Flat Lake completed a rough equilateral triangle with the two locations, and was nearly two hundred miles from either one. He immediately ruled out assigning the case to one of his own staff attorneys. The next option was the public defender for the county. But Ottawa County was so sparsely populated that it had none. Doyle quickly found himself down to his final option: locating a private attorney in the geographical area who had been trained to take these cases.

As encyclopedic as Kevin Doyle's mind is, as he studied the road map that afternoon, not even he could think of anyone from the area who had been through the training sessions. He was forced to call one of the office secretaries who lived in Manhattan, prevail upon her to go downtown, unlock the office, pull out the roster books, and phone him back. Then he had her read off the names of every private lawyer who was qualified to handle capital cases in the five counties closest to Flat Lake. Not that it took her very long to do so: there were only six names.

The first five names failed to ring a bell with Doyle, but he jotted down their phone numbers as they were read off. It was only the sixth name that brought a wry smile to his face.

"Bingo," he said softly.

4

FIELDER

MATTHEW FIELDER WAS out behind his cabin splitting firewood when the call came in. He heard the phone, but chose
to let it ring away—that was what the answering machine
was for, after all. Besides which, Fielder had a hard time
imagining that the call could be from anyone he wanted to
talk with.

At forty-four, Matt Fielder was a dropout of sorts. A
criminal defense lawyer with the Legal Aid Society in Manhattan for sixteen years, he'd been good enough to have
earned a promotion to the rank of supervisor. What that
meant was, they'd taken him out of the courtroom—which
was the only place he'd ever felt at home—and put him
behind a desk, where he was supposed to push paper. When
the Society had gone up against the mayor two years later
over a contract dispute, the results had been disastrous. Instead of pay increases, there had been cuts. When it became
obvious that heads would have to roll, Fielder had willingly
offered up his own. He'd taken a buyout package consisting
of the pension he'd accrued, plus three months' severance
pay. The total amount came to $43,562.19. The public-
service version of a golden parachute.

With the check he'd paid off the last of the alimony
arrears he owed his ex-wife, taken care of a couple of long-
overdue credit-card balances, and bought back his rusting
Suzuki Sidekick from the finance company, who'd repos-

sessed it for the third time the month before. With a little over $18,000 left from the buyout, he'd come across an ad offering 10-acre parcels of undeveloped land in the Adirondacks for $1,000 an acre. The photo showed deer drinking from a crystal-clear pond, surrounded by a forest of evergreens. Sight unseen, he'd written out a check and mailed it off.

Next he'd gotten himself appointed to the Assigned Counsel Plan, qualifying him to represent indigent defendants—the only thing he knew how to do after eighteen years of lawyering. The cases paid a whopping $40 an hour for in-court work, and $25 an hour out-of-court. He was responsible for his own overhead: office rent, phone, fax, copy machine, library, insurance, stationery, postage, and medical coverage. Because he couldn't afford to hire a secretary, he bought a second-hand computer and did his own paperwork.

The first year he netted $4,562.38.

Just when Fielder was consoling himself with the good news—that at least he'd owe little or nothing in the way of income taxes—he received a notice from Internal Revenue informing him that since he'd neglected to roll over his pension fund, he now owed them an additional $11,000.

It was about that time that he decided to pull the plug.

He called the Assigned Counsel Plan to tell them he was packing it in. Laura Held, the administrator of the Plan, got on the phone. Matt and Laura had been colleagues at Legal Aid and friends for a dozen years or so, ever since Laura had cajoled him into representing a deaf-mute who couldn't read, write, or converse in sign language.

Laura tried her best to talk Matt out of quitting, but this time he managed to resist her charms. He told her he was determined to head for the woods.

"This means you'll have plenty of free time?" she asked him.

He should have seen it coming, but he didn't. "I sure hope so," he said.

"Then I'm signing you up for Death School," she announced.

"Say what?"

FIELDER FINISHED SPLITTING the last of the wood, and tossed the sledgehammer and wedges to the side. He figured he'd done about a quarter of a face cord in two hours. He loved splitting ash. It was a good, hard wood for burning, but it was less work than either oak or maple, both of which tended to resist coming apart cleanly. Elm was the worst: the fibers clung and held on forever. Not like ash. With ash, you hit it right, it rewarded you. Life itself ought to be like that. But there sure did seem to be a lot of elm out there lately.

Fielder dried the sweat off his face and upper body with the sweatshirt he'd stripped off earlier. In the quiet of the clearing, he became aware of a faint beeping noise coming from inside the cabin. He remembered the phone call. Looking up at the sky through the branches, he figured he still had another half hour of daylight to stack the wood. He brushed the chips out of his hair and off his jeans, and headed for the cabin door.

"One . . . new . . . message," the robot inside the answering machine told him. A push of a button retrieved it.

"Matt, this is Kevin Doyle. We've got a double murder up in Ottawa County that's going to be arraigned tomorrow morning in Cedar Falls. The DA's a meateater. This could be the real thing. I'm hoping you can take it. Call me as soon as you can, at (516) 555–7282. Thanks."

DEATH SCHOOL," LAURA Held had explained, was the intensive training program run by the CDO to qualify attorneys to handle capital murders. It was open to lawyers who had extensive backgrounds in defending murder cases, and offered to only the very best of those, Laura had confided. For the next ten minutes, she'd played up to Fielder's commitment to justice, empathy with the underdog, and—pulling out all the stops—his ego. Fielder, of course, had never had a chance: this was the same Laura Held, after all, who had once convinced him to represent a client so totally impossible to communicate with that he may as well have been from Mars.

Death School had been a grueling three days of lectures, seminars, demonstrations, and participation. Classes had begun at eight in the morning, and discussion groups ran late into the night. Experts from all around the country had come to share their knowledge, strategies, anecdotes, successes, failures, and secrets. David Bruck had flown in from Seattle to re-create his closing argument on behalf of Susan Smith, the mother who had strapped her two young children into her car before rolling it into a lake. Andrea Lyon came from Ann Arbor to discuss the merits of bursting into tears in front of the jury. Cessie Alfonso, a social worker from Jersey City, described going back more than a hundred years to document the recurrence of mental illness, sexual abuse, alcoholism, and drug dependency in every generation of a particular defendant's ancestors.

Fielder had come away from the experience almost shell-shocked. While colleagues all around him rubbed their hands together, eager to get to work on capital cases and the higher hourly rates they were expected to pay, Fielder cringed at the thought of being responsible not only for a client's freedom, but for his very life. When invited to fill out a form, the final question of which asked when he'd be available to take his first case—a question others were answering with replies like "Immediately," "Tomorrow," and "ASAP"—he'd sat for twenty minutes before inking in his response. "I'm not at all certain," he'd finally written, "that I'm emotionally prepared to do this work."

Which was, of course, exactly what Kevin Doyle wanted to hear. So when three young Hispanics were arrested in the Bronx for gunning down a police officer, Fielder had been the first lawyer Doyle had reached out to. When a fifty-five-year-old man had emptied his gun into his girlfriend and her son in their Manhattan apartment, Fielder had again been tapped. But both of those cases had quickly gone "non-death": the Bronx case because the ballistics evidence soon established that it was one of the co-defendants who'd been the actual shooter (he subsequently cheated the system by hanging himself from the bars of his cell), and the Manhattan case because the defendant's age, poor health, good work record, and minimal criminal history made him an unlikely candidate for capital punishment.

"Non-death" was certainly good news for the clients, and Fielder breathed a sigh of relief the moment he knew that while he might be responsible for the defendants' lives, at least he wouldn't be held accountable for their deaths. But "non-death" was bad news for the bank account. It meant back to the old $40 in-court and $25 out-of-court rates. Fielder didn't care; he was happy to have the pressure off. He worked six, and sometimes seven days a week on the two cases, and it was three months before he managed to take a week off and make the six-hour drive up to the Adirondacks to see what his $10,000 had bought him.

What he found was ten acres, all right, and it was certainly undeveloped. The crystal-clear pond turned out to be a low-lying depression that had flooded over in the spring thaw, and was guaranteed to become an ideal hatchery for mosquitoes by summer. But there was a meandering brook, plenty of deer, and the promised forest of evergreens. Counting on borrowing against the money he'd eventually be getting for the two murder cases, Fielder ordered logs from a local lumberyard. After all, he figured, how hard could it be to build a cabin?

The next time he got back upstate was three weeks later. He stopped first at the lumberyard to tell them they better hold off, the bank had turned down his loan.

"Already delivered 'em," said the sawyer.

"Sorry," Fielder said.

"Don't be sorry," he was told. "Build yer cabin. Pay me when you get around to it."

Just like New York City.

*   *   *

FIELDER HIT THE rewind button on the answering machine and listened to the message again. *A double murder.* As he knew from his Manhattan case, that fact alone qualified the case as a capital one; it was what the statute termed an "aggravating factor." *Cedar Falls.* That was Ottawa County, a good hour's drive from Fielder's cabin outside Big Moose. Two hours, if it was snowing. *The DA's a meateater.* Fielder knew Doyle had a "book" on every prosecutor in the state, the way a coach keeps scouting reports on opposing team's tendencies. There was a general rule: The closer the county was to a big city, the less likely it was that the DA was an avid proponent of the death penalty. Fielder's two earlier cases had illustrated the point: In the Bronx, Robert Johnson was so outspokenly opposed to capital punishment that the state attorney general had taken the case away from him; in Manhattan, Robert Morgenthau was also opposed, but was at least going through the motions of evaluating cases on their merits as they came up.

But Ottawa County was about as far away as you could get from a big city, in almost every way imaginable. Demographically it was much like Herkimer County, where Fielder's cabin was. Instead of settling the area vertically in apartment buildings, folks had spread out laterally, and had left a lot of space in between. They drove pickup trucks, owned shotguns, drank beer, voted Republican, and figured that that old "eye for an eye" stuff made pretty good sense. So when Doyle had said, *"This could be the real thing,"* he meant that here was a case that was going to start out death, and probably *stay* death.

Even as he copied down the phone number, Fielder knew he wanted no part of this one.

IT HAD TAKEN Fielder almost a year to build the cabin. Along the way, he'd made every mistake known to carpentry, and even come up with a few innovations of his own. He'd poured the slab in the rain, so that when it had finally set it was uniformly pockmarked. He'd hung the front door upside down and the picture window inside out. He'd cut his knee, hammered both thumbs, broken a toe dropping a log on it, and fallen from the roof, luckily landing in a snowdrift. But by the time he was finished, he could cut a log with one pass of a chainsaw, drive home a ten-penny nail in three swings, and snap a pretty mean chalk line.

And he had his cabin.

True, it was more or less equal parts log and caulking, but it kept out most of the rain and even some of the wind. It had wideboard pine floors, electric lights, and real plumbing. Heat came from a wood-burning stove, which worked with its doors open when atmosphere was called for, or closed when efficiency was needed. Atmosphere tended to end, and efficiency began, around early September.

The checks from the two murder cases finally came in, and Fielder paid off the lumberyard. His apology for the delay was met with an unconcerned shrug and the observation, "Figgered you couldn't git too far with all them logs in that little wind-up car of yours." The next summer, he took his remaining $600, rented a backhoe, and dredged out his swamp. If it didn't look much like a crystal-clear pond quite yet, at least it was a start.

Down to pocket change and faced with the necessity of earning some real money, Fielder turned to legal writing. He took on a handful of appeals, drafting briefs for defendants seeking to overturn their convictions. The same Assigned Counsel Plan that had paid him to go to court for $40 an hour and prepare motions for $25, now paid him $40 to sit at his computer and compose legal arguments. For once, being far from the city proved to be no drawback, particularly when it came time to visit the inmates, who were experiencing their own version of being upstate—in places with names like Dannemora, Malone, Lyon Mountain, and Comstock. He also wrote short stories, even managing to sell one to a regional literary magazine, *St. Lawrence Currents*, for $75. Talk about real money.

Of course, there were certain drawbacks. Slow to make friends under the best of circumstances, Fielder now found himself moving dangerously close to full hermit status.

He'd occasionally force himself to drive into town on the thinnest of pretexts, in search of a two-day-old local newspaper or an extra bag of sugar. At such times, he suspected that what he was really doing was checking to make sure that the town—Big Moose, population 75—was still there, and that he hadn't missed some cataclysmic event that had plunged the rest of the world into nuclear winter while he slept. A few minutes at the general store were generally all it took for reassurance. Somebody'd be complaining about the rising price of kerosene, or debating the merits of sandworms versus hellgrammites, or ordering new sap buckets in time for syrup season. A glance at the headline of the *Adirondack Advertiser*, the regional newspaper/ realty lister/ pennysaver, would serve to bring him up on the important news: locally, there'd been a drunk driving arrest on County Road 19, while on the international scene the bass were taking No. 2 Lazy Ikes up in Little Bog Lake. He'd given up trying to find the *New York Times* except on Sundays, when desperation would take over and compel him to make the 60-mile drive down to Utica.

FIELDER DIALED THE number Doyle had left. He was fully prepared to turn Doyle down on this one. Not that he couldn't use the money. If the case stayed death, he'd get paid at the rate of $175 an hour. Never mind that Wall Street firms were charging $500 an hour these days to take their clients to lunch; to Matt Fielder, the idea of working for $175 an hour was nothing short of winning the lottery.

No, it wasn't the money. And it certainly wasn't the work. Getting his teeth into a murder case was what made this business worthwhile in the first place. It hadn't been the big cases that had ultimately driven Fielder from practice; it had been the little ones—the petty drug possessions, the shoplifts, the car thefts, the turnstile jumpers. That and the business of running a law office.

"Hello." It was a woman's voice.

"Hi. This is Matt Fielder. I'm returning Kevin Doyle's call."

"Just a minute."

Not that he hadn't tried his best to duck the first two cases Doyle had called him on, too: He was on trial; he was too busy; he had a vacation coming up. But both times, Doyle had brushed those excuses aside, seeming to sense immediately that it was only Fielder's uneasiness about doing death work that he was hearing. And it was that very uneasiness, of course, that had caused Doyle to put Fielder on his short list in the first place.

Both times Doyle had succeeded in prevailing upon Fielder. Both times Fielder had managed to overcome his reluctance and hit the ground running, soon finding himself far too involved in the defense of his clients to dwell on what might become of them if things went wrong. And both times, circumstances had fortunately arisen to ensure that things wouldn't go wrong—at least not *fatally* wrong.

But this time promised to be different. Doyle himself had made that clear in his message. *"The DA's a meat-eater,"* he'd said. *"This could be the real thing."*

"Doyle here."

"Hey, Kevin. Matt Fielder."

"Thanks for getting back to me, Matt. How's life in the woods?"

"It's been a learning experience."

So much for the small talk.

"I've got a live one, Matt."

"So it sounds."

"Twenty-eight-year-old kid up in Ottawa County. Far as we know, he's got no priors. Living on an estate with his grandparents in someplace called Flat Lake. Wakes up sometime Sunday night and butchers them in their sleep. State police have an oral confession. They're arraigning him nine o'clock tomorrow morning in Cedar Falls."

"Who's the DA?"

"Guy by the name of Gil Cavanaugh. Don't know too much about him, other than that he calls himself a conservative Republican, he's a friend of the NRA, and every four years he gets reelected on a law-and-order platform tougher than the one before. Got eighty-eight percent of the vote last time he ran."

"Lovely," was all Fielder could think to say.

"One more thing," Doyle added. "He didn't even give us notification. Claimed he wasn't aware of the case."

"Can't your branch office in Flat Lake handle this?"

"Our branch office in Flat Lake?" Doyle laughed. "We don't have anyone within a hundred miles of Ottawa County."

"Except for me."

"Except for you."

Fielder found a clean spot on his sweatshirt to mop his forehead dry again. "I don't want this," he told Doyle. "We both know they're going to try to kill this kid."

"I need you to help me out for now, Matt. If you still want out in a week, say the word. I'll pull you off it. Promise."

"Right," Fielder said. They both knew that by week's end he'd be up to his elbows in it, and there'd be no way he'd let go of it."

"Thanks," said Doyle, exhibiting that rarest skill of all in the legal profession—the good sense to shut up when you're ahead. "Kid's name is Jonathan Hamilton. Cedar Falls, nine o'clock."

"You bastard," said Matt Fielder.

5

CEDAR FALLS

THE OTTAWA COUNTY Courthouse is a two-story brick building located directly on Main Street, about halfway between Maple and Birch. Since there are only a dozen streets in all of Cedar Falls, Fielder had little difficulty finding it. He pulled his ancient Suzuki to the curb, where it obligingly wheezed to a stop of its own accord.

Before slipping into his suit jacket, Fielder gave it a good shake, hoping to rid it of the odor of mothballs that had followed him from the cabin. It had been close to a year since Fielder had felt compelled to dress up in his lawyer costume, and he hadn't missed it a bit. He tightened the knot of his tie as he climbed the three steps, hoping he wouldn't get too much flack over the workboots that were all he'd been able to find that morning. He carried an old attaché case that had been filled with bags of soil samples and jars of suspected termites, until he'd emptied it out the night before in order to make room for a pad of paper, a couple of pens, and some legal forms.

Inside, the building smelled of mildew and dry rot. The wall paint was peeling, and the dark wood floors were stained and uneven. He found a door marked COUNTY CLERK, knocked once, and entered. A gray-haired woman looked up from behind a service window and smiled. If she noticed his boots, she didn't comment on them.

"Good morning," Fielder said.

."Good morning," she echoed, pleasantly enough.

"I'm here to represent Mr. Hamilton, on the murder case. And I'm new around here." Fielder made a habit of announcing his ignorance at the first available opportunity. He'd found that people tend to want to help those unashamed enough to admit they were out of their element.

"Well, don't you worry about that," the woman said. "I'm Dorothy Whipple, the County Clerk. But you can call me Dot— everyone else does."

"Thank you, Dot. I'm Matt, Matt Fielder."

"Hello, Matt. Now, first thing. Are you admitted to practice in New York?"

"Yes, I am."

"Good." He watched as she fished around for a Notice of Appearance. "Are you retained"—she stressed the first syllable, pronouncing it *ree*tained—"or eighteen-b?" By "18-b," she meant appointed by the Assigned Counsel Plan.

"Actually, neither," he said. "I've been brought in by the Capital Defender's Office, which technically makes it section 35-B, of the Judiciary Law."

"Hmmmm," she fretted. "Don't have a box on the form for that. Guess we'll just have to do a write-in."

Fielder found himself hoping that whoever else he'd encounter that morning would be half as accommodating at Dot Whipple, but he knew better. Even in his Bronx and Manhattan capital cases, he'd found judges, clerks, court officers, and stenographers who were completely thrown when they found out he'd been designated by an authority other than one they were accustomed to dealing with on a daily basis. One judge, presented with a simple order seeking the appointment of a mitigation expert to investigate a defendant's background, had literally run from the bench, screaming that she didn't even know what a mitigation expert *was*, let alone whether or not she had the power to appoint one.

Fielder completed the blanks on the Notice of Appearance and handed it back to Dot Whipple. She smiled again and told him the case would be heard in Part One. When he looked at her quizzically for directions, she pointed across the hall.

"It's the only part we have," she confided. "Used to be a Part Two, years back. But seeing as we only have but one judge now, it seemed a little silly to make him run back and forth."

PART ONE OF the Ottawa County Courthouse is a room of modest dimensions, as courtrooms go, with a spectator section that can accommodate perhaps fifty people, less a few, where a folding chair is broken or occasionally missing altogether. The walls are paneled in tongue-and-groove pine, which was stained to look like dark oak, or perhaps light walnut. Portraits of great, white Protestant Americans are hung at irregular intervals, apparently by an extremely tall person. Most prominently on display are Ronald Reagan, Tom Dewey, Nelson Rockefeller, and Lou Gehrig.

Fielder was surprised to find a dozen people already milling about in the well, even though it was still only eight-thirty, and therefore a full half hour from starting time. Seeing no one who looked like a court officer, he approached a uniformed but hatless state trooper.

" 'Morning," he said.

" 'Morning," the trooper returned.

"I'm here to represent the Hamilton kid," Fielder said. "I'm wondering if there's any chance I could meet with him before court begins."

"Don't see why not." The trooper shrugged. "Let me see if they've brought him over." As the trooper disappeared through a side door, Fielder marveled at his good fortune: two contacts with the system, two human beings. If this were a baseball game, he'd be batting 1.000 so far.

A moment later, the trooper stuck his head out of the doorway and said, "This way, Counselor."

THE FIRST THING that struck Fielder about Jonathan Hamilton was how youthful-looking he was, and how very handsome. He had broad facial features, with the unusual combination of prominent cheekbones and thick lips. Except where he needed a shave, his evenly tanned skin looked as though it would be soft to the touch. Even the bristles of his three-day beard looked soft, sprouting through his skin in individual blond hairs, rather than casting a shadowy stubble across his cheeks. A shock of blond hair fell straight down his forehead. But all of those features faded into the background, to some degree; it was Jonathan's eyes that were truly arresting. They were a pale blue—so pale as to almost suggest blindness, and so startling in their openness that Fielder found it difficult to look into them at times, yet impossible not to.

The truth is that Matt Fielder is himself an extremely good-looking man. But his dark hair, nearly black eyes, and chiseled jaw must have presented a stark contrast that morning to Jonathan Hamilton's blond hair, pale blue eyes, and almost beatific features. In the weeks and months to follow, the media would never run a print article, or carry a televised sound bite regarding the case, without displaying a photo of one man or the other, and often of both. A prominent film producer would go on record as hoping for an eventual acquittal, just so both men could get a chance to play themselves in the movie version.

The pen adjacent to Part One is large enough to hold a half-dozen prisoners at once, though it is doubtful that it has ever been called upon to do so. That Tuesday morning, Fielder and Jonathan had it all to themselves. Their initial meeting was conducted standing up and separated by iron bars. Fielder, who is an even six feet tall, found himself looking up into Jonathan's face.

"My name is Matt Fielder," he said, extending a business card between the bars. "If it's all right with you, I'm going to be your lawyer."

Jonathan took the card and frowned at it for a long moment, prompting Fielder to wonder whether his client was able to read at all. Then Jonathan began running his thumb over the card, at a spot where Fielder's own fingers had left a smudge on the surface. When the thumb didn't seem to do the trick, Jonathan switched to the sleeve of his shirt, rubbing in a determined, circular motion, singularly occupied with the business of ridding the card of its imperfection.

Fielder had the feeling that Jonathan could have easily spent the next fifteen minutes absorbed with the card. He displayed none of the urgency most defendants did when first given a chance to confer with a lawyer, and asked none of the usual questions. That left it up to Fielder to shape the conversation.

"Do you know why you're here?" Fielder asked.

Jonathan hesitated, then answered rather sheepishly, "I guess so."

"Tell me," Fielder said, in as gentle a tone as he could muster.

"Grandpa Carter and Grandma Mary Alice?" Looking to Fielder to make sure he'd got the answer right.

"Right," Fielder said. He had the feeling he was talking to a small child, a child who had somehow been outfitted with the body of a very large man. "What about them?"

"They say I hurt them."

"*Hurt* them?"

"K-k-kilt them."

Fielder hesitated before asking the next logical question. There were times you asked a client if he was guilty, and there were times you didn't. Fielder was in the process of trying to figure out which kind of time this was, when Jonathan surprised him with a question of his own.

"Wh-wh-what could they do to me?"

"What do you mean?" Fielder was pretty certain what Jonathan meant, but he wanted to hear how much Jonathan himself knew.

"Can they give me c-capital punishment?"

Fielder's cardinal rule was, Never lie to a client. It wasn't so much a moral thing as a pragmatic one. Get caught in a lie, and you'd never be believed again. He wasn't about to break the rule, not even now. "Yes," he said. "It's possible."

There was a long silence while Jonathan appeared to digest that news. Then he asked, "What *is* capital punishment?"

Fielder explained that capital punishment meant the death penalty.

"When would that be?" he asked.

"First of all," Fielder explained, "I'm here to see that that doesn't happen, ever. But even if I fail, even if I strike out twenty-seven times in a row, I promise you that nothing like that could possibly happen for many, many years."

"So it wouldn't be, like, *tonight*?"

Fielder allowed himself a small smile. As gently as he could, he explained to Jonathan that there could be no execution without all sorts of stuff first—a full investigation, pre-trial hearings, a jury trial, a separate sentencing hearing, and multiple appeals—things that would truly go on for many years.

"So it can't be tonight," said Jonathan. "No matter what."

Fielder gave Jonathan his solemn promise that it couldn't be that night, or any night soon. As soon as the words were out of his mouth, he could detect a visible difference in Jonathan. All of the tension seemed to go out of his body. It was as though he was truly incapable of contemplating the indefinite future: his horizons stretched no farther than morning and night.

During the twenty-five minutes that Fielder was speaking with Jonathan, the courtroom had gradually filled up, and when Fielder returned he found it packed with spectators, reporters, sketch artists, and the just plain curious. As he made his way across the room, he picked up the tail end of a hushed conversation. A tall, silver-haired man was telling a huddle of listeners, ". . . and they're sending some Jew lawyer up here to represent him."

A few moments later, Dot Whipple tapped Fielder on the shoulder. "How 'bout I acquaint you with your adversary?" she said with a wink, leading the way to where the very same silver-haired man stood, still holding court. As

Dot introduced them, the man smiled broadly at Fielder and extended his hand.

"Gil Cavanaugh," he said. "District Attorney."

Fielder looked him in the eye and returned the smile, but let the hand hang there in midair.

"Matt Fielder," he said. "Jew lawyer."

EVEN AS FIELDER and Cavanaugh were getting acquainted in the Ottawa County Courthouse in Cedar Falls, some fifty miles to the north, in the town of Malone, the Franklin County Medical Examiner was beginning her postmortem examination of the bodies of Carter and Mary Alice Hamilton.

Dr. Frances Chu was no stranger to autopsies, having either officiated or assisted at nearly two thousand of them in her eight years as an assistant to the Chief Medical Examiner of New York City. When she'd seen a listing for the Franklin County position, offering escape from the city at a salary only slightly lower than the one she'd been making, while permitting her to maintain a part-time private practice of her own, she'd quickly sent off her résumé. They'd called her three days later and asked her one question: When could she start? Five weeks later, she was wrestling the steering wheel of a Ryder rental truck, her two daughters asleep beside her, her Ford Fiesta in tow, asking herself why she'd never thought to look at a map before accepting the job.

Malone, New York, is about as far north as you can go before you have to start speaking French to be understood. It is farther north than almost all of Vermont and New Hampshire, and much of Maine. It is farther north than Green Bay, Wisconsin, and Minneapolis, Minnesota. It is *one hundred miles* farther north than Toronto. Local folk are fond of saying that there are two seasons in Malone: July and winter. And as Frances Chu and her assistant began work that Tuesday morning, the temperature in the unheated autopsy room was 53 degrees. July was clearly over.

Dr. Chu was hardly the squeamish type. She'd seen just

about everything there was to see during her New York City tour. Multiple-gunshot-wound victims, machete slashings, ritual mutilations, jumpers, floaters, and even a "space case" or two—where the victim had slipped and become pinned in the tiny space between a subway car and the station platform, fully conscious and in virtually no pain, until the train had to be moved—at which time it took about sixty seconds for every internal organ and drop of blood to drain from the body. Since her arrival in Malone, almost all of the violent cases Dr. Chu had seen were hunting accidents or MVAs (motor-vehicle accidents) of one sort or another: head-ons, rollovers, windshield divers, tree-climbers, and moose-stoppers.

But none of her previous cases had readied Frances Chu for her autopsy of the Hamilton bodies. After getting over her initial shock and completing the examinations, she confided to her assistant that in all her years, she had never seen two persons so badly *purposefully* injured at the hand of another person. A small extract from her autopsy report illustrates the nature of her findings.

The male victim . . . exhibits in excess of 100 stab wounds, concentrated in—but by no means limited to—the face, neck, and upper-chest areas. All of the major veins and arteries in the neck are severed, as is the spinal cord. [Two of] the vertebrae of the upper spine are deeply cut, to the point of being nearly severed. . . .

The female victim . . . is almost identically stabbed, except that in [her] case the second and third vertebrae have been completely severed, leaving the [head] attached to what remains of the upper torso by a layer of derma and muscle approximately 3 cm in thickness.

Toward the end of her report, Dr. Chu attempted to draw certain conclusions from her findings.

Because of the number and severity of the wounds, it is difficult to determine with certainty whether the wounds are the result of a single instrument or multiple instruments. However, it appears that none of the wounds is inconsistent with having been caused by a large-bladed knife, smooth near the point and serrated near the handle. The blade must have been approximately 130 cm in length, and 40 cm in width at its the widest point.

To anyone with even a rudimentary knowledge of cutlery and a familiarity with metric equivalents, Dr. Chu was almost certainly describing a hunting knife with a five-inch blade.

ALL RISE!" CALLED Dot Whipple. "The County Court, in and for the county of Ottawa, is now in session, the Honorable Arthur Summerhouse presiding. Please be seated."

The room came to order as a very short man wearing a very long black robe strode in and took his place behind the bench. Arthur Summerhouse was sixty-four at the time, but fighting every day of it. What was left of his hair had been·dyed jet black and combed back-to-front in an obvious attempt to cover up what nature had chosen to reveal. A small mustache, also jet black, adorned his upper lip, perhaps intended as a bit of distraction ·from the battle being waged on top.

"Good morning," said Judge Summerhouse.

"Good morning," echoed those who were accustomed to the drill.

"For arraignment," announced Dot Whipple, "Docket number Nine-seven–slash–three-three-four. People versus Jonathan Hamilton. Two counts of murder in the first degree."

Gil Cavanaugh rose from his seat at one end of the long counsel table. Matt Fielder took his cue and stepped up to the middle of the table. As they gave their appearances to the court reporter, two uniformed troopers escorted Jonathan Hamilton in from the side door and stood him, hand-cuffed behind his back, next to Fielder. They took one step back and remained there, immediately behind Jonathan.

"Your Honor," Fielder said.

Judge Summerhouse looked up from a folder he'd been examining. "Yes?" he said.

"May I respectfully request that the handcuffs be removed from Mr. Hamilton while he's before the court?"

"Who are you?" the judge asked.

"My name is Matthew Fielder. I've been called in by the Capital Defender's Office to represent Mr. Hamilton."

"Would you like an opportunity to speak with him?"

"That won't be necessary," Fielder said. "I've already done so."

Judge Summerhouse rose out of his seat, though the act failed to add much in the way of elevation. "Who authorized you to do that?" he demanded.

Fielder immediately recomputed his batting average at .667. He briefly considered mentioning Dot Whipple's acceptance of his Notice of Appearance, or the accommodating trooper's providing him access to the pen area, but thought better of it. From what he saw of the judge, he knew he was going to need all the friends he could find. He wasn't about to give up anyone who'd been nice enough to have helped him.

"Nobody," he said. "I thought I could save the court a bit of time by speaking with my client before you took the bench."

"Mr.—"

"Fielder."

"—Fielder, I don't know where you're from, or how they do things there. But the way things work around here, you're not this man's lawyer until I assign you. Right?"

"Right."

"And *until* you're his lawyer, you're not authorized to speak with him. Right?"

"Right."

"Now, you want me to assign you?"

"Yes, Your Honor."

"Okay," the judge said. "You're assigned."

"Thank you."

"And don't roll your eyes like that!"

"Sorry, sir."

"Now, what can I do for you, Counselor?"

"I'd like the handcuffs removed from my client," Fielder said.

"Denied."

The tone of the proceedings pretty much followed that pattern. Gil Cavanaugh announced that he was prepared to convene a grand jury and present his evidence to it without delay. Fielder handed Cavanaugh a letter announcing his desire to have Jonathan testify at the grand jury. Then he asked for an adjournment to consider whether he really wanted to do that, and, if so, to prepare for it. Judge Summerhouse reminded Fielder that the defendant had a right to be released if a grand jury hadn't voted an indictment against him within six days of his arrest. Fielder offered to waive that provision of the law and consent to extending it to thirty days. The judge said he didn't know if he had the power to do that. Fielder pointed out that under the statute the period could be extended for "good cause," which certainly included the defendant's consenting. Cavanaugh announced that he didn't care whether the defendant consented or not, or whether the period was extended thirty *years*; he was going to get an indictment the following day.

"So, now, does your client want to testify at the grand jury?" Judge Summerhouse asked.

"I've served written notice that he does," Fielder replied. "But the statute requires that we be given a reasonable time to prepare."

"So take your time," the judge said. "Take all day, if you like."

"All *day*?" Fielder tried to keep his eyes from rolling again. "I met my client a half an hour ago," he said. "I don't even know if he's *competent* to testify at this point."

The judge was ready for that one, too. "Are you asking

for a fitness examination, under Article Seven-thirty of the Mental Hygiene Law?" he asked.

"Not at this point," Fielder replied. There was no way he was going to give some court-appointed psychiatrist or psychologist access to Jonathan at this early stage.

"What does that mean, 'Not at this point'?" the judge wanted to know.

"It simply means that I am not now asking for a Seven-thirty examination."

By this time the judge appeared to be approaching his boiling point. "Mr.—"

"Fielder."

"—Fielder, are you familiar with the expression, 'It's now or never'?"

Fielder muttered something under his breath about being familiar with a song of that name, but the only word the judge was able to pick up was "Elvis." "What did you say?" the judge demanded.

"Nothing, Your Honor."

The judge turned to the court reporter. "What did he say?" he asked her.

"I'm afraid I missed it," she said.

Another friend, thought Fielder. Back up to .750.

The judge turned back to Fielder. "Are you requesting an immediate fitness examination? Yes or no?"

"No."

"Do you understand that by saying no, you forever waive such an examination."

"I understand," Fielder said measuredly, "that that is your ruling."

"And one more thing, Counselor."

"Yes, Your Honor?"

"Don't ever wear those boots in my courtroom again."

Since the sixth day following the arrest would fall on a Saturday, Judge Summerhouse put the case over until Friday, September 5, in order to give Cavanaugh an opportunity to convene his grand jury and get his indictment. Jonathan Hamilton was remanded without bail.

6

HAM SANDWICHES

DEATH IS DIFFERENT.

Those three words, to which Fielder had first been introduced at Death School, have come to form the mantra of the capital defender. When the state makes the decision to kill, that decision immediately and fundamentally transforms the nature of the process from an ordinary one to an extraordinary one. According to some advocates of the death penalty, the transformation arises out of a distinction that is both morally misguided and legally unnecessary, a mistake responsible for the many long, and seemingly endless delays encountered before the meting-out of a punishment that is rooted in biblical tradition, has been authorized by the legislature, approved by the governor, sanctioned by the courts, and continues to be supported by a sizable majority of the public. Nonetheless, this transformation from the ordinary to the extraordinary is recognized by the courts, including a Supreme Court that, even as it has upheld capital punishment against challenges that it is inherently "cruel and unusual," has insisted that, before an execution may be carried out, exacting standards must be adhered to at every step of the way, from arrest to execution. And in determining on a case-by-case review whether those standards have been met, the justices have time and again taken note of the extreme and irrevocable nature of death as punishment, and have fashioned new yardsticks to measure compliance, adding terms like "heightened due process" and "strict scrutiny" to the lexicon of judicial analysis.

Exactly when word of this distinction—that death is indeed different—found its way to Cedar Falls, New York, is a bit unclear. As the only sitting judge in the county, Arthur Summerhouse had almost certainly been invited to at least one of several training sessions conducted by the Capital Defender's Office as early as the summer and fall of 1995. He will not say if he actually attended or not, and the records of those judges who did can no longer be located.

But by the time Matt Fielder knocked on the door to the judge's chambers—which was somewhere around two-thirty in the afternoon of the same day as the initial court appearance, he found a somewhat changed man. Perhaps the difference was no more than the one that exists between the public Arthur Summerhouse and the private one: those who know the judge are quick to point out that as feisty and difficult as he can be on the bench, once out of his robes he is friendly and indeed quite charming. It is also possible that the five-hour interval had provided the judge an opportunity for reflection, giving him sufficient time to realize on his own that it would be prudent to accommodate some of Fielder's more reasonable concerns. But rumors persist that it was neither of these factors that was responsible for the change, so much as an intervening act: the placement of a private phone call by Judge Summerhouse to a colleague in Rochester who had sat for a time on a capital case the year before until it had been resolved by the defendant's acceptance of a plea offer to life without the possibility of parole. This colleague, who does not deny the conversation, but has insisted that his name be withheld, appears to have imparted the considerable benefits of his "learning curve" to Judge Summerhouse, explaining in no uncertain terms that the idea behind the game was a simple one: Whenever in doubt, you give the defense pretty much everything it asks for. At the same time, you help out the prosecution only in those ways that aren't too obvious and heavy-handed. What you'll end up with is a "clean" conviction and death sentence—one that will be upheld on appeal, all the way up to and including the Supreme Court, where it's undoubtedly going to wind up, sooner or later.

By the time Fielder emerged from his meeting with the judge, he was clutching a handful of signed and sealed orders, granting him the assistance of various experts—a private investigator, a mental-health professional, a mitigation team, and a consulting pathologist—all of whom would eventually be reimbursed with state funds. He also had authorization to obtain a typewritten transcript of the morning's court proceedings. This last item would perform a dual function: The transcript itself would be used as an exhibit to be attached to motion papers the defense would be submitting at a later date. But beyond that, the very act of Fielder's obtaining it served notice upon the court that every ruling it made, and every application it denied, would be collected, scrutinized, and preserved—initially for the benefit of the defense, but ultimately for review by appellate judges in the event of a conviction, and particularly in the event of a death sentence.

With the newly signed orders in hand and the barest suggestion of a smile on his face, Fielder took a short walk around the corner of Maple Street to the building's annex, which for nearly a hundred years has housed the Ottawa County Detention Facility, better known as the Cedar Falls jail.

It was time for a sit-down visit with Jonathan Hamilton.

AT THE SAME time that Matthew Fielder was preparing for his first serious interview with his client, across Main Street, in the Harriman Office Building—begrudgingly named in honor of a member of the opposition party that had funded its construction some forty years earlier—Gil Cavanaugh was assembling his team of assistants and investigators for a meeting to discuss what evidence the prosecution would be presenting to a grand jury the following day.

With no regular grand jury in session, Cavanaugh had already notified the County Commissioner of Jurors to assemble a panel for nine o'clock the following morning. The County Commissioner of Jurors was actually nothing more than a title, a second hat—and there were three or four more on the rack after that—donned from time to time by the County Clerk, Dot Whipple. She had been on the phone since noon, doing her best to round up thirty or so registered voters, from whom Judge Summerhouse would select twenty-three to comprise a special grand jury, which in turn would hear the prosecution's evidence the following day. The procedure would later come under attack by Matt Fielder, who would demand a list of the grand jurors, names—normally kept secret—so he could ensure that none of those who had voted to indict Jonathan Hamilton would wind up on the jury eventually selected to try him.

Cavanaugh knew that the likelihood of the defendant's testifying at the grand jury was so slim that he could discount it altogether. There was simply no way Fielder was going to expose his client to cross-examination at this early stage of the case. There is no judge present in a grand-jury room to oversee the proceedings; the district attorney assumes the dual role of prosecutor and "legal advisor" to the jurors. The function of the defense attorney is narrowly circumscribed: counsel may be present only during the testimony of the defendant, and only as a silent observer. Finally, the rules under which a grand jury deliberates are very different from those governing a trial jury: instead of the strict "proof beyond a reasonable doubt" standard required to convict a defendant, only "reasonable cause" need be established to indict him; and whereas a trial jury must reach a unanimous verdict before it can convict, a mere majority—twelve out of twenty-three—is sufficient to indict. It is therefore little wonder that we are left with the oft-repeated phrase, "A grand jury will indict a ham sandwich if asked to."

What all this meant to Gil Cavanaugh was that however abundant his evidence against Jonathan Hamilton might be, he had no need—and therefore absolutely no desire—to present more than a bare minimum of it to the grand jury. And, knowing that the defense would eventually be entitled to a transcript of the testimony of any trial witness who had appeared before the grand jury, Cavanaugh, like any good prosecutor, would want to call as few witnesses as possible, ask them the smallest number of questions necessary, and restrict even those questions to the highly suggestive (or "leading") variety, ones that could easily be answered with a simple yes or no: "Now, is it a fact, Officer, that the defendant appeared to have blood on his forehead when you first observed him?"

Gathered with Cavanaugh in his office that afternoon were two assistant district attorneys, a paralegal, and four investigators from the state police—Deke Stanton, Hank Carlson, Gerard LeFevre, and Everett Wells. Stanton and Carlson, of course, had been the first officers on the scene, and it was Stanton who had done the initial investigation, claimed to have elicited an oral confession from Jonathan Hamilton, and subsequently arrested him. Wells and LeFevre had arrived at the scene first thing Tuesday morning, carrying a search warrant that had been signed by Judge Arthur Summerhouse in his living room late Monday night. While the judge, the prosecution, and the defense had been busy arguing in court the following morning, Investigators Wells and LeFevre had driven to the Hamilton estate, entered the cottage in which Jonathan had lived, and gone over every inch of it, taking photographs, collecting blood, hair, and fiber samples, and seizing physical evidence. They had returned to Cedar Falls and gone straight to the meeting at Cavanaugh's office with the fruits of their labors. It would take some time for the photographs to be developed, enlarged, and catalogued. The samples would have to be submitted to various crime and forensic labs for analysis and comparison. But the items of physical evidence would pay much more immediate and obvious dividends. Topping the list were two badly bloodstained towels, retrieved from behind a vanity compartment underneath the sink in Jonathan's bathroom. Wrapped in one of the bloody towels was a hunting knife. It had a genuine staghorn handle, and a five-inch tempered-steel blade that was smooth near the point and serrated near the handle. It appeared to have been wiped clean of any blood or fingermarks.

Cavanaugh and his team met for the better part of two hours. The bare-bones presentation they finally settled on consisted of the calling of four witnesses: Investigator Deke Stanton, for the arrest and confession of Jonathan Hamilton; Medical Examiner Frances Chu, to describe the wounds sustained by the victims, the probable time of death, and the nature of the weapon that appeared to have been used; Investigator Gerard LeFevre, to introduce the knife and describe the circumstances of its recovery; and one civilian witness, Bass McClure, to relate his early-morning phone call from the defendant, and his subsequent discovery of the bodies.

ACCORDING TO ENTRIES in the visitor's log book, Matt Fielder's first sit-down interview with Jonathan Hamilton lasted a little bit over two hours. Yet by his own admission, Fielder learned very little of substance during the meeting, and later calculated that if he were to add up the actual words said, they would have filled up less than a half an hour, all told. He'd come to think of the experience, in fact, as something like watching a ball game on television: You got about three minutes of commercials for every minute of actual play. With Jonathan, you got about three minutes of silence for every minute of conversation.

To begin with, Jonathan's demeanor was such that Fielder believed him to be in a virtual state of shock. He seemed aware of his surroundings, but barely so. The word that keeps coming back to Fielder, even today, is *bewildered*. Having already noted Jonathan's apparent inability to project into the future beyond the very day and night in which he found himself, Fielder was now struck by the flatness of Jonathan's affect—how inappropriately he was reacting to the fact that, rightly or wrongly, he'd just been arrested for, and accused of, hacking his grandparents to death.

Fielder asked Jonathan a lot of questions and, eventually, managed to extract a fair amount of information. But the questions Fielder asked, and the answers Jonathan supplied, were almost entirely limited to the subject of Jonathan's background—his childhood, his family life, his schooling, his growing-up. For example, Fielder asked what, if anything, Jonathan did for work and during his spare time. He wanted to know if Jonathan had ever been in trouble before, and, conversely, if he had any accomplishments he could list, things he was proud of. Fielder knew he was going to need all this information sooner or later. For one thing, it was easier to get Jonathan to talk about his past than it was to get him to talk about why he suddenly found himself sitting in jail. And Fielder knew that just getting Jonathan to talk was important in itself. As much as anything else, a sense of trust needed to be established. Talking about the crime could wait. The one thing they were going to have plenty of was time.

To a layman, the notion that Fielder would avoid pressing his client at the earliest possible opportunity on the ultimate issue—that of guilt or innocence—may sound strange indeed. But there are good reasons for this strategy, and Fielder was mindful of them. The defense lawyer, and particularly the court-appointed defense lawyer, learns to exercise caution in the early days of his relationship with his client. Asking a defendant right off the bat whether he's guilty or innocent is something like starting out a blind date with the question, "So, have you slept with other people?" When he first meets the lawyer who's been sent in to represent him, the defendant is naturally wary. *Who is this guy?* he's wondering. *Who's paying him? How do I know he's not part of the same bunch of people who are trying to put me away? After all, they seemed friendly, too, and told me it would be in my best interest to tell* them *every-*

thing. And, if he's somehow able to get beyond that initial paranoia and believe that his lawyer's really on his side, his next thought is still likely to be, *If I tell him I'm guilty, there's no way he's going to fight for me the same way as if he believes I'm innocent*—a fear that's not too difficult to understand, and probably even well-founded, in some cases. As a result, many defense lawyers, when dealing with a defendant who certainly *seems* to have committed the crime he's charged with, will never get around to posing the ultimate question, *Did you do it?* Perhaps here we are witnessing the original application of the "Don't ask, don't tell" policy.

There was another reason why Fielder felt he had no need to know the whole story that first day. The immediate decision that had to be made was whether or not Jonathan should testify before the grand jury. From the available evidence, Fielder strongly suspected that Jonathan had indeed killed his grandparents. What he would ultimately need to know was *why*. And whatever the reason, it couldn't possibly be sufficient enough, or compelling enough, for Fielder to want to have his client walk into the grand jury the following day and talk about it.

The homeowner who shoots the intruder, the battered wife who kills her drunk and abusive husband, the shopkeeper who defends his store the twentieth time he's robbed—those are the defendants you send into the grand jury. Even if the law says that such an individual wasn't entirely justified in doing what he did, if he can tell his story in a sympathetic enough way, chances are good he's going to walk out of there. He'll either be cleared altogether, or charged with some lesser crime, such as the possession of an unlicensed gun in his home or place of business, a misdemeanor requiring no jail time.

No grand jury was going to buy the proposition that Jonathan Hamilton had killed his grandparents in self-defense, or to prevent them from robbing him or abusing him.

His story could wait.

But beyond that, and beyond the need to establish a sense of trust between client and attorney, there was yet another reason altogether that kept Fielder from pushing Jonathan to talk about the crime early on in their relationship. As early as that first afternoon, Matt Fielder was beginning to sense, however tentatively and vaguely, that not only did Jonathan Hamilton not know *why* he had killed his grandparents, but that it was entirely possible he didn't even know *whether* he had killed them.

So they spent those two hours, Matt Fielder and Jonathan Hamilton, getting acquainted. For Jonathan, it was the first real chance to get to know this man who was going to be his lawyer, whatever that strange title may have meant to him. For Fielder, it marked the point at which he truly began caring about Jonathan, not just as another client who needed his help, but as an utterly defenseless, overgrown child of heartbreaking innocence, whose very survival was now placed squarely in Fielder's hands. And though the process would prove a slow and sometimes painful one, given Jonathan's severely limited vocabulary and generally poor verbal skills, a picture began to emerge that afternoon, a picture that would gradually be enlarged upon, filled in, and fleshed out in the many afternoons of the weeks and months to follow.

7

JONATHAN

JONATHAN PORTER HAMILTON came into the world on the twelfth day of August, 1969. By the time of Jonathan's birth, his parents, Porter Hamilton and Elizabeth Greenhall Hamilton, had been through more than their share of marital difficulties. Separated twice, and twice reunited, they had finally reached an accommodation of sorts that involved separate bedrooms in opposite wings of the greathouse on the estate Porter's father, Carter Hamilton, had inherited from his own father, Meriwether Hamilton. Meriwether had made his fortune selling old-growth timber to the sawmills and paper factories at the turn of the century. At one point he had owned nearly a quarter of a million acres of forest in the heart of what is today known as Adirondack Park. When he threatened to cut down every tree standing, the state stepped in and bought him out in order to stop him, making his timber fortune look like small change. Meriwether kept a single 250-acre "parcel" for himself, on which he set about building the seven structures that today comprise the Hamilton estate.

Carter Hamilton, Jonathan's grandfather, grew up on the estate and, save for a half-dozen years spent away at college and in the military, spent his whole life on it. He became a junior partner of sorts in Meriwether Hamilton's financial empire, which grew to include real-estate holdings, oil and gas leases, and a chain of newspapers. When Carter married

Mary Alice Poindexter in 1930, he left Flat Lake only long enough to spend a two-week honeymoon in the Caribbean, returning with Mary Alice to take up residence in the cottage that would ultimately become Jonathan's home. Carter and Mary Alice had two children: William, who was born in 1938 and died of meningitis in his first year, and Porter, born in 1940.

Porter appears to have been the most adventurous of the Hamiltons. Strikingly handsome and Harvard-educated, he was both a good student and a world-class lacrosse player. He won a Rhodes Scholarship, which took him to Oxford, where he lived and studied for two years. When he returned, he brought with him Elizabeth Greenhall, the woman who would become his wife. They promptly moved into one of the upstairs suites in the estate, where they, too, became permanent residents.

Just what the nature of the differences between Jonathan's parents was, is hard to pinpoint. Porter Hamilton was widely known to have been a ladies' man. There is one story, difficult to confirm but likely true, that the ink on his wedding license had scarcely dried when he returned from the church with the maid of honor, and disappeared with her in an upstairs bedroom for the better part of the evening. The maid of honor was none other than Margaret Greenhall, the younger sister of Elizabeth Greenhall Hamilton, Porter's bride of two hours.

Just how Elizabeth continued to put up with Porter's womanizing for nearly forty years invites speculation. By all accounts she was a soft-spoken, timid woman, who was waited upon by servants—a German couple, Elna and Klaus Armbrust, who attended to the housekeeping and the grounds, respectively. Seldom was Elizabeth seen outside her home. It appears that she never managed to obtain a driver's license or a social-security card, and had little or no money of her own, instead depending upon her husband for a weekly allowance to cover her needs. Even then, Porter—who by that time was running most of the family's businesses—would have to take time out to chauffeur her to the store so she could make her purchases, granting or withholding his personal approval when it came to each of her selections.

This much is known about Elizabeth: Not too long after her marriage to Porter, she began to drink, and by the time of Jonathan's birth she had become something of an alcoholic. Not that she ever turned into a public embarrassment, of course: She did her drinking upstairs, in the privacy of her own bedroom, sipping sherry from a crystal glass. Only her mother, Mary Alice Hamilton, and her physician, a fellow named Dr. Nash (the brother of Walter Nash, the longtime Flat Lake Town Supervisor), seem to have been aware of the dimensions of her problem.

Back in 1969, when Jonathan was born, little was known about the subject of fetal alcoholism. Today we are first beginning to understand just how prevalent the problem is, and how indelibly it marks its victims. Researchers have come to identify a number of physical, mental, and emotional symptoms that, taken together, comprise a condition that is officially recognized in diagnostic manuals as FAS, or fetal alcohol syndrome, an organic disorder that has been referred to colloquially as the "incurable hangover." Physically, it may include a somewhat pronounced forehead; a short, upturned nose; a smooth philtrum (the area beneath the nose that is normally ridged); a thin vermillion (upper-lip border); eyes that are small and wide-set; an abnormally small jaw; minor differences in the ears; and a brain that is often somewhat smaller than average. Mentally, there is a slight but definitely noticeable statistical drop in test scores, and an increase in the type of behavior generally associated with ADD, or attention deficit disorder. But it is in the emotional area that some of the subtlest, but deepest scarring seems to show up, with victims exhibiting a characteristic innocence and naiveté that tends to leave them at the mercy of those looking to introduce them to drugs, sex, and a variety of criminal activities.

Even with the strides currently being made to identify the disorder, determine its frequency, and educate the public to the dangers of drinking during pregnancy, comparatively little research has been done to track those suffering from FAS in order to monitor its effects in later life. Part of the difficulty is that, with the disease only recently recognized, researchers lack a clearly defined database of older individuals affected by it. Jonathan Hamilton's situation is a perfect illustration of the problem.

With Elizabeth Greenhall Porter dead almost ten years, there is no way to document with certainty that she drank in the first trimester of Jonathan's pregnancy. But knowing her history of drinking, and looking at Jonathan, it is extremely tempting to conclude that he exhibits at least a mild case of the disorder, a *forme fruste* referred to in the literature as FAE, or fetal alcohol effect. A positive diagnosis is further complicated by the fact that Jonathan is known to have suffered severe smoke inhalation—and therefore probably carbon monoxide poisoning as well—at the time of the fire that destroyed part of the greathouse and took the lives of both of his parents in the winter of 1988. In any event, he does have wide-set eyes, a slightly hypoplastic philtrum, and ears that—at least according to photographs—differ in shape from those of all his immediate ancestors; he scored substantially below average on standardized tests; and those familiar with him describe him as lacking in insight, unable to maintain concentration, and guileless in the extreme.

According to records obtained from Mercy Hospital in Cedar Falls, Jonathan was carried to full term by his mother; nonetheless, he weighed only 4 pounds 11 ounces at birth, and was measured at less than 18 inches long—figures fully consistent with the pattern of prenatal growth deficiency commonly associated with FAS and FAE. But pediatric records tell us that Jonathan soon began to thrive, at least in terms of postnatal growth and overall physical appearance. By the time he entered Cedar Falls Elementary School, he was one of the tallest in his class, although at seven, he may also have been one of the oldest. Family photographs reveal a boy who was extremely good-looking, but who at the same time was seldom caught smiling. In snapshot after snapshot, he can be seen staring into the camera with something eerily suggestive of a fashion model's detachment.

Because the Cedar Falls school system was not a particularly progressive or competitive one—less than thirty percent of its high-school graduates go on to attend college even today—Jonathan's behavior and learning difficulties went largely unnoticed for several years. But by fifth grade, when he was eleven, Jonathan was exhibiting both antisocial traits and cognitive deficiencies. Despite being tall, good-looking, and reasonably athletic, he seems to have developed few friends. His reading comprehension was likened to that of a first-grader, a description which appears to have been a charitable euphemism for saying that he simply couldn't read. According to the comments of various teachers, he had "difficulty focusing and concentrating, [was] either unable or unwilling to follow even basic rules and instructions, . . . show[ed] poor control of his impulses, [could] not accept any degree of responsibility, . . . and require[d] individualized supervision on an almost constant basis."

Twice Jonathan was left back from his class, being required to repeat both fifth and seventh grades. By the time he entered high school—which in Cedar Falls meant ninth grade—he was seventeen years old. A written evaluation by a clinical psychologist, called in by the school's principal on a consulting basis, reads like something straight out of a diagnostic manual for FAS/FAE.

Subject exhibits a marked-to-profound degree of subnormal intellectual functioning, with a specific deficiency in both reading level and mathematical skills. He has great difficulty with abstractions (e.g., time and space, cause and effect, etc.). His attention span, ability to concentrate, and memory retention are all well below normal levels for his age.

Maladaptive social functioning is present and manifested in terms of swings between periods of hyperactivity and lethargy, as well as impulsiveness and occasional oppositional behavior.

Because of poor reading ability, subject was measured with a non-verbal test protocol, scoring 82 (low normal–to–subnormal on the WISC scale), and borderline infantile on his Rorschach (inkblot) responses.

Within a year, Jonathan had dropped out of school altogether. Unsuited to hold down the most menial of jobs, he spent almost all of his time on the estate, venturing off the grounds only in the supervision of an adult, which usually meant his father or grandfather.

If Elizabeth Hamilton's drinking had been the cause of her son's problems, now it became the effect, as well. Jonathan the small boy had been a handful, a high-maintenance child whose unpredictable mood swings and resistance to learning frustrated his mother's limited parenting skills. Gradually she had simply turned away from him.

But even as Jonathan's intellectual and emotional development stagnated, his physical growth continued unchecked. To some observers, it was almost as though his outer body were overcompensating for whatever deficiencies lay buried within his damaged brain. By the age of fourteen, his height had already equalled that of his mother; by sixteen, he towered over her. There is some suggestion in the literature that FAS/FAE delays the onset of those secondary sex characteristics normally associated with puberty. In Jonathan's case, this factor may have been responsible for a late growth spurt that appears to have continued past the age of eighteen, and left him just a shade under six-four by the time it was done with him.

If Jonathan the child confounded Elizabeth Hamilton, Jonathan the adult positively frightened her. Although there is no record of his ever having actually attacked or harmed her, it is not altogether unthinkable that he may have. Evidence continues to mount, that postpubescent sufferers of

FAS/FAE tend to get into trouble because of their inability to adapt socially: They demand attention and gratification, they lie, they steal. Sexually, they are alternately vulnerable and aggressive; and occasionally they can even be physically assaultive. It is not unusual for them to have frequent encounters with the criminal justice system, both as perpetrators and victims. In Jonathan's case, this apparently did not happen; at least no public record can be found of his ever having been arrested prior to the deaths of his grandparents. But this anomaly may be largely explained by the extraordinary extent to which he was kept insulated from the real world that lay just beyond the stone walls of the Flat Lake estate.

In any event, as Jonathan neared twenty, Elizabeth seems to have become increasingly removed from him and the rest of the family, retreating to the four corners of her room, and her faithful companion the sherry bottle. Jonathan's grandparents, Carter and Mary Alice, found their daughter-in-law's withdrawal too painful to watch, and they moved out—but only as far as the cottage. The greathouse became a place of monumental sadness. Elizabeth stayed in her upstairs room; her husband came and went as he pleased; and Jonathan, who had his own quarters on the main floor, was pretty much left to fend for himself. Once a day, the three generations of Hamiltons would gather at the dinner table, to share their meal, either in superficial banter or melancholy silence.

Then one night, during the winter of 1989—more precisely the early morning hours of February 17—tragedy struck. The Armbrusts were awakened by the sound of a smoke detector coming from the greathouse. Just how long the alarm had been ringing could not be determined, but in the investigation that followed, it was calculated that for the sound to have been heard in the servants' cabin, the wind would have had to have shifted almost 180 degrees from the prevalent direction. By the time Klaus Armbrust could break into the house, the entire upstairs was engulfed in smoke. He somehow roused Jonathan and pulled him

from the building, but was unable to make his way back
inside.

The Cedar Falls Volunteer Rescue Squad responded in
time to save the house, but not its upstairs inhabitants. A
stunned Jonathan watched in the freezing February night as
his parents were carried out in body bags. The medical
examiner determined that both victims had died from
smoke inhalation and carbon monoxide poisoning sustained
as they slept. The investigation that followed, traced the
origin of the fire to Elizabeth's bedroom, and concluded
that apparently she had draped a shawl or bedjacket of some
sort over an electric space heater before falling asleep.

Jonathan himself spent eight days in Mercy Hospital,
recovering from severe damage to both of his lungs, ag-
gravated by pneumonia, a fairly frequent complication associated with smoke inhalation. Upon his discharge, he was
brought home to the estate, where he was moved into the
cottage with his grandparents, while the second floor of the
greathouse underwent repairs for extensive fire, smoke, and
water damage.

Because Jonathan's contacts with the outside world after
the fire continued to be so limited, it is difficult to assess
the extent of the impact the event had upon him, both physically and emotionally. Elna and Klaus Armbrust are tight-
lipped people, not given to expressing themselves regarding
Jonathan Hamilton, or any other subject, for that matter.
One of the few remaining outsiders who had occasion to
see Jonathan on anything approaching a regular basis is
Bass McClure, a sometime visitor to the Hamilton estate.
McClure had been a welcome guest on the property for
many years, hiking its trails and fishing its ponds with the
blessings of the owners. Several times he and Porter had
posted the land with notices that hunters and other tres-
passers would be prosecuted. Now, with Porter and Elizabeth dead, McClure made it his business to stop by
whenever he could, just to check on the needs of Jonathan
and his grandparents.

"The fire left its mark on the boy," McClure says, "and

he was a long time recovering from the physical effects of it. As to the mental aspect of the thing—well, I don't believe he ever did get over that. For one thing, he developed that stutter of his—there was no sign of that beforehand. For another, it's like the fire took all the mischief out of him. Before, he was quiet some of the time, and real overactive at other times—kind of like you'd expect from a three-year-old, or maybe a puppy. After, he was quiet *all* of the time. He'd just sit there and look at his hands, or down at his shoes, or stare at you with those pale blue eyes of his. I never did know what he was seeing, or what he was thinking. It was unnerving, it was. It was like all the fight was gone out of him, all the restlessness. You know?"

With all the fight gone out of him, Jonathan became less of a handful for his grandparents. When the repairs to the greathouse had been completed and the upstairs was fit to be lived in again, it was Carter and Mary Alice who moved back in. Jonathan stayed on in the cottage, whether by stubbornness on his part, mutual agreement, or some other process of determination. Reasonably good with his hands, he fixed up the smaller of two bedrooms, fashioning a fairly handsome cabinet out of scrap wood for his television set. Somehow he managed to keep his quarters respectably neat, if slightly less than clean. He came to the greathouse three times each day, where Elna Armbrust served him and his grandparents their meals. It must have been a silent ritual, and a terribly sad one.

8

UP AND RUNNING

FRIDAY'S COURT APPEARANCE was something of a non-
event. Fielder had managed to locate a pair of black loafers
to replace his workboots, but if the change was noticed by
Judge Summerhouse, it drew no comment from him. Jonathan Hamilton was again brought into court handcuffed,
again Fielder registered his objection (as he would continue
to do on all future court dates), and again it was overruled.
Gil Cavanaugh announced that the grand jury had met,
heard the evidence, and "returned a true bill," meaning that
a majority of the jurors had voted to indict Jonathan, though
Cavanaugh—citing rules of confidentiality—would not
specify precisely what it was they had indicted him for. But
no one in the courtroom had the slightest doubt that it was
for two counts of murder in the first degree.

Upon Cavanaugh's application, the case was adjourned
a week, for him to assemble copies of the indictment and
other legal papers he would be required to provide the defense at the official arraignment, the appearance at which
Jonathan would enter his initial plea of not guilty.

From start to finish, the entire proceeding took just over
two minutes. Not that its brevity prevented Gil Cavanaugh
from spending the next half hour on the courthouse steps,
posing for the cameras and telling every microphone in
sight that the citizens of Ottawa County could count on him
to uphold the law of the land. "It is my duty," he intoned

at one point, "my solemn, sworn duty, to see that we send out a message, for all to hear, that the good men and women of this county will not tolerate this type of animal-istic barbarianism. Scripture teaches us that it's God's will to take an eye for an eye, a life for a life. Though in this case, unfortunately, that'll still leave us one life behind. But we'll do what we have to do, I promise you that. I don't know how many of you know it, but I'm a grandparent myself."

Nobody had ever accused Gil Cavanaugh of using few words where many would do.

MATT FIELDER USED his second sit-down meeting with Jonathan Hamilton to ask Jonathan to tell him what he knew about the stabbings. He was prepared to back off if Jonathan showed any signs of balking; he didn't want to undo the trust he'd worked so hard to establish at their earlier meeting. But Jonathan didn't balk—that wasn't the problem. The problem was that his recollection of the events was so spotty.

"I remember waking up in the m-m-middle of the night," he said. "But th-that's all. I can't remember anything else about it. Then I woke up again, later. It was just starting to get l-l-light out, just a little bit. I n-needed to go to the bathroom, and I had to f-feel my way there. In the bath-room, it was even d-d-darker, 'cause there's no window there. But I d-didn't want to turn the light on, 'cause it would hurt my eyes. I p-p-peed. When I went to flush, the handle was all sticky. I thought m-maybe I missed the b-b-bowl. I was thirsty, too, so I w-went to the sink. The f-faucet was sticky, too. I made a c-c-cup with my hands." He demonstrated to Fielder how he'd done that.

"When I put my hands under the sp-spout, the sink was full. I d-d-didn't know why. So I turned the light on."

Jonathan didn't seem to want to go on. Fielder had to prompt him. "What did you see?" he asked.

"The w-w-water."

"Yes?"

"It was all r-r-red."

Jonathan's first thought was that somebody had been painting. There was red paint in the bowl, red paint on the outside of the sink, on the mirror, on the wall, on the light switch, on the floor—everywhere. In the bowl it was a light-color red, like somebody had been washing out a paintbrush. Everywhere else it was dark red. In some places it was so dark it looked black.

"I t-t-touched it," he said. "I held it up to my nose, so I c-could smell it. It didn't smell like paint. So I put some on the t-t-tip of my tongue. It was s-salty."

After a while his eyes had got used to the light. He saw that there was a trail of red, leading from the bathroom to the front door.

"Did you know what it was by that time?" Fielder asked him.

"B-b-blood?"

Fielder nodded. "What did you do next?"

"I w-went to check on Grandpa Carter and Grandma Mary Alice."

"And what did you find?"

Jonathan didn't answer.

"What did you find, Jonathan?" Fielder asked it as gently as he could.

"Th-th-th-they was all cut up."

That's when he'd made the phone call, and reached Bass McClure.

BACK AT HIS CABIN that evening, Fielder changed out of his lawyer clothes and back into jeans and a sweatshirt. He'd gotten over his initial annoyance at having to drive an hour and a half—and that was one way—for a two-minute court appearance of no consequence. But his meeting with Jonathan had certainly been interesting enough. Even if little had come of it in terms of factual revelations about the killings themselves, at least he'd got Jonathan to talk about what he did remember. Fielder figured it would only be a matter of time before the rest of it surfaced too.

In that respect, though, he'd be wrong. Whatever terrible things Jonathan had done that night were apparently buried too deep for him to dredge up, then or ever. Fielder could understand that; after all, he had the crime-scene photos, in full, glossy color. The sights they depicted were enough to make anyone want to forget.

Jonathan had done his best, and that would have to do.

Aside from that, Fielder was actually relieved to have the one week's adjournment: Under the law, he had only five days following arraignment to submit a written motion attacking the indictment because of Cavanaugh's failure to provide the defendant a reasonable time to prepare to testify before the grand jury. The extra week meant that much more additional time to work on his papers.

Not to mention the money.

The way Fielder figured it, counting driving time, he'd put in eleven hours by the time he got back home. At $175 an hour, that came to almost $2,000! To someone whose bank balance tended to resemble nothing so much as a fuel gauge constantly hovering just over the EMPTY line, the sum was nothing short of unreal. Pay a man pauper's wages long enough, and he'll eventually come around to thinking that they're all he's worth.

In fashioning its version of the death penalty, the battle over the allocation of resources for capital defenders had turned out to be one of the stickiest issues the legislature had been required to deal with. To opponents of the death penalty, the worst part of the system is that it pits the vast power and wealth of the state against those who are almost invariably its very poorest members—in terms of economics, education, and intellect. The history of capital-punishment litigation in the modern era can be read as a study of just how far a state shall be permitted to go before the Supreme Court steps in and says that the system has failed to satisfactorily safeguard the process by which it determines which of its accused will live, and which will die. Posed as a question, it comes down to this: What minimum rules must the state promulgate and follow before it may kill?

One of the cardinal rules is that it must provide the accused with the effective assistance of counsel. And the key word is *effective*.

IN 1972, IN the landmark case of *Furman v. Georgia*, the Court had swept the slate clean, voiding every single capital statute on the books at the time—those of thirty-nine states and the District of Columbia, as well as that of the federal government itself. In all, some six hundred death sentences were vacated.

Furman didn't go so far as to rule that the states could not have death penalties. Instead, it found fault with how Georgia, and (in the longest written decision ever handed down by the Court, in which, for the first and only time in history each of the nine justices wrote a separate opinion) how every other jurisdiction with a death penalty had failed to administer it properly and fairly. But in doing so, the Court also showed the way how a death sentence could be enacted and enforced so as to pass constitutional muster.

No sooner was the ink on the decision dry, than states began the process of rewriting their laws, attempting as they did so to follow the blueprint laid out in *Furman*. The first efforts encountered unforeseen problems, renewed challenges, and frequent setbacks. But with each setback, the state legislatures learned something, and each subsequent law had the benefit of those experiences. By the end of the decade, death rows began filling up again, and in 1977, when a man named Gary Gilmore successfully insisted that his lawyers curtail their fight to prolong his life, death regained a foothold in American jurisprudence. By the mid-nineties, executions had become commonplace, and it was no longer unusual to pick up a newspaper and read that two or three prisoners had been put to death the evening before.

Following *Furman*, more than two decades passed before New York State enacted a new version of capital punishment, to go into effect in September 1995. Not that the legislature hadn't tried; but every law they passed in the interim had been effectively, if narrowly, vetoed by a staunchly opposed Democrat governor named Mario Cuomo. It was only with Cuomo's upset defeat in 1994 at the hands of a conservative, law-and-order Republican, George Pataki, that the way was cleared for the return of capital punishment in New York.

Accordingly, by the time the legislature put the finishing touches on what would become the state's new death penalty, it had the considerable advantage of a vast learning curve derived from the various successes and failures of nearly forty other jurisdictions. And the result, as even the most vocal critics of capital punishment must grudgingly admit, is a statute that is about as enlightened as any that might be found, in terms of the protections it affords those it seeks to kill.

In addition to providing reasonable rates of pay to lawyers appointed to represent those accused of capital crimes, the law recognizes the state's obligation to see to it that the lawyers are provided the tools that are reasonably necessary to *effectively* represent their clients. Under this reasoning (which is New York's reasoning, of course, purely because cases since *Furman* clearly establish that it is the Supreme Court's reasoning), the defense is authorized to retain the services of private investigators, psychiatrists and psychologists, consultants, interpreters, social workers, and a host of other experts, all to be reimbursed out of state funds. When appropriate, travel and lodging expenses are covered. If a transcript is needed, the state must pay for it. If photographs are required, a professional photographer may be brought in. If copies of lengthy documents must be made, so be it.

Not that the law is drawn in such a way as to benefit only the defense. Under a specific provision of the statute, the district attorney prosecuting a capital case is eligible for huge additional infusions of state money, but *only for so long as he opts to pursue a death sentence in the case.* One can easily be sanguine about a system that seeks to balance available resources between adversaries; but it is equally tempting to be cynical about a law that makes state-sanctioned killing profitable, and to wonder about the message being sent out to prosecutors, particularly those laboring under the strictures of county budgets that are already strained.

When it comes right down to it, death is not only different, it is also expensive—hugely so. And, as always, it is the taxpayer who ends up footing the bill.

HAVING SECURED THE necessary signatures from Judge Summerhouse on the afternoon of his first court appearance in the case, Matt Fielder needed to get a team up and running. Looking for a local private investigator, he'd asked around first at the courthouse, then at the jail, and finally at a bar up the block and across the street. The name that kept coming up was that of Pearson J. Gunn, a man who reportedly lived in an A-frame in nearby Tupper Lake, but spent many of his afternoons, and most of his evenings, right there in Cedar Falls. Fielder found the bar, a small place shamelessly called the Dew Drop Inn, and was told by the bartender, a pleasant man who answered to the name Pete, that if he sat down and waited twenty-five minutes, he'd have his chance to meet Gunn right there.

Sure enough, at exactly four o'clock, the door swung open, causing a cluster of little bells above it to break into a chorus of chimes. They were "bear bells," Pete had explained when Fielder had first commented on them. You wore them when you were out on the trail, so a bear could hear you coming and have a chance to take his leave. What you didn't want to do was surprise him.

Now, without looking up from the glassware he was washing, Pete said, "That'll be him now." Fielder swung around in time to behold a huge hulk of a man, who—perhaps because of Fielder's subliminal association with the bells—struck Fielder as absolutely ursine, in terms of height, heft, and hairiness.

Fielder and Gunn headed to a corner in the back, where

they shared a table and a pitcher of something local called Adirondack Amber Ale. Fielder did most of the talking, Gunn most of the drinking. By the end of an hour, Gunn had a few pages of scribbled notes, a pretty good understanding of the facts of the case, and what had to have been a remarkably full bladder. Fielder himself had a pleasant buzz for company on the drive home, as well as a new private investigator.

For a mitigation team—so called because its assignment would be to dig up information sufficient to persuade a jury that various mitigating factors in the background of the accused outweighed aggravating factors in the crime, and therefore that death was not the appropriate sentence—Fielder had already reached all the way down to Albany, to tap the firm of Miller and Munson, better known in the business as M&M, from the logo with which they adorned their cards and stationery. Although he'd met one of the M's, he'd never worked with them, a fact which had left him a bit uneasy. But he'd tried to reassure himself with the knowledge that "M & M" had a nice ring to it. There were the candies, of course—those pleasing little coated bits of chocolate, of which the browns, being closest to natural, had always been Fielder's favorites. And then there was the famous Yankee duo of Mantle and Maris, who between them had managed to hit 115 home runs in a single season.

He'd need only one from Miller and Munson.

Baseball was on the very short list of Matt Fielder's true loves. But for a bad break, he might have been a professional ballplayer, major-league material. He'd played college ball on full scholarship at the University of Michigan, a fixture in center field, batting in the third spot. He'd led the Wolverines in hitting three years in a row, with a college career average of .396. Senior year he'd hit .456 and made the starting All–Big Ten team, as well as several first team All-America lists. He'd been drafted twenty-third overall by the Boston Red Sox organization, and assigned to their Class B farm team in Galveston, Texas. His bad break had been of the literal variety. It had come seven weeks into the season, at a time when he was batting a league-leading .429 and waiting to be called up any day to the AA team in Sarasota, Florida. An inside fastball had caught him on the right elbow, shattering the cubital bone into eleven pieces. Three surgeries, six titanium screws, and one year later, he'd finally "hung up his spikes," gone back to Ann Arbor, and tried his hand at law school. For the most part, he'd hated it. Contracts and property and creditors' rights interested him not at all; torts was torture, bankruptcy a bore. But criminal law was intriguing, and it was the idea of fighting for the underdog—being the one voice to still the vengeful mob—that had finally lit a fire under him and turned him from a mediocre student to a possessed advocate.

With a private investigator and a mitigation team on board, Fielder was pretty much up and running. Soon he'd need a mental-health professional—either a psychiatrist or a psychologist, or both—but he wanted to take his time and get the right person. For already he had a pretty good idea that whatever the source of Jonathan Hamilton's apparent slowness, the result could quite possibly rise to the level of "mental retardation." Under the New York statute, Fielder knew that would be the ball game: The legislature, to its credit, had decreed that death was always an inappropriate punishment in such a case, no matter how heinous the crime or how compelling the aggravating circumstances. (Still, there was a serious catch here. In order to constitute "mental retardation" under New York's law, a defendant's diminished capacity must have manifested itself before the age of eighteen. In Jonathan's case, at least part of his mental problems were traceable to injuries he'd sustained during the fire. That had been in 1989, when Jonathan was already nineteen.)

Next, Fielder figured he'd need a pathologist to review and interpret the autopsy reports. But that could wait a bit, too. He figured he wouldn't be getting the material for at least several weeks, and his own familiarity with medical terms would be sufficient for a while after that.

Just who or what else he might need, would to a certain extent be determined by what evidence the prosecution unearthed. In time, Fielder might want to bring in a fingerprint expert, a footprint man, a blood-splatter specialist, or a hair-and-fiber analyst. It might turn out he needed his own lab to do independent DNA testing, or even an exhumation order to permit reexamination of the bodies. But all of that was for another day. He knew better than to go running to Judge Summerhouse with an elaborate laundry list of demands that were, at this point at least, arguably speculative. There are those who counsel defense lawyers to use the scatter-gun approach and immediately demand absolutely everything that might ever conceivably be needed; but they tend to be professors who lecture at universities and write in law journals. In the trenches, Fielder had learned, sometimes it pays to save your shots.

Finally, Fielder knew he had the right to request the assignment of an associate counsel, another defense lawyer to work alongside him, at a rate only slightly lower than his own lead-counsel rate. But here, too, he decided to hold off. It wasn't for nothing that Matt Fielder had chosen to make his new home in a remote section of the Adirondack Mountains. He'd come to like living alone, and he'd always preferred working alone. If the CDO felt he needed associate counsel, they wouldn't be bashful about letting him know. In the meantime he'd wait for Kevin Doyle to call and suggest it. Doyle knew where to find Fielder, after all. That much was clear.

THAT NIGHT, FIELDER sat in front of his wood-burning stove. It was warm enough to keep the doors of the stove half open. He watched as the flames licked at logs of ash, oak, maple, and birch. The first summer he'd bought the land, he'd marked the dead trees with bands of red ribbon, so they'd be easy to spot even after the living ones had dropped their leaves and were indistinguishable from the dead ones. When he hadn't been building his cabin, he'd been busy cutting, splitting, and stacking wood, until he had a pile high enough to get him through the most ferocious winter imaginable.

He could tell you the story behind every log he burned. Not only what kind of wood it was, but precisely which tree it had come from, and which section of the trunk. Whether he'd had to top the tree before felling it; whether it had fallen true or fooled him (which was rare, but had happened once or twice); how difficult it had been to cut up, split, and haul; how solid or rotten it was inside; what insect infestation or other blight had caused it to die in the first place; and how long it had had a chance to season.

He'd come to feel the same way about burning wood that he imagined a hunter must feel about eating meat. He'd never learned to lay a log on a fire without suffering some degree of pain over the realization that he was about to destroy it forever. No wonder some groups of Native Americans had solemnly begged their prey for forgiveness even as they sat down to feast upon it. It was a love-hate thing, a struggle over the desire to preserve, and the need to survive. But Fielder the wood-burner had also come to feel a slight but significant moral edge over the meat-eaters, at least so long as he had a good supply of red-ribboned trees to fell: He spared the living. But what did that make him? A scavenger, reduced to picking at the carcasses of the already-dead. Was that any better?

His thoughts turned to Jonathan Hamilton, alone in his cell at the Cedar Falls jail, with no fire to warm him. What was it, he wondered, that had gone so horribly wrong in Jonathan's poor, damaged brain, that had suddenly compelled him to lash out at the two people he should have loved and respected more than anyone else in the world? What on earth could possibly have triggered such terrible, murderous rage?

If Matt Fielder had no answers to those questions, it was reasonable to speculate that neither did Jonathan Hamilton himself. At that very moment—at least according to the entries in the log kept by the night-duty officer—he lay fast asleep on the cot that, when folded down, took up a third of the six-by-nine cell that had become his home a week earlier. If Jonathan was at the eye of the storm that was just then beginning to brew over the nation's youngest death-penalty statute, he certainly gave no sign of recognition of his special status. Not that that fact is altogether surprising; ask any meteorologist, and he'll tell you that one of the very first lessons you learn about truly violent weather is that there's often a dead calm at the center.

But if Jonathan slept that evening, his lawyer did not. Sixty miles to the southeast, Fielder sat fully awake, staring at the flames and embers of the fire in the stove in front of him, but all the while composing in his mind endless lists of things he'd be needing to do for a client so profoundly ill-equipped that he was unable to help himself. And so the process was already at work: the process which some twenty-five years earlier had driven Fielder from a minor-league baseball park in Galveston, Texas, to a major law school in Ann Arbor, Michigan; that had caused him to suddenly come awake one day and lift his head in the middle of a first-year criminal-law class; that had put him to work for underdog after miserable underdog in his Legal Aid days; that had sent him off to something they called Death School, only to leave him convinced he was emotionally unprepared to do the work they were asking him to do. The same process that, when he'd listened to the message from Kevin Doyle that Monday afternoon, had forced his hand to pick up the phone, return the call, and grudgingly agree to be the one to do whatever it was that had to be done, to put every bit of learning, experience, wisdom, and strength he'd ever acquired—in other words, every ounce of his being—into a struggle that, in the most literal sense imaginable, was nothing less than a matter of life and death.

9

THE ROCK CRUSHER

WHEN MATT FIELDER had risen from the corner table in the Cedar Falls bar to bid Pearson Gunn good-bye, Gunn had also stood up, extended a large paw of a hand toward Fielder, and grunted something that sounded like, "Seeya." Then, as soon as Fielder was out the door, Gunn had caught Pete's eye, signaled his need for another pitcher, and sat back down. If Matt Fielder did his best thinking in front of a fire, Pearson Gunn did his over a seemingly endless supply of Adirondack Amber. He'd sat there for the next two and a half hours—drinking, staring straight ahead, and scheming. Around eleven, Pete had called Molly's Cab Service and told Molly Molloy that it was time for what they referred to as the "Gunn run."

When Gunn woke up the following day, he had no trace of a hangover. He prepared and downed his usual breakfast of six eggs, a dozen slices of bacon, and four slabs of bread, washed down with three cups of black coffee hot enough to lift the skin off a rabbit.

That out of the way, Gunn got ready to go to work.

HILLARY MUNSON HAS what she likes to call a no-frills education. She is a product of the New York City public school system, where she learned reading, writing, arithmetic, and how to fend off an attacker wielding a box-cutter. She earned an undergraduate degree in psychology from SUNY/New Paltz, and an M.S.W. from Albany State. While in school, she wasn't a member of the debating team or the thespian society; she didn't play field hockey; and she didn't date. What she did do was to work full-time at a women's shelter and a drug rehabilitation program. In the process, she paid her tuition, room, and board, and managed to help more than a few people along the way.

After getting her M.S.W., Hillary had teamed up with another graduate, Lois Miller. Together they'd founded Miller and Munson, a psychology social work team offering its assistance to corporations, municipalities, schools, and other entities in need of programs for individuals with problems in areas such as substance abuse, job retraining, child rearing, and crisis intervention. They opened a small, windowless office on the second floor of a run-down building in downtown Albany.

In their first full year of operation, 1992, they landed three clients and netted $2,170.

By mid-1993, they were deep in debt and three months behind in their rent. Then Hillary's younger brother got arrested for breaking and entering a storefront on Eagle Street. He was promptly indicted for burglary in the third degree, a Class D felony carrying as much as two-and-a-third to seven years in state prison. Hillary went to see her brother's lawyer, an earnest but overworked young public defender who figured that, with plea-bargaining, he might be able to keep the damage down to one-to-three. Hillary proposed that she present the court with a comprehensive alternative sentencing proposal, including counseling, job training, and community service. The lawyer told her to give it a try, it probably couldn't hurt.

The proposal ran to eleven pages, neatly typed and single-spaced. It included a thorough case history of the defendant, an assessment of his needs, and a strategy for his rehabilitation. The judge was so impressed that he placed the defendant on probation, with the special condition that he be monitored by Miller and Munson, who would issue periodic reports directly to the judge. Their services were to be paid out of public funds.

Within two years time, the firm had become a staple of the court system, with a broad range of clients from County Court, Family Court, and Juvenile Hall. Every lawyer in Albany County came to know that if you wanted to keep a defendant out of prison, gain custody of a child, or rescue a budding delinquent, you picked up the phone and called the gals at M&M.

By 1995, with New York's capital-punishment statute about to become law, Hillary Munson had been one of a select few non-lawyers invited by Kevin Doyle to attend Death School. Arriving late to one of the lectures, she'd tripped over a briefcase and scattered her notes in the aisle. The lawyer who'd helped her retrieve her notes (who also happened to be the culprit who had carelessly left his briefcase protruding into the aisle) took her to lunch by way of apology. He was single, and was hardly the first man to be taken with Hillary's good looks. She has a small face with delicate features and a captivating smile, framed by a mane of dark curly hair that bounces as she moves. The two of them got along well, and at the end of the meal they traded business cards.

The name on his card was Matthew J. Fielder.

THE WAY PEARSON Gunn figured it, his first job was to rule out the possibility, however slight, that anyone other than Jonathan Hamilton had committed the murders. With that in mind, he picked up the phone and dialed a number he knew by heart. The reason Gunn still had a rotary phone was that he was firmly convinced that the push-button ones were a passing fad that would soon go out of style, along with digital clocks, air conditioners, and cars with automatic transmissions. The number that Gunn dialed belonged to a source of his at the state police barracks in Saranac Lake. Although Gunn refuses to this day to name his source, it was likely none other than Captain Roger Duquesne, the same man who had been rather vaguely identified as "the responding supervising officer" to show up at the Hamilton estate the morning of the killings.

Gunn himself had been a trooper for fifteen years, before he'd been forced out of the ranks in the aftermath of a severe beating administered to a suspect arrested in connection with the rape/murder of a six-year-old girl at the Blue Mountain Lake campground. Gunn and Duquesne had been partners at the time. Gunn had "taken the fall" for the beating, testifying at a departmental hearing that Duquesne had been nowhere in the vicinity when the suspect had injured himself by falling down a flight of stairs, three times. The hearing examiners found the story incredible, but without Gunn's implication of Duquesne, Gunn's was the only head to roll. As a result, Gunn became an extrooper and a private investigator, while Duquesne eventually rose to the rank of captain. But loyalty is a virtue second to none in law enforcement, and from that day on, Pearson Gunn has never lacked for a confidential source within the barracks.

So while Gunn refuses to confirm the fact, and Duquesne steadfastly denies it in both English and French, it is highly probable that the two men met sometime over that weekend, most likely late Saturday night. What is certain is that on Monday morning (to Gunn, anytime before three P.M. still counts as morning), Gunn showed up at Matt Fielder's cabin near Big Moose and presented his report.

Gunn's "report" was an oral one. He'd learned as a trooper that whenever you took notes, sooner or later some smart-ass defense lawyer was going to get ahold of them, put them under a microscope, and manage to make a fool out of you and a choirboy out of his client. Later, as a defense witness, he'd found the rules were pretty much the same, only reversed—there, it was the DA who ended up with the defense's notes. So Gunn had learned to store almost everything in his head. And as long as he stuck to his limit of three pitchers of Adirondack Amber in the space of any twenty-four-hour period, his system seemed to work pretty well.

What Gunn reported orally to Fielder was that in the

minds of the state police and the district attorney, this one was a no-brainer, an absolute lock, a *rock crusher*. The investigators had found and photographed a blood trail that began in the victims' bedroom, led down the stairs and out the door, and continued all the way to the bathroom in Jonathan Hamilton's cottage. In the back of a vanity cabinet that contained Jonathan's sink, they'd found two blood-soaked towels. Wrapped in one of the towels was a large hunting knife. Preliminary typing tests conducted on the blood indicated that it was a mixture of types O+ and A−. According to the medical examiner, blood drawn from the victims established that Carter Hamilton was type O+, while Mary Alice Hamilton was A−. Many of the samples had been sent for DNA testing, and although the results wouldn't be known for about four to five weeks, it was a foregone conclusion that the blood would test out as being that of the two victims, to a nearly mathematical certainty.

In addition to the blood-drop trail, there was also a bloody footprint trail, though contamination had made interpretation of it more difficult. A barefooted person, with a foot consistent with size-12 shoes, had tracked blood both entering and leaving the crime scene. The problem was that, according to a statement taken from one Brian McClure, aka "Bass," McClure had accompanied Jonathan Hamilton in and out of the house, at a time when Jonathan was barefooted. Furthermore, Hamilton, in his first account of discovering the bodies, made to McClure, had apparently indicated he had been barefooted at that time, as well.

Several pairs of shoes had been found in Jonathan Hamilton's cottage, and seized. All were size 12.

Next, in their examination of the crime scene, the investigators had lifted a number of latent fingerprints. Matches had been made with known prints of both victims, supplied by the medical examiner, and with those of Jonathan Hamilton, taken during his processing. A number of hairs and fibers had also been recovered, including seven long blond hairs that, at least when grossly examined, appeared to be consistent with Jonathan Hamilton's hair.

A canvass of the neighboring houses had been conducted. The closest people were a husband and wife, Klaus and Elna Armbrust, who lived on the estate, a quarter of a mile away, and were employees of the Hamiltons—he as a groundskeeper, she as a cook and housekeeper. Neither of them reported hearing anything during the night, or recalled noticing any suspicious vehicles in the area. Possibly because the ground was so dry from lack of recent rainfall, the investigators had discovered no shoeprints or tire tracks of value. Besides the Armbrusts, no one lived within a mile of the house, or had seen or heard anything out of the ordinary.

Finally, Gunn told Fielder that, according to his information, the Cedar Falls grand jury had indicted Jonathan Hamilton for two counts of murder in the first degree, and that it was an absolute certainty that Gil Cavanaugh would be seeking the death penalty.

HILLARY MUNSON LEFT Albany at seven o'clock Monday morning, driving north on Route 87 in a light rain. By nine she was at the Cedar Falls jail. By nine-thirty, she was sitting across from Jonathan Hamilton in a visiting booth, looking up into his face. Hillary is an even five feet tall. Jonathan is about that tall sitting down.

Hillary's objectives at this first meeting with Jonathan were severalfold. First, like Matt Fielder, she wanted to win the client's trust and confidence. This she found harder than she'd expected, despite her experience in dealing with a variety of individuals endowed with limited communication skills. Second, she needed Jonathan to sign a number of release forms, so that she could begin to gather documents from schools, hospitals, and other agencies. It was Hillary's belief that if you collected enough paper on a person, sooner or later you were bound to strike gold. She liked to tell a story of hunting for medical records on a young man, only to be told that all that could be found were a few old dental reports. "Send them over," she'd sighed. When they'd arrived, she'd looked through them and discovered that the man had had all his teeth extracted when he was fourteen years old. When she asked him why, he'd explained they'd all rotted, because no one had ever told him to brush them. Beginning with that single fact, Hillary had painted a picture of extreme childhood neglect, sufficient to save the man from a ten-year prison sentence.

Jonathan's teeth looked fine to her. He signed the forms agreeably but slowly, without so much as pretending to read them. Hillary made a mental note that Jonathan seemed rather guileless.

Then Hillary turned to the real task at hand—getting Jonathan to give her as many "contacts" as he could. By contacts, she meant family members, friends, and other individuals who could be leads to finding out everything there was to know about Jonathan. It was her job to draft as comprehensive a case history of the defendant as she possibly could. Who were his ancestors? What dysfunctional behavior had been programmed into him even before conception? What sort of pregnancy had his mother experienced? Had his birth been uneventful or traumatic? What impact had various family members had upon his first few years? What had his early childhood been like? How had he done in school?

Fielder had already broken the news to Hillary that the process was going to be a difficult one. With no parents or grandparents around to help, and severely limited insights on his own, Jonathan was going to be a "hard case." Not because he was determined to be uncooperative—neither Fielder nor Hillary found that to be true—but simply because he was so terribly isolated from the rest of the world, in so many ways.

Over the course of the next two hours, Jonathan described a total of three living relatives. His two namesake uncles had moved away some years ago. Nathan, he believed, had died of "ammonia." When asked to elaborate, Jonathan had placed both of his hands on his chest, and had mimicked a person having difficulty breathing. As for his other uncle, John, he'd reportedly moved far away, though Jonathan didn't know where.

"Do you ever hear from him?" Hillary asked.

"He sends us postcards sometimes."

"Who do you mean by 'us'?"

"M-me and my grandparents."

Hillary noticed that Jonathan referred to his grandparents as though they were still alive. "What kind of postcards?" she asked.

"Pictures," he said.

"What kind of pictures?" She was hoping for something like the Statue of Liberty, or Niagara Falls, or the Baseball Hall of Fame, that might give her a city to begin with, at least.

"Animals."

Animals. Hillary almost let it go at that. But she'd learned it was always better to ask the next question, even if it seemed pointless and stupid, and nine times out of ten brought nothing but another stupid answer.

"What kind of animals?"

To Hillary's eye, Jonathan's face lit up just a bit. Apparently he liked animals.

"K-k-kangaroo," he said.

Not quite what Hillary had expected. Perhaps Uncle John worked in zoo somewhere. "Any others?"

Jonathan knitted his brow. With great difficulty, he managed to pull up another name and force it out. "P-p-plattypussy."

"Platypus?"

Jonathan smiled broadly.

Hillary didn't. She was busy imagining what it would be like trying to find a man named John Greenhall in Australia.

When Hillary asked about brothers or sisters, Jonathan told her he once had an older brother named Porter, whom nobody had seen or heard from in many years. Asked if he had any idea where Porter might be now, Jonathan shook his head slowly from side to side. "Dead," he guessed.

Hillary didn't pursue it.

"Anybody else?" she asked.

This one seemed to stump Jonathan. For a moment he didn't do or say anything. Then, in a barely audible voice—so soft that Hillary Munson later couldn't say for sure if she'd heard him correctly or not—Jonathan said something that sounded to her like, "Maybe." But when pressed, it was as though he hadn't said it at all: one moment it was there, the next it was gone.

In all, Hillary spent just over three hours with Jonathan during their first meeting. She left exhausted, so difficult had been the process of extracting the bits and pieces of information that Jonathan was able and willing to share with her. But she was heartened by the knowledge that she'd gotten along with him quite well, had his signatures on her various release forms, and knew a little something about his background.

That said, looking back now through the prism of hindsight, it can probably be said that the meeting was most notable for what Hillary Munson missed.

PEARSON GUNN DOESN'T miss much. Or so he likes to think. Gunn went to see Jonathan Hamilton on Tuesday, when Matt Fielder was busy at his computer, working on his motion to dismiss the indictment, and Hillary Munson was back down in Albany, firing off requests for records.

Gunn—who brushes off any notions of privileged communications with a wave of his huge hand and a bellowed, "Do I look like a lawyer to you?"—is far more ready to talk about meetings with Jonathan than either Fielder or Munson. While he won't quote Jonathan directly, Gunn is willing to summarize the conversation that took place between the two of them that day.

"I found the kid sorta dazed-like," Gunn reports. "It was like he'd woken up in jail all of a sudden one day, and couldn't really say just why. When I asked him if he knew anything about what had happened to his grandparents, he nodded and let me know he knew they'd been killed. I asked him how he felt about that, and he told me he loved them and he missed them a lot. He didn't quite choke up at that point, but he came damn close. I thought it was real. I mean, I see people lying and acting all the time. When Jonathan said that, I thought it was real.

"Next I asked him if he knew who'd done it. He said he wasn't sure. When he said that, I didn't say anything else right away. I wanted to see if he'd volunteer anything without me asking another question. And he did. After a minute he like shrugged his shoulders and went, 'Me?'

"The thing about it was, for the life of me, I couldn't tell if he was saying that he thought he was the one who had done it, or if he was just guessing. I had the feeling that he was trying his hardest to come up with the right answer, just so he could please me. It was weird in a way, it really was."

Asked what his overall impression of Jonathan was at that first meeting, Gunn narrows his eyes. "I remember thinking to myself that this was a kid who hadn't been dealt a full deck. I didn't think he was lying to me. I didn't think he was *smart enough* to lie to me. And yet everything about the case pointed to him, in spades, five times over. So I ended up thinking something like this: He did it. In a way, he *knows* he did it. But for some reason he really can't *recall* doing it.

"I remember reading once that sometimes a person can do something so terrible, so out of character, that afterwards it's so painful for them to think about that they have to bury it to go on living. But I mean *really* bury it. Gets to the point where they honestly don't remember it anymore. Put 'em on a polygraph and they'll deny doing it, and the needles'll back 'em up every time. Absofuckinglutely amazing, the things the human mind can do."

With Gunn so forthcoming about his impressions even now, it is a virtual certainty that he wasn't bashful about sharing those same impressions with Matt Fielder at the time he'd formed them. And if one looks back at the operation of the defense team in those early days and weeks of the case, it's easy to see that Fielder, Gunn, and Munson were all pretty much on the same page. In the face of overwhelming evidence pointing at Jonathan, they'd come to accept the fact that he had in fact killed his grandparents. They had no idea *why* he'd done it; however, and they'd quickly found themselves at a dead end of sorts: If Jonathan himself didn't remember committing the murders—and they were ready to accept that he didn't—how on earth were they ever going to find out just what it was that had driven him to do it?

Here they were, three people desperate to save the life of a fourth person. Only, that fourth person was totally unable to help them. Looking back at their early frustration some months later, Fielder would put it this way: "It was like we were trying our hardest to reach out to this drowning man, who was sinking out of sight before our very eyes. All we needed was for him to reach out a hand to us, so we'd have something to grab on to. And it turned out he didn't have any arms."

10

VEGETARIAN CHILI

AN ICY RAIN accompanied Matt Fielder on his drive to Cedar Falls that Friday morning. The rain was just heavy enough so that he needed his wipers, but light enough so that if he kept them on, the windshield would begin to streak. The Suzuki was a base model: four cylinders, five speeds, two doors, and not much else. He'd passed up shelling out an additional $2,000 for something they called a "convenience package," that would have given him tinted glass, a rear-window defroster, intermittent wipers, a locking center console, a lighted vanity mirror, and a couple of other things that had struck him at the time as totally frivolous. He'd have liked the intermittent wipers, but naturally they wouldn't sell him those without the rest of the deal—they knew what they were doing. So now he drove with one hand on the steering wheel and one on the wiper control, flicking it on and off every five seconds or so, so that the blades would make a single pass across the windshield before returning to rest. *Manual* intermittent wipers, he called them.

The icy rain had turned to the regular variety by the time Fielder reached the courthouse, but he saw right away that it hadn't kept the public away. He had to drive around the corner to find a parking place, finally settling for a spot in front of the jail. By the time he made it back to the entrance, his suit was spotted and his socks were soaked through his loafers.

The court appearance was brief but significant. Gil Cavanaugh presented the indictment he'd obtained from the grand jury. To nobody's surprise, it charged Jonathan Hamilton with two counts of murder in the first degree, as well as various lesser included crimes—second-degree murder, burglary (for illegally entering the victims' home with the intent of committing a crime), and the illegal possession of a weapon (the knife) with the intent to use it unlawfully.

Asked how the defendant pleaded, Fielder responded on Jonathan's behalf. "Not guilty," he said.

Next, Cavanaugh handed up a motion requesting that the defendant be required to submit to the taking of blood and hair samples, as well as having his footprints taken, all, no doubt, to compare to evidence recovered at the scene. Fielder asked for time to respond, but he knew this was one round he was going to lose. Unlike statements, which may be refused under the Fifth Amendment's prohibition against compelling an individual to give testimony against himself, the items Cavanaugh was seeking were "nontestimonial." Unless Fielder could show that supplying them endangered his client's life (as he might be able to do, for example, if the issue was one of removing a bullet lodged near the brain) or "shocked the conscience" (such as pumping the contents of his client's stomach), all Cavanaugh had to do was demonstrate that there was "probable cause" to believe that the defendant had committed a crime—something the grand jury conveniently now had done for him by voting its indictment.

Turning to the offensive, Fielder submitted papers of his own—the motion to dismiss the indictment, based upon Cavanaugh's failure to give the defense a reasonable time to decide whether to have Jonathan testify before the grand jury, and to prepare him to do so. But there, too, Fielder knew he had a loser. Still, he was doing what he had to do. What was reasonable in an ordinary case might turn out to be unreasonable in a capital case. One of Fielder's jobs was to make a record at every step of the proceedings, so appellate courts could one day decide just how different death was going to be in New York. Even in non-capital cases, every lawyer's nightmare is the discovery that his client's rights were in fact violated—but, that in failing to preserve the issue by registering a proper and timely objection the defense waived the defect.

Prisons are full of defendants whose lawyers didn't bother to object.

With no further business, Judge Summerhouse adjourned the case for three weeks, for each side to respond in writing to the other's moving papers.

THE RAIN DID little to dampen Cavanaugh's impromptu press conference, held on the courthouse steps following the arraignment. "Today is September twelfth," he said into the microphones. "As the district attorney elected by the citizens of Ottawa County, I have one hundred twenty days from today to decide whether it is my intention to seek the ultimate penalty in this case. As horrible as these murders are, and as defenseless as these poor victims were, I am going to extend to the defendant a courtesy that he certainly never offered the victims. I am going to hold off a bit, to give the defense the opportunity to try to convince me why I should *not* seek the death penalty in this case. I will consider anything they present to me in the next three weeks. I'm a tough man, but I'm also a fair man. So, you see, I've now served public notice. The burden's on them."

As cameramen jockeyed for position, Cavanaugh stood under an umbrella held by an aide, and answered a few softball questions lobbed at him by reporters. No, he had never seen a more gruesome crime in all of his years in public service. Yes, he was certain the right man was locked up, and yes, the good folks who lived in the county could sleep well at night. No, offhand he couldn't imagine anything the defense could possibly tell him that would persuade him not to ask for death, but he wanted to give them the chance, just the same. And yes, he expected to be reelected handily the following November.

Then he excused himself and left, with his entourage in tow.

When the reporters made their way over to Fielder, who'd been watching the performance from one side, he held up a hand and told them he had no comment for them. He hated to do it. For one thing, reporters can be helpful: they live in a world where information is currency, and are generally eager to trade a good lead for a bit of background material and an unconfirmed rumor, with maybe a future piece of gossip thrown in. Besides that, Cavanaugh's antics infuriated Fielder, who would have loved to be able to say something to balance the scales. But what was he going to tell them? That his client didn't know whether he was guilty or not? That he was having trouble remembering if he'd murdered his grandparents? Or maybe, that if he'd done it, he couldn't say why?

"Sorry," he said three or four times.

"Are you going to try to talk the DA out of asking for death?"

"Sorry."

"*Is* there anything good about your client?"

"Sorry."

"When *will* you talk with us?"

"I'll have a statement at the appropriate time," was about all he came up with. Public relations has never been Matt Fielder's strong suit.

He broke away from them and made it around the corner to his car, just in time to see a uniformed officer placing a parking ticket underneath one of his manual intermittent wiper blades.

He was starting to get the feeling that it wasn't his day.

AROUND THE SAME time Matt Fielder was beginning the drive back to his cabin near Big Moose, a technician was getting to work some 150 miles to the west, in the Rochester suburb of Rigney Bluff. The technician's name was

Yvonne St. Germaine, and she worked for a company called GenType. GenType is a commercial testing laboratory that had been in business only three years at the time, but was already employing eighty-five people and grossing over seven million dollars a year in receipts. Along with a handful of similar labs like CellMark, LabCorp, and BioTest (it was beginning to become apparent that a prerequisite to success in the field was having a two-syllable name that could be cleverly SplitUp), GenType's claim to fame was that it was a well-known and widely accepted tester of DNA samples.

Less than a decade earlier, the discovery of the value of deoxyribonucleic acid as a nearly unique genetic marker had revolutionized the science of identification. And only two years ago, a celebrated West Coast trial had made DNA a household term. The fact that few people even knew what the initials stood for, and that fewer still had any inkling of the theory behind the application, made no difference; it was no longer sufficient simply to tell a jury that something looked like blood, or *was* blood, or was *human* blood, or was even *type AB−* human blood. By 1997, every prosecutor in America knew that henceforth it would be necessary to explain to the jurors that DNA testing had been performed, and had conclusively established that the odds of the blood's having come from anyone other than the accused were precisely 1 in 46,351,562,837. And, so long as the accused wasn't some sort of a celebrity golf player, chances are, that would pretty much do the trick.

Yvonne St. Germaine opened the Express Mail package that had arrived that morning from someplace called Cedar Falls, New York. Inside, she found an inner container that, when slit open, revealed twenty-seven small items. Each item was separately wrapped. Each contained either a cotton swab, a red smear on a slide, a small swatch of cloth, or what appeared to be a human hair, complete with the follicle. Each was marked with a number. The numbers were all different, but each was preceded by the letter *X*. In Yvonne St. Germaine's language, *X* stood for "unknown." She also found, separately protected in plastic bubble-wrap, two test tubes containing blood. From the fact that the test tubes were plugged with purple stoppers and the blood inside them was still liquid, she knew that it had been properly mixed with an anticoagulant. The tubes were marked K-1 and K-2. The *K* designation meant that these were "known" samples for comparison against the unknown ones.

Finally, there was a letter typed on the letterhead of the Ottawa County District Attorney, requesting analysis of all the items, and explaining that additional samples, to be collectively labeled K-3, would be forwarded to GenType in several weeks.

Yvonne checked her watch, entered the exact time in her notebook, and, using a sterile forceps, lifted the first item, X-1, from its envelope. To Yvonne, it looked like a small portion of terrycloth material, perhaps snipped from a towel or a bathrobe. The material itself may have been white at one time, or perhaps a light gray or beige. It was hard to tell for sure, though, so thoroughly was it soaked in what certainly appeared to Yvonne's trained eye to be blood.

MATT FIELDER SPENT Saturday pouring the footings for a small barn he hoped to raise before winter set in, and cooking up a large pot of chili. To anyone watching Fielder cook—and nobody was—it would have been apparent that he was having company for dinner, and that the company was female.

They would have been only half right.

The chili recipe was something that had evolved gradually since Fielder's meat-eating days, now some ten years behind him. It called for dried lentils and soaked black beans, fresh onions, leeks, celery, carrots, tomatoes, and whatever wild mushrooms were to be found. A half dozen different varieties of peppers, ranging all the way from sweet red bells to chemically unstable black habaneras, provided both depth and fire. By the time it was ready, it was thick enough to stand a fork up in it, and so dark and rich that vegetarians drew back from it in disbelief.

The truth was, Fielder certainly could have used a little female company. Married at twenty-three, single again by thirty, he'd been on his own ever since. There had been women in his life, to be sure, but something in him had always managed to keep them at arm's length. Perhaps it had been the trauma of divorce, or the comfort he took in retreating into his own protective shell, or the multitude of little idiosyncrasies he'd developed over so many years of doing things his way. Whatever it was, those who knew him well—and there were precious few in that category— had pretty much given Fielder up as a "lost cause" who was destined to live out his days alone. His sister, herself happily married and surrounded by a houseful of kids, joked that he was searching for the perfect "elationship," so afraid was he of the "*r*-word."

But that Saturday, Fielder wasn't looking for an elation- ship. The chili he'd prepared was for a business dinner. The business at hand was Jonathan Hamilton, and the din- ner guest was Fielder's investigator, Pearson Gunn.

Gunn showed up around seven, driving a '57 Chevy Impala, the kind with the huge seagull-wing tail fins. It brought with it a cloud of blue smoke, which would hang in the air a good ten minutes after the engine had been killed. Gunn climbed out, a gallon of red wine suspended from one index finger, which looked like it barely fit through the glass ring at the neck of the jug. Fielder, whose own taste in reds ran to dry merlots and cabernets, noticed that when Gunn swung the bottle, the wine didn't slosh around so much as it *oozed,* the way a heavy-duty motor oil might do in the middle of winter. He accepted the of- fering graciously, but refrained from looking at the label, just in case it turned out to be from someplace called Val- voline Vineyards, or Château Chevron.

In the vouchers for payment the two men would submit many months later, they would claim to have worked only two hours that evening, but it is likely they were simply being prudent about the way in which they billed. The fact is that they ate around nine, drank until midnight, and sat up well past three, reviewing what they knew about the case, what they *didn't* know, and what they needed to do next.

Carter and Mary Alice Hamilton had no known enemies. Both were well into their eighties at the time of the murders. Since the deaths of their son and daughter-in-law in the fire a decade earlier, their world had gradually closed in around them. In recent years, they had seldom ventured beyond the stone walls of the estate. They had few friends they hadn't outlived, and those they kept in touch with by phone, or through the occasional exchange of letters.

Gunn had thoroughly investigated the Armbrusts, the German couple who lived on the estate and had been taking care of the Hamiltons. Everything about them checked out. They'd worked for the family for close to thirty years, tending to the needs of the land and three generations of its owners. Klaus had had one arrest, at age seventeen, for driving without a license; Elna had no record whatsoever. By all accounts, they'd gotten along well with Jonathan's grandparents, and were not only griefstricken by the murders, but appropriately concerned for their own safety. Financially, their needs were modest, and had always been met. It seemed they had nothing to gain from the deaths, and everything to lose.

Gunn had spoken briefly on the phone with Bass McClure. McClure was the one Jonathan had reached by phone the morning of the killings, and it was McClure who'd been the first person to view the crime scene, other than Jonathan himself. Gunn knew McClure, and liked him. He also sensed from his undisclosed law-enforcement contact (again, this was almost certainly Captain Roger Duquesne) that the prosecution was less than happy with McClure. Whether this displeasure was simply the result of McClure's failure to safeguard the integrity of the crime scene, or whether it went beyond that, was something Fielder wanted Gunn to look into further. A reluctant prosecution witness can sometimes turn out to be the defense's best friend.

Finally, the conversation focused on Jonathan Hamilton himself. Neither Fielder nor Gunn came right out and said it, but both men were privately convinced that Jonathan had committed the murders. What they didn't know was *why*. Furthermore, they had every reason to believe that the prosecution was in exactly the same position. Other than Jonathan, no one alive had witnessed the killings. There was Jonathan's "confession" to Deke Stanton, but that had been oral, unpreserved on tape, and not witnessed by anyone other than Stanton. It was consequently somewhat limited in terms of its value, even if the prosecution could convince Judge Summerhouse that it was admissible. Except for that, Gil Cavanaugh was left with a purely circumstantial case.

Just why prosecutors worry about circumstantial proof is somewhat a case of the tail wagging the dog. Proof can be divided into two types, direct and circumstantial. Direct proof is an eyewitness account: *I saw that it was raining.* Circumstantial proof is the proof of some fact which, once established, leads to a logical inference of a second fact: *I saw water on the pavement, and there were people carrying open umbrellas.*

It turns out that the vast majority of what we call "miscarriages of justice" occur in direct-evidence cases. The culprit is almost always human error—faulty eyewitness identifications, lapses of memory, or imperfect accounts of observations. In contrast, there is nothing stronger than a compelling set of circumstances that point inexorably at the accused.

But juries don't think so.

Somewhere along the line, somebody juxtaposed the words "purely" and "circumstantial," and trials have never quite been the same since. For some reason, a jury will accept the word of a confused, traumatized, biased, and error-prone witness who gets up on the witness stand and insists under oath that he'll "never forget that face," over a trail of scientific evidence and deductive logic that leads to an accused with almost mathematical certainty.

And prosecutors have learned this. So, lacking an eye-witness, they cringe in fear over the possibility that the jury will reject their case as "purely circumstantial." They instinctively look for what they consider to be the next best thing to an eyewitness identification.

A motive.

A motive is something that never has to be proved. In that respect, it is not to be confused with *intent*. Many laws, including murder, may require proof of intent. But "intent" merely refers to a person's immediate objective: *The defendant shot the victim with the intent of causing his death.* "Motive," on the other hand, refers to what produced the intent in the first place: *The defendant, motivated by his anger at having been betrayed, shot the victim with the intent of causing his death.*

But a prosecutor without a motive is left feeling a little something like a lion without a mane. Sure, he's got his claws, his teeth, his strength, his speed, and his cunning. But no *mane*? Panic immediately sets in. And, the more important the case, the greater the panic becomes.

FIELDER POURED SOME more wine from the gallon jug. In a moment of weakness, he'd peeked at the label and noticed the modifiers *Ruby Red,* followed by a third R beginning yet another word. He'd immediately looked away, not wanting to know just what it was he'd been drinking all night. But the mind loves to fill in blanks: Ruby Red Rotgut? Ruby Red Roof Tar? Ruby Red Rain Sealant? Ruby Red Rear Axle Grease?

"You better believe Cavanaugh and his team are worrying about motive jush as hard as we are," Fielder said.

"Jush?" Gunn wasn't going to let Fielder's slurring go unnoticed.

Ignoring him, Fielder pressed on. "We've got to beat him to the punch on this," he told Gunn.

"Hey, no problem," said Gunn, watching the reflection of the fire in his glass. "I'll get on it. So what if it's fuckin' impossible? You want it, I'll do it. Where there's a will, there's a way."

Fielder, who was by that time lagging behind Gunn by a good quart or so of Ruby Red, and an equal amount of mental clarity, tried hard to digest what he'd just heard, but his mind refused to cooperate.

"Whajoosay?"

Alcohol was Pearson Gunn's briar patch: He was never more at home than when he was seriously tanked. Now he simply pressed some internal button, and rewound his mind to the spot that had been requested. "I'll get on it," he repeated. "So what—"

"No, no." Fielder sat up. "The last part."

Gunn fast-forwarded a bit. "Where there's a will, there's a way."

"That's it."

"What's it?"

"A *will*," Fielder said. "These were wealthy people. They've gotta have wills lying around somewhere. Sooner or later, even a clown like Cavanaugh's going to figure that out and try to find 'em, see who they left their money to. If it turns out to be Jonathan—*bango!* There's his motive."

" 'Bango'?"

IN TAKING THE measure of his adversary, Matt Fielder had formed an initial impression shared by most of Gil Cavanaugh's opponents, both before and since. Having watched the district attorney pirouette before the cameras and pander shamelessly to his constituents, Fielder had sized up Cavanaugh as half demagogue, half buffoon. That was a serious underestimation on Fielder's part. For all of Cavanaugh's theatrics, he is a smart man who misses very little and knows how to play the angles.

Even as Fielder and Gunn sat in front of their fire, pleased at their cleverness in having stumbled upon the notion of a last will and testament as a possible motive for the killings, Gil Cavanaugh slept soundly in his bed, seventy-five miles away. He'd thought about a will a full week earlier, and already had had one of his assistants move for an ex parte court order to gain access to it.

Not only that, but Cavanaugh was well ahead of Hillary Munson, too, in terms of subpoenaing records relating to Jonathan Hamilton. Still unknown to the defense was the fact that, as part of the initial "processing" of his prisoner, Deke Stanton had had Jonathan sign a number of forms. Included had been several fingerprint cards and a personal-property receipt, both standard-enough stuff. Not so standard were the blank authorization forms, the same type of forms Hillary Munson had presented to Jonathan a week later. The only difference was that Hillary had explained to Jonathan exactly what it was that he was agreeing to, and why it was important that he do so; Stanton had simply instructed him to sign his name on the dotted line. Jonathan, with his limited reading skills and compliant nature, had of course done as he'd been told. Stanton had turned the signed forms over to Cavanaugh, who promptly stapled them to subpoenas and had them served on the appropriate agencies.

FIELDER WOULD FIND out about all of this in due time, when recipients of his own subpoenas began calling him to tell him they'd already furnished the material he was looking for to the district attorney. The discovery would lead Fielder to fire off an angry letter to Cavanaugh, rescinding his client's prior authorization. Which was, of course, a little like closing the barn door after the horses had left. It would also cause him to change his estimation of Cavanaugh, and to realize, soberly, that the defense investigation was running well behind that of the district attorney.

But as annoying as that realization might be, it would hardly be a novel position in which Fielder would find himself. The truth is, the defense almost always lags behind the prosecution; it's the very nature of the process, in which the prosecution tends to act, while the defense tends to re-act. But, ironically enough, it's also one of the aspects of the game that appealed to Fielder and got his competitive juices going. Being cast in the underdog role was one of the things that had drawn Matt Fielder to criminal defense work in the first place. Like many defense attorneys, he takes pride in the knowledge that he does some of his best work when things look bleakest, and when the odds against his succeeding seem absolutely overwhelming—right around the time the prosecutor is thinking about putting a bottle of champagne on ice for his victory party.

"Man, you're some cook." Pearson Gunn's voice brought Fielder out of his trance. "What kind of meat did you use to make that chili so rich?"

This from a man whose investigative prowess Fielder was counting on in order to save a man's life.

"Venison, I bet, huh?"

So there they sat, the captain and co-captain of a ragtag, three-member pickup team who'd never played a game together in their lives, up against a seasoned, all-star roster of veteran heavy-hitters. Not only were they seriously over-matched, but they were also playing in the other team's ballpark, in front of a hostile crowd, and under the eye of a biased umpire. And before long they'd find out they'd already spotted the home team a couple of runs before even coming up to bat.

The way Matt Fielder figured it, pretty soon he'd have Gil Cavanaugh right where he wanted him.

11

HILLARY

By Monday, Matt Fielder had pretty much gotten over his hangover. He'd slept past nine Sunday morning, a full three hours later than his usual rising hour. By the time he'd finally gotten his bearings, there was no sign of Pearson Gunn, who—as best Fielder could remember—had lapsed into a deep coma on the couch sometime around three in the morning. But the disappearance of the Impala from the driveway told him that Gunn had somehow returned to life and driven off.

The rest of the day had been something of a fog for Fielder. His tongue felt like it had fur on it and was too big for his mouth. There had been alternating waves of nausea, throbbing headaches, and a dryness in his throat that made it painful to swallow. He felt thirsty, but every time he took a sip of liquid, his stomach threatened to turn itself inside out.

Around two in the afternoon, he'd decided that some activity was called for. He'd found some shoes, climbed into the Suzuki, and headed down Route 28 for Utica. Twice he'd almost gone off the road trying to negotiate routine turns; each time, the ensuing adrenaline surge had sustained him for the next ten minutes or so.

In Utica, he'd bought coffee and a bagel, and found a copy of the Sunday *Times*. Heading back north, he'd driven with the window wide open to stay awake. To keep from freezing, he'd turned the heater up full-blast. Somehow he'd made it back, but it must have been pretty much on automatic pilot; afterward he could barely remember driving.

Straightening up his cabin that evening, Fielder had come across the culprit lying on its side by the couch: the gallon jug, frighteningly close to empty. He'd summoned up his courage and forced himself to read the label in full. Ruby Red Port. He'd gagged and had tasted a mixture of coffee, bagel, and pulverized fermented grapes.

It would be more than two years before he dared drink anything stronger than cider.

He'd glanced through Sports Sunday, checking the baseball scores. The cartoons in The Week in Review had failed to strike him as particularly amusing; one of them he didn't get at all. He'd spent twenty minutes with the crossword puzzle, but had trouble making out the fine print of the clues, especially the absurdly tiny numbers in the boxes. Twice he'd written answers in the wrong place. And, to top it off, the puzzle was a stepquote. He *hated* stepquotes.

By seven-thirty that evening, he'd climbed into bed, begged for forgiveness, and prayed for sleep. Around ten, some merciful god had finally relented.

PEARSON GUNN SPENT most of Monday trying to track down the last wills of Carter and Mary Alice Hamilton. Because they'd been dead only two weeks, he knew that nothing would be probated yet. That meant he'd have to find the lawyer who'd drawn up the wills in the first place, and who, hopefully, had retained a copy of them in his or her files.

There were about fifteen lawyers who practiced in and around Cedar Falls, and Gunn knew most of them, having worked for many of them at one time or another. But the Hamiltons had lived over by Flat Lake, and Gunn didn't know any lawyers from around there, or indeed if there even *were* any. Worse yet, there was no village of Flat Lake to speak of, so any lawyer in the vicinity would have to be working out of his home. And you couldn't very well drive around knocking on doors, asking if there was a lawyer in the house.

He called every lawyer he knew of in Cedar Falls. No one had written a will for the Hamiltons. He tried the yellow pages, looking under ATTORNEYS. There were none with addresses in Flat Lake. Running out of ideas, he went to see Dot Whipple at the courthouse, and she let him look in a red book that had a lawyers' directory in it.

"Used to be, they listed the names by county," Dot told him. "But they changed things a few years back, and now it's simply one big list containing all the lawyers in the state in alphabetical order."

Which made it no use at all.

"Help me out here, Dot," Gunn pleaded. He'd learned long ago that the surest way to get assistance was to come right out and ask for it. Made people feel needed.

Dot scrunched up her face for a moment. "How about Jonathan's parents?" she asked him.

"Gonna be hard to ask them," Gunn said. "Both of 'em burned up in that fire. Gotta be ten years now."

"I know that," snapped Dot, who kept track of just about everybody in the county, and certainly knew that Jonathan's parents had died in the fire, which had been in 1989, actually. February.

"So?"

"So they're dead." She stated the obvious.

"Yeah?"

"Which means *their* wills got probated long ago."

WITH PEARSON GUNN busy Monday in Cedar Falls, trying to hunt down the wills of Jonathan's grandparents, Matt Fielder decided it would a good time for a road trip. He'd called Gil Cavanaugh that morning with a request to examine the physical evidence in the case—whatever items had been recovered at the crime scene, taken from Jonathan at the time of his arrest, or later seized from his cottage pursuant to the search warrant. Cavanaugh had been helpful to a point. The good news was that Fielder was welcome to inspect the evidence (though any other answer would have amounted to a violation of law, as well as etiquette). The bad news was that it was all currently being held for safekeeping by the troopers at Troop H. Troop H houses the New York State Police Headquarters and Training Academy, and happens to be in Albany. For Fielder, that meant a drive of 130 miles. Each way.

Then again, it was a nice day for a ride. And as long as Fielder was going to be in Albany, he decided to make a day of it. He phoned Hillary Munson, and arranged to meet her at her office that afternoon. He figured they'd better get started putting together a mitigation letter to present to Cavanaugh. Not that it would do any good, of course: Cavanaugh was going to do what he was going to do, and they both knew what that was. But that couldn't stop Fielder from trying.

Beyond that, Fielder almost certainly had an ulterior motive in mind. It had been almost two years since he'd seen Hillary. Ever since the day of their lunch together, he'd kept her business card in his wallet, and a vivid picture of her in his mind. It was that picture of Hillary Munson—of her pixie smile and her soft, curly hair—that now caused the miles to fly by for Matt Fielder and his trusty Suzuki Sidekick.

He reached Albany around one o'clock, and managed to find the State Police Headquarters without too much difficulty. It was a large, modern building, with lots of new brick, glass, blond wood, and recessed lighting. It reminded Fielder more of a suburban library than it did of the crumbling, filthy NYPD precinct houses he was accustomed to. Apparently when you were upstate, the home team got a better clubhouse.

The trooper who assisted Fielder looked about thirteen years old, but he was courteous and helpful. He lugged a large blue duffle bag out from the back, set it down on the counter, and began to empty its contents.

"This is the Hamilton case, huh?" he asked Fielder.

"Yes."

"Word is, they're going to fry the kid. Lieutenant's giving ten-to-one odds he'll end up in the chair."

"Never happen," Fielder said. "Take the odds."

"Think so?" the trooper asked earnestly, looking around to make certain nobody was eavesdropping on this unexpected transmission of inside information.

"Know so."

"Well, good luck." The trooper said it with such genuineness that Fielder didn't have the heart to tell him that the ten-to-one odds in favor of Jonathan's being executed actually sounded just about right to him. It was only when it came to the method of death that the lieutenant was wrong. Under New York's enlightened new capital-punishment law, electrocution was out, having been replaced by the more humane choice of lethal injection. It seems there were too many accounts of prisoners' heads bursting into blue flames, or their eyeballs being forcibly ejected from their sockets.

It took some doing, but between Dot Whipple's know-how and Pearson Gunn's physical strength, by noon they'd examined the contents of 164 cartons of records in the courthouse's basement storage closet, known in official circles as the Archives. Midway through the 165th carton, they found the worn accordion-file they were looking for: WILLS PROBATED—1989. Inside were about thirty documents, among them were the wills of Porter and Elizabeth Hamilton. Dot turned it over, so they could read the printing on the blueback.

WILBUR H. MAPLE, Esq.

Attorney and Counselor-at-Law

40 Front Street

Saranac Lake, New York

"You got a subpoena for these?" Dot suddenly remembered to ask.

"Think I just might," Gunn replied. But it is difficult to imagine that Dot wouldn't have made him copies of them anyway. It would seem too silly to refuse at that point, given all they'd been through running down the document. Besides, Dot has always been quite partial to Pearson Gunn, and more than once over the years she's been heard to say that were she twenty years younger, the man wouldn't stand a chance against her.

Twenty minutes later, Gunn was on his way over to Saranac Lake, to have a little chat with Wilbur H. Maple, Esquire, Attorney and Counselor-at-Law, to try to find out if, by any chance, Mr. Maple had also drawn up a will for Jonathan Hamilton's grandparents.

Gunn was pleased with himself, and understandably so. He is a solid investigator who possesses good instincts, and he usually gets the job at hand done, one way or another. But on this particular day, he'd missed something. Although he had copies of Jonathan's parents' probated wills sitting next to him on the seat of his Impala, he'd made the mistake of regarding them purely as a means to an end— the end being the unprobated wills of Jonathan's grandparents, the ones that might ultimately shed some light on the motive behind the Flat Lake murders.

What Gunn had failed to do was to read the wills themselves.

By the time the trooper had finished emptying the contents of the duffle bag onto the counter, there was an impressive array of items for Fielder to examine. In separate clear plastic envelopes were the hunting knife that had been found under Jonathan's sink, and the two blood-soaked towels, one of which had contained the knife. Only, the blood no longer looked like blood to Fielder: it had dried and turned a dark brown color, almost black in spots. In several areas, squares of the towel were missing, where cuttings had been removed for laboratory analysis.

There also was a lot of clothing that apparently belonged to Jonathan. Of particular note were the shoes: a pair of boots, two pairs of sneakers, and a pair of sandals, all bearing tags that identified them as size 12. Fielder knew that the bloody bare footprints leading from the crime scene to Jonathan's cottage had been determined to have been left by a person whose feet were size 12. Wrapped separately in plastic were a flannel shirt and a pair of shorts. On close examination, Fielder could see what appeared to be smudges of blood on the sides of both of them.

There were sunglasses, eating utensils, a few crude wood carvings, a set of miniature porcelain animals, a Frisbee, and some toilet articles. There was a handful of books, but all of them seemed as though they'd just come from the store. There was a wallet, containing $22, and an envelope filled with $3.27 in change. There were half a dozen flat, oval stones, smooth enough to have come from a brook; Fielder guessed they'd make good skipping-stones. There was a cigar box full of old photographs, which Fielder dumped out and spent a few moments looking through. From the blond hair and facial similarities, he guessed that most, if not all of them, were of relatives. From newspaper photos he'd seen shortly after the murders, he recognized Jonathan's grandparents, posing with Jonathan in front of what looked like an authentic birchbark canoe, in what had certainly been happier times. There were shots of another couple, most likely Jonathan's parents. There were several of a dog—an Irish setter, it looked like. And one of a child, no more than a year old, squinting into the sunlight. It was worn and faded, and looked old enough to be a photo of Jonathan himself as a boy, though it was hard to tell for sure.

But it was the last two items to come out of the duffle bag that caused Fielder the most difficulty. One was a honing stone, used to put a sharp edge on a knife. From its uneven shape, it looked as though it had seen plenty of use. The other was an empty leather sheath. Fielder located the hunting knife, still encased in plastic, and set it down next to the sheath, so that the two items lined up side by side.

It looked to be a perfect fit.

* * *

WILBUR H. MAPLE, Esquire, Attorney and Counselor-at-Law, turned out to be an octogenarian straight out of the pages of a Dickens novel. He was barely five feet tall in his elevator shoes, ruddy-faced and totally bald save for a fringe of snow-white hair that ran around the back of his head, connecting a pair of long, bushy sideburns. He wore a three-piece suit that once had been navy blue, but somewhere along the line had faded to purple, and easily could have been as ancient as Maple himself.

"And what can I do for you, sir?" he asked Pearson Gunn following introductions.

"You can tell me if you wrote a will for a man named Carter Hamilton." Gunn figured he'd keep things simple, talk about one will first.

"I most certainly did," Maple beamed.

"I was wondering if I could get a look at it," Gunn said.

" 'Fraid not."

"Why's that?"

"You're too late, sonny."

"Excuse me?"

"Already turned it over to the DA," Maple explained. "Fella from his office showed up middle of last week, with a subpoena *duces tecum*. And he *tecum*ed it, if you know what I mean."

"Did you keep a copy?" Gunn looked around hopefully, but there was no sign of a copy machine. The most modern piece of machinery in sight was a portable manual Smith-Corona typewriter, circa 1935.

"Nope. Don't need one."

"Why's that?"

"Two reasons," said Maple, tapping one finger against the side of his head. "First off, I got it all in here."

"Okay," said Gunn, who was willing to play. "What's it say?"

"In the event Carter and his wife died together, everything goes to the boy, Jonathan. That's your client, right?"

"Right."

"Lucky fella."

"Well—"

" 'Course, I wrote the bank in as trustee and all that," Maple said, "seeing as the boy's a bit on the slow side, if you catch my drift."

"And if the estate couldn't go to Jonathan?" asked Gunn, who remembered reading somewhere about a law that barred convicted murderers from inheriting anything from the victims of their crimes.

"Normal stuff." Maple shrugged. "Estate would go to any great-grandchildren living at the time of the testators' deaths, on a per capita basis. Seeing as there aren't any, then I s'pose we'll have to look a little further. I seem to remember the boy's got an uncle off somewhere or other. Austria, maybe?"

"I see," said Gunn. "You said something about a second reason you didn't make a copy of the will."

"Yup," said Maple.

"What was that?"

"I wrote Carter and Mary Alice joint and mutual wills. So hers is the same as his, 'cept for the signatures."

Gunn had never heard of joint and mutual wills, which had gone out of vogue some forty years earlier, primarily because they tended to afford insufficient protection in the event of joint and mutual deaths. But he knew enough to frame the next question. "Think I could have hers?" he asked.

"Don't see why not," Maple said, " 'long as you get it back to me, so's I can file it for probate."

Gunn gladly traded his promise for Mary Alice Hamilton's will. But his victory had been a Pyrrhic one: Like every other piece of evidence in the case, it led directly and inexorably to Jonathan. Worse yet, it was, for all practical purposes, already in the hands of the enemy.

Matt Fielder had his will, all right.

But Gil Cavanaugh had his motive.

*   *   *

ON THE WAY from state police headquarters to the offices of Miller and Munson, Fielder found himself whistling, checking his appearance in his rearview mirror, and smoothing down his hair, which had become windblown and disheveled from the drive. But it wasn't until he caught himself stroking his chin to feel how closely he'd shaved, that he finally realized precisely who and what all these little mannerisms were about. Who they were about, of course, was Hillary Munson. What they were about, came down to a single word.

Horny.

As much as Fielder hated to admit it, his solitary life in the woods didn't fulfill quite all of his needs. He would deny the point adamantly, insisting that he was every bit as content to be away from civilization as Thoreau ever had been. But at moments like this, he knew better.

He tried to focus by asking himself what he knew about Hillary. That she was cute and petite, smart as a whip, and full of life? Fine for starters. What he didn't know was whether she had a boyfriend, or even a husband. After all, he hadn't seen her in nearly two years. The way things worked these days, a cute young thing like her wouldn't stay single on the open market for two months. She could have kids by now. She could be nine months pregnant! He told himself to calm down and think logically.

But horniness can be a funny thing, and it is seldom, if ever, affected by logic. As he drove through the streets of Albany that afternoon, trying in vain to think pure thoughts and concentrate on the business at hand, Matt Fielder was already busy scheming.

Much has been written on the subject of just what it is that makes a person an effective lawyer and, in particular, an effective litigator. Contrary to popular perception, it is not merely a gift for oratory that is required. The fact is that, statistically speaking, precious few cases ever go to trial; the overwhelming majority test skills quite different from those ultimately needed in front of a jury. An analytical mind, a talent for organizing, and a willingness to put in long hours of preparation—all of these attributes are certainly important. But perhaps the most essential ingredient of all is one that carries a slightly derogatory label. "Show me an effective lawyer," someone once said, "and I'll show you a master manipulator." Lawyers manipulate. They manipulate not only jurors, but judges, witnesses, other lawyers, court personnel, probation officers, parole boards, their own clients . . . *everyone*. A *"master manipulator"* is one whose victims aren't even aware they're being manipulated. A *"grand master"* takes it one step further: His victims praise him specifically for being so *straightforward* and *unmanipulative*.

None of this thought process went through Matt Fielder's conscious mind, naturally, during his drive to meet Hillary Munson. What did occur to him was that it would be a smart thing to skip lunch. Right off, he'd have nothing to fear from embarrassing tuna breath or dreaded lettuce-stuck-between-the-teeth syndrome. What's more, he'd be able to tell Hillary that he hadn't had a chance to eat all day, and inquire if perhaps she might know of a quiet place where they could adjourn for a bite of dinner, while, of course, continuing to talk strategy.

Unless, that is, she was nine months pregnant.

AROUND THREE-FORTY THAT afternoon, some ancient circadian rhythm deep inside Pearson Gunn's body told him it was time to head over to the Dew Drop and check in with Pete. It has been Gunn's general experience that bartenders can supply late-breaking stories, tips, gossip, rumors, local color, and important background information. Failing all that, they can at very least supply cold mugs of Adirondack Amber Ale.

Twenty minutes later, the bear-bells above the door of the Dew Drop jangled twice, and Gunn walked in. Pete reflexively glanced up at his clock and noticed that it was running a minute slow.

*   *   *

HILLARY MUNSON DEFINITELY was not nine months pregnant. To Matt Fielder, she looked better than ever. What's more, she seemed genuinely happy to see him, and if her greeting hug struck him as being a bit on the sisterly side, he figured he had all evening to work on that. Besides which, they weren't exactly alone. There was a secretary working at a computer station ten feet away, and a third woman, an attractive blonde, not much taller than Hillary.

"Matt Fielder"—Hillary did the honors—"this is my partner, Lois Miller."

They exchanged handshakes. Lois's was pleasantly firm.

"Looks like you guys have a live one here," she said.

"So far," Fielder said, hoping to amuse them with his clever gallows humor.

He followed Hillary to a back office, where they proceeded to spend the next two hours working on the task of trying to save Jonathan Hamilton's life. Specifically, they outlined the written presentation Fielder would submit to Gil Cavanaugh, in which he'd set forth what he believed to be the case for mitigation—the various reasons why the prosecution should decide against seeking the death penalty for this particular defendant.

Never mind that they both knew it was an all-but-foregone conclusion that their plea would fall on deaf ears; they knew they couldn't let that knowledge deter them from their work. What they did have to be careful about was tipping their hand too much. First they had to guard against implicitly conceding that Jonathan had in fact committed the crimes. That called for a liberal dose of such phrases as "alleged," "purported," and "assuming *arguendo*." Second, they had to steer clear altogether from subjects like *motive, intent*, and *remorse*—areas which lay too close to the border of factual guilt. This left them with Jonathan himself: who he was, what was redeeming or sympathetic about him, and why a person like him simply was not an appropriate candidate for the state to kill.

At the top of their list was Jonathan's limited level of intellectual functioning. They needed to talk about it—in-

deed, they realized it was their very strongest argument—
but at the same time they wanted to avoid making an outright claim at this stage that Jonathan was "mentally retarded" in the eyes of the law. Such a claim, made in
writing, would rise to the level of an outright defense, and
might prompt Cavanaugh to invoke his right to have his
own mental-health experts examine Jonathan, so that the
DA might test—and ultimately refute—the claim. That opportunity was the last thing the defense wanted to give him.
Long before acceding to it, they wanted to find what examinations of Jonathan had been made in the past, and precisely what the results had been. If previous findings
conclusively showed retardation, the defense might very
well want to rely on them, much the way a blackjack player
sticks with a hand of seventeen or eighteen showing. Even
if the earlier exams proved to have been more equivocal,
suggesting that a new series ought to be conducted, the
defense wanted to have their own experts do the testing,
rather than leave it to some Dr. Death selected from Cavanaugh's Rolodex.

And again, there was the problem of the origin of Jonathan's possible retardation. If it predated his carbon monoxide poisoning during the fire, all was well and good. But
if it didn't, the defense was going to find itself up against
the rule that, in order to exempt him from death, Jonathan's
retardation must have manifested itself before he turned
eighteen.

As a result, in describing Jonathan's mental capacity,
they restricted themselves to words like "slow," "compromised," "limited," and "restricted." They spoke of low
reading levels, poor learning skills, and minor behavioral
problems, of concrete ideation and difficulty in adjustment.
But never did they come right out and state what they
would have loved to and what Matt Fielder knew he'd
probably end up having to argue to a jury at the eleventh
hour, at a point where they'd already convicted Jonathan,
and when their only remaining decision was whether he

lived out his life in prison, or went to his death. "You can't kill this kid, because he's retarded."

Next Hillary and Fielder turned to other areas of mitigation. The tragic deaths of Jonathan's parents were high on their list, coming as they had when Jonathan was only eighteen. So, too, was the fact that, with his grandparents now dead, Jonathan was left with no family whatever. But the irony here wasn't lost on Fielder: the claim they were making was dangerously close to the joke about the child who murders his parents and then asks for leniency because he's an orphan.

Jonathan's lack of any prior record or history of violence was certainly worthy of mention, particularly when weighed against the lengthy and violent records of most death-row inmates. Similarly, Jonathan's behavior in the hours following the crimes was noteworthy: Even assuming that he'd committed the crimes, he'd made no attempt to flee, and had barely tried to hide what appeared to be the weapon. Then he himself had called the authorities and waited there until someone arrived. Hardly the acts one might expect from a vicious killer.

The list went on. By the end of two hours, they had compiled an outline of some dozen mitigators, each carefully phrased so as to avoid giving the prosecution more ammunition than it already had, or provoking Cavanaugh to react with any increased zeal. The whole time, Fielder never once let his thoughts stray from the business at hand, with the possible exception of noting at one point that Hillary Munson wore no ring on the fourth finger of her left hand, and a little later deciding that whatever perfume she was wearing reminded him of jasmine. Up near Big Moose, the only women he'd run into smelled of sawdust and chain oil.

"I've got a splitting headache," Fielder finally said, only slightly exaggerating. "Do you have any aspirin?"

"I think I may have some Midol," Hillary offered, reaching for her handbag and beginning to rummage around in it.

"I don't have cramps, or my period, or anything like that," Fielder told her. "I just want some aspirin," he said. "Good, old-fashioned aspirin."

"On second thought," Hillary said, "maybe we've got something around here for grumpiness."

"I'm not grumpy."

She raised an eyebrow. For some reason, Fielder found the act highly seductive. If his headache complaint had been genuine, and not simply step one of his Master Plan (and to this day Fielder insists with a straight face that it was the former), then the sight of Hillary's one raised eyebrow brought about an immediate shift of gears, no less so than had it been a skirt or a blouse that she'd raised instead.

The Plan, of course, called for Fielder to somehow segue gracefully and unobtrusively to the topic of dinner. The headache certainly provided him an ideal jumping-off spot. The cause of the headache was the fact that he hadn't eaten a thing all day; the remedy was all too obvious.

The problem was Hillary's raised eyebrow. It had the immediate effect of shattering Fielder's concentration.

Looking back at what happened next, it is reasonable to accept Fielder's claim that what he meant to do was to repeat "I'm not grumpy," followed by the words "I'm just hungry." From there, dinner would be a done deal.

Instead, the words that actually came out of Fielder's mouth were, "I'm not grumpy, I'm just horny."

PEARSON GUNN SAT at the bar for a while, catching up on local news with Pete, and gradually lowering the level of Adirondack Amber in his pitcher. But the bar stools at the Dew Drop were too small—or Gunn's butt was too big—for true comfort, and eventually he repaired to one of the tables, somehow managing to make it in one trip—pitcher, glass, briefcase, hat, and all.

The problem was, at the table there was no Pete to talk with. True, from time to time, folks would come into the place, and if they knew Gunn (and almost all of them did), they'd stop by to chat, and maybe even sit awhile. But sooner or later they'd move on, leaving Gunn to himself. In fact, it was during one such period of solitude that Gunn decided to pass the time by reaching for his briefcase and extracting a file he'd been working on earlier that day. The file, of course, was that of Jonathan Hamilton. Gunn found a dry spot on the table and spread the papers out in front of him.

The first document he came to was the will of Mary Alice Hamilton, the one Wilbur Maple had recited to him from memory. Gunn looked through it; it was exactly as Maple had described it.

Underneath it were the wills of Jonathan's parents, the ones that had been probated after their deaths eight years ago and had led Gunn to Maple in the first place. Gunn began leafing through one of them. It was Porter's. It, too, was of the "joint and mutual" variety, apparently a Maple specialty. It had been drawn up in August 1988, revoking all prior wills and codicils. A stamp on the cover indicated that it had been probated in November 1989. Stapled to it was the death certificate of the deceased, reflecting the date of death—February 17, 1989—and the cause—a "fire of accidental origin."

Gunn returned to the text of the will. It recited that Porter was of sound mind and body, but mindful of the tenuousness of human life. Accordingly, he'd left his estate to his wife, Elizabeth. Next he'd addressed the possibility (which of course had become a reality) that the two of them might die together. In that event, Porter's parents, as the current holders of the bulk of the Hamilton inheritance, were "well enough situated in their own rights" that the will would leave them only a few personal effects. A small sum was left to Elizabeth's surviving brother, John Greenhall, said to be living in Sydney, Australia. Gunn recalled Maple saying something about Jonathan's having an uncle in Austria. Not much of an expert when it came to matters of global geography, Gunn assumed the two places might be one and the same. Austria, Australia. They certainly couldn't be too far apart.

Next came the modest sums left to the heirs of Elizabeth's other brother, Nathan, who had died "with issue." Gunn wasn't exactly certain what that meant. Figured maybe he had some sort of unresolved conflict when he'd bought the farm.

After that, the entire estate was to be divided equally among Porter and Elizabeth's two sons, Jonathan and Porter Jr., and their issue, if any.

As soon as Matt Fielder said "horny," instead of "hungry," the damage had been done, as baseball broadcasters like to say. Not that he didn't try to *unsay* it, to inhale the word back from whence it had come. Failing that, he blushed, grimaced, and tried desperately to compose an apology. But trying to apologize for using a disastrously wrong word is something like trying to regrow a redwood forest. The destruction is accomplished in a heartbeat; the restoration takes many lifetimes.

By this time, Hillary was wearing a broad grin. "Excuse me?" she said, hand on hip, lips pressed together tightly to hold back the laughter, eyebrow raised higher than ever.

"Sorry," Fielder managed to mumble.

"For what?" Hillary laughed.

"For the slip. I meant to say, 'I'm *hungry*.' "

"Freud would be proud."

"Sorry," he said again. "It's not just that I'm horny, though God knows it's probably true. The truth is, it's *you*. I'm like, attracted—very attracted—to you." It came out sounding like a line from a soap opera. "Hell," he said. "I want to go to bed with you." Maybe if he tried hard enough, he could parlay mere defeat into total disaster.

"I'm flattered."

Flattered? Here Fielder had bared his soul, confessed everything, and made a total fool of himself in the process. He expected nothing short of an extreme reaction in return—either on-the-spot swooning, or outraged, indignant rejection.

" '*Flattered*'?" he heard, from a voice sounding very much like his own.

"Quite," she said, apparently also having heard the ventriloquist. "And, under different circumstances, I might even consider the invitation."

Fielder did his best to ignore the less-than-enthusiastic "might even consider" part. Instead he repeated her phrase, " '*Different circumstances*'?"

"Yes," Hillary said. "I'm—"

"—Seeing someone?"

"Ah, that too."

"That's nice for you," Fielder allowed. "Who is he?"

"He isn't."

"Excuse me?"

"*He* is actually a *she*," Hillary explained. "You met her a little while ago."

Fielder groped helplessly. "Lois?"

"Lois."

"You're—"

"Gay." She nodded. "When I introduced Lois to you as my 'partner,' I thought you might get a clue."

"Hey," he said, "they don't call me 'Myopic Matt' for nothing."

"You're not myopic, Matt. You've just been living in the woods too long."

PEARSON GUNN STARED at the words he had just read. Jonathan had a brother. A brother named Porter Jr. A brother who had been included in the wills of their parents, but later omitted from that of their grandparents, the ones with the real money.

Even in his two-pitcher Amber haze, Gunn found that to be an interesting set of circumstances. He drained his glass, rose to his feet, and ambled over to the pay phone, where he proceeded to dial Matt Fielder's number. He listened to four rings, before the answering machine picked up, offering him nothing but Fielder's recorded voice.

*   *   *

THE REST OF Fielder was at that moment 120 miles to the south, at a small restaurant in downtown Albany, sitting down to what would turn out to be a very pleasant dinner with Hillary Munson and her partner, Lois Miller. The news about Jonathan Hamilton's having a brother would have to wait until the following day.

12

SPOTTED·DARTERS

THERE IS A tiny speckled chameleon, indigenous to the very northern reaches of the Adirondacks, called the spotted darter. If you watch one of them for any length of time, you come away convinced that it is physically incapable of moving forward in a straight line. Instead, it zigs first this way and then that, frenetically advancing three steps, only to retreat two. It seems such a study in pure paranoia that the local Franch Canadians have dubbed it *le lezard luna-tique*, "the crazy lizard."

With the discovery of the existence of Porter Hamilton, Jr., the defense team members began acting very much like spotted darters. On Tuesday, after speaking with Pearson Gunn and learning for the first time that Jonathan had a brother, Fielder assigned Gunn the task of locating Porter. It was a natural-enough selection, given the fact that Gunn was the team's fact-investigator. Besides which, Fielder needed Hillary to continue helping him with the mitigation letter.

On Wednesday, Fielder pulled Gunn off the detail, and replaced him with Hillary. He'd decided Hillary might be in a better position to track Porter down, inasmuch as tracing family members was one of her specialties. He told Gunn to help him assemble facts for the letter.

By Thursday, when Porter still hadn't been found, Fielder put Gunn back on it, figuring that with Hillary and

Gunn working on it together, they couldn't fail. He'd write the mitigation letter himself.

HILLARY MANAGED TO come up with a birth certificate, reflecting the fact that a Porter Hamilton, Jr., had been born at Mercy Hospital in Cedar Falls, on June 26, 1964. From there, she came up with a social-security number, a driver's license, and a stack of school records, which she sifted through for some clue to Porter's current whereabouts. Meanwhile, Gunn went back to the Flat Lake estate and re-interviewed Klaus and Elna Armbrust, the caretaker couple who lived on the grounds.

Gunn had found in his first meeting with the Armbrusts, that they were people who didn't tend to volunteer a lot of information. Once again he had to prod them to find out what they knew. Yes, they told him, they did remember Jonathan's older brother, whom the family had always referred to as "Junior." He'd been a bit of a troublemaker, according to Elna Armbrust, an angry boy who'd "got into the drugs" as a teenager. He'd left home sometime around 1985 or 1986, which would have made him twenty-one or twenty-two at the time. No, they hadn't seen or heard of him since.

Anyone who was angry and "into the drugs" ought to have a rap sheet, Gunn theorized. He called a source (and once again, we are invited to speculate that it might have been Captain Roger Duquesne of the state police, though it is reasonable to believe that, as a private investigator, Gunn had other contacts capable of helping him out in this area), and asked for a name and date-of-birth check. He got his response sometime Saturday afternoon. To his surprise, it came back negative: the New York State Criminal Justice System computer in Albany had no record of any Porter Hamilton, Junior or Senior, let alone one with a DOB of 06/26/64.

Stymied for the time being, out of habit Gunn headed for familiar surroundings. The Dew Drop Inn is not only the place where Gunn does his best drinking; it is also the place where he does some of his more creative thinking, and almost all of his networking (not that the nineties term "networking" has a place in Gunn's vocabulary, any more than does Fielder's term for it—"schmoozing").

As Gunn sat at his customary table with his familiar pitcher and glass, the usual Dew Drop denizens came and went. As luck would have it, one who came in that afternoon was Bass McClure. McClure and Gunn knew one another and got along well enough. Gunn already had interviewed McClure regarding the early-morning telephone call from Jonathan the morning of the murders, and McClure's subsequent visit to the Flat Lake estate. Both men were aware that, as the first person on the scene other than Jonathan himself, McClure was a prosecution witness. Whether or not at that point Gunn actually knew that McClure had testified at the grand jury is uncertain; in any event, something of an arm's-length relationship had resulted, with each man just a bit wary of the other.

But alcohol has been known to lower inhibitions on occasion, and on this particular Saturday afternoon, Gunn hesitated only a moment before inviting McClure over to join him at his table. And if McClure had any second thoughts about the idea, he didn't seem to show them.

The two traded small talk for a while, noting how the days were already getting shorter and the leaves beginning to turn, and how it wouldn't be too long before there'd be snow in the air. They compared notes on the coming hunting season, the level of water over in Stillwater Reservoir, the bald-eagle nests up at Wolf Pond, and the relative merits of full-time four-wheel drive versus part-time. Those topics of great importance out of the way, they fell silent.

Gunn figured it was as good a time as any. "What do you know 'bout Jonathan Hamilton's older brother?" he asked.

McClure shrugged. "Junior?"

"Yup."

"Haven't seen him in ages," McClure said. "He cut out a couple a years before the fire, if I remember correctly."

"Any idea where I might find him?"

McClure furrowed his forehead.

"Background info," Gunn explained, "that sorta stuff."

That seemed good enough for McClure. "Not really," McClure said. "Last I heard, he'd got himself jammed up on a series of robberies of some sort."

"Whereabouts?"

"Syracuse area maybe," McClure said. "Or Rochester. Someplace like that."

"What kinda time did he get?"

"Dunno."

And that was all McClure knew. Fifteen minutes and a beer later, he was on his way.

HILLARY MUNSON WASN'T doing much better. She'd checked social-security records, but according to those, Porter Hamilton, Jr., hadn't worked in almost ten years. On the books, anyway. Nor had he filed a state or federal tax return, registered a car in New York, or renewed his driver's license. He had no post-office box or telephone (listed or unlisted) in the dozen upstate counties she checked, wasn't on the welfare rolls, and hadn't applied for Medicaid or food stamps. None of the branches of the military knew of him, other than the fact that he'd registered for the draft when he'd turned eighteen, back in 1982.

It was as though he'd left Flat Lake eleven or twelve years ago and promptly fell off the face of the earth.

WHILE HILLARY MUNSON and Pearson Gunn were exhausting their leads, Matt Fielder sat in front of his fire, putting together the first draft of his mitigation letter.

Reducing an emotional appeal to a written presentation is an art, and it is an art that Fielder happened to be very good at. He'd been doing it in one form or another for all of his professional life—in pre-sentencing and pre-pleading memorandums, and in letters to prosecutors, judges, probation officers, and parole boards. He'd reached the point where he could write so persuasively that he'd invariably end up convincing himself of the merits of his position, no matter how tenuous that position might be.

Now, reading the pages over, Fielder found himself succumbing to the old magic once again. How could anyone fail to agree with him? How could anyone seriously think of seeking the death penalty against this overgrown child-man, who'd never harmed anyone before, who'd turned himself in to the authorities, and who barely seemed to understand what he'd done? Surely even a Gil Cavanaugh would have to see how totally inappropriate death would be for this case.

Around eleven, Fielder fell asleep on the floor in front of his fire, daring to believe in the persuasive power of his words. In his efforts to persuade Cavanaugh to spare Jonathan's life, the evening would mark perhaps the highest point in terms of Fielder's optimism, and certainly the lowest point for his realism.

SITTING WITH HIS third and final pitcher of ale shortly before midnight, Pearson Gunn was truly perplexed. How could it be that an angry, drug-abusing man—for some time now old enough to be treated as an adult in the eyes of the law—could get "jammed up on a series of robberies of some sort," and yet still not come back with a criminal record? Especially when the robberies had been committed in Syracuse or Rochester, both of which were definitely within New York State, last Gunn had heard.

He emptied the last of the pitcher into his glass. No matter how he looked at it, it just didn't make any sense. One robbery you might beat. Even two, if you were lucky enough. But a series? He drained his glass. *Nobody* beat a series of robberies. That just didn't happen—it was the kind of thing you could take to the bank.

Gunn's jaw dropped open, in a move that might have gone largely unnoticed but for the fact that his mouth happened to be full of ale at the time.

"That's it!" he gurgled.

Anybody who turned to look in his direction would have

seen him drooling ale from his beard onto his lap. But Pearson Gunn couldn't care less. The robberies were *bank* robberies, he'd suddenly realized. Almost all banks are insured by the FDIC, which means the U.S. Government shares jurisdiction over them along with the states.

The reason New York had no record of Junior was suddenly very clear.

The feds had him.

FOLLOWING GUNN'S SATURDAY-NIGHT epiphany, locating Porter Hamilton, Jr., was almost anticlimactic. On Sunday, Gunn telephoned the U.S. Bureau of Prisons and convinced someone to punch a name and date of birth into his computer; in less than a minute, Gunn learned that Porter was an guest of the Federal Correctional Institution in Atlanta, Georgia.

"What's he doing?" Gunn asked.

"Stamping out D.C. license plates, probably," came the reply.

"No," Gunn said. "What kinda *time*?"

"Oh." There was a pause, punctuated by the sound of more computer keys being hit. "Three hundred sixty months."

Which translated to just over twenty-six years, if you took time off for good behavior. Just as Gunn had figured all along: nobody beats a series of robberies. Especially against the feds.

FOLLOWING THE CALL, Gunn had reported to Fielder, who fired off a letter to Porter the very next morning, informing him that his brother Jonathan was in serious trouble, and asking that Porter call collect at his earliest opportunity so that arrangements could be made to have a member of the defense team fly down to interview him.

Porter called three days later, to say he'd be happy to meet with whoever came down. Fielder declined to fill him in on the nature of the trouble Jonathan was in, explaining that the call was probably being monitored. The truth was,

Fielder didn't want to reveal what had happened; he wanted whoever flew down to be able to confront Porter with the news face-to-face, in order to gauge his reaction. Despite the fact that everything about the murders pointed to Jonathan, Fielder knew that he, of all people, had to try to keep his mind open to other possibilities. Sure, Porter's involvement was a long shot. But when your chances are down to slim and none, you go with slim.

Later that day, Fielder took a drive over to Cedar Falls. It was a spectacular afternoon, crisp and cloudless, and the sun lit up the colors of the turning leaves the entire way. He passed red sumacs, purple maples, orange oaks, yellow birches, and a variety of other tans, ochers, and browns, all interspersed among the evergreens, which in turn ranged from darkest green to palest blue-gray.

He found Judge Arthur Summerhouse in his chambers, and presented him an order authorizing travel expenses for Pearson Gunn and Hillary Munson to interview a witness in Atlanta.

"What's the matter, he can't fly up?" the judge joked. "You going to tell me he's indisposed, or something like that?"

"Something like that." Fielder smiled.

"Why do they both have to go down there?"

Fielder had anticipated this question, ever since he'd decided against making the trip himself. On the one-in-a-million chance that Porter were to say something incriminating to himself, Fielder didn't want to be the one to hear it. He didn't want to risk becoming a witness to some aspect of the case, and end up having to recuse himself as Jonathan's lawyer. The next best thing, he'd decided, was to send both Gunn and Hillary; that way there'd be two witnesses, and not just one, to anything Porter might say.

"Actually," he now told Judge Summerhouse, "I should be going with them. I was hoping to save the taxpayers a few dollars. But now that I think of it—"

"That won't be necessary," said the judge, hastily signing the order before Fielder could add his own name to it.

FOUR DAYS LATER, Pearson Gunn and Hillary Munson sat side by side in a small cubicle, facing a Plexiglas partition and holding telephone receivers to their ears. The man who sat across from them on the other side of the Plexiglas, holding his own receiver to his own ear, bore little physical resemblance to Jonathan Hamilton. To his visitors, Porter James Hamilton, Jr.—or Junior (or "P. J.," according to both his stated preference and the crude tattoo that adorned the two middle knuckles of his left hand)—looked pretty much like Hollywood's idea of a typical thirty-something, burned-out white convict. Sean Penn might have gotten the call, or maybe Kevin Bacon. P. J. was blond, like Jonathan; but while Jonathan was clean-shaven, this man sported a wispy mustache and matching chin whiskers. In place of Jonathan's clear blue eyes were smoky gray ones that peered out darkly beneath sleepy, hooded lids. An old scar that began at one corner of his mouth disappeared somewhere under his jawline, vaguely suggesting that his chin might be mechanically attached to the rest of his face, like that of a ventriloquist's puppet.

Mostly, it was the man's size that hinted at the family relationship, but even that resemblance disappeared when P. J. slouched back on the visiting-room chair.

"So, Saint Jonathan's got himself jammed up, huh?" were P. J.'s first words, following the introductions.

"That's right," Gunn acknowledged. "Your brother's been arrested."

"What kinda beef?"

"Murder."

P. J. shifted into an upright position. "You're shittin' me," he said.

"We didn't fly down here to shit you," Hillary assured him.

"Who'd he do?"

Hillary was momentarily put off by the con talk, but

Gunn didn't miss a beat. "They claim he 'did' your grand-parents," he said.

The hooded lids disappeared, and P. J. stared wide-eyed and open-mouthed, in a display of astonishment that Gunn and Munson would later agree was so authentically spon-taneous as to be almost comical. The *"No fuckin' way!"* that came from P. J.'s lips was all but superfluous.

They spent a few minutes filling him in on some of the details, before turning to the subject of P. J.'s own troubles. If his reaction to the news hadn't been enough to convince them of his lack of involvement, there was also the little matter of his alibi: P. J. had been picked up outside of Syr-acuse in October 1996 and had been in custody ever since. He'd finally copped out to four bank robberies, but they'd pinned another dozen on him. Even with his guilty plea, it had added up to thirty years under the guidelines.

"Coulda been worse." He shrugged. "At least I'm in a federal joint. Food's better. Hey, they coulda sent me to Marion, Illinois, to give blow jobs to John Gotti. Pardon my French," he added with a crooked smile, for Hillary's benefit.

They pumped him for information about Jonathan's for-mative years, anything that might prove useful to Matt Fielder in his attempt to establish mitigating circumstances. It seemed to them that P. J. wanted to be helpful. It was clear he considered his younger brother something of a pampered brat—calling his brother "Saint Jonathan" had established that at the outset. Still, he tried his best to help, particularly after they told him that Jonathan was a candi-date for the death penalty. But the truth was, there wasn't too much he was able to tell them. Just as Elna Armbrust had said, P. J. had begun abusing drugs, as well as alcohol, early in his teens, at a time when Jonathan was still a boy. By the age of twenty, Junior had already had committed a dozen petty offenses, but had yet to be arrested. At twenty-two, he'd left home, never to return. He'd learned of his parents' deaths three years later from an item on the TV news. He'd tried to get to the funeral, but was in jail somewhere in northwestern Pennsylvania at the time, and they refused his request for an accompanied furlough.

"If they woulda, I was goin' to make a break for it," he admitted with a smile.

There seemed to be nothing left to talk about. "Well," Hillary said, putting her pen into her briefcase, "we appreciate your help."

"Glad to be of service to you, ma'am."

"Not that you were an easy guy to find," Gunn added. "For a while there, we didn't even know you existed. We thought Jonathan was an only child."

"Oh, no," P. J. said. "There was the three of us."

AROUND THE SAME time that Pearson Gunn and Hillary Munson were finding it was their turn to open their eyes wide and let their lower jaws drop, Matt Fielder was sitting at his computer, putting final touches on his mitigation letter to Gil Cavanaugh. He'd read it over so many times that he knew it by heart. He'd faxed a copy of it to Kevin Doyle at the Capital Defender's Office, to make sure he wasn't including anything that might be used against Jonathan in any way. Doyle had phoned him with his approval, but also with a sobering comment.

"It's a great letter, Matt," he'd said. "But from everything I know about Cavanaugh, he'd go death against his own mother if it'd get him reelected."

But, hey, what did Doyle know? After all, he was only the leading authority, the number-one capital defender in the state. Who was *he* to say?

Fielder printed out a final draft, signed his name at the bottom, and folded it into an envelope. Then he took a drive into Big Moose, where he handed it to the postal clerk.

"I want this sent by Express Mail," he told her. "Overnight. Return receipt requested."

"The works, huh?"

"The works."

"We don't get too many of those," she admitted. "Must

be a matter of life and death or something, huh?"

"You might say so," said Matt Fielder.

THREE OF YOU?" said Pearson Gunn and Hillary Munson in tandem.

"Sure," P. J. replied, looking surprised at their ignorance. "There's me, there's Jonathan, and there's Jennifer."

"Jennifer?"

Hillary retrieved her pen from her briefcase. The interview would continue for another half hour.

Jennifer was the middle of the three Hamilton children, born in 1967, making her thirty—three years younger than P. J., but still two years older than Jonathan. Physically she was said to favor Jonathan, in that she was blonde and fair and—at least according to P. J.—"drop-dead gorgeous." Then again, it had been some time since P. J. had seen her, and also some time since he'd seen any "snatch" (as he so eloquently phrased it) at all.

Like her older brother, Jennifer was apparently something of a black sheep in the Hamilton family. From the bits and pieces P. J. had picked up over the years since his departure, he was able to report that she, too, had left home never to return, about two years after he did. Last he'd heard, she was living somewhere in Vermont, or maybe New Hampshire, under a different name. He didn't know just where, and couldn't remember what the name was. About the best he could do was supply her birthday, September 6. But he seriously doubted that she had a criminal record.

"Not *that* kinda black sheep." He smiled.

"What kind, then?" Hillary asked.

"You know," he said, looking her up and down, and smiling crookedly. "She always had a little bit of a *taste* for things."

And that was about it. Jennifer Somebody, thirty years old, living somewhere in Vermont, or maybe New Hampshire. With a little bit of a *taste* for things.

*   *   *

SITTING TOGETHER ON the last leg of their flight back to Albany, Gunn and Munson compared notes. They'd certainly learned enough to rule out P. J. Hamilton as a suspect; that much they could tell Fielder. But when it came to shedding any new light on Jonathan, Junior had proved to be of very little use. On the other hand, he'd surprised them by revealing the existence of a third sibling. But once again, he knew so little about her that it seemed all but certain she'd turn out to be nothing but another dead end.

That is, if they were ever lucky enough to find her.

Gunn suddenly leaned across Hillary to get the attention of a passing flight attendant. "Excuse me," he said. "I've got this medical condition. Do you happen to have any ale on board?"

13

FLAT LAKE

THE CASE WAS back in court on Friday, October 3. The media was there, but this time in modest numbers. The parties had settled into motion practice, which rarely produces sound bites worthy of the six o'clock news. So it was only those present, or those diligent enough to read the next day's local newsprint, who would learn that while Judge Summerhouse, predictably, had denied the defense's motion to dismiss the indictment because of the prosecution's refusal to give them extra time to participate in the grand-jury process, just as predictably he'd granted the prosecution's request that the defendant provide blood and hair samples, and submit to the taking of footprints.

Nor would the news viewers be treated to the sight of Matt Fielder's objecting when Judge Summerhouse ordered him to have the rest of his motions filed within the normal forty-five-day period allowed by the statute for non-capital cases. "That's plenty of time," he told Fielder. "You get 'em in. Case is adjourned till November seventeenth."

What the viewers *would* see and hear, as usual, was Gil Cavanaugh. He'd received Fielder's mitigation letter three days earlier. "That," he now told the courtroom and the pool camera, "has given me more than an ample opportunity to review it and consider it fully."

Never mind that it had taken Fielder almost three days just to type the thing.

"The defense has asked me to refrain from seeking the death penalty in this case," Cavanaugh intoned in his most resonating baritone voice, "as is their prerogative. But my orders come from the people of this county, and it is my sworn duty to uphold the law of this state. The defense points out that Mr. Hamilton had no prior criminal record before the commission of these crimes. Well, that may be true in a *technical* sense," he allowed. "But once he killed the first victim, as far as *I'm* concerned, he was a murderer. If he'd stopped at that point, he wouldn't have been *eligible* for the death penalty, though if it was up to me to write the laws, he sure would have been. But no, it's only after he goes and kills the *second* victim, takes a *second* human life, that we're allowed to seek true justice. In *my* book, Mr. Hamilton *already* had his criminal record at that point. He killed two God-fearing people. The law doesn't require me to wait until he kills a third—maybe one of *you*—before I fulfill my obligation.

"Next thing they tell me, Mr. Hamilton is supposed to be a bit on the *slow* side. Like that should constitute some sort of an excuse for what he's gone and done. Well, folks, the way *I* was always brought up to believe, being slow may be an excuse for reading poorly, or for not getting good grades in school. But it's not an excuse for murder. No, sir. We will treat Mr. Hamilton the same way we will treat any other citizen of this county. We will not treat him any worse because he may have had a little trouble in his classes; that could have happened to anybody. But we won't treat him any *better*, either. That's simply the American way, folks: equal justice under the law.

"And so," and here Cavanaugh raised his voice theatrically, "I have come to the conclusion that the mandate of the legislature, the will of the God-fearing people who elected me, and my own personal conscience require that I do my duty, however unpleasant that duty may be. Therefore, I, Francis Gilmore Cavanaugh, the duly elected District Attorney of Ottawa County, do hereby solemnly certify that, in the event that the defendant should be convicted of these heinous and unforgivable crimes, I shall ask a jury of his peers to impose the only appropriate sentence, that of death."

If Cavanaugh's decision surprised nobody, it certainly topped the evening news, and made headlines across the state. Even the unflappable *New York Times* found room on the bottom of page one for a small item.

UPSTATE PROSECUTOR SEEKS DEATH IN KILLING OF TWO

Slowness Is No Excuse, Says Ottawa County D.A.

CEDAR FALLS—A twenty-eight-year-old man could face the death penalty in connection with the August 31 stabbing deaths of his grandparents.

Jonathan Hamilton, of Flat Lake, NY, was indicted last month for two counts of first-degree murder. Today Gilmore Cavanaugh, the Ottawa County District Attorney, announced his intention to ask for death in the event of a conviction.

Rejecting the defense's argument that Hamilton is not an appropriate candidate for capital punishment because of his lack of prior criminal history and his borderline level of comprehension, Cavanaugh countered by insisting that "slowness is no excuse for murder."

The defendant's lawyer had no comment on the development.

Should the district attorney get his wish, Hamilton could be the first person sentenced to death under the state's two-year-old capital-punishment law. The last execution in New York took place more than thirty years ago.

Because the story had run in Saturday's edition, Matt Fielder missed it. But a copy of it arrived in the mail three days later, courtesy of Kevin Doyle. The Capital Defender's Office makes it their business to clip all stories bearing on the death penalty.

Reading the article infuriated Fielder. In the first place, trial lawyers take second place to no one when it comes to the ego department. So, seeing Cavanaugh's name mentioned twice, and his not at all, was annoying enough. But the real sting came from the reporting of his failure to comment on the matter. What did they expect him to say? Didn't they realize he was thrust on the horns of a dilemma here? If he climbed up onto a soapbox and argued that his client should be spared because he barely knew what was going on, that was tantamount to admitting that Jonathan was guilty. On the other hand, if he reminded them that there was nothing more than circumstantial proof against Jonathan, that might be held against him later. He hated lawyers who used the "fallback" approach: "My client didn't do it. But if he did, it was self-defense. And even if it wasn't self-defense, then he was drunk at the time, or insane. Yeah, insane, that's it!"

He looked at the clipping. In the margin, Doyle had inked in the words, *Talk about a rock and a hard place!* At least *he* understood. Then again, what were the chances of getting twelve Kevin Doyles on a jury? What were the chances of getting *one*? He'd seen the public-opinion polls. According to the latest survey, something like eighty percent of the voters in Ottawa County approved of capital punishment. And most thought a death sentence was appropriate in *all* murder cases, let alone those the legislature deemed qualified because they contained aggravating circumstances. When the pollsters tried to find out what sort of defendants people might be willing to spare, the results were downright scary. They'd get responses like, "Well, I don't think there should be a death sentence if the defendant acted in self-defense," or "I'm not in favor of it if the death was the result of an accident," or Fielder's personal favorite, "I probably wouldn't vote for death in a case where I didn't think the defendant was guilty."

* * *

WITH THE DIE officially cast, Fielder turned to the task of preparing the remainder of his written motions. Forty-five days might seem like a lot of time, but he knew that he couldn't afford to chance leaving things for the last minute, as he had routinely done in his Legal Aid days. At stake here were several things of vital importance to the defense: the sufficiency of the evidence presented before the grand jury; the legality of the property seized by the state police; the admissibility of the statement Jonathan had allegedly made to Deke Stanton; and the broad issue of what evidence, documents, scientific test results, and photographs the prosecution would be required to turn over to the defense in advance of trial.

Pearson Gunn and Hillary Munson, meanwhile, were directed to set all other assignments aside and devote their collective energies to locating the whereabouts of Jennifer Hamilton. Fielder felt personally responsible that, for the second time in a matter of weeks, the defense had been embarrassed by an inadvertent discovery—first that Jonathan had a brother, and now that he had a sister.

If P. J. hadn't proved to be of much help, that could be explained by the fact that he'd left home as early as 1986, when Jonathan had been only 17. And by that time, P. J. himself had already been drinking, abusing drugs, and committing crimes with some regularity—all matters that would have directed his attention away from a brother five years younger. Jennifer might be a different story. If P. J. was to be believed—and this, of course, might be a big "if"—she hadn't left until two years later, in 1988, when Jonathan had been 19. As the middle child, she'd been closer in age to him, and presumably more a part of the family dynamic. Hopefully, she'd therefore be in a better position than P. J. to shed some light on Jonathan's early development.

Besides which, she was about all they had left.

With the defense's division of labor thus mapped out, Matt Fielder sat down at his computer, with every intention of getting started on his motion papers. But as things turned

out, the sun, slanting through his cabin windows at a pe-
culiar angle that Sunday morning, made it hard for him to
read the characters on his screen. It occurred to Fielder that
he could close the shutters, but the windowsill was filled
with all sorts of clutter—sunglasses, pens, spare keys, loose
change, and little empty bottles for collecting and testing
his well-water. Besides, the thought of trading natural light
for artificial struck him as much too harsh. The days were
growing noticeably shorter as it was, and already the leaves
were falling. Soon enough, the combination of darkness and
cold would place severe restrictions upon the number of
hours he could spend outdoors. And, after all, he did have
forty-five days to get his motions in; he figured he could
afford a bit of procrastination. So instead of closing the
shutters, he shut down his computer.

And he took a drive.

He could have headed northeast, up to Stillwater Reservoir, where he probably would have a pretty good chance
of spotting a bald eagle or two. He'd come to know where
a pair of them was nesting, high up in one of the tallest
trees, and one summer day he'd been lucky enough to
watch a young eaglet make its first flight. The parents had
coaxed it out, first by withholding food, and finally by making a series of passes at the nest, each one closer than the
one before. Then they'd taken up stations in a lower branch
of a nearby tree, and took turns screeching taunts at the
eaglet until, precariously perched on the edge of the nest,
it had finally either summoned up the courage to push off
on its own, or simply lost its balance and been forced to
improvise in midair. In flight, it had looked almost equal
in size to the adult birds. Its first attempts at navigating had
been a bit on the clumsy side, but within an hour it was
soaring, diving, and gliding in for landings as though it had
been airborne all its life.

But he didn't head up to Stillwater Reservoir.

He could have headed southeast, down to Little Moose
Mountain, the tallest peak for miles around, which would
have given him a commanding view of the lakes and rivers

and autumn colors spread out beneath it in all directions. If he was quiet enough, there was a fair chance he'd see black bear up there this time of year, gorging themselves on shoots and berries and wildflowers, in preparation for the coming winter hibernation.

But he didn't head southeast.

He could even have taken his canoe and driven west with it to Beaver Falls, where there was an easy spot to launch it, and where, for ten bucks, he could find someone at Stuckley's Amoco Station to drive his car down to Otter Creek so it would be waiting for him by the time he paddled down there. On the way, it was a good bet he'd pass deer grazing by the riverbanks, or maybe even a moose feeding on the vegetation that grew on the bottoms of the still pools the river made as it meandered.

But he didn't do that, either.

Instead, he headed northeast, farther up into lake country. He took his time as he drove, taking in the sights and breathing in the smells, knowing there was no hurry to scale a mountain while the sun was still high, and no rush to make it downstream to a landing before nightfall. He knew he'd be seeing no bald eagles this day, no black bear or feeding moose. For he'd lowered his goal to a far more modest one. He was headed to Flat Lake, to the Hamilton estate.

To the scene of the crime.

THE WAY PEARSON Gunn and Hillary Munson had chosen to divide up the job of trying to find Jennifer Hamilton was a simple one: Munson would look in Vermont, Gunn in New Hampshire. Of course, the word *look* was something of a misnomer, because most of their looking would be done over the phone. And, since they were still feeling somewhat guilty about their belated discovery of Jonathan's brother—and then that he had a sister as well—they'd decided to add some incentive to the quest, in the form of a friendly bet. The winner would be the first one to come up with a correct current address for Jennifer. The stakes were high: If Gunn won, Hillary would have to buy him a pitcher of ale; if Hillary prevailed, Gunn would owe her a dinner. Whether Gunn was on the road to committing the same blunder Matt Fielder had made, remains uncertain to this day. As things turned out, it was Hillary, and not he, who ended up having to pay off.

It was quickly established that nobody with the name Jennifer Hamilton and the birthdate September 6, 1967, had a criminal record—in either New York, Vermont, or New Hampshire, or with the federal authorities. Nor was any Jennifer Hamilton a licensed driver, or the owner of a motor vehicle registered in any of the three states. No phone company had a record of her, and no gas or electric company was supplying service to her.

But computers, Pearson Gunn had discovered a while back, were funny things, which could be made to work backward as well as forward. Thus, if you had someone's date of birth, you could sometimes plug it in, and get the machine to spit out the names of all the people on various lists who shared that particular birthday. Gunn didn't tell Hillary about this little trick right away. He figured he'd try it with New Hampshire first, and see if he got a hit. If he struck out, then he could always suggest she try it with Vermont.

He knew an investigator over in Manchester, who had a friend in Laconia, who in turn had a contact in Concord, who agreed to let them into his office that Sunday morning and run the date of birth. There the two of them spent four full hours running drivers' licenses, car registrations, criminal records (though Gunn had done that once already), jury rolls, state employment rosters, gun permits, hunting licenses, fishing tags, doctors' and nurses' registries, welfare recipients, and lists of teachers, barbers, and beauticians. Thousand of 09/06/67's came back, but none for a Jennifer Hamilton.

It was only when they ran a list of licensed day-care-center operators that they came up with anything of interest. That particular printout was one of the shorter ones, actually, containing only 72 names. (By way of contrast, there were some 1,860 state employees, 2,356 gun owners, and 3,111 fishermen.) It wasn't until they got to the third and final page of day-care operators that they hit what they considered a "possible."

LICENSED DAY-CARE-CENTER
OPERATORS—DOB 09/06/67

(Page 3 OF 3)

Sundberg, Mary Ann
Sutherland, Anne Howell
Talmadge, Marjorie S.
Tennyson, Patricia Sewell
Todd, Edward L.
Twyning, Carolyn McMaster
Tyson Charlene
Underwood, Susan W.
Untermeyer, Clifford B.
Van der Haas, Judith A.
Walker, Jennifer H.
Wendover, Kathleen Bryson
Westerlake, Hope
Williams, Cynthia Claridge
Williams, Ned
Wysor, T. Forest
Yates, Priscilla Osgood
Yelverton, Harriet C.
Zeller, Laura Greene
Zucker, Pamela T.

It wasn't a lock by any means, but any "Jennifer H." born on September 6, 1967, certainly was worth checking out. They did just that by pulling up her file. It dated back to July of 1991, when she'd applied to run a Class 3 center, for five children or less, out of her home in Keene. She'd been given a temporary provisional certificate to begin operating that September, and a full Class 3 license the following May. But she'd failed to renew it in 1994, and there'd been no activity since. Still, she'd provided an address, a tax number, and a telephone. And, best of all, her original application listed her full name: Jennifer Hamilton Walker

Evidently, Jennifer had gone and gotten herself married. The problem was, when Gunn and Hillary called the phone number, nobody there had ever heard of a Jennifer Walker, or a Jennifer Hamilton, or a Jennifer Hamilton Walker. The man who answered said it was a new listing they'd obtained when they moved in two years ago. And it was in Portsmouth, not Keene.

They didn't do any better with the phone directory. But, by running the name Jennifer Walker forward through the computer, they came up with all sorts of stuff: a driver's license, a welfare identification number, a jury summons (never answered), and—best of all—a current address. It seemed that Jennifer Hamilton Walker lived in Nashua, at 14 Nightingale Court.

The phone was an unlisted one, but that didn't stop them for long. Within twenty minutes, Gunn was listening to a woman's voice on an answering machine recording. "Hi," it said. "You've reached Jennifer. Leave a message at the tone, and I'll get back to you as soon as possible."

Gunn hung up without saying anything. He couldn't think of anything clever, and he preferred to catch Jennifer Hamilton in person. But the real reason was that he was too busy tasting his winnings.

IN MATT FIELDER'S, book, there were two types of lakes. The first type was where they let people build roads and houses right up to the edge of the water, and—as if that wasn't bad enough—then they let them build docks and rafts right out *on* the water. The second type was where they left the lake alone, where if you wanted to see it you had to hike through the forest to reach it, and if you wanted to be on it you had to remember to pack a canoe on your back. To Fielder, the difference meant everything in the world. It was that difference, in fact, that had brought him to the Adirondacks in the first place.

Flat Lake was definitely of the second type.

Anyone who spends only summers in Ottawa County—and the rigors of the winter months make it easy to forgive one for doing so—could easily assume that Flat Lake derives its name from how still its waters are in summer. And indeed they are, the result of an unbroken barrier of foliage that grows right up to the shoreline. Oak, maple, and ash form a backdrop to cedar, pine, spruce, and fir, which in turn frame shorter juniper, mountain laurel, andromeda, and wild fern. Sprinkled throughout is a generous helping of birch, slender trunks so white against the darker shades as to be almost startling when first seen. In autumn, the deciduous trees are well enough sheltered from the wind that they hold their leaves long after they've dried and turned. The overall result is a rich riot of color, spectacular enough in itself, but more often than not doubly enhanced by the presence of a perfect reflection on the still surface of the lake.

Yet the stillness is only an illusion. In fact, Flat Lake is constantly fed. But its nourishment comes not from the muddy spilloff of some sediment-filled creek or debris-choked brook. Instead, a natural artesian spring, located at the very center of the crater that carved out the lake in the last ice age, forever bubbles up from the bottom, supplying a constant source of water so cold and clear and pure that the freeholders in Cedar Falls long ago declared it a permanent county treasure, so as to protect it from the greed of outside bottling companies that have coveted it since the turn of the century.

And because any body of water that is continuously fed must have a runoff of its own, Flat Lake has a dam at its very southern tip, a steel gate that, if one knows exactly where to look, marks the only visible evidence of man's intervention. The gate is mechanically lowered each spring. The process is a laborious one, requiring two strong men, since the operation must be done entirely by hand, as no power supply is permitted to reach the lake. The height of the gate is set just below that of the water line itself, so as to act like the skimmer of some huge swimming pool. The result is that any leaf, twig, acorn, or other matter that alights on the surface is swiftly swept over the dam and out of sight, restoring to the beholder the illusion of a perfect, unbroken stillness.

Fielder found a large boulder at the edge of the lake and sat, enchanted by the beauty, mesmerized by the quiet. In the short space of an hour, he counted two deer, three rabbits, and an entire family of seven raccoons, all of them drawn there to drink from the water. He would have stayed longer, but he'd called ahead to make an appointment with Klaus Armbrust to see the Hamilton estate, and he didn't want to be late. Rising, his boot broke off a sliver of the rock he'd been sitting on. He decided it must be slate of some sort, the way it was formed in thin layers. He picked up the sliver and nestled it into the curve made by the thumb and index finger of his right hand. Then, with a sidearm delivery so pronounced that his knuckles brushed the ferns by the water's edge, he skipped the stone across the lake. One, two, three, four, five, six, *seven!* He watched with a broad smile as the ripples spread and collided, until the surface of the water gradually healed and grew still once again.

KLAUS ARMBRUST UNLOCKED the front door of the main building and stood aside, letting Fielder enter first. A faint musty smell greeted them, a suggestion that Nature had already begun the process of reclaiming the now empty house.

"This place has certainly seen its share of tragedy," Fielder observed.

"It surely has," Klaus agreed.

The tour took no more than twenty minutes. Fielder hadn't expected to uncover any revelations. After all, the state police had been over the scene three times, each time more thorough than the one before, and Pearson Gunn had been there twice on behalf of the defense. Still, Fielder wanted to get his own feel for the place where Carter and Mary Alice Hamilton had been murdered, and where, eight and a half years earlier, their son and daughter-in-law had lost their own lives in the fire.

The interior was all stone and wood, built a century ago at a time when craftsmanship was a virtue to be cherished. From the massive oak timbers and beams, the huge stone fireplaces, the recessed bookshelves and cabinets, all the way down to the wideboard pine floors, everything whispered of a day in which fine homes had been built with painstaking, loving care, instead of being slapped up to meet calendar deadlines and avoid cost overruns. Here there was no evidence of Sheetrock, plastic, vinyl, or Formica. Everything was *real*. Everything had come from the earth and, when in due time it would finally collapse and crumble under its own weight, everything would return to the earth.

Upstairs, Fielder could see that Elna Armbrust had succeeded in washing away most of the carnage, but even her best efforts had failed to hide the faint remnants of bloodstains on the walls and floors of the master bedroom. What possible madness, Fielder found himself wondering, could have possessed Jonathan that night? What unimaginable rage could have taken such a gentle child of a man, and turned him into a machine of murder?

From the main house, they walked to the cottage that had been Jonathan's. By comparison, it was tiny, but the same care in construction was evident. Fielder was struck by the sparseness of Jonathan's quarters, by how little he'd chosen to surround himself with. Someone had made up his bed, even fluffed his pillow and turned down the covers at one corner, as though expecting he might return any day. Lastly, they stopped in the bathroom, where Fielder examined the vanity cabinet that housed the sink. Only a fool would be stupid enough to hide a murder weapon there, a fool or a child. In Fielder's eyes, Jonathan Hamilton fit into both categories pretty well.

It was something of a relief to step back out into the

sunlight, and Fielder breathed the autumn air deeply into his lungs, as he waited for Klaus to padlock the cottage door behind them.

"Tell me, Klaus," he said. "What was Jonathan's sister like?"

"Jennifer?"

Fielder nodded.

"Pretty girl," Klaus said wistfully, almost as if he were trying to picture her after all these years. "Very pretty."

"What was she like?"

He seemed to reflect for a moment. "Quiet. . . . Smart," he added.

"Anything else?"

Klaus looked down at his shoes. "Unhappy," he said, with visible difficulty.

"Oh?"

"Unhappy," Klaus repeated, as though there was simply no more to say on the subject.

But Fielder wasn't quite finished. "You and your wife told Mr. Gunn about Jonathan's brother, right?"

"Yes, sir."

"Why didn't you ever mention his sister?"

Klaus shrugged easily. "He never asked us about her, sir."

And though Fielder would think about that response more than once on the drive back home, he was finally forced to acknowledge that it made pretty good sense. Here were two people who'd spent their entire adult lives in the shadows of those they served, who'd probably been taught to keep their silence around strangers, and whose command of English was limited to begin with. They hardly would have been the sort to volunteer information.

But if that part made sense, what of the comment that Jennifer had been an unhappy girl? Why had that been so? What was it that had driven one son of a wealthy, privileged family to a life of drugs, alcohol, crime, and finally prison? What was it that had brought a full measure of physical beauty and material comforts to a daughter, only to leave her unhappy enough to disappear with hardly a trace? And where in the strange puzzle that was Jonathan Hamilton did that particular piece fit in?

It was, as they say, something to think about.

14

NIGHTINGALE COURT

As it turns out, there are two New Hampshires. One is the New Hampshire of picture postcards, movie backdrops, and travel videos. It is the New Hampshire of the north, dominated by the sprawling White Mountain National Forest, an area that covers tens of thousands of acres and contains some of the most ruggedly beautiful terrain in all of North America. Here the traveler comes upon such sights as Mount Washington, the tallest peak east of the Rockies, which boasts the highest wind velocity ever measured on the face of the earth, and which each year claims the lives of climbers foolish enough to underestimate its dangers. Here, too, are the state's world-famous tourist attractions, bearing names like the Old Man of the Mountains, the Cog Railway, the Flume, Franconia Notch, Cannon Mountain, Tuckerman Ravine, Lost River, and Castle in the Clouds. Here lakes and rivers of every imaginable size, shape, and temperament abound, from the raging white water of the Androscoggin to the vast expanse of Winnipesaukee.

But there is another New Hampshire as well.

To the south, no mountains soar. No flumes, ravines, notches, lost rivers, or castles in the clouds are to be found. Wake up in Manchester or Concord or Keene or Jaffrey or Derry, and you might as well be in suburban New Jersey or Long Island. Here the mother-daughter houses sit side by side on quarter-acre lots, the blacktop driveways sprout basketball hoops, and the fastest-moving water can be found down at the local car wash. Here the sights have names like McDonald's, Burger King, Taco Bell, Texaco, and Jiffy Lube, and the prime attractions tend to be shopping malls, bowling alleys, and pizza joints. And it is here that the city of Nashua is to be found, less than ten miles from the Massachusetts line, and light-years away from the White Mountains.

Matt Fielder hadn't known any of that, of course, when Pearson Gunn and Hillary Munson had come to him to announce that they'd located Jennifer Hamilton in Nashua, New Hampshire, living at someplace called 14 Nightingale Court. Since it had been Gunn and Munson who'd made the journey to Atlanta, Matt Fielder had argued that it was now his turn for a road trip. "Besides," he'd pointed out, "I need a break from working on motion papers."

" 'Besides,' my ass," Gunn laughed. "You just want to go 'cause you hear this Jennifer is a babe."

"Leave him alone," Hillary said. "If anyone needs a babe, it's Matt. Trust me." Fielder shot her a look, and she'd said no more.

Two days later, he was on the road.

NIGHTINGALE COURT, WHICH held such promise with its fetching name, turned out to be a small trailer park located off Route 3A, on the northern outskirts of town. Fielder pulled up to the place around three, having been on the road for almost five hours. He spotted number 14, a small but well-kept white trailer, its cinderblock foundation tastefully hidden by white wooden trelliswork, and decorated with potted red chrysanthemums.

Fielder had passed the time on the way over trying to come up with the best plan on approaching Jennifer. Gunn, ever the sleuth, had advised him to "sit on the place" until she either came out or showed up. Then, once he saw her, if he had any doubts about whether she was the right person, he had several choices: He could call out her name and watch to see how she responded. He could find a cop to pull her over on some pretext and, in the process, check her identification. Or he could drive up behind her car and tap her just hard enough so that they'd have to get out and exchange licenses.

All of this seemed a bit too cloak-and-dagger for Fielder, however, and he'd decided instead on a more direct tack. He climbed down from his Suzuki, and was about to head for the trailer, when a slowing schoolbus pulled up so close to him that he had to step back to avoid being brushed by it. The door hissed open, and five or six children, ranging in age anywhere from around six to sixteen, poured out and dispersed in the direction of various trailer sites. One of them immediately caught Fielder's eye. He looked to be about twelve or thirteen, with striking facial features capped by blond hair that fell across his forehead. Even before he got close to his destination, Fielder knew exactly where he was going. He watched as the boy passed numbers 11 and 12—there was no number 13—and headed directly for the small white trailer with the trelliswork and the red mums. Just before he reached it, the door swung open, and out stepped Jennifer Hamilton Walker.

Despite his desire to avoid staring, Fielder found himself incapable of looking away from her. She was tall, perhaps five-eight or -nine, and slender. Like the boy, she was blonde, with hair worn long and straight. And, like both her brother and her son, she was beautiful, arrestingly beautiful. Pearson Gunn's prediction that she'd turn out to be a "babe" failed to do her justice. P. J. Hamilton's characterization of his sister as "drop-dead gorgeous" was closer to the mark, perhaps, but even his phrase fell short. It didn't capture the evenly tanned skin, the wide-set blue eyes, or the mouth that was just a bit too full for the rest of her face. It didn't take into account the way she cocked her head just so, causing her hair to fall to one side. Or the way she instinctively drew her son around behind her, so that she ended up standing protectively between him and the stranger. And it didn't say anything about how she stood her ground, almost defiantly, as Fielder began approaching them.

IT IS DIFFICULT to be a serious student of sports without at the same time being a firm believer in momentum. For the easiest lesson on the subject, simply turn on a basketball game on your TV. You'll soon learn that teams don't tend to *trade* baskets so much as they do to score in spurts. *"The Knicks are on a 17–2 run,"* the announcer will tell you, or, *"The Bulls have scored 12 unanswered."* There even is a tailor-made antidote for such sprees—a momentum-stopping device called the 20-second timeout.

As far back as high school, Fielder had learned firsthand how crucial it was to seize control of the flow of a baseball game, and how hugely and decisively doing so could affect the outcome.

He'd been playing in a Saturday-afternoon pickup game, batting with one out in the bottom of the third. Fielder's team was down 6–0. In fact, they didn't have a single hit to that point. Fielder's best friend, Whitey Ryan, had just earned a walk, and had advanced to second on a wild pitch. Fielder, batting next, worked the count to two-and-two. The pitcher, a tall, gangly kid with a big-league fastball, threw him a high hard one. With a different count, Fielder would've taken it. But, with two strikes on him, he knew he had to protect the plate. He chopped at it and managed to get his bat on it, but could do no better than to send a soft grounder between first and second. The second baseman, a little kid called Goober Wilson, scooped it up cleanly. But instead of throwing Fielder out at first, he decided to get cute and make the play at third. His hurried throw sailed over the third baseman's head and on into the parking lot. Whitey Ryan scored, and Fielder was awarded second. But far more significantly, in that instant, Fielder's team had seized the *momentum*. The next eight batters reached base safely, five of them tagging the previously untouchable pitcher for clean base hits. By the time the inning was over, Fielder's team had scored seven runs. They went on to win the game 8–6.

Afterward Fielder boasted that it had been his hit that had broken the ice. But Whitey Ryan, who knew even more about the intricacies of the game than Fielder did, was quick to correct him. "That doesn't get scored as a hit," he said. "Goober coulda got you at first, easy. So it goes down as a fielder's choice, is all. Same as an out."

Never mind that for weeks, Fielder had gone around thinking the term was a personalized one, custom-tailored to whoever happened to have been at bat. As he understood it, it got called a "Fielder's choice" because he'd been the one who'd hit the grounder; had it been Whitey, it would have been a "Ryan's choice."

But the real lesson he'd learned that day wasn't about which base to throw to, or about the virtue of playing it safe and going for the sure out. It wasn't even about the strange language of official scoring. It was about *momentum*—about how a snap decision on a routine play could decide not only the fate of a particular batter, but could sometimes change the course of the entire game, and determine its very outcome.

It was a lesson he'd never forgotten.

To Matt Fielder's way of thinking, the point at which the momentum in Jonathan Hamilton's case first began shifting toward the defense will always be the instant he first locked eyes with Jonathan's sister, Jennifer.

It is entirely possible, of course, that the initial look that crossed Jennifer's face at that moment reflected nothing more than the predictable level of concern a mother might be expected to feel at the sight of a total stranger staring at her and her child. Who was this man? What was he doing there? Did he mean them some harm? Was he a police officer of some sort? Had he followed her boy home from school? Had he spent the past week stalking one or both of them?

Any of those reactions would have been ample cause for

alarm. But to Fielder, Jennifer's look went way beyond mere alarm; it went almost to the point of panic. And in the weeks and months that followed, Fielder would find himself drawn back again and again to the moment, as he struggled to fathom this strange and striking young woman who would have such a profound effect on both the case and him personally, and as he tried his best to understand just where she fit into the growing mystery of the Hamilton family. And the answer that he would eventually come to settle on went something like this: It had been nearly a decade since Jennifer had left home. She'd moved two states away, changed her name, and begun life all over again. In the years that followed, she hadn't gone back home once for so much as an afternoon's visit, picked up a phone to call, or even dropped a postcard in the mail to say that she was alive. She'd taken a life of plush comfort and certain affluence, and traded it in for a concrete slab in a trailer park.

And she'd stuck it out.

But now, hard as she'd worked to put her former family behind her, it was suddenly apparent that they'd succeeded in hunting her down and finding her. For Jennifer no doubt had heard the sound bites and read the news stories. She'd seen that her younger brother had been arrested in connection with the brutal murders of her grandparents. And she'd known it would be just a matter of time until they came to her. The police, the press, the defense—it didn't matter who. What mattered was that her ten-year struggle to re-create her life had come to nothing. Despite everything— her flight and her fight, her adopted state, her new home and her changed name—the sight of the stranger standing there staring at her, told her that she was about to be drawn back into the web of the family she'd tried so hard to leave behind.

For in the split second in which Jennifer had looked up and locked eyes with the tall dark man standing by the funny-looking car, she'd known full well that whoever he was, it could be only Jonathan that he'd come about. And for Matt Fielder, his response to her reaction; as he later would put it, was, "There was something there, all right. I knew right away I hadn't driven all those hours for nothing."

THEY SAT AROUND a fold-down aluminum tabletop, and drank tea from mugs that didn't match. The boy had gone out back to play with friends, promising earnestly to be back before dark. He was nine, it turned out, and his name was Troy. People took him for older because he was tall for his age, she explained.

"My name is Fielder," he'd told her when he'd first walked up to them. "Matt Fielder. I'm the lawyer for your brother Jonathan."

He'd half expected her to deny that she had a brother named Jonathan, to tell him there must be some mistake. Or, at very least, to feign surprise that her brother would need a lawyer. But she hadn't. Instead, she'd simply turned to the boy and told him to go inside and wash up.

Now Fielder sat sipping his tea. It was bland and lukewarm, but he was grateful to have something to distract him from the face he found so hard to look away from.

"How long have you lived here?" he asked her, taking in the interior of the trailer. It was all Formica and plastic and aluminum, benches that opened into beds and hid storage bins beneath them, tabletops that swung up to reveal cooking surfaces, and chairs that folded flat for stowing. The best that could be said about it was that it was compact, functional, and clean.

"About two years," she said, without apology.

"And before?"

"Different places."

There was an uncomfortable silence. They both knew he hadn't come to talk about her travels.

"How's my brother?" she finally asked.

He assumed she meant Jonathan. Fielder figured there was enough family tragedy to talk about without bringing up P. J. and the thirty years he was doing for the feds in

Atlanta. "About as good as can be expected," he said. "He seems to share your ability to survive in small spaces."

"We share lots of things," she said.

"Yes," Fielder agreed. "The resemblance is quite striking." But it came out sounding much too formal. What he wanted to tell her was how pretty she was, how absolutely gorgeous. He wanted to tell her how he found it all but impossible to keep from staring at her. But a tiny voice in his head whispered to him to slow down, lest he make a total idiot of himself. He couldn't be certain, but the voice sounded remarkably like that of Hillary Munson.

Jennifer turned and peered out the window, to where a group of children were busy kicking an old soccer ball around. She would continue to repeat the gesture every few minutes, for as long as the two of them sat there talking.

"Your husband must be blond, too," Fielder said.

"I'm not married," she said.

"The boy's father, then," he corrected himself. "Mr. Walker."

"There is no Mr. Walker. It's just a name I took, to help me . . ."

"To help you disappear."

"Yes."

He sipped at his tea. It was almost room-temperature by now, and he was tempted to ask her for an ice cube or two to complete the transformation to iced tea. But looking at the motel-type refrigerator tucked underneath the countertop, he doubted that it would be large enough to include much of a freezer compartment, let alone ice-cube trays.

"Why the disappearance?" he asked her.

She laughed, but it was a dry, humorless laugh, as though in response to some long-ago joke at her own expense. "Are you familiar with the phrase 'dysfunctional family'?"

It was his turn to say yes.

She sighed deeply. "You can't really want to hear about it," she told him.

"You may be right," he said. "But I need to. It may be

all I have to work with to try to save your brother's life."

She looked out the window again. "Could they really kill him?"

"They sure intend to give it their best."

When she looked back at him, her eyes had filled, and as he watched, a single tear spilled over and ran down one cheek. He wanted to reach out and brush it away. He wanted to come around to her side of the tabletop and put his arms around her. He wanted to do whatever he could to make things better. Instead, he sat with his hands locked tightly together in his lap, afraid that any gesture he might make would be taken the wrong way. The truth was, Fielder had no way of knowing if the tear was shed for Jonathan's plight, or for Jennifer herself as she permitted her thoughts to reach back to her own past, a past she was now about to unlock—not only for him, but for herself as well—after nearly a decade of determined, deliberate denial.

Perhaps, he decided, it was for both of them.

15

JENNIFER

THE WAY SHE told it, Jennifer Hamilton had grown up in a household dominated by a controlling and sometimes abusive father, who rendered almost irrelevant a timid alcoholic of a mother. As for her grandparents, they'd thrown up their hands and abandoned the house to the younger generations, preferring to live under their own roof in the cottage that would eventually become Jonathan's. They would joined the family at mealtimes, but otherwise they kept mostly to themselves. Maybe, Jennifer speculated, they'd seen too much already.

With an older brother who seemed born to raise hell, and a younger one who came into the world smiling but damaged, Jennifer tried her hardest to find a place for herself in the family dynamic. But, as many middle children of troubled homes find, the pickings were slim. With their father often physically absent, and their mother emotionally removed, what little energy the parents did bring to the business of child-rearing was largely devoted to keeping P. J. in check or Jonathan occupied. Jennifer, by far the soundest of the three children, was rewarded with neglect.

And yet she thrived. She made friends at school (though she didn't dare invite them home), got good grades in her subjects, and immersed herself in the hundreds of books that filled the shelves of the study—books the rest of the family regarded as part of the decor. She read everything from Shakespeare to Salinger, from Hawthorne to Hemingway. She read of faraway places, of tall cities and vast oceans, and of people who laughed and loved and lived happily ever after. And all the while, she dreamed of the day when her own prince would come riding up to the door on a white horse to carry her off. He wouldn't even have to be handsome, she told herself. She'd already seen enough of handsome, in her short life.

As a teenager, she was the tallest in her class; a freak too tall to attract boys, who were scared off by her intimidating height, even as they were intrigued by her developing breasts. In order to stop growing, she gave up eating altogether one summer, and, when forced by her father to put food in her mouth, she'd comply only to excuse herself afterward in order to go upstairs to her bathroom, where she could run the water to drown out the sounds of her regurgitating the food—food that threatened to deprive her of being petite and normal, like the rest of her classmates. Only much later in life did she come across such terms as *anorexia* and *bulimia* in her reading, long after she'd outgrown her bouts of self-starvation and purging.

She wanted to go off to college, but her father sat her down one afternoon and told her how fragile her mother's health was. By then P. J. was already into alcohol and drugs and becoming something of a problem; as for Jonathan, he'd turned out to be little more than a dreamy child in an oversized body of his own. "Your leaving home will be the death of your mother," her father warned her. "You're all she has left."

Whether it was true or not, Jennifer couldn't defy her father and risk killing her mother. She enrolled in Cedar Falls Community College, where Klaus Armbrust drove her each morning and picked her up each afternoon. She found the work easy and the other day students friendly. The best thing about it was, by that time she was no longer the tallest in her class. The boys, at least, had caught up to her. But she'd been sheltered so long that she'd developed no social graces or self-esteem, and she rejected their advances, soon gaining the reputation of being aloof and indifferent. She earned her associate's degree in English in a year and a half instead of the customary two, intending to transfer her credits to a four-year institution.

But right around that time P. J. left home, sending their mother into deeper depression and increased drinking. Again Jennifer's father prevailed on her to stay home "where she was needed," though he never specified who it was that needed her, or precisely what needs she was expected to fulfill. But stay home she did.

"What did you do with yourself?" Fielder asked her.

"Oh, I got a job. My father knew the man who ran the lumberyard over in Pine Creek, and he got him to let me keep the books there three days a week. He figured it would also be a way to give Jonathan something to do."

Each day Klaus dropped Jennifer off at work, he'd drop off Jonathan with her. While Jennifer worked on balance sheets and bank statements in the office, Jonathan would amuse himself out back, in the fenced-in yard that contained stacks of two-by-fours, sheets of plywood and paneling, and huge mounds of wood chips and sawdust. If there were chores to be done, like restacking lumber, he'd occasionally help out; at eighteen, he was strong enough to work alongside the hired men, and he could pull his own weight, so long as he didn't have to keep count of pieces or make decisions on his own. But more often than not, he just sat around in the sun, or passed the time by playing with the dogs that had the run of the yard.

Jennifer glanced out the window. It was growing late in the afternoon, and as the length of the shadows increased, so did her level of agitation. Finally she stood, unable to continue her narrative any longer. But she needn't have worried; as though on cue, there was a sound of footsteps outside, the door to the trailer opened, and Troy bounced in, filthy and out of breath.

She hugged him close and tousled his hair, undeterred by dirt and sweat. "Wash up before you touch anything," she told him, and he obeyed without complaint, heading directly to the bathroom. Jennifer turned back to Fielder. "Will you stay for dinner?" she asked.

"No," he said. "You weren't counting on company. Besides which, I want to find a place to stay, before it gets too late. But I'd like to come back and talk some more tomorrow, if it's okay with you."

"You can stay here if you like," she said, pointing at the benches. "But I don't get home from work 'til one in the afternoon."

"How about I come by around then?"

She shrugged noncommittally. If listening to Jennifer's story had been enlightening stuff for Fielder, it was apparent that telling it was hardly a labor of love for Jennifer. Still, she hadn't said no.

"I'll see you tomorrow, then." He was careful to make it sound like a statement, rather than a question.

PULLING BACK ONTO Route 3A, Fielder was relieved to get away. As beautiful as he found Jennifer, and as much as the notion of sleeping ten feet away from her excited him, the trailer made him feel claustrophobic; and the thought of spending the morning cooped up there waiting for her to come home from whatever work she did, was not an enticement.

He found a Motel 6 outside of a town called Merrimack, and paid $26 cash for a night's stay, remembering to ask for a receipt so he'd be able to submit it with his voucher someday, if he didn't lose it first. Then he took a drive north, toward Manchester, hoping to find a place to eat. A McDonald's had a big yellow banner up, advertising a 99¢ special on Big Macs. He decided to forget being a vegetarian, and he bought two of them to go, along with a large Coke.

Back in his room, he propped himself up against the headboard of the bed and clicked on the remote control of the TV set. Letters moving across the bottom of the screen told him that the World Series game had been rained out; in its place they were showing a tape of the Yankees' Game

6 clincher from a year ago. There were two other channels to chose from. One was all local news programming, the other was showing an old *Cheers* rerun. He clicked off the set, and turned to his food. The Coke turned out to be watery and flat, to the point where it was almost undrinkable..

But the Big Macs were awesome.

He fell asleep around nine thinking of Jennifer, half of him grateful to have a good bed beneath him, the other half regretting that he'd passed on her offer to spend the night in her trailer. After all, who was to say what wonderful things might have happened once her son had fallen asleep.

Yet even in his dream, she never once smiled.

16

GOD'S WILL

WHERE WERE WE?" Jennifer asked.

They were sitting on the stoop of the trailer, warm in the afternoon sun despite temperatures in the forties. Always cold during the winters he'd spent in New York, Fielder had gradually become acclimated to the weather of the north country. A good part of it was simply learning how to dress. The first thing you did was to trade in your silly city shoes for a pair of good, lined, waterproof Rockports. Then you wore heavy denim jeans, instead of lightweight cotton twills. Next you went out and bought yourself some good thermal bottoms and a serious down vest. And finally you got over your vanity and your urban fear of hat hair, and you put on a wool cap.

But the other part of it was *attitude*. You told yourself you didn't need it to be 68 degrees to be comfortable—that it was okay, even fun, to be outside in the cold. When your body felt like shivering, you took a couple of deep breaths, and started *moving* instead. Every once in a while, you took your gloves off, just to see how long you could go without them before your fingers started to get numb. And gradually you became acclimated. You got to the point where you came to regard the cold as your companion, if not quite your friend. You became one of *them*.

"You were working at the lumberyard," he said, "and Jonathan was hanging out there."

"Right," she said.

The arrangement had worked for a while. Three times a week, Klaus would drop the two of them off in the morning and pick them up in the afternoon. They'd ride in silence both ways—the caretaker uncommunicative as always, the boy off in his strange, private world somewhere, and Jennifer left to herself.

Until, one afternoon, the car broke down as Klaus was on his way to pick them up. Without a car phone or a CB radio, he had no way of calling them, and by the time Jennifer decided he wasn't coming for them, the place was empty, and there was nobody left to give them a lift home. So they'd set out walking, Jennifer figuring either they'd meet Klaus along the way, or they'd be lucky enough to hitch a ride. If not, it was only about eight miles, a distance she guessed they could cover in a couple of hours.

She guessed wrong.

After about a mile, Jonathan complained that he had to pee. They left the roadside and found him a wooded area where he couldn't be seen, an act of precaution on Jennifer's part, since modesty was simply not in Jonathan's range of behavior. But, obediently enough, he wandered off a bit and found a tree that seemed to suit him. But as the minutes went by, Jennifer grew impatient.

"What are you *doing*?" she called out to him.

There was no immediate reply, but that was often the case with Jonathan. So she called out a second time.

This time he answered, or at least spoke. "Need help," was what he said, as best as she could tell.

She headed over to where he stood, his back turned to her. It was only when she reached his side that she realized his problem. He had a huge erection, which he held in both hands as though it were some creature that wasn't a part of him.

"Need help," he said again, a look of total bewilderment on his face.

"I think I may have laughed at him," Jennifer said now, shielding her eyes from the sun, as though she were somehow trying to peer back over the years. "I made him let go of it, figuring it would go down of its own accord. But it didn't."

Fielder felt a chill that the weather couldn't quite account for. He wanted to hear the story, but at the same time he didn't. A feeling of uneasiness spread through his body.

"Go on," he said. Closing the distance between them, so she could lean against him if she wanted to.

"I'd heard somewhere that when it happens to a patient in a hospital or a doctor's office, they give it a good rap, and it goes away. So," she said, "I tried to do that. But I guess I was afraid to hurt him, and I must not have done it hard enough. It only seemed to make things worse."

By that time Jonathan appeared to be in real physical pain, so excruciating the sensation must have been. Moreover, he was so frightened by what was suddenly happening to him that he appeared to be on the verge of panic, his eyes darting about wildly as he grunted for his sister to help him.

"I couldn't think of anything else to do but to try to bring him off," she said. "So I began rubbing him. At the same time, I kept telling him to take it easy, that it was going to be okay. I figured at some point he'd have to begin to calm down and enjoy it, instead of being so scared by it. And for a time, he seemed to. He let me sort of push him down onto the ground, where I could do it better for him. I kept thinking it would all work out: he'd relax and get into it, he'd be able to come, and then he'd be okay.

"But it didn't work that way. He just kept getting bigger and bigger," she said, "and harder and harder. And the panic never seemed to go out of him. Then, before I knew it, he was pushing *me* over, climbing on top of me, pounding me with his fists, crushing me. He was trying to get it inside me, but he didn't seem to understand that he couldn't, because of my clothes. And the more he tried and failed, the more panicked and angry he got, until it reached the point where I was truly afraid he was going to kill me."

"So?" Fielder asked. But already he knew the rest.

"So," she said. "So I let him do it. I pulled off my pants, and I showed him what to do. And, he . . . did it."

Only then did she allow her body to collapse against Fielder's. He took her weight, reaching one arm around her far shoulder, so as to draw her up close to him. When she didn't resist, he began to rock her softly.

But there was more.

"Afterward, I must have bled for an hour. I think we both thought I was going to die. Jonathan couldn't take his eyes off the blood. I'm sure he was even more frightened than I was. At one point, we saw Klaus drive by on the road; he'd managed to get the car working. But I was too scared to flag him down, and we let him pass a second time, heading back toward home."

Eventually she got the bleeding to stop, but she was still in too much pain to walk. So Jonathan—the same Jonathan who'd just finished brutally raping her—lifted her up, cradling her in his arms, and carried her home, never once putting her down to rest for the two hours it took them to cover the seven miles.

"It was dark by the time we got back. Somehow I made it to my room and into my bed. I threw away the ruined clothes I'd used to stop the bleeding, but Elna found them the next morning and showed them to my parents.

"My father stormed into my room and made me tell him the whole story. Instead of being sympathetic, he was livid. He refused to blame Jonathan; he said Jonathan was just a child who didn't know any better. He blamed Klaus, and most of all he blamed me. He laughed at my mother's request to let me see a doctor, insisting that a little bleeding was a normal thing in a virgin. That night, he gathered us all together and made us swear on a Bible never to talk about the incident, to carry on as though none of it had ever happened."

"And?" Fielder asked.

"And it might have worked," Jennifer said, "if I hadn't gotten pregnant."

"My God," Fielder heard himself saying. "Troy." Suddenly it all came together for him: the boy who looked so much like Jonathan that instinctively Fielder had known he had to be a Hamilton the moment he'd seen him step down from the schoolbus.

Jennifer nodded.

"Why?" he asked. What he meant was, *Why didn't you have an abortion?* But he realized that was a question her couldn't ask her now, not with her son growing up apparently normal, and so obviously loved.

"I *wanted* an abortion," she said, as though she'd read his thoughts. "But my father wouldn't hear of it. He was a religious man. 'It was God's will,' he told me, and God would strike me down if I went against his wishes. The only thing I didn't know was which 'his' he meant."

So one day several weeks later, without so much as saying good-bye or leaving a note, she'd packed a few things into an overnight bag, taken $200 from her father's dresser drawer, and walked out onto the road. The first ride she got took her Cedar Falls. At a diner, she struck up a conversation with an elderly couple who were heading for Portland, Maine. She convinced them to take her with them, but had to get out the following morning, when she became too sick to continue. At a service station, she asked where she was.

"Lebanon," someone told her.

"Where's Lebanon?"

"Not far from Hanover. White River Junction."

"No," she said. "What *state*?"

"New Hampshire."

She'd taken the $200 to pay for the abortion, but now she had to use it to pay for food, and for a motel room. "But by that time," she explained, "I'd already thought about keeping the baby. It was like, as soon as I'd run away, I knew I'd never go back. There was no longer any shame to feel. Instead, what I mostly felt was *lonely*. I know it sounds crazy, but more than anything else, I think I decided to keep my baby so I wouldn't feel so *alone*."

"And you never went back?"

"Never," she said, "not to this day. Not even to New York *State*. I'd been gone about six months when Troy was born. I cried for two full days when they told me he was normal; they couldn't understand why I'd been so worried. Then I needed to tell somebody, so I called Sue Ellen Simms, one of the few girlfriends I'd made back in Flat Lake. She told me she'd heard that my family had disinherited me, and that my father refused to mention my name in public. As far as he was concerned, it was as if I were dead. Worse. It was as if I'd never existed.

"By that time, I was staying with a family in Enfield, living in a room above their garage. I gave Sue Ellen their phone number, making her promise on her eyesight that she wouldn't tell anybody else. A few months later, she called to say there'd been a fire, that my parents were dead. Part of me was glad to hear it, I hated them so much. But part of me felt guilty for feeling that way. Sue Ellen said at first there was some talk that Jonathan had lit it."

Fielder stiffened. "I never heard that," he said.

"About the fire?"

"No," he said. "About Jonathan's being a suspect. I was told it was an accident."

Jennifer shrugged. "Maybe it was," she said. "But it's hard to know. My family's always been pretty good when it comes to keeping secrets. Until now, at least."

"I guess a double stabbing is kind of hard to keep secret," Fielder observed.

"Doesn't look too much like an accident, huh?"

He let her attempt at humor go. "Where did the new name come from?" he asked her. "Walker."

"I had to pick *something*," she said. "When I went to the Department of Motor Vehicles to get my New York driver's license changed to a New Hampshire one, I asked them if they could switch the name over to my married one. The woman didn't want to do it without seeing a marriage certificate, but when she looked at my belly, I guess she decided that was proof enough. I was eight months pregnant at the time, and pretty big. But she insisted on keeping Hamilton as my middle name."

"Good thing she did. I never would have found you otherwise."

"I'm glad you did," she said. She reached up for the hand he'd wrapped around her shoulders, and took it in both of her own.

"Why 'Walker'?" he asked her.

"I don't know," she said, with another of her shrugs. "I saw it somewhere. It reminded me of Jonathan a little. The way he'd walked that day, carrying me. By that time I'd pretty much forgiven him, and I wanted my baby to have some connection to him, I guess."

"Does Troy have any idea who his father is?"

"No," she said. "I told him I was married a long time ago. He thinks his father died in a hunting accident. It's why he humors me, I think, and allows me to be so over-protective of him."

The story was winding down. He knew how difficult it must have been for her, but he also sensed that telling it had been something of a catharsis for Jennifer, a letting-go of things held too close for too long.

"Does that car of yours really run?" she asked, eyeing it suspiciously.

"It got me here, didn't it?"

"Take me for a ride," said Jennifer Hamilton Walker.

THEY HAD TO be back by three, when the schoolbus would arrive with Troy, so they couldn't go far. But Jennifer seemed to want to get away from the trailer park for a bit, as though the story, once told, could now somehow be left behind there. They drove around aimlessly for a while, the windows open wide, the heat turned up full-blast to compensate.

"Turn in there," Jennifer said, at a sign marked Silver Lake Beach.

Fielder swung the wheel hard, and the Sidekick screeched its tires and threatened to roll over before complying. They drove past an unattended gate, and parked in a blacktop lot next to a lake. It was definitely of the southern New Hampshire variety—small and overdeveloped—and the sight of it made Fielder wonder if Jennifer didn't miss the unspoiled beauty of Flat Lake, back in a world she'd once called home.

They got out and walked down to the water. There were hundreds of ducks and geese—either stopovers pausing to rest on their southern migration, or year-rounds who'd lost the instinct, and learned instead to survive the winter on handouts from the locals.

At the water's edge, Jennifer again took his hand in hers, and they stood on the bank, watching the birds fluttering about, preening themselves and searching for anything that seemed remotely edible.

"Will you be staying the night?" she asked him.

He didn't know whether she meant with her, or in the state. And his confusion must have been transparent, because Jennifer quickly smiled and added, "Here in New Hampshire."

"I don't know," he said.

"Is there anybody you've got to get back to?"

"Just your brother."

"Stay one more night," she told him. "I'll make us all a nice dinner. I'm a pretty good cook, actually. Then I'll get a sitter for Troy. There are all sorts of people back at the park who've been after me to let them watch him, so I can go out on a date." She smiled conspiratorially. "I'd love to give them something to gossip about."

"Is that what you think I am?" He laughed. "Someone to gossip about?"

"No," she said softly. "I think you're maybe someone to love."

It took a moment for that to register. But she held his eyes with her own. And in that moment, and from her look, he understood that it wasn't just about sex, either, any more than it was about gossip. Here was this thirty-year-old woman, as beautiful a person as he'd ever set eyes on, with all this love to give. In her entire life, the only person she'd ever loved was her own son. And now she was asking him, Matt Fielder, to stay a bit, and let her try to love him.

He guessed her brother could wait another day.

He freed his hand from hers just long enough to put his arms around her and pull her close to him. The nearby ducks scattered, as though they'd seen enough to know there'd be no handouts here.

17

TOO SCARED TO SCREAM

JENNIFER TURNED OUT to be more than a "pretty good" cook. She made chicken breasts stuffed with sautéed mushrooms and wild rice, fresh asparagus, and a pie made from local wild blueberries—ingredients Fielder had insisted on paying for at the checkout counter.

"They're paying me serious money to represent your brother," he'd told her. "Think of this as my way of giving something back to the community."

"So I'm a 'community' now?" She'd laughed. A part of her had begun to emerge that Fielder hadn't seen before, a part that dared to smile openly, laugh out loud, and even flirt on occasion. It was as though she'd been required to grow up and become an adult too quickly, and now Fielder's presence somehow managed to unlock the little girl that always was in her but never had been permitted to surface.

Dinner in the trailer was itself something of an intimate experience. The three of them sat around the folding table-top, which all but disappeared under plates, glasses, flat-ware, and paper towels folded to imitate linen napkins. They talked about work and school and Little League and teachers, about whether rap was really music or not, about which cars were fastest, and which sneakers were coolest. Troy wanted to get a tattoo—just a small one, no dirty words or anything—and his mother had forbidden it. They agreed to give Matt the deciding vote. When he sided with Jennifer, Troy moaned "Grown-ups!" and smacked the palm of his hand against his forehead in mock exasperation. But from the boy's smile, Fielder could tell he was secretly pleased that they cared enough to intervene.

Sharing the after-dinner chores was something of a gesture, since the kitchenette barely had room for one person. But they managed to pull it off anyway—Jennifer washing, Fielder drying, and Troy putting things away.

Around seven, the youth-sitter showed up—Troy objected to the term *baby-sitter*—and they said their goodnights.

"Where are you going?" he asked.

"The movies," Jennifer told him.

"What movie?"

"Don't know yet."

"What's playing?" he asked.

"Not sure."

"How can you be going to a movie, if you don't even know what's playing?"

She threw him one of her shrugs, topped off with a smile.

"Hey, Mom," he said. "Is this like a *date*?"

She laughed. "And what if it is?"

That stumped him, but only for a moment. "Don't be home too late," he warned them sternly.

As almost any single parent could have told Fielder, you can't do much better than that on the approval scale.

So," FIELDER SAID, pulling the Sidekick out onto the highway, "were you serious about a movie?"

"No way."

"What'll it be, then?" he asked.

"What would *you* like?"

"What I would like," he said, "is to make love with you." And then he held his breath and prayed she wouldn't tell him to turn around and drive her back home.

"God," she said instead. "This must be what it's like to feel seventeen years old."

"Yeah, well, don't get your hopes up too high. You haven't seen the honeymoon suite at the Motel Six yet."

"How do you know?" she said, with a wicked wink.

"Touché." He laughed. But the truth was, he did know; everything about her told him tonight wasn't just a date for Jennifer.

To Fielder, the evening would turn out to be what making love was always supposed to have been about, but never quite was. It would become the single moment in his life when tantalizing anticipation, excruciating eroticism, and breathtaking love would manage to lay aside their differences for a few short hours and come together in perfect, magnificent symphony.

To Jennifer, it would be everything she'd ever dreamed about and more, for as long as she could remember. Never mind that she'd had to wait until the autumn of her thirtieth year for her handsome prince to come calling. Never mind that he'd finally found her, not at some castle in the clouds, but at a trailer park in someplace called Nashua, New Hampshire; or that he'd ridden up not on a white steed champing at its bit, but in an old green Suzuki with torn mud flaps.

At the door of his room, he swung her into his arms and carried her inside before remembering that the gesture might have brought back memories that could have ruined it all. But if she remembered she showed no sign of it; she threw her head back and laughed like a child.

She was shy when it came to undressing in front of him, but it struck Fielder as an honest shyness, as her brash boldness at shamelessly planning the evening suddenly collided with her long years of privacy. She wanted the lights off; he needed to see her. They compromised on a small desk lamp.

He stopped her from unbuttoning her top, so he could do it for her. Underneath, he discovered some sort of strange, frilly undershirt thing.

"It's a teddy," she told him. "I bought it years ago, through a mail-order catalog. After that, they kept sending me ads for all sorts of other stuff—mesh stockings, sequined g-strings, and cutout panties. I was so afraid Troy would come across one of them, we had to move. Anyway, you're supposed to like it. It's supposed to be sexy."

"And it is," he assured her. "But it belongs on the chair over there."

At which point she misunderstood him completely, got up, and proceeded to move to the chair. Which didn't turn out to be so terrible, either, once she realized her mistake.

It was like that. Just when they'd get so deeply involved with their bodies and their passions that there didn't seem anywhere else to go, something would happen to make them laugh, to slow things down, to calm them so they could start all over again.

If she was nervous, she was also eager; if she was inexperienced, she was also quick to learn. If he was worried about when to be gentle and when to be forceful, at some point he forgot to worry, and he was both. And, when at last they lay quietly side by side, aware of precious time running out, he knew he'd been somewhere he'd never been before.

"What do you like most about me?" she asked him.

He thought of her face, her eyes, her too-full mouth, her smile, her long blonde hair that fell a certain way, her little-girl breasts, her flat tummy, her bottom that he hadn't been able to keep his hands off of, her long legs . . .

"Well?"

"The way you kiss me," he said.

"I like your voice," she said. "More than anything else, I love listening to your voice."

They dressed in silence for the fifteen-minute ride back to Nightingale Court and reality, each of them forever changed, each of them wondering what the next day would bring. Holding the door open for her on the way out of the motel room, Fielder saw, for the first time that night, how bare and cheerless the place looked, his $26-a-night Motel

6 room, and he wondered what it would be like coming
back to it alone in half an hour, for the mundane business
of sleeping. When Jennifer reached to flick off the wall
switch, he caught her hand.

"Leave the light on for me," he said, in his best imitation
of a midwestern twang. But if she caught the joke, she
didn't smile.

RIDING BACK TO the trailer park, Jennifer seemed every
bit as far removed as Fielder was from the evening they'd
spent together. But where his thoughts dwelled on the shab-
biness of the motel room, hers turned to her son.

"Do you think he's all right?" she worried aloud.

"I'm sure he is."

"How do you know?"

"The sitter seemed very competent. She'd said she'd
raised three children of her own."

"I know," she said. "But I didn't tell her he likes to read
before he goes to bed. Or that he needs to be reminded to
brush his teeth, and wash his face. Suppose he should get
up and walk around in his sleep, like . . ." But there her
voice trailed off, her mind apparently preoccupied with a
myriad of other terrors that might lie in wait for her child.

"Listen," he said. "Troy's all right, and you're a wonderful mother. You need to stop worrying about him so
much."

She looked up at him, and he took her hand and
squeezed it, and gave her his most reassuring smile. It
seemed to do the trick.

"I'm sorry," she said. "It's just that I've never left him
before. Not at night."

And, of course, Troy was just fine.

Fielder drove the sitter home, all of a hundred yards or
so, and headed back to the motel. But not before promising
Jennifer to come by for breakfast before he headed home
the following day.

*   *   *

IN HIS DREAM that night, Fielder replayed his evening of making love with Jennifer. Only, each time they came together, some part of her would hold back. Just as he'd be on the verge of entering her, she'd panic and stop him, to ask if Troy had been permitted to read before bedtime, or if he'd been reminded to brush his teeth. "Suppose he gets up," she cried at one point. "Suppose he should get up and walk around in his sleep, like . . ."

"Like what?" he asked her.

Only to awaken and realize he was lying awake in the dark motel room, alone, and that he'd spoken the words aloud, to himself.

"Like what?" he repeated softly, trying to force his dream to resurface, to come back to him. *Making love . . . Jennifer holding back . . . worrying about Troy . . . reading, brushing his teeth, getting up and walking around in his sleep, like—*

Like what?

But sleep closed over him again.

BREAKFAST IS A difficult time for those unaccustomed to eating before the afternoon, but Fielder did his best to cope with English muffins and orange juice. Troy raced off to catch the schoolbus, leaving the two of them in sudden quiet. Fielder motioned for Jennifer to come around to his side of the tabletop, and when she did, he took her in his arms and pulled her onto his lap. Her kiss tasted of crumbs and butter and jelly, and he wondered if maybe he could learn to change his meal schedule after all.

"How'd you sleep?" he asked her.

"Like a baby." She grinned. "You?"

"Good," he said. But something tugged at him, as though from far away.

"I was bad," she confided.

"You were *wonderful.*"

"No," she insisted, "I was bad. I called in sick to work."

"You were bad," he agreed with a laugh. "But I've got to be getting back."

"I know. But I needed the day to myself. I haven't taken a sick day in five years."

They did the dishes, but he kept grabbing her from behind, and they ended up on her bed. At one point Fielder thought the trailer might slip off its foundation, but it held up. They laughed about it afterward.

"Do you think your neighbors wondered why it was rocking?" he asked.

"I hope so." She smiled. She looked at her watch. "Hey, it's almost ten," she said. "I suppose we should get up and—"

And in that instant it all came back to him. The dream. What was it she'd said? *Suppose he should get up*, she'd said. *Suppose he should get up and walk around in his sleep, like—*

Like what?

"Does Troy really walk in his sleep?"

"No," she admitted, after a moment's hesitation. "But it's one of the things I worry about."

"Why?"

"Have you ever seen someone who does it?" she asked him. "It's scary," she said. "Their eyes are open, and they can do all sorts of things. But they're still asleep, and in the morning they honestly can't remember anything about it."

But what about the "like"? Where had that come from? Something in him kept telling him that the "like" was important.

"What does it remind you of?" he asked her.

She shrugged and looked away from him, as though to check on her son through the window. But he wasn't out there—he was at school by now—and it hadn't been her usual, easy shrug. It had been something quite different: a deliberate avoidance of his eyes, and of his question. And in that difference, and from that avoidance, he knew it wasn't just his imagination that was at work here.

"What does it remind you of?" he asked her again. Still

she looked away, even as he reached out for her. "What?" he pressed her.

When at last she turned back to face him, there was a strange, glassy look in her eyes, a faraway look he hadn't seen since she'd finished reliving the story of her childhood for him the afternoon before.

"Not 'what,' " she whispered. *"Who."*

The lawyer in Matt Fielder eased up then, and he let her off the hook, his cross-examination done. He'd been taught long ago, when you got the answer you've been looking for, try to avoid the temptation of overkill. So, instead of forcing her to speak the name herself, he did it for her.

"Jonathan," is what he said.

She nodded weakly.

JONATHAN WAS A sleepwalker. He'd been walking in his sleep since early childhood. Sometimes they'd find him downstairs, or curled up in the bathroom, or even outside on the lawn once or twice, before they had special locks installed to keep him in. He would seem to be awake. His eyes would be open, he could see, he could do things; but he never spoke. In the morning, he'd have absolutely no recollection of the things he'd done, or how he'd managed to end up where they'd found him.

"After the day—the day Klaus's car broke down," she said, "Jonathan began coming to my room during the night. The first time, I thought he was awake, and just wanted to talk. Then I realized he was asleep, and it wasn't talk he wanted. After that, I'd lock my door, but the lock was so flimsy he'd push his way in anyway. I was too scared to scream, too scared to say anything."

"So you . . ."

She nodded. "So I'd let him. He was never violent again, like the first time. I found it was just easier to rub him, or whatever, until he was finished. It never took long. Then I'd walk him back to his room. I don't think he knows about any of it, even to this day."

But Jennifer had certainly known about it. She couldn't

say if she'd gotten pregnant that first day, or from one of Jonathan's subsequent nighttime visits; it didn't seem to matter much to her. What mattered was, there soon came a time when she could no longer live under the same roof as her brother, or her indifferent parents.

Fielder was positively dumbstruck. "Do you understand what you're telling me?" he asked her.

"What? That I was a whore?"

"A whore?" He grabbed by the shoulders and shook her. "You were a *saint.* You did the only thing you possibly could have done, to save your life. But that's not all."

"There's more?"

"Yes, there's more. Don't you see, Jennifer? Don't you get it? Your brother killed your grandparents *in his sleep.* He doesn't even know he did it."

18

HITTING THE BOOKS

THE REVELATION THAT Jonathan Hamilton was a sleep-walker had an immediate and dramatic impact on his defense team. Before leaving to return home, Matt Fielder spent another two hours with Jennifer, grilling her for every minute detail she could supply about her brother's disorder. It seemed she'd been one of the last in the family to learn of it. Around the time Jonathan was making his periodic nighttime visits to her room, she'd brought up the subject of his wanderings with her mother and both her grandparents, but only in veiled, general terms. All three of them, it turned out, had been aware of the behavior for many years—since the time Jonathan had been about five or six. It had been harmless enough at the beginning, comical stuff such as his wandering about the house, peeing into the kitchen wastebasket, or winding up in someone else's occupied bed. Later, there'd been occasional episodes involving violence, but nothing had ever been reported to the authorities. Once, Jonathan had fallen down a flight of steps in his sleep; a doctor was summoned, but hadn't been told the true circumstances surrounding the incident. Another time, Jonathan had lashed out and struck his mother hard enough to give her a black eye that lasted the better part of a week. And once or twice he'd hurt his hands punching some imagined enemy in the middle of the night, unaware that it was a wall or a door. Jennifer had never talked to her father about the problem; by the time she knew about it, the two of them had all but ceased talking about anything. But she'd found out from several conversations with her mother that the family's code of silence applied more than ever. Her father reportedly warned the rest of them that if even a rumor got out, the police would be sure to come take Jonathan away, lock him up in an insane asylum, and throw away the key.

The only person Jennifer ever dared tell, over all the years, had been her friend Sue Ellen, whom she'd sworn to secrecy. Fielder was now the second person she'd trusted enough to confide in; and even so, he found the process of extracting the information from her somewhat akin to old-fashioned dentistry.

She doubted that either Klaus or Elna Armbrust had known of Jonathan's condition. As for her older brother, she couldn't say. She'd had no contact with him since he'd moved out of the house a couple of years before she had, and they'd never discussed it before that.

Still, Jennifer had presented Fielder with a veritable gold mine of information, and even as he held her tightly and kissed her good-bye, he needed to tell her how important it might prove to be.

"I want you know," he said, "that what you've told me just may be enough to save your brother's life. And I really mean that."

"I hope so," she said. "I should hate him, you know. I should want him dead. But for some reason, I've never been able to stay angry at him."

ARMED WITH HIS discovery, Fielder drove back to Big Moose in a state approaching absolute exhilaration. His thoughts raced off in all directions. He knew first off that he had a bunch of reading to do regarding both the scientific literature on sleepwalking, and its legal applications. He realized he'd have to go back to Judge Summerhouse to get more orders signed for experts. Earlier he'd gotten authorization for a mental-health expert; now he'd need to get a bit more specific. He figured he'd need both a psychiatrist and a psychologist—one to examine Jonathan, another to provide expert testimony. He also might want a neurologist to take X rays and hook Jonathan up to needles and machines, to do CAT scans and MRIs and EEGs and whatever other tests they had these days, in order to find out what strange things went on in Jonathan's brain while he slept. He'd have to check with the jail, subpoena their records to see if there'd been any reports of unusual nighttime activity on Jonathan's part. He'd need to have the Armbrusts re-interviewed, as well as P. J. down in Atlanta. He'd want to look into the 1989 investigation of the fire that claimed the lives of Porter and Elizabeth Hamilton, to see if it really had been an accident, or if the rumor Sue Ellen Simms had heard about Jonathan's being responsible held any truth. And he'd need to try to track down Sue Ellen herself, to see if she could remember hearing anything about the sleep-walking from Jennifer, after all these years.

Above all, it was time to sit down and have another conversation with Jonathan, time to introduce him to a part of himself he might not even know existed.

OVER THE WEEKEND, Fielder got together with Pearson Gunn and Hillary Munson, to discuss developments. They met at Lake George, which was pretty much the geographical midpoint of the triangle created by their homes, and they spent a long afternoon sitting on the deck of a restaurant overlooking the lake, picking at their food, sipping at their drinks, enjoying the sun, and bringing each other up-to-date on developments.

Excited as Gunn and Munson were to learn of Jonathan Hamilton's sleepwalking, they insisted that Fielder first tell them about Jennifer. They were investigators, after all, and it hadn't been lost on either of them that Fielder had been gone from Wednesday morning to late Friday afternoon.

"Must've taken you an awful long time to find her," Gunn theorized.

Fielder said nothing. He'd expected them to rub it in a

bit, though not literally, until Hillary leaned across the table and ran the palm of her hand across the top of his head.

"Aha!" she exclaimed. "Those antlers are *history*!"

And even Fielder had to laugh.

From Gunn came word that the state police had completed their preliminary testing of the evidence recovered from the crime scene, and how it compared to exemplars provided by Jonathan. The towels discovered in his vanity cabinet, as well as smears found on his bathroom walls, his flannel shirt, and his undershorts, contained a mixture of blood that, according to highly reliable RFLP DNA testing, was genetically identical to that of known samples drawn from the two victims. Ditto for the trail of drops leading from the main house to the cottage. Jonathan's own blood sample was still undergoing DNA testing.

Jonathan's fingerprints had been found in various places in the main house, on the sheath that matched the knife, and on his bathroom wall—and there it had actually been left in the same mixture of his grandparents' blood. The bloody footprints in the main house also definitely belonged to Jonathan—both the booted set and the barefoot ones.

Several dozen human hairs had been recovered at the main house, including a number of blond ones that, upon microscopic examination, proved to be consistent with hair samples pulled from Jonathan's scalp. Seven of the hairs had intact or partial follicles attached, and therefore had been submitted for DNA testing. In the absence of sufficient genetic material, the PCR method would be used instead of the slightly more definitive RFLP method, and the results, when received, would likely point to Jonathan only to the exclusion of something like one-in-a-million odds, instead of one-in-a-*billion*.

"Thanks for all the good news," Fielder said.

Hillary had begun receiving records in response to her subpoenas. Jonathan was, by all accounts, "borderline low-normal" in his intellectual capacity. Whether this level translated out as "retarded" was questionable, according to some experts, and doubtful according to others. And, under the death-penalty statute, *retarded* was the magic word. It still looked like a judgment call whether they should risk having Jonathan retested—it had been almost fifteen years since his last evaluation—or stick with the old scores. Fielder pointed out that the sleepwalking theory might make that decision unnecessary, at least for now. What it had done was provide them with an option, a new basket in which to put some of their eggs. In death cases, he reminded them, you generally had nothing to work with; now they found themselves confronted with the luxury of choosing between retardation and sleepwalking, or even *both*. In the most wretched of all neighborhoods, they'd suddenly been showered with an embarrassment of riches.

Together, they parceled out new work assignments. Hillary would use her contacts to reach out to doctors who could examine Jonathan and provide expertise regarding sleepwalking; after that, she'd see if she could find Sue Ellen Simms. Gunn would check to see if there'd been any episodes since Jonathan had been in jail; he'd also reinterview the Armbrusts and P. J.—the latter, hopefully, by phone—and see if he could find out more about the origins of the fire that had claimed the lives of Jonathan's parents. That would leave Fielder to read up on sleepwalking, get new orders for the experts, and conduct his sit-down with Jonathan. And, should he happen to find himself with too much time on his hands, there were always motion papers to keep him out of trouble.

It was going to be a busy autumn for all of them.

JONATHAN HAD BEEN locked up for six weeks—a blink of the eye in the life span of a murder prosecution—but to Fielder, it looked like it had been more like six months. His hair was unkempt and seemed less blond than before. He'd lost weight, and his prison jumpsuit hung on him, instead of fitting him. Most noticeably, his eyes—which earlier had been an arresting pale blue—were dull and lifeless. He reminded Fielder of an animal that was failing to thrive in captivity, or a plant that had been uprooted and moved indoors, and wasn't getting enough sunlight.

Fielder greeted him with, "Hello, Jonathan," once they were seated across from each other.

"Hello, Mr. Fielder."

"Matt." If Fielder addressed someone informally, he insisted on reciprocity.

"M-Matt."

"How are you doing?"

"Okay, I guess."

"Are you sure?" Fielder asked him. "Are you eating enough?"

Jonathan shrugged, the identical shrug Jennifer had used. The Hamilton family shrug. It was scary to Fielder how much, and in how many ways, Jonathan resembled his sister, and how much Troy resembled the both of them.

"The f-food's not too good," he admitted. "And I'm not s-sleeping so good."

"How come?"

"Bad dreams. I saw the d-doctor yesterday. He gave me pills, said they'd m-make me sleep better."

"What kind of pills?"

"Little ones. White."

Fielder asked what the dreams were about. He wanted to know whether Jonathan was experiencing flashbacks regarding the discovery of his grandparents' bodies, or, possibly, even reliving the commission of the crime itself. But Jonathan replied that he couldn't remember. If his subconscious was struggling with what he'd done that night, his conscious mind wanted no part of it.

Their meeting lasted an hour and half. Not unsurprisingly, it was Fielder who did most of the talking. He wanted Jonathan to know how hard he and his associates were working, how much they cared about him, and how he shouldn't give up hope. He tried hard to draw Jonathan out, coaxing him to talk about his fears, and inviting him to be an active part of the defense team. Though his motives were laudable, the extent to which he succeeded was questionable. Characteristically, Jonathan's concerns were with *little* things: What time did they want him to wake up in the morning? When was he expected to brush his teeth? How could he keep track of which days were shower days? Who was taking care of the squirrels he'd been feeding each day back home? Why wouldn't they let him have laces for his shoes?

Toward the end of the session, Fielder decided to take a more active approach. "I met your sister," he said.

"Jennifer."

It was uttered as a statement, but Fielder treated it as a question. "Yes," he said.

"Baby."

That one took Fielder by surprise. Hillary Munson had understood Jonathan to say the word "Maybe" when asked if he had surviving relatives other than his brother P. J. In hindsight it is likely that Jonathan had actually said, "Baby." But Fielder caught Jonathan's response quite clearly. He didn't know for a fact if Jonathan had ever known of his sister's pregnancy, let alone that she'd given birth after leaving home. But then he remembered having seen a photograph of a baby, stuck among the belongings seized from Jonathan's cottage. He'd assumed at the time that it had been a childhood photo taken of Jonathan himself. Now he wasn't so sure.

"What baby?" he asked.

But it was too late; Jonathan's eyes had already glazed over. Whatever baby had visited his thoughts a moment ago was now far removed, well beyond the young man's powers of recall.

Fielder moved on. "Did you used to have any trouble sleeping when you were back home, at Flat Lake?"

The question drew another shrug from Jonathan.

"Ever wake up in a strange place?"

A blank stare.

This was getting him nowhere. He decided to take one good swing for the fences. "Jonathan," he said, "do you remember ever walking around the house when you were asleep? Or hearing anybody talk about your doing that?"

The same blank stare.

"Anything like that?"

Finally, the shy curl of a smile, as though Jonathan had belatedly caught on to the joke. "How c-can you be walkin' around," Jonathan asked, "wh-wh-when you're *asleep*?"

It was a pretty good question.

THE ANSWER, IT turned out, was not quite so mysterious as Fielder first suspected. Or so he learned on the first of two full days spent holed up at the Cedar Falls Free Library. He actually hadn't intended to start his reading so soon. He'd figured on taking a day off for tree-felling and log-splitting, activities that let his body take over for his brain, and served to rejuvenate him and remind him why he'd fled the city and moved up to the mountains.

But he hadn't counted on the rain.

An unusually dry August and September had suddenly turned into a wet October. The day after his meeting with Gunn and Munson at Lake George, Fielder had awakened to a freezing rain. By nine, it had changed to a steady downpour. The radio told him it was here to stay for a while, and a look at his own barometer had confirmed the prediction. Operating a wet chainsaw wasn't Matt Fielder's idea of a good time, any more than swinging a 12-pound sledgehammer at a rainslicked wedge.

So, the library it was.

According to the scientific literature, nearly one percent of the adult population is said to suffer from some form of sleepwalking or "night terrors." Most instances occur during the deeper, "slow-wave" portions of sleep, typically Stage Three or Four. Both children and adults may suffer from the condition. It is not to be confused with nightmares, which are simply a type of dreaming and more often take place during the earlier, first and second stages of sleep. In dream sleep—often called REM sleep, for the rapid eye movements that characterize the continued functioning of a limited number of the body's smaller muscles—the larger muscles are literally paralyzed, and gross motor functions are shut down; hence, the individual is unable to talk, walk, or otherwise move about.

But during non-REM sleep (or in those rare cases of persons suffering from a condition known as REM sleep behavior disorder), tests indicate that the potential for full locomotion is there. The recent use of a technique called polysomnography—the recording, by electrodes, of brain waves and muscle activity, and the mapping of the interaction between the two—confirms that a subject can actually get up and walk about, thus becoming a *somnambulist*, one who, in the very truest sense, can be said to be a "sleepwalker." The same individual is fully capable of running, jumping, talking, kicking, throwing punches, wielding a knife, aiming and firing a gun, and engaging in all sorts of other physical activity—and all the while, recordings of his brain waves clearly establish that he is asleep.

Fielder found the literature full of dramatic cases, some of them merely anecdotal, but others carefully and clinically documented. There was, for example, the tale of a retired detective recovering from a nervous disorder, who was asked to assist in a case of an apparently motiveless murder on a beach in southern France, only to realize from a unique four-toed footprint left in the sand that it was he himself who had committed the crime, while in the throes of an episode of sleepwalking.

Or the story of a man, by all accounts quite happily married, who chased his wife from their bed in the middle of the night, caught up with her, stabbed her repeatedly as she lay in the middle of the street, and then—to the horror of onlookers—smashed her head against the pavement, killing her.

Or the twenty-four-year-old Toronto man who arose one night and, still asleep, drove his car fourteen miles to the home of his in-laws, whom he reportedly loved deeply. Upon arriving, he savagely beat his mother-in-law with a tire iron and then stabbed her to death, before attempting to kill his father-in-law as well. Next he drove to the police station, where for the first he noticed time his severely cut hands, and told them he thought he'd just killed some people.

Or the sixty-three-year-old Jewish refugee who, dreaming that Gestapo agents were breaking into his home in Cleveland, Ohio, got up in his sleep and fired a shotgun into the living room, killing his wife of thirty-five years.

The stories went on and on, each more riveting than the one before it. Fielder had heard once that although you could hypnotize a person, you couldn't make him commit some horrible act under hypnosis that he wouldn't normally commit. He learned now that there were no such restraints placed upon the sleepwalker. Each of the cases he read dealt with individuals who were non-aggressive, and even gentle in their waking states, but who became aggressive and violent during their sleepwalking.

By the end of a day's reading, Fielder was convinced that the phenomenon was every bit as real as the chair he was sitting in or the books that lay in front of him. He'd learned terms like "sleep-related violence," "non-insane automatism," "sleep apnea," and "psychomotor epilepsy." He had twenty pages of notes on case histories, polysomnography studies, and other scientific data. He had statistics quantifying disorders by age, gender, education, and profession.

But while the experts were virtually unanimous in their acceptance of the phenomenon, there were disagreements when it came to the subject of causation. There were, to be sure, a number of clues that emerged from the studies. The vast majority of violent sleepwalkers were men. Typically they had irregular sleep patterns. Many were shift workers, whose schedules were constantly changing, requiring them to readjust their hours of sleep. Often they'd been through some recent traumatic or unsettling experience, such as the loss of a loved one, a marriage, or a job. A number of them had previously experienced other, less dramatic, sleep disorders. Some had resorted to the increased use of caffeine, nicotine, and other drugs. Many, when tested, demonstrated a greatly reduced ability to be roused during their deep-sleep stages.

To Fielder, that last finding seemed paradoxical at first. Why, he'd asked himself, should an unusually sound sleeper be prone to sleepwalking? Shouldn't the exact opposite be true? But as he'd read on, he realized that that was exactly the point, at least in the minds of many of the researchers: It is precisely that individual, the one who has the greatest difficulty waking up, who is most prone to sleepwalking, because his motor functions are so much more easily aroused than his consciousness.

What kind of a sleeper, he wondered, was Jonathan Hamilton?

FIELDER FOLLOWED UP his two days at the Cedar Falls Free Library with two more at the library of the Syracuse University Law School. There he pored through hundreds of text books, case reports, and law-review articles, in search of the courts' reaction to sleepwalking when raised as a defense in a criminal prosecution. He read about *mens rea*, about criminal intent and responsibility, about voluntariness, insanity, and all sorts of mental diseases and defects. He read cases involving crimes committed by people with dementia, epilepsy, alcoholism, drug intoxication, and post-traumatic stress disorder. He read about a man who'd strangled his children to death, convinced they were devils bent on destroying the world. He even came across two of the incidents he'd discovered in his earlier reading: the Toronto man who'd killed his mother-in-law had been acquitted by a jury; the Cleveland man hadn't been so lucky.

On the afternoon of the second day, he found what seemed to be an early case of documented sleepwalking violence. An article written back in 1951 by a law professor named Norval Morris, and intriguingly titled "Somnambulistic Homicide: Ghosts, Spiders, and North Koreans," led him to a previously unreported case from Victoria, British Columbia, captioned *The King v. Cogdon*. It seemed that a year earlier, one Mrs. Cogdon had been charged with murdering her nineteen-year-old daughter Pat, an only child she'd been deeply attached to. The night before the killing, she'd dreamed that spiders were in the house and were crawling over her daughter. She'd risen from the bed she shared with her husband, gone into Pat's room, and awakened to find herself violently brushing off her daughter's face.

The next day Mrs. Cogdon recounted the incident to her doctor, along with a previous dream in which ghosts had come to take her daughter away. The doctor prescribed a sedative for her. That night, after participating in a conversation regarding the Korean War, she fell asleep. She dreamed that North Korean soldiers had invaded the house, and that one of them was in her daughter's room, attacking Pat at that very moment. She jumped up, got an ax from the woodpile, ran to Pat's room, and swung the ax twice, striking her daughter on the head and killing her.

All she could remember afterward was the dream, and running from her daughter's room to the home of her sister next door, where she collapsed, crying, "I think I've hurt Patty."

At the trial, Mrs. Cogdon told her story, which the prosecution did not seriously contest. Her lawyers also called to the stand her doctor, as well as a psychiatrist and a psychologist. They all agreed she was not psychotic, and insanity was never raised as a defense. Nevertheless, Mrs. Cogdon was acquitted, the jury apparently concluding that the act of killing had not been, at least in their judgment, her act at all.

But Fielder knew that—however interesting Professor Morris's account might be—officially unreported cases seldom make converts of judges. He needed to find the seminal case, the earliest recorded pronouncement that stood for the proposition that one who kills while asleep cannot be held criminally responsible by the state.

His search took him another eight hours, to nearly midnight, by which time his eyes could barely focus, his muscles ached from sitting, and his stomach growled for fuel.

It took him to a tiny alcove in the sub-basement level, to an ancient, dust-covered volume, one of a leather-bound set of *Queen's Bench Reports*, containing opinions collected from courts that had sat centuries ago, and an ocean away.

But find it he did.

Regina v. Hawkins, it was called.

There was a lot of fine print and old English mumble-jumble Fielder had to wade through, before he reached the point where the writer had finally gotten down to the facts and holding of the case.

Next came before the Court a lad of barely nineteen years, named Thomas Hawkins, of Bedfordshire. Young Hawkins stood accused by the Crown of slaying his own mother, by the act of running her clear through with a sabre.

The LORDS were fully satisfied that the youth had indeed inflicted the fatal wound. It was his state of mind they dwelt upon. By all accounts, he'd been fast asleep at the time. Suddenly he arose from his bed and ran into the study, where he took down the sabre, a war relic that had graced the wall above the mantle. Thence he proceeded straightaway to the quarters of his parents, where with his father too stunned to react, he set upon his mother, in a state that could only be described as possessed. The father then tackled Thomas, and wrested him to the ground, where the boy appeared to awaken for the first time. He had no notion of where he was, what had brought him there, or what it was he'd done.

LORD FLETCHER observed that the lad merited some sort of sanction, but in that he stood alone.

LORDS MERRIWEATHER and SOAMES were both of the opinion that no crime had indeed occurred. If a man is not truly his self when he acts, they asked, shall he be said to be answerable before the Crown? Or is it not as though someone separate and apart from him has committed the offense?

THUS, the prisoner was ordered discharged without delay.

Fielder had to beg the library's security guard for change to feed the copy machine. It was already past closing time, and the poor fellow wanted nothing more than to lock up the building for the night. But in the end, the bloodshot eyes and the desperate look on Fielder's face, combined with his frantic insistence that it was a matter of life and death, finally caused the guard to relent.

By the time Fielder reached his cabin, it was going on three o'clock in the morning, and the rain was changing over to a heavy, wet sleet. He pulled his boots off and collapsed onto his couch, too tired to undress, too weary to make it to the bedroom. His head still spun from shootings, stabbings, bludgeonings, and ax murders; from ghosts, spiders, Gestapo agents, and North Korean invaders.

By the time he'd awake it would be afternoon, almost twelve hours later, and the ground and trees would be covered with the season's first snowfall. His clothes would smell, his body would ache from stiffness and hunger, and he'd have a scratchy three-day stubble of a beard.

But he'd also have his case.

19

THE SMOKING GUN

Do you get CBS up there in the woods?"

"Some days I don't even get my toaster," Fielder answered. "Who is this?"

"Laura Held. Turn on your TV."

He did as he was told. Laura Held was now one of Kevin Doyle's assistants at the Capital Defender's Office down in New York City. As the set warmed up—it was nineteen years old—Fielder found the right channel, just in time to see a close-up of Gil Cavanaugh.

"—bring us up on any other developments in the case?" an interviewer was asking.

"Yes, I can," said Cavanaugh. He looked even better in makeup, Fielder decided. "I can tell you that senior members of my investigation team have tracked down the last wills and testaments of the murder victims." Here he paused for dramatic effect.

"And?"

"And the sole living beneficiary," he announced, "to all those millions, just happens to be the defendant—though, I might add to the taxpayers, not if *I* can do anything about it."

The camera drew back, and a split screen added the image of the interviewer, a pretty woman sitting in a studio somewhere. "And there you have it, Mike. Gil Cavanaugh, the Ottawa County District Attorney, confirming that DNA testing has positively established Jonathan Hamilton's presence at the scene of his grandparents' double murder. And further, that it was Hamilton himself who stood to benefit financially from the deaths. Back to you in the studio."

"Back to the drawing board?" Laura asked Fielder.

"Did I ever tell you about the time he called me a Jew lawyer?"

"No. Down here we call that redundant."

They shared a laugh.

"Are you sure you wouldn't like associate counsel on this one, Matt?"

"Who do you have in mind?"

"No one. There isn't anyone qualified within a hundred miles of you."

"Thanks for asking," he said.

The DNA results Cavanaugh was referring to, would turn out to be based upon analysis of the blood sample taken from Jonathan, according to Pearson Gunn's confidential source. Six of the hairs collected at the scene of the killings had yielded genetic material which, when enhanced by PCR technology, had proven identical to Jonathan's. According to the tables, the odds of that being a mere coincidence were exactly 1 in 31,468,225.

But Matt Fielder took it all in stride. As far as he was concerned, the case was no longer a whodunnit, if ever it had been. It was now a full-fledged psychodrama. And whatever physical evidence and DNA statistics Cavanaugh might have on his side, the defense had its own ace in the hole:

Young Thomas Hawkins, of Bedfordshire.

HILLARY MUNSON REPORTED that she'd prepared a short list of psychiatrists and psychologists to examine Jonathan and testify about sleepwalking. They went over the list, discussing each expert's credentials, temperament, and availability, before settling on one of each. To Fielder, the experience reminded him of ordering from a Chinese menu; one from column A, one from column B.

He drew up orders and took them Judge Summerhouse, who gave him the expected hard time.

"This is a fraud on the taxpayers," the judge said. "No wonder the governor wants to cut your rates."

Fielder smiled. There was a school of thought among death-penalty defense lawyers, that you hoped judges *wouldn't* authorize funds for experts, thereby creating grounds for successful appeals in otherwise hopeless cases. But Fielder wasn't interested in creating appellate issues at this point; he wanted the experts. So his smile was actually a bluff, a theatrical dare to Judge Summerhouse to turn him down and risk reversible error.

The judge signed the orders.

PEARSON GUNN CHECKED with a couple of the corrections officers at the county jail, and even got a peek at the records. There'd been no reports of sleepwalking or other unusual behavior on Jonathan Hamilton's part. By all accounts, however, he did seem an unusually sound sleeper, who often slept through the bells announcing mealtimes, or the clamoring of other inmates.

Gunn re-interviewed the Armbrusts, who had nothing to offer on the subject of Jonathan's sleepwalking. Either they weren't aware of it or weren't saying. But Klaus Armbrust did confirm Jennifer's account of special locks he himself had fitted to the doors of the main house. He showed Gunn his handiwork, large bolts that could only be opened with keys from the inside. "They were something of a problem the night of the fire," Klaus confided. "I had to break a window to get in and pull the boy out. The parents, they were asleep upstairs. I couldn't get to them. Too much smoke."

A phone hookup with Jonathan's brother in Atlanta proved to be little help. P. J. had either left home too soon, or had been otherwise occupied, to be aware of any episodes of sleepwalking. "But, hey," P. J. said cheerfully, "you want me to come say it, I'll do it. Things are pretty dull around here, you know. I could sure use a change of scenery."

THE SNOW MELTED and disappeared, but the early Adirondack frost had caused many of the leaves to drop, and now threatened pumpkin patches and winter squash vines. Halloween came and went, and with it October and, for all practical purposes, fall. There was frost on the cabin windows each morning, and up in the mountains, nighttime temperatures were already dipping into the teens.

With no time to cut and split the trees he'd marked that summer, Fielder was compelled to order a cord of firewood. It killed him to do it, but already he was walking around the cabin in a heavy wool sweater, while still burning upward of a dozen logs a night. Both the *Old Farmer's Almanac* and the meteorologists with their high-tech radar, were calling for an unusually cold winter, with plenty of snow to make up for last year's drought. So far, they were looking pretty smart.

Fielder turned to his motion papers. He sat himself down at his computer and composed the usual list of requests— to dismiss the indictment because the evidence presented to the grand jury might have been insufficient (always a hard thing for a defense attorney to do, inasmuch as he's prohibited by law from observing the proceedings); to throw out the physical evidence taken from Jonathan and seized from his cottage, because there hadn't been probable cause to arrest him or to get the search warrant; to suppress the statements he'd supposedly made to Deke Stanton, because they flowed from the illegal arrest, and also because Jonathan had never knowingly and intelligently waived his constitutional right to silence; and to compel the prosecution to provide the defense with pre-trial discovery: inspections of physical evidence; copies of autopsy reports, scientific tests, search-warrant papers, property vouchers, photographs, and the like; and any information the prosecution had that suggested the defendant's innocence (and was willing to own up to).

Then Fielder expanded his wish list, so as to include things that he knew Judge Summerhouse would routinely turn down in an ordinary case, but would have to think twice about in a death prosecution. He wanted copies of all police reports, not on the eve of trial, but now. He wanted the investigators' rough notes, lists of witnesses, transcripts of grand-jury testimony. He wanted a change of venue to another county, to avoid the prejudice of Gil Cavanaugh's press-conference pronouncements. He wanted additional jury challenges. He wanted Judge Summerhouse to recuse himself, because of his close relationship with Cavanaugh. And so on.

The Capital Defender's Office preaches that pushing the envelope is an absolute virtue here, and bashfulness a liability. Judges, who hate seeing even their least significant convictions reversed, will occasionally give you more than you may be entitled to in a death case, in order to avoid the pitfall of giving you less than some appellate court decides they should have. So it becomes that rarest of all things for the defense, a win-win situation. *When in doubt*, goes the prevailing wisdom, *ask for it*. You'll either get it, or you'll have created a possible point for appeal. And as everyone knows, it's appeals that keep inmates alive on death row. Which, for better or for worse, is the job of the capital defender.

WITH HER ASSIGNMENT of locating psychiatrists and psychologists completed, Hillary Munson turned her efforts to trying to locate Jennifer's former friend, Sue Ellen Simms. The task seemed a simple-enough one, particularly in comparison to the recent hunts for P. J. Hamilton and Jennifer herself. And this time, Hillary had a major head start: she already knew Sue Ellen existed.

It had been Fielder who insisted Sue Ellen be found. To his way of thinking, she could supply valuable corroboration to Jonathan's history of sleepwalking. Early on in his Legal Aid days, Fielder had represented a defendant accused of a brutal assault. The man's claim was that at the

time of the incident, he'd been under the influence of phen-
cyclidine, a powerful hallucinogenic drug better known by
its street names—PCP, angel dust, or simply "dust." Fielder
had found a psychiatrist at Kings County Hospital who was
an expert in pharmacology. He'd testified that a sufficient
amount of PCP definitely could render an individual incapable of forming criminal intent. The prosecutor had tried
in vain to discredit him on cross-examination.

Nevertheless the jurors had convicted the defendant in
short order. Talking to them afterward, Fielder had learned
they'd fully accepted the doctor's testimony. It was the defendant they doubted; they simply rejected his assertion that
he'd taken the drug the day of the incident.

Once bitten, twice shy, Fielder had come away from the
experience determined never to make the same mistake.
Now, almost twenty years later, he wanted *proof* that Jonathan had been in a somnambulistic state the night of the
killings. And, knowing he'd probably never come up with
that, he figured the next best thing was to find an independent witness who could at least confirm that Jonathan had
been known to walk in his sleep on occasion. From there,
he felt the bizarre circumstances of the crime itself would
do the rest—the absence of a compelling motive (the existence of the wills notwithstanding), the excessive nature
of the wounds inflicted upon the victims, and Jonathan's
confused and compliant demeanor afterward.

Sue Ellen Simms had been a gawky, unattractive girl, at
least according to a yearbook photo Hillary Munson dug
up at the high-school library. Just the kind of girl the shy,
too-tall Jennifer Hamilton would have sought out as a
friend. Both girls sang in the school choir, and were members of the cooking club; neither, it seemed, had been voted
most likely to do much of anything after graduation.

And if Sue Ellen had gone on to exceed expectations,
she apparently hadn't selected world travel as her venue. A
visit to the home of her parents in Oak Forest revealed that
while Sue Ellen now had a husband, a new last name, and
three daughters of her own, she was still living right there

in Ottawa County, in the town of Silver Falls.

Armed with an address and a phone number, Hillary thanked the Simms for their help, and drove off. *First Matt Fielder gets himself laid,* she smiled to herself. *Then he gets his sleepwalking theory. Now he's going to get his corroborating witness.*

Things were definitely looking a little bit brighter in the defense camp.

PEARSON GUNN KNEW just about everybody there was to know in Ottawa County. One of those he knew was Donovan McNamara. McNamara was a heavy-equipment operator who was equally adept at leveling a house with a bulldozer, dredging out a pond with a backhoe, raising a roof with a crane, or plucking a cat from a treetop with a cherry picker. Like Gunn, Donnie was a regular at the Dew Drop Inn in Cedar Falls. The two men's taste in beverages differed only slightly: while Gunn had long extolled the virtues of Adirondack Amber Ale, Donnie was partial to Molson's Ice. But on this particular Friday evening, Gunn's interest in his drinking buddy transcended such differences. For, in addition to driving heavy equipment by day, Donnie McNamara also drove the pumper for the Cedar Falls Volunteer Rescue Company at night. And it had been that very outfit which, some eight and a half years earlier, had responded to the call from the Hamilton estate near Flat Lake, and had later assisted in conducting the investigation into the cause of the fire.

Gunn waited until he was well into his second pitcher to bring up the subject. By that time, Donnie was clutching his sixth Molson Ice. It was easy to keep track, because Donnie liked to keep the empties on the table as a reminder to not overdo it. When he'd hit double figures, he'd quit. Or at least slow down.

"Remember that fire years ago, up at the Hamilton place?" Gunn asked him, in as casual a voice as he could manage.

"Yup," Donnie belched. " 'Ninety-one, it musta been. Or 'ninety-two."

"Something like that." Actually, it had been 1989, but Gunn didn't argue the point.

"Smoky sonafabitch," Donnie recalled.

"Yeah. Were you in on the investigation?"

"Me? No."

"Remember who was?"

"How come?"

"Nothin' special," Gunn said. "Got a client who'd like to know."

"How bad does he need to know?"

Gunn had the private investigator's sixth sense for knowing a shakedown when he heard one. He reached for his wallet, and took a peek inside, noticed he was a little on the light side.

"Not all *that* bad," he said. "Maybe a couple of Jacksons bad."

"Make it a Grant," Donnie said, "and I think I might be able to remember who it was looked into the thing."

"You're one greedy mick," Gunn said to his fellow Irishman, handing him a fifty. "It's not enough they pay you a million dollars an hour to play with Tonka toys all day."

"Hey, the wife's expectin' again."

"The wife's *always* expecting." Donnie already had about fifty kids, it seemed. "This better be good," Gunn said.

Donnie slipped the fifty into his shirt pocket. "Was ackshully *two* guys who handled the followup," he said. "They sent up some guy named Meacham, from the Schenectady arson squad. I hear he passed, though."

"Passed what?"

"*Passed,*" Donnie repeated. "Like *dead.*"

"Great," Gunn groaned. "How about the other guy?"

Donnie hesitated a moment.

"No fucking *way*!" Gunn told him.

"Okay, okay. Lemme see. The other guy was the fire

marshal from our outfit. I'm just tryin' to remember his name, is all."

"*Remember* it."

"Hey, lighten up," Donnie protested. But he suddenly managed to recall the name. "Squitieri," he said. "Jimmy Squitieri, that's it. Used to call him Spider."

"Where can I find him now?" Gunn asked.

"Jeez, I don't know. He retired, went down to Florida somewhere."

"Florida's a big place, Donnie."

"Saratoga?"

"That's right here in New York, over on the Northway."

"Shit. *Sounds* like Saratoga."

"How about *Sarasota*?"

"Yeah," Donnie said, "that could be it. Saratoga, Sarasota. Same thing."

Which actually wasn't so bad, Gunn had to admit later, as he thought about it. Locating a James Squitieri in Sarasota, Florida, might not be a piece of cake. But it sure beat looking for a Jennifer H. Somebody in Vermont, or maybe New Hampshire.

FIELDER AWOKE TO a loud ringing noise in his ears. After a moment's disorientation, he realized he'd fallen asleep on his couch, in front of the woodburning stove, for a change. The ringing noise turned out to be the phone. He found it under a cushion, and answered on what must have been the fifth ring.

"I was about to give up," said a familiar female voice.

"Who's this?" he asked. He'd learned some time ago to ask right away, rather than to play along pretending to know until it was too late to ask.

"How soon we forget."

"Jennifer."

"I miss you," she said.

"I miss you, too. I've been kinda busy, I guess."

"How is it going?"

"Better," he said. "Thanks to you."

"Matthew?" She'd told him she preferred it over Matt, which reminded her of a sheriff with a droopy mustache.

"Yes?"

"Would it be all right if I visited Jonathan?"

"Visit Jonathan. . . ." he echoed. For some reason, it had never occurred to him that she might want to, given the original reason for her leaving, and the fact that she hadn't been back in all these years. But now that she was asking, he guessed it was the most natural thing in the world. Here was her younger brother (not to mention the father of her child!) locked up for murder, possibly looking at a death sentence. Aside from P. J., she was the only family he had left. And P. J. wasn't in much of a position to be visiting anybody, his offer to Gunn notwithstanding.

But as Fielder thought about it, he realized maybe it wasn't such a good idea, after all. "I'm torn," he told her. "I know you'd like to, and it might be nice for Jonathan. Only thing is, I may end up having to put you on the witness stand someday. When I do, the DA is going to want to show that you're just trying to help your brother because you love him. One way of showing that is to ask you if you've been to see him. From there, it's a short step to suggesting you went there to get your stories together, or to coach him."

"I could deny it," she offered, "say I wasn't there."

"He'll subpoena the visiting records from the jail. It'll look even worse if he catches you in a lie."

"So I guess it would be better from me to stay away, huh?"

"From that standpoint, yes."

"How about *you?* Can I come see *you?*"

Fielder was caught off guard.

"Here?" That would not go down in history as one of the great recoveries of all time.

"There, here," she said. "Wherever."

The word *relationship* gradually came into focus. Fielder reminded himself how self-sufficient he'd become, how happy he was being alone in his cabin in the woods. He wasn't so sure he was ready for any of this.

"I really miss you, Matthew."

Then again . . .

"Look," he said. "I want to see you, too. But for the same reason it might be better for you to stay away from Jonathan, it might not be the best thing for you and I to be, you know—"

"Linked romantically?"

The phrase reminded him of one of those television entertainment shows, or the newspapers they sold at the supermarket checkout counters. He could picture their photos on the cover of the *National Enquirer*, under three-inch headlines.

DEATH ROW INMATE SWEATS IT OUT WHILE LAWYER, SIS GET IT ON

"Right," he said. "Listen, I've got to finish some paperwork. But by next weekend, I may need to take a drive, and—"

"Interview me again?"

"Yeah. Something like that."

FIELDER PUT THE finishing touches on his motions. He'd ended up asking for everything he could possibly think of, all the way down to disciplinary records of any state troopers and investigators who might be called to testify at trial. Then he drove to Cedar Falls, where he served a copy of his papers on the District Attorney's Office, and filed the original with Dot Whipple at the courthouse. While he was there, he dropped into the jail to see Jonathan again. He wanted to prepare him for visits from the various doctors who'd soon be coming in to talk to him.

Jonathan had been talking to doctors since early childhood, it turned out, and he seemed to take the news pretty much in stride. But Jonathan seemed to take everything pretty much in stride.

Again, at some point during their conversation, he muttered the word "Baby." Again he drifted off when Fielder tried to follow up on it. And again, he looked pale, thin, and tired. And even more withdrawn than he had at the previous visit. Fielder had the strange sensation that they were starting to lose him.

Sure, I remember Jennifer," said Sue Ellen Blodgett. She'd dropped the Simms when she'd gotten married. "It was just too much of a mouthful," she'd explained. "Sue Ellen Simms Blodgett. Know what I mean?"

Hillary Munson had smiled and assured her she knew what she meant. Hillary looked across the Formica kitchen table at Sue Ellen. The gawky, unattractive girl had grown up into a slightly less gawky woman, but the addition of fifty pounds hadn't done much for her unattractiveness. She balanced her youngest daughter on one knee as she gazed back at Hillary through purple-framed glasses.

"When was the last time you saw her?" Hillary asked.

"Oh, not for years. But we've talked on the phone a couple of times. And exchanged a letter or two."

"Do you remember her brothers?"

"Yup. Porter, he was a hell-raiser. Jonathan, he was always real quiet-like." She paused to wipe a glob of purple jelly from her daughter's chin. "Are they really going to, you know, give him one of those lethal injections, like?"

"They aim to try," Hillary said. "What else do you remember about him?"

Sue Ellen did her best, but it was clear from listening to her that she had never spent much time at the Flat Lake estate, and hadn't seen anything of Jonathan in the ten years since his sister had left the state. She recalled the boy's good looks, his shyness, and, above all, his slowness.

"He was one step above a *retard*, if you ask me. No offense, but he was always pickin' up sticks or rocks or pine cones, or going, 'Can we play now?' or 'Can we eat now?' He could barely take care of his self, like."

A second of Sue Ellen's daughters wandered into the

room and began tugging at her mother's sleeve. "When can we *go out*?" she whined.

Hillary decided to cut to the point. "Do you remember anything about Jonathan's sleeping?" she asked.

"He used to wet the bed, if that's what you mean. Then, later on, he started walkin' in his sleep."

Hillary sat up. "Walking in his sleep?"

"Yup," Sue Ellen nodded. "What do they call that, Sominex, or something? Got so they had to put special locks on the doors. I even heard he was the one who lit the fire. Prob'ly did it in his sleep, huh?"

"Where'd you hear that?" Hillary asked her.

"I think there was talk," Sue Ellen said. "And of course you know about how he used to come into Jennifer's room?"

Hillary nodded noncommittally.

"She musta told you about that?"

"How did *you* find out about that?" Hillary asked her.

"Oh, she told me," Sue Ellen answered. "We were best friends, like. I mean, I always had other friends. But I don't think Jennifer did. I was her only friend, far as I know."

"What do you know about her child?"

"Troy? I know Jonathan's the father, if that's what you mean."

"How do you know that?"

"She told me. She even sent me a snapshot. I might still have it somewhere."

"Do you think you could take a look?"

Hillary meant sometime after the meeting, but Sue Ellen stood right up, shifted her baby to one hip, and walked into the next room. When she reappeared a few moments later, her second daughter was holding on to her skirt, and a third one had somehow materialized, and was trailing a few feet behind them. But Sue Ellen was carrying a cardboard carton under one arm.

"Some of my memorabilia," she explained, setting the carton down. "I'm very organized." She rummaged through the contents for a minute or so, before extracting a worn envelope, which she raised above her head with a triumphant "Da-*dahh!*" and presented to Hillary. Inside was a photograph of a baby, who could have been Jonathan himself, and a letter, written in fading blue ink.

December 19, 1989

Dear Sue Ellen:

Here are the photos of Troy I promised to send you. Isn't he the most precious thing in the world? What's more, he's smart and not afflicted in any way, like you-know-who.

We're living with a nice family here, and I've got a pretty good job. There's never enough money, of course, what with rent, car payments and insurance, food, pampers, etc. But I can't complain. At least we're safe here.

How are you and R. B. getting along? Do I hear wedding bells? I'm so jealous, but I'm also truly happy for you. Give him a kiss for me, a big wet one!

As for J. I guess I can forgive him, more or less. Except for that once, I know he really was asleep. And even that first time, I understand he can't be blamed entirely. (Even if he almost killed me!)

As for my parents, I know I should be upset, being an orphan and all now. But you, of all people, know how horrible they were, each in their own way. Do you really think J. started the fire in his sleep? God!

Sue Ellen, I'm never coming back. That part of my life is over. But I promise to be your best friend,

Always and forever,
Jennifer

P.S. I know how you're always saving things. But if you keep this letter, please make sure you hide it somewhere safe, so my address never gets back to my grandparents.

P.P.S. I miss you so.

"Can I keep this?" Hillary asked.

"I guess so," Sue Ellen said. "She's moved a couple of times since then, anyway. But the other part, you'll keep that quiet-like?"

" 'The other part'?"

"About who Troy's father is."

"Mum's the word."

HEADING BACK TO Albany, Hillary figured it was a deal she could live with. From what she knew of Matt Fielder, given enough time, he'd be able to convince Jennifer Hamilton to testify on her brother's behalf, even if meant delving into the dark recesses of her own past, and reliving such things as rape, incest, and illegitimacy. But that would only be Jennifer's word. The letter corroborated Jennifer's testimony. It described Jonathan's sleepwalking in writing, a full nine years prior to the Flat Lake murders—long before there was any possible motive on the part of lawyers, doctors, and loved ones to put their heads together and concoct some clever defense that might play at trial.

That was its importance. And in that respect, it became the first piece of solid physical evidence with which they'd be able to fend off claims that their defense had been fabricated.

Hillary Munson had come up with the smoking gun.

20

BATS, BIRDS, AND GRIZZLIES

JONATHAN HAMILTON'S CASE was back in court on November 17, the forty-fifth and final day Judge Summerhouse had given the defense to get its motions in. Since Fielder had already submitted his papers the week before, the judge could do nothing but adjourn things for the prosecution's response. He gave Cavanaugh five weeks, until December 22.

"See that?" the judge told Fielder. "You got forty-five days. I'm only giving the DA thirty-five. Talk about being *fair*."

Talk about being *disingenuous*. All three of them—Summerhouse, Fielder, and Cavanaugh—knew full well that prosecutors are routinely given two weeks or less to answer motions, which is more than sufficient time for them to print out computerized responses reciting their opposition to whatever the defense asks for. On top of that, it had already been close to a week since Cavanaugh actually received the papers.

But Fielder held his silence. There was certainly nothing improper about the judge's giving Cavanaugh a cushion. Besides, the doctors could use the extra time to conduct their interviews of Jonathan and start preparing their reports. Gunn was trying to find a Florida address for somebody called Spider, and Fielder himself was anxious to take another drive to New Hampshire.

Jonathan struck Fielder as a little improved. They spent an hour talking in the lockup area off the courtroom. Again, Jonathan's worries didn't seem to be particularly case-oriented. Instead, he complained of the cold and of being tired much of the time. He thought it might have something to do with the food, or the pills they gave him each morning. Fielder promised to look into both matters. Other than that, however, Jonathan seemed to be holding his own. Fielder told him to be patient, that things were moving along about as fast as could be expected. But the repeated delays didn't appear to bother Jonathan. In fact, it was hard to know if he even had a sense of time, the way most people do. It was more like dealing with a child in that respect. You talked about today; "tomorrow" tended to be a tricky concept.

From the courthouse, Fielder took a walk around the corner to an army-navy surplus store he'd noticed earlier on Maple Street. There he bought a couple of woolen blankets, which he brought around to the jail and left for Jonathan. That, too, was the kind of thing they'd talked about at Death School—winning your client's trust by tending to his personal needs. The cost involved was often minimal, and sometimes even reimbursable. But even when it wasn't, it was well worth the effort. Take the blankets, for example. They'd come to a little over $30 counting tax, an expenditure well within Fielder's budget. And for once he'd even remembered to ask for a receipt, which he placed on his dashboard when he reached his car, just so he wouldn't lose it.

Driving back to his cabin, he realized for the first time that Cavanaugh had had no official statement to make following the court appearance. No death-penalty decisions to trumpet, no DNA test results to celebrate, no motives to reveal. As for Fielder, silence was still the order of the day. There might come a time when he'd want to go public with the defense of sleepwalking, but that time was still off in the future.

As the Suzuki's ancient heater finally began to warm up,

Fielder loosened the knot of his tie and cracked the window an inch in order to get some fresh air. The receipt which he'd placed on the dashboard immediately lifted off and became airborne. It fluttered about for a second, before being sucked out the opening.

Fielder broke into a grin. Had some watchful god detected his ulterior motive of hoping to be reimbursed for his $30, and punished him for being less than completely selfless? Well, easy come, easy go. Now he could feel truly noble about his investment.

THE FIRST DOCTOR to interview Jonathan was a board-certified psychiatrist named George Goldstein. Goldstein was a nationally known professor of forensic medicine at Yale, with a seven-page curriculum vitae and a subspecialty in sleep disorders. He was also an accomplished hypnotist, though he shared Fielder's concern that, at least at this stage, it might be too risky to use the technique with Jonathan, both legally and medically.

He showed up at the Cedar Falls jail the day following Jonathan's most recent court appearance, a day when the mercury would drop to 11 degrees Fahrenheit while the sun was still up. The first thing Dr. Goldstein noticed about the young inmate was his manner of dress. He would comment on it in his written evaluation, which he submitted some time later.

> Patient presents himself dressed in the usual prison garb, consisting of a lightweight, one-piece jumpsuit. He is further wrapped, Native American style, in a handsome, two-tone, woolen blanket. A cheerful smile on his face suggests that although he may be confined, he is nonetheless warm.

IF ATLANTA HAD been a pleasant place to visit at the end of September, Florida was positively heaven in the third week of November. Pearson Gunn stepped off the plane at the Sarasota-Bradenton International Airport and made his way to the Thrifty Car Rental counter. Before leaving New York, he'd checked with the CDO to see if they'd reimburse him for Hertz rates. Not exactly, he'd been told.

Jimmy Squitieri didn't really live in Sarasota, any more than he lived in Saratoga. Only golf pros lived in Sarasota, it turned out, while tennis pros lived a bit to the north, in Bradenton. Jimmy Squitieri lived in someplace called Fruitville, just off Route 75—which might go a long way toward explaining why he told people he lived in Sarasota.

Gunn found the house and pulled up to the curb. It was a one-level stucco thing, very white. In front was a small lawn that to Gunn was surprisingly green for November, some neatly trimmed bushes, and a couple of pink plastic flamingos complete with whirlygig wings that spun in the breeze. Where the garage should have been, there was an open-sided structure that looked as if it had been custom-framed around a powder blue Chevy Monte Carlo that sat in its midst. A wiry, gray-haired man with a cigarette dangling from his lower lip was tying vines of some sort to the framing. He wore a permanent squint from either the sun or the smoke, it was hard to tell which. Gunn walked over to introduce himself. Before he could say anything, the man spoke.

"It's a carport," he explained, the cigarette waving up and down like a conductor's baton, but somehow managing to stay put. "It's to protect the vehicle's baked-on metallic finish from the harmful ultraviolet rays of the sun." This was clearly a man who'd written too many reports in his day.

"We don't see too many of them back north," Gunn commented.

"Monte Carlos?"

"Them too."

Inside, they sat on matching white Naugahyde Barcaloungers, above canary-yellow carpeting, Spider gripping a Stoli and tonic over ice. Gunn had refused a drink, noticing it was still before one in the afternoon.

"Got any orange juice?" he'd asked on impulse.

"Never touch the stuff," Spider had assured him.

Yes, Spider remembered the Flat Lake fire. It had been his investigation, his and Eddie Meacham's. "Good guy, Eddie, but a stickler. Wanted to call it suspicious. I hadda talk him out of it."

"Was it suspicious?" Gunn asked.

"Sure it was. You had your charring on the rafters, you had your alligatoring on the floorboards—"

"'Alligatoring'?" Gunn was beginning to think maybe Spider had been in Florida too long.

"Yeah. That's when you get a crosshatched pattern from where the heat is most intense. Ends up looking like alligator hide."

"The papers said it was an electric space heater caught fire," Gunn said.

"Yeah, I know. But the papers didn't explain how come there was damage *beneath* the floor where the heater was, did they?"

"No."

"Funny thing," Spider said. "I always thought heat was s'posed to *rise*. Know what I mean?"

Gunn nodded. "But you signed off on it," he said.

"Yes and no," said Spider, taking a long drink of Stoli. "We interviewed the kid. He was a retard. What was his name? Johnny?"

"Jonathan."

"Yeah. Jonathan. So I ask him if he's been playin' with matches, maybe had a little accident? He says, 'I don't know. I don't think so.' You hear me? *'I don't think so.'* Not 'Fuck no!' or 'Who, me? But *'I don't think so.'* So I talk to the grandfather. I can see he's in charge now, know what I mean? I tell him it don't look too good. We call it arson, we gotta lock the kid up. Next thing, the adjuster from the insurance carrier shows up, starts sniffin' around for accelerant fumes. I suggest he and Grandpa take a little walk together up the path, see if maybe they can work somethin' out. Know what I mean?"

Gunn nodded.

"You sure I can't get you somethin'?" Spider asked, rising to refill his glass.

"No, thanks."

"About twenty minutes, they come back. Grandpa's decided not to put in a claim on the life policies. That's the big money, see? But the family's loaded; they don't need it. To make it look good, the adjuster agrees to cover the damage to the premises. What could thata come to? A coupla grand, tops? Everybody's happy. We can all go home."

"Except," Gunn said, "Meacham still wanted to call it suspicious."

"Yeah," Spider said. "Good old Eddie, may he rest in peace. Listen, you were on the job, right?"

Gunn nodded. "State trooper," he said.

"Soon as we walked into the place, Eddie took a sniff around, smelled sumpin. But he didn't smell no accelerant. He smelled *money*. Thought right away we could make a score. Know what I mean?"

Gunn nodded. He knew what a score was.

"Eddie figgered if we threatened to call it arson, or even suspicious . . . Well, you know what I mean."

Another nod from Gunn.

"But the way I was lookin' at it, the family had had about enough *agita* for one day. Retard kid gets up in the middle of the night, starts a fire, kills his parents. On toppa that, they just found out they gotta let the life policies walk. Way I saw things, enough was enough. It was no time for the old Shake 'n' Bake." Spider drained his glass again. "Know what I mean?" he said.

Is THIS THE Princess of Nightingale Court?"

"Matthew?"

"I always feel like an apostle when you call me that. Or a saint."

"Yes, but you're *my* saint. God, I miss you!"

"I've missed you, too," he said.

"When can you come?"

"Should take me about twelve minutes."

"Don't tease," she scolded him. "And don't be gross. It's not nice."

"I'm not teasing or being gross," he said. "I'm at my trusty Motel Six. I really can be there in twelve minutes."

"No," she said. "Stay right where you are. I'll throw on some clothes and get someone to come over and watch Troy."

"Don't worry too much about the clothes," he told her.

Around the same time Fielder was waiting in his motel room for Jennifer, Pearson Gunn was ordering his first pitcher of ale at the Dew Drop Inn. Gunn had flown back from Sarasota that afternoon, making it a total of four flights in two days. Flying disoriented Gunn, who much preferred the feel of solid ground beneath him. Ale, on the other hand, tended to restore equilibrium, even as it produced a general sense of well-being.

"*Bonjour, étranger.*"

Gunn looked to his right, the direction the voice had come from. But he knew it had to be that of Roger Duquesne, the state police captain who'd once been his partner, and now (though Gunn will not confirm the fact) was his prime law-enforcement source.

"Roger!" Gunn called.

Duquesne was out of uniform, but he sometimes worked in civvies, making it hard to tell whether he was on the taxpayers' time right now or his own. Whichever it was, he had a drink in his hand and a glow on his face.

It being a Friday night, there were no empty tables, so they stayed at the bar. There they soon fell into their regular routine of trading war stories and hoisting a few for the old days.

As much as Matt Fielder was taken with Jennifer, he'd managed to keep his thoughts about her under control during the weeks he'd been back home working on her brother's case. That control disappeared the moment she walked into his motel room.

The clothes she'd thrown on were a faded pair of jeans, an oversized pullover sweater, a pair of sneakers, and a wristwatch. That was it. Nothing on top of that, and—as Fielder discovered soon enough—nothing underneath. He tried to imagine just what it was she must have been wearing when he'd called.

An hour later, they lay together trying to catch their breath, their bodies coated with sweat. "Tell me again," he said. "Why is it that I live alone in a cabin in the woods?"

A laugh bubbled up from somewhere inside her. "You decided on that before we met?" she offered. Which was about as good an answer as anything he could come up with.

"How's the case going?" she asked.

"Not too bad, actually. We found Sue Ellen. She confirms that Jonathan was known as a sleepwalker. It seems she even saved an old letter of yours, in which you talked about it. If the DA tries to show our defense is a recent fabrication, we can use that in rebuttal."

"So that's good?"

"Very good," he said, kissing the tip of her nose as a reward. "The doctors have begun interviewing Jonathan. We'll know more about that in a week or two. And it seems the rumors about the fire were right."

"Oh?"

"It certainly looks like Jonathan's doing. Middle of the night, definite signs of arson, doors locked inside and out. And then, when they asked him about it, he couldn't say if he'd set it or not. Sound familiar?"

"I'm sure he didn't *mean* to do it," she said.

"Exactly the point."

"So what do you do now?" she asked.

"Now," he answered, reaching out for her, "is when I take you in my arms, and tell you how terribly much I love you."

Had he really said that?

*   *   *

So it's really a lock?" Pearson Gunn asked Roger Duquesne, forty-five minutes and a pitcher later.

"A lock? It is the lock of all locks, *mon ami*," Duquesne confided. "A *fait accompli*."

"No loose ends?"

"*Bien sur*, there are loose ends," said Duquesne. "*Toujours* there are loose ends. Otherwise, private dickheads like you would scream that it is all *trop parfait*, it must be a *frame*!"

"Like what?" Gunn asked.

"What 'Like what?' "

"What kinda loose ends?"

"*Caca* stuff, *mon ami*. Like *peut-être* Deke Stanton didn't read the young man his rights *très bien*. Or that Bass fellow messed up the footprint trail *un petit peu*. Or only six out of seven hairs were found to be a DNA match. Or crime scene got a little sloppy, handled the knife too much, so by the time the latent-print people got ahold of it, they came up with *rien de tout*. Tell me, *mon ami*. Is that kind of *merde* going to spring your guy?"

"No," said Gunn. "It sure ain't."

But it was good to know about, just the same.

It was the conclusion of the psychiatrist George Goldstein that Jonathan Hamilton honestly had no recollection whatsoever of stabbing his grandparents to death. That same lack of recollection, however, according to Dr. Goldstein, was "entirely consistent in every respect with Jonathan's having committed the crime while in a somnambulistic state."

Jonathan's first post-event awareness was when he awoke to urinate sometime later in the early-morning hours, and discovered blood on his hands. His first reaction had been confusion. As he'd followed the blood trail to the main house, he'd experienced a growing sense of dread. That dread had changed to full-fledged horror when he reached the scene of the crime and beheld the results of his acts. All of those reactions were typical to incidents of sleep-related violence, as was Jonathan's prompt phone call to the authorities, in which he'd related that his grandparents had been "hurt real bad."

To Dr. Goldstein, Jonathan Hamilton presented a classic profile of a sleepwalker. Having familiarized himself with the results of Hillary Munson's findings, he knew Jonathan had a probable history of fetal alcohol syndrome, or at least its less pronounced cousin, fetal alcohol effect. On top of that, he had reportedly suffered some significant degree of organic brain damage as a young adult, the result of smoke inhalation and carbon monoxide poisoning during a fire.

Dr. Goldstein found that Jonathan himself seemed to have some awareness that he'd had sleepwalking episodes at various times in the past, though he was characteristically vague when it came to the source of that awareness. As to why the jail records contained no accounts of unusual nighttime activities, that fact could easily be attributed to the medication that had been ordered for Jonathan to combat his sleeplessness. The log entries showed it to be clonazepam, a Valiumlike drug Dr. Goldstein often had prescribed to his own patients *specifically for the suppression of night terrors.*

Dr. Goldstein concluded by suggesting that a variety of tests be performed. Among his recommendations was first to take Jonathan off all medication, then hook him up to a polysomnograph machine, and—by applying a low-voltage electrical current to the large motor muscles—attempt to artificially induce a sleepwalking episode.

Such an experiment, of course, would require the consent of the jail authorities. Because of that, there'd be no way of keeping it secret from the prosecution; and for now at least, it would remain in the suggestion box.

EVEN AS MATT Fielder spent the weekend playing family with Jennifer and Troy, the defense continued to work. Pearson Gunn crossed off a few things from his list of "Things to Do," and added a few others. He also started a

new checklist, which he called "Things to Think About."
It began modestly enough.

- ✔ Turkey or duck for Thanksgiving?
- ✔ Miranda rights ever read to Jonathan?
- ✔ Why no prints on knife?
- ✔ Cut back on ale consumption?
- ✔ Why only 6 out of 7 hairs?
- ✔ Enough antifreeze in car radiator?

Taking a look at the list, Gunn decided that maybe he'd
simply been looking at things the same way for too long.
Perhaps it was time for a new approach, a little creativity.
They even had a phrase for it these days, like everything
else. "Out-of-the-box thinking," they called it. So why
shouldn't *he* give it a try? After all, what did he have to
lose?

Duck it would be.

HILLARY MUNSON WORKED late into the night to put the
finishing touches on the report of her meeting with Sue
Ellen Blodgett. She knew how important Sue Ellen's testimony could be in terms of establishing a historical record
of Jonathan Hamilton's sleepwalking. She also wanted to
memorialize in writing the chain of custody of Jennifer
Hamilton's letter to Sue Ellen, so as to preempt any attack
on its admissibility at trial. And she wanted to have everything finished so she could overnight it to Matt Fielder before the holiday weekend began.

Hillary was actually a little bit nervous about the holidays. She was driving down to New York (more specifically to Whitestone, Queens) to spend the weekend with
her parents, her brother, and her aunts and uncles and cous-
ins—all of whom she hadn't seen in almost two years. And,
at her mother's urging, she'd agreed to bring that "special
friend" she'd been talking about for some time, but whose
name she'd kept secret all this time.

Oh, were they in for a surprise!

*   *   *

THE SECOND DOCTOR to go into the Cedar Falls jail and interview Jonathan Hamilton was a clinical psychologist by the name of Margaret Litwiller. Dr. Litwiller brought with her a briefcase full of materials—standardized test forms, blank paper, crayons, playing cards, stick-figure drawings, black-and-white photographs, ink-blot cards, anatomically correct dolls, and tiny colored blocks shaped like houses, cars, and other everyday objects.

She spent nearly three hours with Jonathan, during which time (at least according to the visiting-room guard's observations, dutifully noted in the log book) the two of them "did proseed to play with alot of little toys."

In the confidential report she would submit to Matt Fielder some two weeks later, Dr. Litwiller would conclude that Jonathan, "while marginally oriented to person, place, and time, possesses only the most primitive level of insight into his own ideation and thought processes. . . . In particular, his MMI profile reflects almost childlike responses to his surroundings. . . . Notably, however, his Rorschach responses reveal surprising levels of hostility. Confronted with cards in the series 6-a through 11-c, normally suggestive of butterflies, songbirds, and teddy bears, Jonathan instead sees bats, birds of prey, and grizzlies. This hostility, while deeply suppressed, seems largely directed toward authority figures, in particular parents and grandparents."

In Dr. Litwiller's considered opinion, it was quite evident that while asleep, and accordingly freed from the constraints of his superego, Jonathan had simply "acted out" his anger against the most convenient authority targets available.

THANKSGIVING DAY FELL on the twenty-seventh of November. A low cloud cover blanketed the Northeast, but a promised cold front stayed just above the Canadian border. Matt Fielder joined hands with Jennifer Walker and her son Troy as they said grace over the fold-down aluminum tabletop in the trailer park just north of Nashua, New

Hampshire, before feasting on a small turkey. In Tupper Lake, New York, Pearson Gunn carved crisp duckling, stuffed with homemade venison sausage, for his wife and himself in their A-frame. Hillary Munson and her companion, Lois Miller, sat down with a roomful of slightly stunned family members, to a five-course dinner featuring rock Cornish game hen, in a split-level in Whitestone, Queens.

And in Cedar Falls, New York, Jonathan Hamilton was slipped a plastic tray through the bars of his cell. The tray was machine-stamped with little compartments, which this day had been filled with breaded chicken nuggets, mashed potatoes, frozen peas, and jellied cranberry sauce. Some jailer's version of a Thanksgiving Special.

21

CABIN FEVER

ON THE MONDAY following Thanksgiving, Matt Fielder drove west from Nashua to Albany, and attended a meeting at Hillary Munson's office. Mitch Dinnerstein, of the Capital Defender's Office, had driven up from New York for the occasion, representing Kevin Doyle. Pearson Gunn was there, as well as Drs. George Goldstein and Margaret Litwiller.

It was Fielder who had called the meeting, and he spoke first. He'd brought the group together, he explained, because he wanted to address a problem, and get the reaction of everybody present to a possible solution. The problem was the adverse publicity they were getting in the press. With each passing day and every court appearance, Gil Cavanaugh was consolidating his manipulation of public opinion. The defense camp, meanwhile, had so far remained silent, fearful that anything they said could only make things worse for Jonathan.

It took the group all of a minute and a half to reach a consensus that they were indeed taking a beating from the media. The discussion quickly shifted to the remedy Fielder now proposed: floating the sleepwalking defense to see how it might play out there.

The two doctors spoke first. Both were completely convinced that Jonathan had held no conscious malice toward his victims, and that the killings could only be explained as an act of somnambulistic violence, for which he should not be held criminally responsible. Both were satisfied beyond any doubt that Jonathan was neither malingering nor attempting to dupe them; he simply lacked the intellectual capacity necessary to pull off that sort of deception. Both were willing to stake their reputations on their findings, and both voted wholeheartedly in favor of going public.

Hillary Munson agreed in principle, but raised a yellow flag. Defense lawyers, she cautioned, lately had been feeding the public an ever-increasing diet of exotic defenses. Over the past decade or so, there'd been high-profile trials attributing sensational crimes to insanity, alcohol abuse, drug dependency, gambling addiction, spousal violence, childhood sexual abuse, multiple personalty disorders, post-traumatic stress disorder, racial injustice, and a variety of other claims. Alan Dershowitz had even published a book on the subject, titled *The Abuse Excuse*. Hillary's fear was that a saturation point was being approached and that society might well be headed for a period of backlash, in which juries might finally reach the point of not caring *why* a particular defendant had committed a crime, so long as he had in fact committed it.

Mitch Dinnerstein spoke up. First he wanted to know if they weren't jumping the gun. "Are you sure you're ready to concede factual guilt?" he asked.

Fielder looked across the room, in the direction of Pearson Gunn. After all, Gunn had conducted the bulk of the defense investigation, and it was Gunn who had a confidential source close to the prosecution's team. But Gunn was gazing off to one side, and Fielder failed to catch his eye. He wondered if the investigator might be feeling just a bit intimidated by the others in the room. Gunn was a high-school dropout, surrounded by a roomful of advanced-graduate-degree holders. But there was too much at stake to worry about such considerations.

"How about it, Pearson?" he asked. "From what you know, do you have the slightest bit of doubt that Cavanaugh can prove Jonathan did it?"

Gunn shook his head slowly from side to side. "The way his people are talking," he said, "you can stick a fork in the kid right now."

Which was simply another way of saying, *He's done.*

"Then it seems to me," said Dinnerstein, "that you've got nothing to lose. Always try to remember what the goal in these cases is. It's not to *win*, at least not in traditional sense of getting somebody acquitted, walking him out the door. What we're doing comes down to *triage*. It's saving lives. You go public with this, come right out and say your client did it, first thing that happens is you're going to score points for honesty. Then, when you tell them he shouldn't be held fully responsible because he was a *known sleepwalker*, they'll at least be listening to you. Of course, you'll have to be ready to put your money where your mouth is. Can you do that, when push comes to shove?"

"We've got proof," Fielder said, "documentary proof that Jonathan was sleepwalking at least as early as ten or twelve years ago. Probably a lot longer than that."

"And we can back that up with test results," chimed in Dr. Litwiller.

"Then fucking *go* for it," Dinnerstein said. "If you can sell it in the court of public opinion, Cavanaugh will blink. As soon as he sees that Joe Six-pack doesn't want to kill this kid, he'll come to you and offer you elwop."

" 'Elwop'?" asked a confused Dr. Goldstein.

"Life without parole," Fielder translated. "*L-W-O-P.*"

"What we really call it," said Dinnerstein, "is a home run."

But Fielder, whose call it was, still wasn't fully convinced. "Supposing you're right, Mitch: It's all well and good. We get a little public support, force Cavanaugh's hand, see where it all takes us. But suppose Hillary's right: Suppose it turns out the public couldn't care less. How do we know the whole thing's not going to blow up in our faces?"

"That's the chance you take," Dinnerstein said. "But, hell. Wouldn't you rather find out now, instead of down the line, when the jury brings in its verdict?"

"I sure wish," said Fielder, "there was some way we could gauge ahead of time how the public's going to react to this."

"Maybe there is." The voice was Hillary Munson's. "What do politicians do when they want to try out a idea? Or Madison Avenue types, when they need to see how an ad campaign is going to play?"

"They test-market it?" Fielder guessed.

"Exactly." Hillary nodded. "They try it out on a *focus group*."

Fielder inched forward on his chair. "You mean we ought to go out and find a bunch of housewives, ask them what they think of the idea?"

"Something like that," Hillary said, "but be careful some feminist doesn't hear you talking like that."

"Right," said Fielder. "But I can't go to the judge and ask him to sign an order allocating funds for market research. He'd throw me out on my ear. Worse yet, he'd make me tell him what the nature of the defense is, that we want to do the research on. And as soon he knows, Cavanaugh will know. So we can't go to the judge. And if we can't, where else would we ever get the money to do something like that?"

It was at that point that all eyes slowly turned in the direction of Mitch Dinnerstein.

"All right, all right," he said after a moment. "I'll run it by Kevin. Who knows? He might just be crazy enough to go for it."

By the second week of December, autumn in the Adirondacks is already a distant memory. The cold has set in for good by that time, after a series of false starts and temporary reprieves. But it is by no means the cold that is the worst part of an upstate winter. Nor is it the snow, which traditionally falls far more heavily in the western regions of the state. Nor is it even the wind, for that matter, though on a blustery day that can be a pretty serious contender for the honors.

Ask almost anyone who lives in the heart of Adirondack Park to tell you the single thing he or she hates most about winter, and the answer you'll hear isn't the cold, or the snow, or the wind.

It's the *darkness*, hands down.

And when they talk about darkness in the Adirondacks, it isn't simply a matter of the tilt of the earth producing a later sunrise and an earlier sunset as you move farther north. No, the elements have gotten together in a conspiracy that reaches far deeper than that. What little daylight there is in winter comes from a sun that crosses low in the sky, where its path is not only dramatically shorter, but where its rays are often obscured by high mountains, filtered by the boughs of tall evergreens, and angled through an increasingly thick layer of clouds, water vapor, and other atmospheric particles. Instead of being light by five or six in the morning, the sky remains pitch-dark until nearly eight. It takes almost to noon before anything remotely approaching true brightness is achieved, and by then, it seems, the sun is already thinking about setting. By three it is dusk; by four you need your headlights to drive.

For the locals, it all adds up to fewer hours spent outdoors, less opportunity for physical exercise, and a dramatic increase in cases of breathing disorders due to molds, spores, and dry woodsmoke. This is the stuff that depression is made of. The Adirondacks are where the term "cabin fever" originated. It's little wonder that the upstate suicide rate is said to nearly triple during the period from early December to mid-March.

For Matt Fielder, the shortened days brought a slow but steady retreat into the confines of his heated living room. That meant fewer hours of cutting wood, and more of burning wood. As aesthetics gradually yielded to survival, the doors of his stove stayed shut almost around the clock. Fire had become a commodity to be felt, rather than a luxury to be watched.

Beyond that, the diminished daylight provided Fielder with even more time to himself. More time for reading, for writing, and for attending to some much-needed repairs to the interior of his cabin. More time to focus on Jonathan Hamilton's case, and to miss Jonathan Hamilton's sister.

In Fielder's mind, the two things had become hopelessly intertwined. Sure, there were all the usual reasons for wanting to prevail in the case. In spite of what he'd done, Jonathan remained a hugely sympathetic figure, a profoundly damaged boy trapped in a man's body and subjected to forces about which he had little understanding, and over which he had no control. The enemy was a pompous, self-serving politician with an agenda that had nothing at all to do with fairness or justice. And the stakes they were playing for were enormous: Nothing less than Jonathan's life hung in the balance.

As always, there was the driving force of Fielder's own ego at work, the innate competitiveness that had driven him to this strange line of work years ago. Like any criminal-defense lawyer who'd ever walked into a courtroom, Matt Fielder loved to win, and—even more—hated to lose. So the case ended up being one that consumed him like no other. It was a case he took to sleep with him each night, and woke up with each morning.

And yet there was even more.

There was Jennifer.

Here Fielder had finally succeeded in leaving his former life behind him—and with it the never-ending grind of work, the suffocating closeness of the city, and the absurd, complicated strategies of remaining single in a world that seemed created for couples, families, and groups. Here he was, living out his *Walden Pond* fantasy in his cabin in the woods, away from it all, a million miles from civilization, thumbing his nose at the rest of the world. He had everything he needed, and nothing he didn't want. It was the culmination of a dream, a time he should be reveling in and celebrating, as the happiest man on the face of the earth.

And he was miserable.

He was in love.

He knew he didn't want to win this case just so he could save Jonathan, or beat Cavanaugh, or strike a blow for Truth, Justice, and the American Way. He didn't even want to win it just to satisfy his own precious ego. No, he wanted to win it for *her*. He wanted to free the prisoner from the dungeon so that the real prize could be his. In dream after dream, Fielder saw himself scooping up the waiting princess in his arms and carrying her off from her wretched trailer park to his magical clearing in the forest. There he'd even build an addition to his cabin, so there'd be room for her son as well.

Though he figured the one bathroom should still be enough.

As it turned out, Kevin Doyle *was* crazy enough to like the idea of market research into a sleepwalking defense. The problem was, he simply didn't have the money to commit to it. Governor Pataki was already hounding the legislature to cut back funding on defense expenses in capital cases. Why, the governor wanted to know, had the Court of Appeals set the rates for defense lawyers so high? Why couldn't they pay them the same $40 in court and $25 out of court they paid them in other cases? Surely they'd still have plenty of takers, if only for the publicity value generated by the cases. The purpose of the death penalty was to deter murderers, after all, not to enrich defense lawyers. And why take the taxpayers' hard-earned money and spend it on all these fancy, unnecessary defense experts, like mitigation specialists, psychiatrists, psychologists, social workers, and the like? It was all so very simple in the governor's mind: *You really want to deter somebody, you execute him. Then see how quickly he goes out and kills somebody else.*

Doyle was simply too busy trying to hold the line against cutbacks to stick his neck out and allocate funds for what Fielder's team wanted. But he did have a suggestion. "Call Allie Newhart," he said. "She's down in Washington, at the

NJRI. It sounds like the kind of thing they might be interested in."

The NJRI, or National Jury Research Institute, is a privately funded, non-profit group established to analyze the processes by which juries reach their verdicts. Its studies are published in various scientific texts and journals, and are available to any interested party, prosecution and defense alike. Its methodology includes questioning real jurors who have sat on actual cases and are willing to be interviewed, as well as the staging of mock trials during which the mechanics of jury deliberations can be observed.

Capital cases have long been of particular interest to the NJRI, especially the penalty-phase portion of trials, at which jurors are asked to decide whether a convicted defendant will be sentenced to death, or to some lesser punishment. What the NJRI has found is that jurors faced with this most difficult and important task often operate either in ignorance or defiance of the rules that are supposed to govern their decision-making process, and instead routinely resort to methodology never contemplated in the wildest dreams of legislators, judges, and lawyers.

They have found, for example, that capital jurors invariably vote for death because they refuse to believe that "life without the possibility of parole" really means just that; notwithstanding the judge's clear instructions to the contrary, they persist in assuming that unless they vote to execute the defendant, he'll be out in five or ten years to commit more crimes. They vote for death in overwhelming numbers whenever they're told their decision will only be regarded as a "recommendation" to the sentencing judge, assuming that the judge will pay little or no attention to their recommendation—though the truth is, in many states juries' recommendations are legally binding on the court, and almost always are followed even in those states where the judge has the power to ignore them. Juries vote for death because they feel it's required of them once they've found the defendant guilty as charged, since the crime he's accused of is, by very definition, "capital murder." They vote for death because they mistakenly think that if they fail to, their earlier finding of guilt will be overturned, and a new jury will have to begin the entire process all over again. They vote for death because they believe that, given all the appeals and delays built into the system, there's no chance the defendant will ever actually be executed.

Or, if they vote *against* death, they do so for equally bizarre reasons. They vote against death because of "lingering doubt": because they believe the defendant may have been the victim of mistaken identity, or may have acted in self-defense, or might not have been responsible for his acts because he was insane at the time he committed them—all laudable-enough reasons for jurors to hesitate to send a man to his death, but all grounds that should have compelled them to acquit him in the first place!

Fielder flew down to Washington, D.C., a week before Christmas. Five days earlier, he'd overnighted to the NJRI a ten-page confidential proposal for a study to be conducted on the reactions of jurors to a defense of sleepwalking in a capital prosecution. He'd included news articles and editorials from both the *Adirondack Advertiser* and the *Plattsburgh Press*. Both papers had reported public sentiment as running high in favor of executing Jonathan Hamilton for the murder of his grandparents. The clippings read like movie ads. "Brutal," the *Advertiser* had said. "Senseless and depraved acts," according to the *Press*, "fully deserving . . . of death."

"Looks like you're doing just great with the media," said Allie Newhart. She was tall, stocky, and stern-looking, and shook hands like a man. But at least she knew how to be sarcastic.

"I just sent you the highlights," Fielder said. "There's a guy on a talk-radio station out of Saranac Lake who thinks the death penalty's too good for my client. Wants him tortured first, cut up into small pieces—real slowly, so he can experience what the victims must have gone through."

"And I bet he wants front-row seats to watch."

They were joined by Newhart's boss, Graham Taylor, a

towering, gray-haired man whom Fielder was instantly ready to dislike, until Allie introduced him as a fugitive from a Madison Avenue ad agency who'd given up a seven-figure income to run a non-profit study group on a shoestring budget. Fielder decided he could forgive even a good-looking, six-foot-seven Wasp, with credentials like that.

"We've gone over your proposal," Taylor said, "and I must say we're interested in the idea."

"But we have one major reservation," Newhart added.

"What's that?"

"We want to make certain," said Taylor, "that you're not looking to us to find out what type of juror to select at trial. We can't risk getting labeled as a jury-consulting firm, offering our services to the highest bidder. There are plenty of them out there, you know."

Fielder understood the concern. "That's not what I'm looking for," he said. "My client's taking a terrible beating in the press. I'm convinced he's got an honest, legitimate defense. I want to go public with it, to start offsetting some of the damage. I'm afraid if I don't do it soon, it'll be too late by the time we go to trial. It'll look like some lawyer stunt—you know, pulling the rabbit out of the hat at the eleventh hour. But before I do anything, I'd like to know if I'm going to cause more harm to my guy than good."

"If we should decide to go ahead with it," Newhart asked, "how quickly would you need the results?"

"Not for another ten, fifteen minutes," Fielder joked.

Neither of them so much as smiled. "We'll get back to you in a day or two," said Graham Taylor.

It was clear that the meeting was over, and that Fielder was dismissed. He rose and said, "Thank you." What he was thinking was, he was glad he'd never had to make a living on Madison Avenue.

THICK, LOW CLOUDS obscured the sun on the morning of December 22. Driving to Cedar Falls, Fielder could sense a change in the air, and understood for the first time how local folks claimed to be able to smell snow when it was on its way.

In court, Gil Cavanaugh served and submitted his written response to the defense motions. Quite predictably, he opposed just about everything Fielder sought. The evidence presented before the grand jury had been legally sufficient, he assured everyone, and while he submitted an obligatory transcript of the proceedings for the court's inspection, he declined to furnish the defense a copy. All of the evidence had been properly obtained, he contended, from the items recovered at the Hamilton estate to the statements uttered by the defendant. He turned over to the defense only those items which the law required him to: copies of the autopsy, toxicology and serology reports, and the results of other scientific tests. Other items, such as investigators' statements, original notes, and witness lists, he refused to part with. He ridiculed Fielder's requests for a change of venue, additional jury challenges, and a different judge, and opposed all of them as unnecessary.

Judge Summerhouse put the case off to January 12, for his decision on the motions. Then he wished everyone a merry Christmas. There was a murmur from those assembled that came out sounding like a cross between "Thank you" and "Same to you." Jonathan Hamilton, blanketless and shivering beside Matt Fielder, said nothing before being led back to the pens.

FROM CEDAR FALLS, Fielder headed home toward his cabin in Big Moose. The talk back at the courthouse had been of the coming storm and he didn't want to get caught in it. Above him, the sky was now a uniform, solid gray, and there was almost no breeze detectable in the branches of the pines and hemlocks that lined the road on either side. Once or twice a few early flakes appeared and landed on the windshield, but never enough to require a sweep from the wipers. The snow was in no hurry, Fielder could see. Unlike the sudden storms that whipped in with high winds and sometimes even lightning, this snow would come when it was good and ready, when it was time to settle in and stay the night. Until then, there was no need for Fielder to rush home.

So he took a detour. Before Route 30 reached Lake Eaton and the Long Lake Bridge, he turned right onto County Road 18. From there, he found the turnoff to Flat Lake Road, and followed it, as he'd followed it several months ago, back when he'd made his first trip to the estate to see with his own eyes the place where Jonathan Hamilton had risen from his bed that fateful night and ended the lives of the two people he probably loved most in the whole world.

The colors were gone at the lake. The brilliant reds and oranges and yellows of autumn had vanished. The trees they had lit up so spectacularly only months ago were now bare sticks jutting up among the evergreens, starkly silhouetted against the slate gray of the sky. Gone, too, was the perfect reflection of the entire scene upon the still surface of the lake, which had struck Fielder so the first time he'd visited the spot.

But there was a reward, nonetheless.

In place of the autumn colors, in place of the mirror image, winter had provided her quiet answer to autumn's gaudy show, and it was every bit as breathtaking.

Sometime in mid-December, just before the lake freezes over, the same two men who lower the steel gate in spring to create a skimming effect to rid the surface of debris, show up again. Slowly they crank the big wheel a dozen turns or more, gradually raising the gate until its top comes to rest a full foot above the waterline. The result is that the water no longer flows over the top of the dam; instead it spills out under the bottom of the gate. This change causes the skimming action to cease, and the surface of the lake becomes motionless.

And motionless, it turns to ice.

Already well below the freezing point, the water has resisted turning solid until then only because of its rapid movement. As soon as that movement ceases, the surface freezes over, literally within hours, before falling leaves and twigs have a chance to mar its surface, or winds to ripple its smoothness. What is left is a plane of ice so perfectly, geometrically flat that it is startling to behold. Carpenters from miles around have been known to come and place their bubble-levels on it—not to measure the flatness of the lake itself, but to check the accuracy of their equipment.

It is then, at least according to the year-rounders, that the lake is truly at its most beautiful: at that instant just after the freezing, but just before the first snows fall and blanket the ice. And it is then—not in the budding, flowering promise of spring; not in the glorious, sun-drenched days of summer; not even in the spectacular, colorful riot of autumn; but in that exquisite moment that comes only in early winter—that Flat Lake reveals her true self, and earns the name by which she is known.

THAT EVENING, MATT Fielder sat in front of his wood-stove, resigned to the fact that the falling snow had forced him to postpone at least until the weekend his plans to drive to New Hampshire, and sifting through the day's mail. There was a tax bill, a credit-card solicitation, an Eddie Bauer catalog, a law-school alumni bulletin, and an envelope from Washington, D.C. Carefully he slit it open and unfolded the letter inside. The National Jury Research Institute had agreed to conduct a study with a sample of registered jurors in Cascade County, Montana. The locale had been selected because it had been found to resemble Ottawa County in several important respects. To begin with, there were the obvious geographic similarities, with both counties set in the foothills of major mountain ranges. Their respective county seats, Great Falls, Montana, and Cedar Falls, New York, were virtually indistinguishable in many respects. And in terms of demographics—the ethnic composition, the local economies, the regional politics, and the voting histories of residents toward issues involving crime and punishment generally, and the death penalty in particular—the areas turned out to be almost carbon copies of each other. Furthermore, Montana was sufficiently distant from New York to minimize the likelihood that the survey sample would be tainted by news accounts, or that word of the study would leak out and find its way back east.

The methodology would be fairly straightforward. The subjects would be asked their reactions to a hypothetical case involving a young man accused of a brutal murder. During the course of the interviews, the subjects would be informed, bit by bit, of various aspects of the young man's appearance, background, conduct following the crime, and—finally—the circumstances under which he'd committed it. The letter went on to say that the results of the study would be available in four to six weeks.

Fielder allowed himself a smile. Maybe, he dared to think, the momentum was getting ready to shift once more.

DOWN IN ALBANY, Hillary Munson and Lois Miller sang carols as they trimmed a small Douglas fir, happy to be able to celebrate the holidays by themselves, without the well-intentioned assistance of family and friends. At the Dew Drop Inn in Cedar Falls, Pearson Gunn stared into the bottom of an empty pitcher, knowing it was time to head home, but wondering if perhaps he hadn't missed something along the way. And up the block and around the corner, in the Ottawa County Jail, Jonathan Hamilton lay on his back in the half-light of his cell, trying his best to recall a time and a place that kept slipping farther and farther into the distance.

22

GOING PUBLIC

By the second week of January, Judge Summerhouse had ruled on the defense's motions. He decided that the evidence presented to the grand jury had been legally sufficient; he ordered pre-trial hearings into the admissibility of the physical evidence seized, and the statements made by the defendant; and he declined to compel the prosecution to turn over more documents than those which the statute required. There would be no change of venue, and no additional jury challenges. And there certainly wasn't going to be a different judge.

The case was adjourned to the third week of February.

A week later, a large manila envelope marked PERSONAL AND CONFIDENTIAL arrived in the mail at Matt Fielder's cabin. For a moment, Fielder thought he might have ordered something risqué from a mail-order catalog. Then he remembered. He tore open the envelope and found a 200-page bound report bearing an impressive title.

AN INQUIRY INTO THE ATTITUDES OF PROSPECTIVE JURORS IN CASCADE COUNTY, MONTANA, ONCE INFORMED THAT A MURDER SUSPECT MAY HAVE BEEN IN A SLEEPLIKE TRANCE WHEN HE COMMITTED THE ACTS RESULTING IN THE HOMICIDE.

Catchy, it wasn't. But it soon became apparent that the people down at the National Jury Research Institute had done their homework. They'd taken every single fact Fielder had given them in his proposal, fictionalized it slightly, and shaped it into a question that had in turn become part of a comprehensive survey. Researchers had then gone out into the field and interviewed some four hundred citizens of Cascade County, Montana.

The results were nothing short of fascinating.

The subjects were presented with a case of a young man accused of brutally murdering an elderly family member he apparently loved. The evidence pointed overwhelmingly to his guilt. Initially, close to 83 percent of those interviewed believed the man deserved the death penalty. The reasons they cited in support of that belief included the vicious nature of the crime, the age of the victim, and the relationship between the defendant and the victim.

From that point, the NJRI researchers attempted to determine which additional factors, once revealed to the subjects, were likely to reduce the percentage of those favoring death, and which factors were likely to increase it.

Those shown a computer-altered photograph of Jonathan Hamilton were less inclined to execute him. Among those shown a black-and-white photo, the pro-death percentage dropped to 76 percent. But only 59 percent of those shown a color photo, depicting Jonathan's blond hair, blue eyes, and handsome features, felt he should die.

Of that latter group, only 51 percent continued to advocate death when informed that the suspect was borderline retarded. Among those subjects, provided the additional fact that he stuttered badly when he spoke, the figure dropped to 48 percent. Informed that he was orphaned, only 42 percent held out for death.

Next, the subjects were told that while the defense was conceding the certainty that the young man had committed the crime, it was equally convinced that he'd done so while in the midst of a sleeplike trance. He had a long history of such trances, they were told, which could be documented in writing and fully confirmed by medical experts. Those same experts were satisfied that the young man had been totally powerless to control his actions while in the trance, and had awakened with absolutely no recollection of what he'd done. The group of subjects who still wanted to execute the young man now fell to 17 percent.

But one had to be careful, too.

The 42 percent who were anxious to execute the young man despite the fact that he was an orphan suddenly doubled, to a dangerous 83 percent, if the subjects were made aware of a rumor that the young man himself might have had something to do with causing the deaths of his parents, however accidentally and however long ago. And it climbed to over 90 percent if they learned that he'd once raped his sister, had continued to have sex with her thereafter, and had fathered her illegitimate child.

The lessons were all too clear to Matt Fielder. Not only could he go public with the sleepwalking defense, but he *had* to, if Jonathan was to have a fighting chance at trial. The deck was too stacked against him, as things stood. Get the story out, and the public perception would swing in Jonathan's favor. At the same time, he'd have to steer clear of the obvious pitfalls—the origin of the fire, and the relationship Jonathan had carried on with Jennifer.

Two questions immediately crossed Fielder's mind. First, could that be done? Could the helpful part of the story be put out there while the dangerous part was safely contained? And second, if it could, what was the best way to do it?

But all he had to do to find out was to read on. The NJRI questioners had anticipated both of Fielder's concerns. They'd determined, by asking follow-up questions, that if the sleep-trance information came directly from the defense camp, only 44 percent of the public was likely to believe it. Furthermore, a footnote cautioned him, an intense grilling would no doubt follow the revelation, and matters like the fire and Jennifer's disappearance might have to be addressed.

On the other hand, if the information came from some other source, the defense probably wouldn't be subjected to such scrutiny, or at least wouldn't have to respond in detail. At the same time, the results themselves would be far more dramatic. If the story got out through a leak, for example, through "an anonymous source close to the case, but identified with neither the defense nor the prosecution," the number of believers rose from 44 to 78 percent. And, in case you really wanted to dream, if you could somehow manage to make it appear that the story came from the prosecution, either directly or in the form of a leak, the figure jumped to an astounding 96 percent!

Before doing anything else, Matt Fielder sat down at his computer and composed a love letter to Allie Newhart, Graham Taylor, and the rest of the staff at the NJRI. Then he picked up the phone and got Hillary Munson and Pearson Gunn on a conference call.

"We need to meet," he told them. "Tomorrow."

ONE OF THE things that seems to draw lawyers to criminal-defense work is the lack of paperwork the practice tends to generate. In comparison to corporate, tax, real estate, personal injury, and other types of civil work, the average criminal case file is wafer thin.

But that rule seems to gradually apply less and less as one moves up the ladder of seriousness in terms of the crime charged. By the time you get to major felonies, the wafer has expanded some, and it isn't unusual to have a few inch-thick files in your drawer. Move up to homicides, and you'll see some two- and three-inchers, even before trial, and not counting transcripts from earlier proceedings. Take on a capital case, and you can forget about the file drawer altogether; you're going to have to head to the copy room and start collecting empty cartons.

The night before meeting with Munson and Gunn, Fielder went through his entire file on Jonathan Hamilton's case—or rather, his cartons. He went over everything, with the aim of organizing it in preparation for the next day's meeting. This he did, creating files with titles like LEGAL PAPERS, SCIENTIFIC REPORTS, PROSECUTION WITNESSES, DEFENSE WITNESSES, PHOTOGRAPHS, JURY SELECTION, and NEWS CLIPPINGS, and filling them with whatever belonged under the headings. In the process, he reread almost every document he refiled. He didn't start out meaning to do that; it just seemed to turn out that way.

He reread the original complaint and the indictment; his own motion papers and Cavanaugh's response; the autopsy protocol, and the toxicology and serology reports; the blood, fingerprint, footprint, hair, and fiber comparisons; the DNA results; Jonathan's old school records and medical files; his psychiatric and psychological evaluations; Hillary Munson's entire mitigation folder; and the few items Pearson Gunn reluctantly had committed to paper, highlights of interviews with Klaus and Elna Armbrust, Bass McClure, P. J. and Jennifer Hamilton, and Sue Ellen Blodgett. He even tried to decipher Gunn's coded scriblings of rumors he'd picked up from a confidential source—a shadowy figure he referred to only as CS-1, but who seemed to know a great deal about what was going on in the prosecution's camp.

Fielder's fourth-grade teacher was a tall, thin, gray-haired woman named Katherine Sweeny. To this day, he remembered two things about her. The first was that she came from Watertown, a fact imprinted in Fielder's mind ever since the day she'd written it on the blackboard during science class as "H_2O-town." The second was her credo: "If you really want to learn something," she'd always told the class, "write it down."

To this day, Matt Fielder writes it down. He can't help himself; it's as if Miss Sweeny is still standing behind him, peering over his shoulder.

So, as he reread everything in Jonathan Hamilton's files, Fielder wrote things down. But, because he also wanted to get some sleep that night, he limited what he wrote to those things he didn't understand, or had questions about, or wanted to look into a bit more deeply. He ended up with a page and a half of notes, which became the last thing he looked at before turning in. As he studied it, only three items bothered him. The first two were from Pearson Gunn's list of "Things to Think About."

First, why was it that no fingerprints had been lifted from the knife? Surely the state police investigators realized they'd discovered the murder weapon as soon as they'd unwrapped the hunting knife from the bloody towel found in Jonathan's vanity cabinet. How could they possibly have been so sloppy in their handling of it? But then again, Fielder had seen poor police work like that before. He'd won more than his share of cases—cases where defendants almost certainly had been guilty—because cops had screwed up the physical evidence. Maybe that should be his approach in this case. Maybe it was a mistake for him to concede that Jonathan was the killer. But then again, was a conservative, upstate New York jury really going buy into a mishandling-of-the-evidence defense? This wasn't southern California, after all.

Second, what was this business about only six of the seven hairs from the crime scene matching Jonathan's? Wasn't six out of seven pretty good? Perhaps the seventh hair was simply broken off and therefore missing a follicle, so that it contained no DNA material for comparison. Or perhaps it had belonged to one of the victims, or to Mrs. Armbrust (who probably made up the bed every day), or even to one of the investigators who'd been at the scene. Not much to go on, there.

Then there was something in Hillary Munson's report of her interview with Sue Ellen Blodgett. Fielder was every bit as excited about Sue Ellen's contribution to the defense as Hillary was, particularly the 1989 letter in which Jennifer had mentioned Jonathan's sleepwalking. But something about the letter bothered Fielder. In it, Jennifer had said she was enclosing photos of Troy. Yet according to Hillary's report, there'd been only *one* photo in the envelope when Hillary opened it.

Fielder looked at the clock and saw that it was almost

three in the morning. He realized he'd reached the point where he was truly grasping at straws. He put another log in the stove, a piece of dry, unsplit oak, a good all-nighter. Then he flicked off the lights.

LOOK AT THESE statistics!" Hillary Munson exclaimed. "*Seventy-eight percent* will believe us."

"Ninety-six percent," added Gunn, "if it comes from the DA."

The vote had been swift and unanimous. Both Munson and Gunn agreed that, given the numbers the NJRI study had come up with, the defense needed to get the story of Jonathan's sleepwalking defense out to the public as soon as possible.

"Hillary," said Fielder, "I want you to alert both Dr. Goldstein and Dr. Litwiller that we're going to do this. Make sure they know that if anyone contacts them, all they're to is to confirm that they've interviewed Jonathan. And not a word about the fire, the rape, or any of that stuff."

"You got it," Hillary said. "How are you going to do this? A press conference?"

"I don't know." It was the one thing Fielder hadn't figured out yet. He *hated* press conferences, and tended to look down on lawyers who tried their cases in the media. Still, he knew the time had come for him to get over his aversion. His client's life might depend upon it.

Gunn spoke up. "Why don't you give me a day or two to think about that?" he said. "I might be able to come with something."

As grateful as Fielder was for the reprieve, he knew time was running out on them. He agreed to hold off three days, but that was all. If Gunn couldn't figure out a way to do it within that time, he'd call a press conference.

How do you even do that? Fielder wondered.

THE FOLLOWING DAY, Fielder checked in with Kevin Doyle. He wanted to thank Doyle for putting him together with the people at NJRI, and to tell him he was getting ready to air his defense in public.

"Go for it!" Doyle has always been a big believer in what he likes to call the "unified theory of defense" in capital cases. He preaches that you can't go through the motions of insisting your client's factually innocent, and then—once he'd been convicted, and the penalty phase had begun—suddenly switch horses and start telling the same jury, "Yes, he did it, but he was high at the time, and he had a really tough childhood." According to Doyle (and almost everyone else who does this work), you've got to put your money on one horse, and leave it there.

Give me Sleepwalker to win in the seventh, Fielder wanted to say. "Kevin," he said instead, "can I ask you a stupid question?"

"Sure."

"How do you call a press conference?"

Doyle laughed heartily. "Let me know when you're ready," he said. "I think I might have a few friends left in the media."

PEARSON GUNN WAS back at his usual table that evening, and the evening after that. All told, he went through five pitchers in the process. Tough work, as they say, but then somebody's got to do it.

Around eight-thirty on the second evening, Captain Roger Duquesne of the state police wandered in, just off duty from a split shift. He spotted Gunn, and greeted him with a loud, *"Bonjour, mon ami!"*

Gunn waved. At the same time, he used one of his feet to slide an empty chair back from the table. It was a move he'd been practicing for two nights.

The two men sat and talked almost to eleven. As always, Gunn refuses to divulge what it is they discussed. (To this very day, he refuses to confirm that Roger Duquesne and Gunn's source, "CS-1," are one and the same.) But according to Pete the bartender, who was on duty that evening, for once it seemed to be Gunn who was doing most of the talking, and Duquesne most of the listening.

Which is not altogether surprising. Information, after all, is a two-way street. Just as successful private investigators need to have sources within government ranks, so too, do law-enforcement personnel depend upon informants in the private sector to keep them abreast of developments on the street.

Or, looking at it another way, it is entirely possible that both men put in for expenses incurred that night at the Dew Drop Inn, during the course of official investigations. And that the taxpayers ultimately ended up picking up the tab for all three pitchers of ale.

Twice over.

TWO DAYS LATER, an exclusive story appeared on the bottom of the front page of the *Adirondack Advertiser*, under bold headlines.

D. A. GIRDS FOR SLEEPWALKING DEFENSE IN FLAT LAKE MURDER TRIAL

By that evening, all the major networks and their local affiliates had picked up the story. Most of them ran it against a backdrop consisting of a huge photo of Jonathan Hamilton. Copies of the photo had been dropped off earlier that day by messengers of unknown origin. It was in full color, and clearly showed Jonathan's blond hair, pale blue eyes, and handsome features.

Matt Fielder sat in front of his TV set that night, switching from one channel to another, his mouth open, his eyes wide. When the last of the newscasters finally finished her report and signed off, Fielder continued to sit in front of his set for a full twenty minutes, watching the evening sermonette, the playing of the national anthem, a test pattern, and finally a blank screen.

"Holy shit," was all he could think to say. "Holy shit." Over and over again.

23

DIGGING OUT

IN RETROSPECT, IT is extremely difficult to understand the thinking behind Gil Cavanaugh's decision to go to the media with the story of Jonathan Hamilton's sleepwalking. Obviously, he'd somehow learned of the defense's plan to go public, and had figured that the best way to control the damage was to beat them to the punch. The preemptive strike tends to be almost a reflexive action among those accustomed to dealing with the media.

The course Cavanaugh chose was probably doomed from the outset. On top of that, it was carried out with almost astonishing clumsiness.

For a full week, he tried his best to stonewall it. In press conference after press conference (for, unlike Matt Fielder, the district attorney was no stranger to the ways of the media, or what it took to make them come running), Cavanaugh alternately dismissed the notion that Jonathan Hamilton had committed the crimes in his sleep, and blithely insisted that it was something the defense could never prove.

"Nonsense!" was his first response. "This is nothing but the very latest 'Twinkie defense,' the desperate concoction of some clever defense lawyer. I'll bet my last dollar nobody ever heard about Hamilton's walking in his sleep before he killed his grandparents!"

That very same afternoon, the reporters came flocking

back to him. The defense, it seemed, was saying it was in a position to establish that Jonathan had been sleepwalking for many years.

"Sure," Cavanaugh retorted. "They'll get someone to say that. But can they *prove* it?"

Apparently so, they told him the following morning. There was talk of documents that went back almost ten years, and of nationally known psychiatrists and psychologists willing to stake their reputations on their opinions.' Cavanaugh turned to his aides, but their response was a silent chorus of shrugs and quizzical looks. Evidently, they hadn't heard *that*.

In the days that followed, it became clear that just as Cavanaugh's initial response had been ill-conceived, so, too, were his follow-ups. Gradually, he began to change his posture from one of doubting the authenticity of Jonathan's sleepwalking, to one of attacking its relevance. "It's nothing but another red herring," he said. "First they said he wasn't to blame because he was *slow*. Now they want to excuse what he did because he was *asleep*! What are they going to blame it on next? That he's a *victim of society*? I say a man ought to be held accountable for his own acts, fast or slow, awake or asleep!"

The problem was that each time Cavanaugh tried a different line of attack, the defense had an answer ready for it. And the back-and-forth process simply served to prolong the debate, and keep it front and center in the news.

By midweek, the local radio stations began getting wind of the public's reaction to the debate. There was no flood of calls, to be sure, but there was a pretty steady flow, and according to the early reports, sentiment was running as high as ten-to-one in favor of Jonathan. "You can't punish a man for something he does while he's sleepwalking," asserted one listener. "Why would you want to execute someone who's not responsible for what he did?" asked another. Many callers seemed to have friends or relatives who'd been known to walk in their sleep. Others had read of such cases. A woman from Cooperstown phoned to say that she herself had wound up in her own garden once or twice. "Durned if *I* know how," she added.

By the end of the week, Cavanaugh had circled the wagons. In what he said would be his final public pronouncement on the matter, he retreated to his original stance of questioning whether Jonathan had really been sleepwalking at the time of the murders. "This wasn't about being *asleep*," he insisted. "It was about greed and evilness. It was about *money*!" Then, in a fairly transparent case of bet-hedging, he added, "And anyway, we can't be having a lunatic running around in our midst. Who knows what'll happen *next time* he decides to get up in his sleep?"

Then he did what he probably should have done in the first place. He went to Judge Summerhouse and applied for a gag order.

The judge, like just about everybody else, had evidently been following the brouhaha. "And just who is it," he asked wryly, "that you'd like to gag?"

For once, Matt Fielder had to smile. No, he told the judge when asked, the defense had no objection to the order. What he didn't say was that, as far as he was concerned, the damage had already been done, and it was as good a time as any to let things quiet down and sink in, before the reporters' questions became too difficult for him to answer.

IF GIL CAVANAUGH thought the gag order was going to put an end to the uproar, he was mistaken once again. You can gag lawyers, but you can't gag reporters. And you certainly can't gag the public. The talk-radio hosts kept the story alive, and the calls kept coming in to the news stations. A poll of 850 Ottawa County residents over twenty-one years of age was reported in the *Advertiser*. Close to 90 percent of those responding believed the death penalty was inappropriate in Jonathan Hamilton's case, while a full 33 percent maintained that he shouldn't be held criminally responsible at all.

Asked by an *Advertiser* reporter to comment on the results, Fielder replied that he couldn't, seeing as the DA had obtained a gag order. His response was quoted verbatim in the next day's paper, drawing a phone call from Judge Summerhouse, sternly admonishing him that a gag order was a gag order, and neither side was to comment on who'd sought it. "Sorry," said Fielder. But once again, the damage had already been done, and the public's perception was reinforced that it had been the prosecution all along that felt the need to put a lid on things.

FIELDER WAS STARTLED by the ringing of his phone. He picked it up and said, "Hello."

"Matthew Fielder, please," said a woman.

"That's me."

"Please hold for Mr. Cavanaugh," she said.

Not exactly his favorite way of being treated, thought Fielder. But then again, this was the man who'd started off their relationship by referring to him as a "Jew lawyer." He wondered what it was the DA wanted now.

There was a click on the other end, followed by Cavanaugh's voice. "Hello, Matt," he said. "Gil Cavanaugh here. I'm sorry—is this your office, or your home?"

"It's both," Fielder said.

"I see. How've you been?"

"Not bad."

"Quite a ripple we caused there," Cavanaugh said. "In the media."

" 'We'?"

"Well, you know, the case."

"Right."

"I was thinking . . ." said Cavanaugh.

Fielder waited.

"I was wondering, just for the sake of argument, if your man might be interested in some sort of a disposition."

Fielder felt his heart begin to pound, but he held his silence.

"Did you hear me?"

"I heard you," Fielder said. "I thought maybe you were going to tell me what you have in mind."

"Well," said Cavanaugh, "we'd be talking life, of course."

"What kind of life?" There was life, and there was life. There was life without parole, there was twenty-five–to–life, there was fifteen-to-life, and there was everything in between.

"I think the term is le-*wop*," said Cavanaugh, mispronouncing LWOP to make it come out sounding like a Frenchman's slur for an Italian.

"Well," said Fielder, doing his best to conceal his excitement, "if that's an offer, I'll certainly run it by my client."

"Why don't you do that?" Cavanaugh suggested. "You never can tell, he might decide he likes living."

They talked for a minute more before exchanging goodbyes, neither man particularly comfortable. It was clear they had little in the way of small talk to share—the gregarious local country-club politician and the refugee loner from the big city.

As soon as he'd replaced the phone in its cradle, Fielder pumped his fist in the air and let out a full-volume "Yesss!" Whether or not Jonathan Hamilton might be interested in pleading guilty—in exchange for living the rest of his life in prison—wasn't really the point. In fact, as Fielder thought about it, he imagined he'd have a hard time just getting Jonathan to understand the choice presented to him. But that wasn't the point. The point was, there was suddenly a light at the end of the tunnel. From a situation that had seemed utterly hopeless only a week ago, there had been a sudden and dramatic turnaround. And Cavanaugh's phone call marked the first acknowledgment of precisely how meaningful that turnaround had been.

The enemy had blinked.

THE SNOW THAT fell that night began softly, falling in large wet flakes that coated the branches of the evergreens and grasses, but melted when they landed on solid surfaces still warmed by the ground. Gradually, however, the temperatures dipped below the freezing mark, and slid into the high twenties. The change was a matter of only a few degrees, but it was enough to cause the flakes to stick. The result was a rapid accumulation of wet, heavy snow that bent boughs and tree trunks low, even as it raised the white ground up to meet them.

By daybreak, a full foot of snow had fallen in most of the area, even more in the mountains. Near midafternoon, with no letup in sight, some areas were reporting as much as thirty inches. Snowplows began losing the battle to keep roads clear, trees snapped like kindling, and power lines fell with them.

It wasn't until the following morning that the snow let up, or moved out, or just figured it had done enough to remind folks who was in charge of things. By that time, the storm had broken records that had stood for thirty years. The entire Adirondack region lay blanketed under three feet of heavy snow, the kind that bends shovels and gets measured not only in inches and feet, but in strained backs, heart attacks, and deaths. Out on the highways, stranded motorists were plucked from the tops of their cars by helicopters; two thousand homes were reported to be without power and water; and phone service would be out for days. For people and animals alike, life was reduced to a matter of pure, grim survival.

Matt Fielder was in heaven.

Dry in his woolens and warm by his fire, he watched the snow pile up outside until the drifts covered the lower halves of his windows. With his power out, he melted snow for drinking water, and cooked soup on the cast-iron surface of his stove. Twice he had to climb up onto his roof to shovel off the new accumulation, in order to reduce the danger of a cave-in. By the third time, he no longer had to climb; he simply strapped on his snowshoes and walked until he came to his chimney.

This, too, was why Fielder had fled the city and come

to the Adirondacks. The sheer beauty, the majestic quiet, and the awesome display of the elements reminded him how puny and powerless man could be in this world. There was no fighting back against Nature; whenever she decided to play hard, to dig into the batter's box and take a full swing, she won, plain and simple.

But there was room for accommodation.

If you'd built your cabin for strength instead of beauty, and had driven the nails close enough and straight enough, its frame would stand up against the fiercest wind. If you'd triple-caulked the logs, had spent your money on insulation instead of decoration, and had chosen an ugly woodburning stove over a dramatic open fireplace, your walls would keep out the bitterest cold. And if you hadn't been so foolish as to install designer skylights where structural beams belonged, your roof would withstand the crushing weight of even the heaviest snow—provided you were willing to get off your butt now and then, and lend a hand with a shovel.

If you did all that, the storm pretty much lets you be.

What it didn't let you do, was drive the sixty miles to Cedar Falls, to visit your client.

IT WAS A full two days before Fielder's power was restored. With electricity, his pump came back on, and he soon had water flowing from his well. Despite the freezing temperatures, no pipes had clogged or burst. Snow, which *Homo temperatus* tends to think of as cold stuff, actually makes pretty good insulation. Just ask anyone who's ever built an igloo, or watched a sled dog bed down for the night.

Beginning the second day, the phone began showing signs of life. It would ring at odd hours, each time once, or twice at the most. Each time Fielder went to pick it up, the line would be dead. After a while, he figured it had to be work crews out on the roads, testing equipment. He turned the volume down, and learned to ignore the rings.

By the afternoon of third day, he went out with his shovel and made his first serious attempt at digging himself out. His Suzuki had nearly disappeared; it took him almost two hours to clear around it. But after a few jiggles to the carburetor valve, it started right up. The driveway (or what Fielder called his driveway, since in reality it was little more than a twisting path that managed to avoid the largest trees, and a bare majority of rocks and roots) was a different story. He cursed himself for never having bought a plow blade for the Suzuki. He'd actually priced one, a huge, second-hand thing they wanted $350 for at a John Deere place over in Martinsburg. They'd asked him what he was going to put it on, and when Fielder had pointed to his Sidekick, they'd laughed like schoolboys. He'd settled on a shovel instead, $12.

The problem with the snow wasn't just how heavy it was to lift. It was also a matter of what to do with it once you *did* lift it. The drifts were so high that you had to throw the snow *up*, as well as to one side, just to keep it from collapsing back onto the area you were working on. It took him two hours to clear what he guessed was about fifty linear feet. He'd once paced off his driveway, and it had come to just under a fifth of a mile. So, figuring a rate of twenty-five feet an hour, how long could it possibly take him? Another forty hours, tops?

Totally exhausted, he quit after another hour, and dragged himself back inside. He'd just stripped off his boots when the phone rang. More equipment testing, he guessed. But this time, the first ring was followed by not only a second, but a third. He reached for the phone and picked it up, expecting the familiar silence.

"Matt?"

"Yeah," he said, still fighting to catch his breath. "Who's this?"

"Kevin Doyle," the voice said. "Sounds like I caught you in the middle of something important."

"No, no," Fielder managed. "I'm just . . . trying to breathe, is all."

"Well, congratulations," Doyle said.

"For breathing?"

"Okay, that too," said Doyle. "Haven't you heard the news?"

"*News*? I haven't heard anything but my tea kettle for four days. We've had a little snow here."

"So I heard."

"So what's the news?" Fielder asked.

"You really don't know, do you? Cavanaugh decertified."

Fielder's mouth opened, but nothing came out.

"You there, Matt?"

"I'm here."

"Cavanaugh decertified," Doyle repeated. "Threw in the towel on death. Of course, that's the *good* news."

"And the *bad*?"

"Welcome back to eighteen-b rates."

Fielder still couldn't believe it. "Are you *serious*?" he asked.

"I'm afraid so. Forty dollars an hour in court—"

"No, no. Are you really serious that Cavanaugh decertified?"

"Where've you been? It was all over the news this morning. Seems like he was taking too much of a beating from the media, insisting on death in spite of the sleepwalking thing. People were starting to call him bloodthirsty, saying they'd think twice before voting for him again next election."

"He called me and offered us LWOP a couple of days ago," Fielder said. "But it was in exchange for a guilty plea."

"And you turned him down?"

"I never called him back. I—"

"Ballsy move, man! Way to call his bluff!"

"Well—"

"Don't be so modest, Matt. I always said you were cut out for this work."

WITH FIELDER'S PHONE service restored, Kevin Doyle was only the first of many to get through to him that afternoon.

Hillary Munson checked in from her office in Albany, and Pearson Gunn called from someplace with jukebox music playing in the background. Half a dozen reporters phoned, asking Fielder to comment on Cavanaugh's surrender; he dutifully reminded them he was still gagged. Bass Mc-Clure—the same Bass McClure who'd responded to Jonathan's early-morning call—called to tell Fielder how glad he was to hear the news.

"You know," McClure said, "I always did like that boy. Never understood how he coulda hurt his grandma and his grandpa like that. Even in his sleep."

"The human mind's a strange thing," was all Fielder could think to say.

"I guess so," said McClure. "How you doing over there? Dug out yet?"

"Not yet," Fielder said. "But I'm working on it."

THAT NIGHT, JENNIFER called from New Hampshire to add her congratulations. "You did it," she told him. "You really did it."

"I don't know if *I* did it," he said. "But it's done."

"Stop being so modest, Matthew. You saved my brother's life."

"We both did," he allowed.

"What happens now?" she asked.

"I'm not sure. I'll have to call the DA, see if there's something we can work out in the way of a plea. Then I'll need to go talk with Jonathan."

"Does he know yet?"

"I imagine so," Fielder said. "News travels pretty fast in jail. Especially news like this."

What he didn't address—and what Jennifer didn't press him on—was the question of whether Jonathan, once he'd been informed of the development, would even be able to grasp its significance.

"Matthew Fielder," said Jennifer, "you're my hero."

And he remembered his dream, how someday he'd succeed in freeing the prisoner from the dungeon, just so he could scoop up the beautiful princess in his arms, and carry her off to his cabin.

He was halfway there.

"How do I ever thank you?" Jennifer was asking him.

"I don't know. I guess we'll just have to keep you around, see what we can come up with," Fielder said.

And gulped.

FIELDER WAS JOLTED awake by the sound of a laboring engine, and for a moment he thought he was back in the city, listening to the Saturday-morning serenade of garbage trucks. He lifted himself up so that he could see over the snow line, which was still more or less mid-window. What he saw was a huge yellow tractor, belching black diesel smoke as it lifted a gigantic wall of snow in its front-loader.

He threw on clothes and boots, and made it out the front door just as the operator killed the engine and jumped down from the cab.

"Bass? Is that you?"

Not only was it Bass McClure walking toward him, but it was Bass McClure carrying a bag of jelly donuts and a thermos of hot coffee.

"Mornin', Matt," said McClure, as he followed Fielder into the cabin. "Sorry if I woke you."

"I thought you drove a Jeep," Fielder said.

"Oh, that." McClure laughed, waving in the direction of the tractor. "County property. I figured maybe you could use a little help."

"You sure figured right. Thank you."

They sat for a while, content to eat their donuts and drink their coffee. Though the two men had grown up in opposite parts of the state, and had earned their livelihoods doing very different types of work, they shared a trait that seemed to be going pretty much out of style: Neither of them was embarrassed by silence. So for a good twenty minutes, they simply sat and ate and drank, grateful for the fact of each other's companionship, but feeling no need to exploit it. And when McClure finally broke the quiet at one point to say, "Afraid I nicked one of your maples on the way in," Fielder looked up from his coffee and said, "I'll nail a bucket to it," and the matter was forgotten.

McClure stayed a while longer, before he stood up and said he'd better get going, seeing as someone else might need help digging out.

"Well, thanks again," Fielder said. "And for breakfast, too. Good donuts. Where'd you get them?"

"Dunkin' Donuts, up on County Road 27, just past Pine Hollow. Nice folks, only been there about a year or so. Hey, Matt?"

"Yes?"

"I'm glad the DA backed off."

"Me and you both," Fielder agreed.

"There's a family that's sure seen more'n its share of tragedy. The kids' runnin' off, the fire, the incest, the pregnancy. And now this."

"You knew about the incest and the pregnancy?"

"Used to hear a lotta stuff, back then," McClure acknowledged. "Rumors. Can't remember if it was the older brother who was sposed to have been responsible, or the father."

Fielder said nothing. He decided it wasn't his place to correct McClure's understanding and set the record straight about Jennifer and Jonathan.

"So what happens now?" McClure asked.

"We'll put our heads together," Fielder said. "See if we can get together on a sentence that lets Jonathan see daylight someday. If we can't, we'll have to take it to trial."

"Sleepwalkin'?"

Fielder nodded.

"Be careful," McClure cautioned him.

"How's that?"

"Folks were pretty quick to jump on Cavanaugh for still wantin' to execute Jonathan, once it looked like he might not a meant to do what he did. But if push comes to shove, and it looks like the boy's goin' to walk out scot-free, them same folks'll turn on you in a minute, tell you an' your fancy doctors all that sleepwalkin' stuff is pure b.s., that this was nothin' but a case of good old-fashioned *greed*."

"You really think so?"

McClure zipped up his jacket and pulled his cap down over his ears. "There's a saying around these parts," he said. "It goes, 'Things aren't always what they seem to be at first glance. But sometimes they are.' "

24

PLAYING HOUSE

THAT'S GOOD, THAT they d-don't want to kill me no more.
Isn't it?"

"Yes, Jonathan. That's very good."

They were talking over the phones, and through the tiny
round cutout in the Plexiglas partition that separated them.
Fielder had driven over to Cedar Falls shortly after Bass
McClure had left the cabin.

"B-but I still stay in jail. Right?"

"That's right," Fielder said. "At least for now."

"That's okay. As long as I got my b-blankets, to keep
me warm. And they keep feeding me."

"They'll keep feeding you," Fielder assured him.

"Fish."

"Excuse me?"

"Fish," Jonathan repeated.

"They feed you fish?"

"No," Jonathan said. "I sm-smell fish."

Fielder took a deep breath with his nose. Sure enough,
there was a faint odor in the air of fish being cooked.
"You're right," he said.

Jonathan smiled broadly. "Grandpa Carter took me fishing," he said, as though it might have been that very morning he was talking about. "We went out on the lake, in a
boat. I caught two sunnies and a perch. We threw them
back. Grandpa Carter said they would live, that way."

Fielder noticed that Jonathan had put four or five sentences together, without once stuttering. "Did you like Grandpa Carter?" he asked.

Jonathan smiled again. "I *love* Grandpa Carter," he said.

"And Grandma Mary Alice?"

"Her too," he said. "I—I—I loved her, too." His eyes had glazed over, though, and now he stared off into the distance somewhere. It was as though it had all come back to him: His grandparents were dead, and he was here in jail, charged with killing them.

"Jonathan," Fielder said, "we're going to have to make a decision, you and me." But even as he spoke the words, Fielder knew how utterly impossible it was going to be to enlist Jonathan's help in the process.

"What de-decision?"

"We have to decide if we should go to trial, or if we should agree that it's best for you to stay here, or a place like this, for some more time."

"I can stay here," Jonathan said. "Can I k-keep my blankets?"

Not, *"Will I ever get out of this place?"* Or, *"How long will I have to stay here?"* Faced with this monumental decision, all Jonathan wanted to know was, could he keep his blankets?

"Of course you can," Fielder said softly, "of course you can. But you have to decide."

"Decide?"

"Whether you want to stay here awhile, or have a trial."

But how was Jonathan supposed to know what a trial was? All he seemed to be able to do was to look back at Fielder and smile sheepishly. "You decide for me," he finally said.

"I can't do that," said Fielder. But by the time he got around to speaking the words, he was thirty miles away, and halfway home.

HELLO?"

"Hello, Jennifer."

"Matthew! How *are* you?"

"I'm good."

"I didn't expect you to call back so soon."

"Can't a guy miss you?"

"Of course you can." She laughed. "I mean, I'm glad that you do. But is that the only reason you called, just to tell me that?"

"No," he admitted. "I want you to come here."

"Are you sure?"

"I'm very sure."

"You told me to stay away," she reminded him. "Why the sudden change?" she asked.

"Two reasons," he said. "First, because I miss you terribly. Second, because I want you to help me talk to Jonathan."

There was only a momentary pause. Then Jennifer said, "Okay, if you think it's best."

"I think it's best."

"What made you change your mind?"

"It's time for us to start figuring out if we're going to insist on a trial for your brother, or if we're better off seeing if we can to work out some kind of a plea bargain that gets him out in a reasonable amount of time."

"Like how much?"

"I don't know yet. I'll have to talk to the DA."

"So how can I help with Jonathan?"

"I'm not at all sure you can," he admitted. "But I don't seem to be getting anywhere on my own. So I figured it might be worth your going into the jail with me, see what happens."

"And Troy?"

"Bring him, too, of course. But I don't think he should go in with us. That might be too much for Jonathan. And for Troy, too."

"We can be there tomorrow night," she said, "if that's soon enough."

"That's perfect."

*   *   *

WHEN FIELDER'S PHONE rang later that afternoon, it was Gil Cavanaugh. "Tried you three or four times," the DA said. "Your answering machine must've been off."

"*Everything* was off."

"I wanted to tell you personally that I was decertifying the case, Matt. But I'm sure you've heard, by this time."

"Yes, I have. But I appreciate the call. And my client and I are certainly very grateful."

"One for the visiting team," Cavanaugh said.

"Well, at least we've avoided a shutout."

"Just remember," the DA reminded him. "If you insist on playing things out, it's the home team that gets last licks."

"And if we don't?"

"I'm not going to lie to you, Matt. I've taken quite a beating in the polls over this case. My favorable rating is down to forty-two percent. It's never been below seventy, before this. I just want this thing to go away, and go away quick."

"And therefore—"

"And therefore, I'm ready to offer your client a plea. Murder Two, minimum sentences, to run concurrent."

Second-degree murder started at fifteen-to-life. Jonathan would serve fifteen years in a state prison. After that, his freedom would rest in the hands of a parole board, never a comforting thought. Fielder said nothing.

"I might even consider Man One, but only if he's willing to take it right away."

"With what kind of time?" Fielder asked. First-degree manslaughter carried as little as two-to-six, or as much as eight-and-a-third–to–twenty-five. Since there'd been two victims, the judge could double the time if he wanted to, by imposing the sentences consecutively. But he didn't have to.

"I'm willing leave it up to the judge," Cavanaugh said.

"You might be," said Fielder. "But I'm not."

"You're asking a lot," Cavanaugh said. "Let me think

about it, see what I could live with. In the meantime, why don't you talk to your client?"

"I did," Fielder told him. "This morning."

"And?"

"And he left it up to me."

Cavanaugh chuckled. "Don't you love having a client like that?"

"No. As a matter of fact, I hate it."

"He's going to have to do some real time here, Matt. Suppose he comes out after a few years, does something again? How'm I going to look then?"

"He's taking medication," Fielder explained. "It suppresses the sleepwalking. With that under control, he's a puppy dog."

"Tell me something, Matt. You really believe this sleepwalking crap?"

"I believe he was sleepwalking, yes."

"Sheeet," said Cavanaugh. "You guys got the story out pretty good, you really did. Then the media folks took it and ran with it. Before I knew it, I found myself painted into a corner. Hey, Matt, I've been around for a few years. I'm smart enough to recognize when I've got a no-win situation on my hands. So I'll do whatever I have to, in order to cut my losses. But do me a favor, Matt?"

"What's that?"

"Don't give me this *sleepwalking* bullshit. I know a murder for money when I see one."

For a moment, Fielder almost took the bait, almost launched into a long speech about how Jonathan was incapable of being greedy, that to him there was no difference between a ten-dollar bill and a ten-million-dollar estate. But he avoided the impulse.

"Whatever you say, Gil," he said instead. "You come up with the right numbers, we can call it anything you like."

Long after he'd hung up the phone, the words *"murder for money"* continued to ring in Fielder's ears. Weren't they almost the same words Bass McClure had used that very morning?

*   *   *

THE FOLLOWING DAY Fielder devoted almost exclusively to two of his least favorite things, shopping and cleaning, and one of his most favorite, cooking. He took an inventory of his food cabinets, and discovered that they were just about empty. He'd consumed just about everything edible in the cabin by the time the snowstorm had ended, and probably would've started in on his shoes pretty soon if it hadn't.

Shopping consisted of taking a drive to Blue Mountain Lake, where there was what passed for a supermarket, but in reality was a midsized deli that sold items at campground-store prices. There Fielder restocked on staples, picked out ingredients for a few days' worth of meals, and tried to imagine what kind of snacks a nine-year-old boy might be into. He settled on pretzels, peanut butter, bags of crackers shaped like little fish, a gallon of chocolate ice cream, and marshmallows to toast over the fire.

Back at the cabin, he put the groceries away, made up the couch as a guest bed, put clean towels in the bathroom, and began straightening things up. "Straightening up" is about as far as Fielder's version of cleaning goes. Vacuuming floors, dusting furniture, and washing windows are all high on the list of reasons why he left the city. In the country, there is little in the way of dust to speak of. You sweep the ashes out from under the woodburning stove from time to time, and you pick up any leaves and twigs that have wandered inside, but that's pretty much it. Other than that, you adopt what environmentalists like to call "natural solutions" to problems. Bothered by flies? Leave the spiderwebs alone for a week, and you'll be surprised how well the spiders take care of your fly problem. Crumbs get under the couch, or in some other hard-to-reach place? Relax, the mice will find them. The mice start getting out of hand? No problem; you borrow a neighbor's cat for a few days.

By early afternoon, Fielder was peeling and chopping vegetables, cooking chicken, and shaping meatballs out of ground turkey. He'd decided on pasta for dinner that night, since he wasn't sure what time Jennifer and Troy would be getting there, and chicken pot pie for the next day. He'd toyed with the idea of fish, but imagined a nine-year-old boy might turn up his nose at the thought, or pinch it shut from the odor. Then again, Fielder knew the aroma could produce a bonus of its own. One time he'd been simmering a seafood stew, complete with shrimp, scallops, and two or three kinds of fish, when a mother bear, with two cubs in tow, had ambled up to his front door. Fielder had obligingly divided the stew into four portions, but the bears had apparently been hoping for dessert, as well. He'd ended up having to shoo them away with a broom. When he'd told the story later to some local people, they'd taken him to task for feeding the bears, explaining that he wasn't doing them any favors. The lesson would only serve to embolden the animals, they pointed out, and cause trouble for everyone down the line. Still, sharing dinner with bears had been quite an experience for a city kid, and the memory of it had prompted Fielder to pick up some frozen shrimp at the supermarket that morning, just in case Troy was game.

As the afternoon wore on, Fielder realized that his anticipation went far beyond what Hillary Munson would have called his horniness for Jennifer. Certainly he wanted to go to bed with her again; he wasn't going to deny that. But a good part of the excitement was the thought of being in *his* bed with her, in *his* cabin. He realized, of course, that with Troy along, none of that would be possible. But the interesting thing was that it didn't seem to bother him too much. His preparations seemed to be extending well beyond his sexual desire for Jennifer; they included planning outings for the three of them, coming up with little touches around the cabin to please Jennifer, and taking pains to make Troy feel at home.

Home?

Was that what he was doing here? Playing family with Jennifer and her son? Setting up some sort of a trial run for a new life he was envisioning? *Nesting?* The realization was one that normally would have sent Matt Fielder into a total panic.

What was really scary was that it didn't.

JENNIFER AND TROY arrived around nine o'clock. There were hugs and kisses all around; apparently Troy hadn't yet reached the stage where such things were to be avoided like the plague. They seemed to love the cabin, and particularly the setting, though it was hard to see much outside in the darkness. The pasta and meatballs were a big hit, and Troy showed no sign of suspecting that it was really ground turkey he was eating.

When the subject of sleeping arrangements came up, it was Troy who asked if he could camp out on the floor, in front of the woodburning stove. He'd brought his sleeping bag along, hoping to spend a night in the woods, but the amount of snow on the ground convinced him not to. He was promptly awarded the floor.

That left the bedroom and the couch.

"You take the bed," Fielder told Jennifer. "I sleep on the couch half the time, as it is."

"No way," she said. "It's *your* bed."

"C'mon," he said. "I even changed the *sheets*. I do that every couple of months, whether they need it or not. Well, maybe not *that* often." He shut up at that point, suddenly aware that he'd been doing a standup comic routine for Jennifer's benefit.

She lay down on the couch and curled up, as if trying it out for size. "I'm fine right here," she announced.

Looking down at her, he had to admit that it looked like a pretty good fit. So it was decided, without another word. Or, put slightly differently, Fielder had lost their first argument, and it felt just fine.

"How does the fire stay hot all night?" Troy asked.

"Good question," said Fielder. "Grab a couple of those biggest logs over there. We'll stoke her up real good, and shut the doors tight. Then you'll see what happens."

Troy watched as Fielder placed the logs just so, leaving

a small amount of space between them for sufficient draft. "That should do it," he said, closing the doors and stepping back. Almost immediately, there was an audible clanking from the cast iron, as it began expanding from the sudden increase in heat.

"Good *stoking*," Troy said, pleased at the addition of a new, outdoorsy word to his vocabulary.

IN HIS DREAM, Fielder found himself locked in a fierce struggle to the death between the armies of good and evil. He was Saint Matthew, the defender of the hearth, the protector of the holy family unit. Pitted against him were the dark forces of lust, temptation, and sensuality. He alone could withstand their onslaughts. Vastly outnumbered by their legions, he continued to fight on valiantly, until the hordes drove him back and pinned him against the castle gates. On and on he battled, but to no avail. At last he was knocked from his feet and toppled backward. He lay helplessly on his back, awaiting the moment of his death. As the first of them set upon his defenseless body, he was able to make out a face. It was the beautiful female face of a Nordic vixen Fury, her blonde hair framing her perfect features, her red mouth opened wide, her white teeth gleaming in the moonlight. At first she seemed intent on going for his jugular, or clamping her jaws around the entire width of his throat. But even as she fell upon him, she dropped her head and aimed it toward his chest. Was it, then, his heart she intended to rip from his breast? Lower still her head sank. Did she mean instead to wrench out his stomach, his liver, to devour his very entrails? And would he be forced to watch, a modern-day Prometheus, doomed to eternal torture for the unpardonable sin of bringing fire into his cabin?

But no! Even lower her mouth sank, until at last he could feel it clamp onto its final target, and begin to gorge itself upon the naked flesh of his groin! He readied himself to cry out in agony from the unbearable pain of her bite—

only to feel instead the soft, wet warmth of her mouth, as it rose and fell rhythmically.

Reflexively his upper body jerked up into a sitting position. In the darkness, he felt a hand cup itself over his mouth to quiet him, and another press itself gently but firmly against his chest, gradually pushing him back down on the bed.

When at last his body convulsed, and the insides of his eyelids lit up in flashes of red and white and purple, he bit into his lower lip hard enough to taste blood, in order to keep from crying out. But he felt no pain.

It took him a long time before he could finally utter "my God" between gasps for air. Jennifer's muffled giggle from beside him told him she'd settle for even such an inarticulate expression of appreciation. And Fielder's very last thought, before he drifted back off to sleep, was that poor, long-suffering Prometheus simply might have misunderstood his orders; had he listened just a bit more carefully, he might be remembered to this day as the one who *stoked* fire.

25

DONUTS AND DOUBTS

ARE YOU SURE you're okay with this, Jennifer?"

"Yes, I'm okay. Just a little nervous, is all."

They were sitting in the visiting room of the jail, sharing a booth on one side of the plastic partition, waiting for Jonathan to be led into the other side. They'd dropped Troy off at the courthouse, in the capable hands of Dot Whipple, who'd promised to take him on a tour of the building. There were phone sets for both of them, an arrangement that had taken a bit of doing on Fielder's part. He'd asked the guard what they would have done if he'd brought along an interpreter, to help him converse, say, with a Spanish-speaking inmate. The guard had looked at him as though he were crazy. Apparently there *were* no Spanish-speaking inmates in Ottawa County. But he'd agreed to hook up another phone for them, anyway.

A door on the other side of the partition swung open, and Jonathan was led in. Fielder knew that his only warning of the visit would have been a piece of paper he'd been shown five minutes earlier, containing the names of the two people who'd come to visit him. He watched now as Jonathan, wrapped in his familiar blanket, sat down and smiled shyly at the sister he hadn't seen in almost ten years.

"Hello, Jonathan," said Jennifer into her phone.

Fielder had to point to Jonathan's phone, to remind him to pick it up.

"Hello," he said.

"Do you remember me?" she asked him.

"J-Jennifer," he said, by way of answer.

"How are you?" she asked.

"Warm." He smiled, touching his blanket.

"I've missed you."

"M-miss you, too," he said. Then a look of concern crossed his face, a knitting of his brow and a narrowing of eyes, as though he'd suddenly remembered something from long ago. And though he'd let the phone slip down against his chest, the word he now formed silently with his mouth was easy to read.

"Baby."

It was the same word he'd spoken to Fielder, back in October, when the subject of Jennifer had come up for the first time. The same word, in all likelihood, that Jonathan had uttered to Hillary Munson as early as September, when he'd been asked about surviving members of his family other than his brother. It struck Fielder as a classic example of association: You mentioned Jennifer—or even vaguely referred to her—and Jonathan immediately was reminded of his baby.

"He's not a baby anymore," Jennifer said. "He's a big boy now."

A look of confusion spread over Jonathan's face now, replacing the expression of concern that had been there only a moment earlier. In Jonathan's mind, it was as if his child had been forever frozen in time, and to him would always be a baby.

Fielder asked Jennifer if she had a photo. She nodded, set down her phone, and rummaged through her handbag. After a moment she found a wallet, and extracted from it a photo of Troy, blond-haired, smiling, and nine years old. She passed it through the opening in the partition to Jonathan. He stared at it for a long moment, as though totally unable to make the connection.

"Troy," she said. "His name is Troy. He's your son."

"Troy," Jonathan repeated, continuing to stare at the

photo. For an instant his eyes narrowed just a bit, as though he appeared to see something in it for the first time; Fielder dared to believe that it was true recognition they were witnessing. But then Jonathan took a corner of his blanket, and began rubbing it against the glossy surface of the photo, where some smudge or fingermark had evidently caught his attention. Watching the act sent a tiny shiver through Fielder's body, and took him back across the months to one of their earliest meetings together, when Jonathan had done the very same thing with a business card Fielder had handed him. For all of his failings and shortcomings, for all of his inabilities, Jonathan had a streak of compulsive cleanliness in him, a streak that compelled him to rub things clean. A streak, no doubt, that went a long way toward explaining the mystery of why no fingerprints had been found on his hunting knife. Even in his sleep, even in his unconscious, murderous rage, the strange compulsion to wipe things clean had manifested itself.

Jonathan went to pass the photo back to his sister, but she motioned that it was for him to keep. He pressed it against his chest, or where the blanket covered his chest. But to Fielder, it seemed that he still had absolutely no clue who the boy in the picture was.

"Jennifer's here to help us decide what we should do," Fielder explained. "Whether we want to have a trial and fight the case, or see if they'll let you plead guilty and come out in a few years."

Jonathan stared at Jennifer, as though waiting for her to announce what it was he was supposed to do. The two of them looked so much alike to Fielder that they could have been twins, this pair of stunningly beautiful, blond people, both of whom had now become so much a part of his life, in such very different ways.

"Can you stay here a while longer?" Jennifer asked her brother through the phone.

"It wouldn't be here," Fielder corrected her. "It might be somewhere not as nice." But as soon as he'd said it, he realized he was only complicating matters, making them harder for Jonathan to comprehend.

"Can you wait?" Jennifer asked her brother. She, at least, understood he needed things simplified, stripped to the basics.

He nodded. "I'm okay," he said. "They f-feed me, and Mr. Matt brings me b-blankets, k-keep me warm."

"I'll come visit you," she said. "And Troy, too."

"Troy," Jonathan repeated, as though trying out the sound of the name.

"I will, too," Fielder added.

But Jonathan was off somewhere in the distance, unreachable. Perhaps he was trying to make some sort of sense of things. Perhaps he was still trying to figure out, in his poor, damaged, child's mind, just what the connection might be between two people he knew only from their photographs—one of whom was named Baby, the other Troy.

It was hard to know.

THAT AFTERNOON, WHILE Jennifer, Troy, and Dot Whipple went up the block to the diner to get some lunch, Fielder dropped in on Gil Cavanaugh.

"Well, well, Matt. What brings you here?" The district attorney extended a hand, and this time Fielder took it. It had been four months since he'd caught Cavanaugh referring to him as a "Jew lawyer," and though he'd never forget the incident, he figured it was about time to forgive. Besides, he wanted something, and he knew he couldn't afford to let personal battles get in his client's way.

"I'm here to see if we can work out a disposition," he said.

Cavanaugh motioned to a chair, and Fielder took it. "What do you have in mind?" he asked.

"What I have in mind," Fielder said slowly, "is Man One, two-to-six, to be served in a hospital."

Cavanaugh smiled his politician's smile. "Even if I thought that was an appropriate disposition," he said, "the judge would never go for it."

Fielder looked him in the eye. "The judge will go for it," he said, "if you tell him to."

"What makes you think so?"

"I'm new around these parts,". said Fielder, trying his best to sound like Bass McClure, "but unless I miss my bet, you're the one in charge here. I may be wrong about that, of course, but I don't think so." With that he stood up, thanked Cavanaugh for the meeting, and walked out the door.

The idea, of course, was to play directly to the man's ego. If Cavanaugh really *was* in charge, he'd want to talk the judge into accepting the plea, just to prove how much clout he had. And on top of that, hadn't Cavanaugh said only a couple of days ago that he wanted the case to go away, and go away quickly? Well, now Fielder was giving him a chance, a guilty plea in a case the district attorney could lose at trial, if enough people bought that sleepwalking stuff the media kept talking about. Come election time, he could run as a softer, gentler Gil Cavanaugh, who knew when to go easy on a poor, unfortunate soul. Who knows? It might even get him 90 percent of the vote, next time around.

Fielder found Jennifer, Troy, and Dot Whipple at the diner, just in time to pick up the check. He shot Jennifer a wink, trying to tell her that things had gone as well as he'd hoped at his meeting with the DA. But it was difficult to read her return wink, which might have signaled that she understood, or might have related to the night before, for all he knew.

Whichever was the case, for Matt Fielder it had been a pretty good twelve hours, all things considered.

DRIVING BACK TO his cabin that day, Fielder had every reason to feel on top of the world. Sitting in the car alongside him was the woman he was in love with. In the backseat was a boy who, in Fielder's mind, had already begun to look up to him as the father he'd never known. An hour ago, Fielder had taken a bold first step toward successfully resolving the most serious case he'd ever handled, involving a truly deserving client he cared very much about. The early indications were that he might actually be able to pull off a result that would have seemed nothing short of miraculous, only two weeks ago.

In a word, he had *momentum* on his side.

But students of momentum know what a fickle creature she can be, how she can shift her affections as quickly and as unpredictably as an April breeze. And in this particular case, the amount of time Fielder would have to savor his good fortune would be measured not in days or weeks, but in mere minutes.

They were heading south on Route 30. Fielder turned to his passengers. "Anybody need anything before we leave civilization?" he asked.

Jennifer laughed, but said nothing. Perhaps it was her way of saying that, like Fielder, she had everything in the world she needed at the moment.

But apparently not so for Troy. "Food?" he asked.

"Food?" Fielder was incredulous. "You just finished eating, ten minutes ago!"

"But I didn't have *dessert.*"

"I'm afraid you've got a lot to learn about nine-year-old boys," said Jennifer.

"I guess so," Fielder admitted. "There's a bakery over in Raquette Lake, might be open."

"If I remember correctly," Jennifer said, "there's an all-night Dunkin' Donuts place near Pine Hollow, if you take County Twenty-seven. If it's still there."

And that was it, right there. The single blink in time when things changed yet again. Changed ever so slightly, ever so subtly. But changed in such a way that from that instant on, for Matt Fielder, nothing would ever be quite the same.

The point, in other words, when the momentum shifted once again.

*   *   *

THEY WENT FOR donuts, and ended up buying a baker's dozen—chocolate cream and jelly-filled and sugar-coated and the special of the day, key lime. Troy worked it out so that no two of the thirteen flavors they ended up with were the same. He even included a Dutch apple just to make things work out, despite the fact that he hated cinnamon. He began sampling his favorites even before they were out of the store, giving high marks to the blueberry and black raspberry, but thumbs down to the lemon and banana.

Out in the parking lot, Fielder took a bite out of the key lime. Pale green filling oozed out and dripped onto his jacket. "Damn!" he said. "I'm going back in to get some water, see if I can wipe this stuff off before it stains."

Heading back to the store, he was vaguely aware of Jennifer calling after him, but he couldn't make out what it was she wanted. All he kept hearing, over and over again, were the words of Bass McClure, describing the very same Dunkin' Donuts place. *"Nice folks,"* McClure had told him. *"Only been there about a year or so."* If McClure had been right about that, how was it that Jennifer, who claimed not to have set foot in the state in almost ten years, could possibly remember the place?

Unless, of course, she was lying.

Back inside, he dabbed at the spot with a moist paper napkin. "So tell me," he said to the woman behind the counter. "How long you folks been open here?"

"Come the first of March," she said, "it'll be just a year."

"What was here before then?"

"Oh, it was a donut place, but not a *Dunkin' Donuts* place. There's a big diff'rence, you know."

"I sure do," he said.

THEY STAYED ANOTHER day, Jennifer and Troy. The chicken pot pie that night was good, even if no bears showed up to share it with them. In the middle of the night, Jennifer again came into Fielder's bed, whispering to him that Troy was a sound sleeper who wouldn't wake up. They made love slowly, silently, falling asleep afterward in each other's arms. When Fielder awoke sometime later, it was still dark, but his arms were empty.

IN THE MORNING they drove up to the north end of Stillwater Reservoir, where they hiked a five-mile loop. They saw deer, moose, and bald eagles. And when Jennifer and Troy left that afternoon for New Hampshire, it was with hugs and kisses, declarations of love, and solemn promises to see one another as soon possible.

And through it all, Fielder had the bizarre sensation of being outside of himself, of watching his body going through the motions. He desperately wanted to say something to her, to ask her about the donut place, to clear up what he hoped was nothing but a silly mistake on her part.

But he didn't.

LATER THAT DAY, after Jennifer and Troy were gone, and quiet had returned to the cabin, Fielder phoned Hillary Munson in Albany.

"Remember how that letter from Jennifer to Sue Ellen referred to *photos*?" he asked her. "As in more than one?"

Hillary remembered.

"I want you to find out what Sue Ellen did with the photo she didn't save," he said. "I want to know if that's the one Jonathan ended up with."

"First thing tomorrow," Hillary said. "Mind telling me what's going on?"

"I really don't know," he said.

Which was pretty much the truth.

THE FOLLOWING DAY Fielder got a phone call from Gil Cavanaugh. Judge Summerhouse was away, he said. The beginning of February each year, he and his wife flew down to the Florida keys, where they had a time-share in a condominium. The judge was a big sport fisherman, Cavanaugh said. He'd probably come back with a sailfish, or a marlin.

Great, Fielder thought. So Jonathan's fate lay in the

hands of a man whose idea of fun was taking beautiful fish and killing them—not for food, but because they might look good hanging on the walls of his chambers.

He thanked Cavanaugh for the call.

THAT SAME DAY, Hillary Munson drove three hours from Albany to Silver Falls, to re-interview Sue Ellen Blodgett. Once again, the meeting took place in Sue Ellen's kitchen, and once again it was attended by Sue Ellen's three daughters.

"There's one thing we'd like to clear up," Hillary said. "From the letter Jennifer sent you, it looks like she enclosed more than one photo of Troy. But there was only one in the envelope."

"Right," Sue Ellen said, lacing up one of her daughter's sneakers. "I brought the other one to Jonathan."

"How come?"

"I don't know if I can tell you," she said. "Jennifer swore me to silence about this."

"Jennifer needs you to tell us," Hillary lied. "And so does Jonathan."

"God's honest truth?"

"God's honest truth."

"Jennifer called me a short time after she sent me the letter," Sue Ellen explained. "She asked me to bring one of the snapshots to Jonathan. She wanted him to have it, to keep."

"So you did?"

Sue Ellen nodded, as she began brushing the hair of a second daughter. "It was like a trade," she said.

"A trade?"

"Jennifer had asked me if I could get something of Jonathan's, in exchange, like, for her to keep."

"And you did that?" Hillary asked.

"You sure it's okay for me to be telling you this?" Sue Ellen asked.

"I'm very sure."

"Well, okay. She asked me to get a lock of his hair."

"Oh?"

"Only we didn't have a scissors or a knife, or anything else to cut with," Sue Ellen said. "So I pulled some hairs out of his head. He let me," she added. "He didn't seem to mind the pain none."

"And what did you do with them?" Hillary asked.

There was a pause while Sue Ellen held her daughter's barrette in her mouth. "I put 'em in a little Ziploc baggie, and mailed 'em to Jennifer."

"How many of them were there?"

"Oh, I don't know. A dozen, I guess."

"And that was it?"

Sue Ellen nodded. "You won't tell Jennifer I told, will you?"

"No," said Hillary. "I won't tell Jennifer."

BUT SHE DID tell Matt Fielder, first chance she got, from a pay phone at a Mobil station. And as soon as he heard about it, Fielder called Pearson Gunn.

"Remember that business about only six of the seven hairs from the crime scene matching Jonathan's?" he said.

Gunn remembered. It had bothered him, too.

"What's the story with the seventh hair?"

"I don't know," Gunn said.

"I need you to find out," Fielder told him.

THE URGENCY IN Fielder's voice made it clear to Gunn that more was called for than an evening at the Dew Drop Inn in Cedar Falls. Ever protective of his confidential source, CS-1, Gunn still hems and haws when asked to reveal exactly what it was he did that day, or perhaps that night, in pursuit of the solution to what by that time had become known in the defense camp as the Mystery of the Seventh Hair. What is certain, however, is that when Gunn dropped in at Matt Fielder's cabin the following afternoon, he had some answers.

"The hairs were all collected from the immediate area," he reported. "Either picked up from the bed itself, or the floor right next to it. There were maybe two dozen, all told. Most of them matched up with samples later taken from the victims. Of the remaining seven, all were blond, and all had roots, meaning the lab people were able to extract DNA from the follicles. Six proved to be positive matches with DNA found in Jonathan's blood sample."

"And the seventh?"

Gunn looked at his notes. "They've ruled out the Armbrusts, both of whom have gray hair. Turned out one of the crime-scene investigators was blond, but they took his blood and compared DNA, and it's not a match. So they're still classifying it as an X, for 'unknown.' Cavanaugh and his people think there mighta been contamination in the collection process. Or the lab mighta messed up, or something like that."

"Why's that?" Fielder asked.

"According to the lab, the DNA from the seventh hair is *similar* to Jonathan's, but not *identical*."

"What the hell is *that* supposed to mean?"

"Funny," said Gunn, stroking his beard. "I wondered the same thing. So this morning, before coming over here, I looked through the DNA reports the DA supplied us, found the name of the lab that did the testing, and gave them a call."

"And?"

Gunn leafed through his notes some more. "Got ahold of a woman named Yvonne," he said. "Yvonne St. Germaine. Works for an outfit called GenType, someplace near Rochester. She's the one who did most of the testing. And I gotta tell you," Gunn observed, "it's pretty interesting stuff."

Fielder sat back. Gunn generally liked to tell a story when he reported in with results, and there was never any use in rushing him. Sooner or later, he'd get down to the important part.

"Yvonne sticks to what she told the troopers," Gunn said. "Number seven is *similar* to numbers one through six, but it's not *identical*. So I asked her the significance of that.

She said it could very well be be nothing but pure coincidence. Or there might possibly be—let's see—'a genetic relationship between the donors,' " he read. "That might explain it, too." Gunn paused to look up from his notes, to make certain Fielder was still following him. "You know," he said, "like parent and child?"

Or, for that matter, like brother and sister.

THE SUN CAME out that afternoon, and the temperature rose uncharacteristically, causing what snow was left on the ground to melt and puddle. By nightfall, with the mercury still up in the mid-forties, the local radio station was broadcasting predictions of an early spring.

That night, Fielder allowed himself the luxury of an open stove for the first time in what seemed like ages. He turned off all the lights in his cabin and sat in front of the fire, hypnotized by the licking flames and dancing sparks. And he thought about the unthinkable.

For weeks now, indeed for months, he and his team had been operating on the assumption that Jonathan Hamilton had killed his grandparents in his sleep. They'd unearthed an ancient letter that documented his propensity to sleepwalk. They'd searched for precedents in the literature, and found them, both in medical publications and case law. From there, it was as if the idea had suddenly sprouted wings and taken flight. They'd brought in experts to test the likelihood of the scenario, and the experts had agreed with everything they'd suggested. Next they'd gone to the public and asked whether, since Jonathan wasn't awake at the time, he ought to be held criminally accountable for his actions nevertheless. The public had answered with a resounding no. That answer had convinced the prosecutor as well, who in turn now was going to try to sell it to the judge. Thus, from a tiny scrap of information, they'd succeeded in taking a surefire candidate for death row, and transformed him into a poster boy for forgiveness.

But where had it all come from?

It had come from Jennifer.

It had been Jennifer who'd casually let slip her fear that Troy might turn into a sleepwalker, and made Fielder coax out the basis of that fear, which turned out to be Jonathan's sleepwalking. It had been Jennifer who'd sent them looking for Sue Ellen Simms for corroboration; Jennifer who'd mailed the letter off to Sue Ellen years before, knowing her friend well enough to know she'd save it. Sue Ellen herself knew nothing of Jonathan's sleepwalking, other than what she knew from Jennifer. The Armbrusts knew nothing of it, either, only that special locks had been installed on the doors. Jonathan's own *brother*, P. J. (who certainly should have known about it if anyone did), knew nothing about it, despite his willingness to come and testify. Even Jonathan himself knew nothing about it.

It all went back to Jennifer.

Every single bit of it.

Then there'd been her slip about the Dunkin' Donuts place. If she hadn't set foot in the state since fleeing her family almost a decade ago, how on earth did she know about a place that had been there less than a year?

Or had she been back?

Had she been back on the night of the murders?

What was it that had possessed Jennifer to ask Sue Ellen for a lock of her brother's hair? Did she have some diabolical plan in mind way back then? Some plan she knew she'd need it for, someday? It seemed almost too crazy to be thinkable. Yet why else would she have gone to such lengths, and sworn her friend to such secrecy, over something that seemed so innocent? And why else would she have omitted any mention of it from the letter (the letter she knew Sue Ellen would obediently save), choosing instead to phone with separate instructions? Certainly she'd meant all along for one of the photos to be delivered to Jonathan. Otherwise, why would she have placed two of them in the envelope in the first place?

What was it she'd really wanted with her brother's hairs? Had she simply been interested in a keepsake from her past—the same past she'd fled and vowed never to return to, going so far as to change her name to cover her tracks? A keepsake from the very one who'd raped her, continued to carry on his incestuous relationship with her, and fathered her illegitimate child?

Or had she wanted the hairs for some far darker purpose, preserving them in their little plastic bag over the years as part of her grand design? Had she then slipped the bag into her pocket one evening, toward the very end of August, and driven through the night to the place she cursed for all her misfortune? Had she fingered the plastic bag nervously as she sipped coffee in an all-night donut place, where she tried to summon up the courage to continue on to her destination? Had she later sprinkled them over the mutilated bodies of her grandparents, even as they lay dying of their wounds? And had she perhaps grown careless during the process, and lost one of own hairs?

But *why*?

Whatever could have driven her to destroy her grandparents and, at the same time, ensure that Jonathan would be blamed? Hadn't she said she'd forgiven him for what he'd done to her?

Or had that, too, been a lie?

And it was Bass McClure's words that came flooding back to Fielder once again. *"Can't remember if it was the older brother who was responsible, or the father."* Fielder had held his tongue at the time, knowing that McClure was wrong, but respecting what little was left of Jennifer's privacy.

But maybe McClure had been right. Maybe it was P. J. who was Jonathan's father—P. J., who'd smiled crookedly at Pearson Gunn and Hillary Munson when the subject of Jennifer had come up, and told them that his sister had always had "a little bit of taste for things."

Or maybe it was Jennifer's own father.

Which was a notion that opened up a whole new can of worms. The fire—the fire that Spider Squitieri insisted had been no accident. Suppose it *hadn't* been a matter of Jonathan's sleepwalking and playing with matches? Suppose it had been Jennifer, bent on revenge? And had Jonathan himself been meant to die in it, along with his parents? Hadn't Klaus Armbrust had to break through a window in order to pull him out, and even then, not in time to save Jonathan from further brain damage? And when had the fire been, for that matter? Not too long after Jennifer's flight to New Hampshire, just after the birth of her son, when her anger was still simmering, perhaps even boiling over.

Fielder got up from the floor and walked over to the woodpile. He picked up couple of pieces of maple, and placed them on the fire. He gave them a shove with the poker, and there was a bright spray of sparks. After a moment, the lower log ignited into orange-and-blue flames. Fielder sank back down to the floor, resumed his position, and tried to pick up his train of thought.

But it was difficult. The problem was, it was all so iffy, so far-fetched, so utterly preposterous. Was Jennifer really capable of murdering four people over the course of eight and a half years? Had she decided finally to spare Jonathan's life only so that he could become the scapegoat, ensuring that she herself would never be suspected of anything? Did her lust for revenge against a dysfunctional family really run that deep?

This time it wasn't just something Bass McClure had said that came back to him. It was the words of Gil Cavanaugh—Fielder's two-faced adversary, whom Fielder had so successfully outmaneuvered and duped and painted into a corner, until now he was all but ready to surrender. *"I'll do whatever I have to,"* Cavanaugh had said, *"in order to cut my losses. But do me a favor, Matt. Don't give me this sleepwalking bullshit. I know a murder for money when I see one."*

Was Cavanaugh right, after all? Were these killings the result not of sleepwalking, and not even of revenge? Had Jennifer acted out of nothing but good, old-fashioned greed? Fielder thought back to the wills. Jennifer had known that both she and P. J. had been disinherited by their family, that neither of them would see any of the millions that had been handed down from generation to generation of Hamiltons. There, at least, she'd been telling the truth. Next she must have figured out that, upon the deaths of her grandparents, everything would go to Jonathan, as the only one who'd stayed on at the estate. But if Jonathan happened to be convicted of the murders—even if he pleaded guilty and received the short sentence Fielder was trying to work out for him—he'd be disqualified from inheriting a penny.

It would all go to Troy.

And, therefore, to Jennifer.

Was that what had consumed her all these years? Was that what had fueled her plan, day in and day out, as she scraped her pennies together on her fold-down aluminum table top, in her miserable, godforsaken trailer park? Struggling to make her car payments the first of every month, while knowing that back at Flat Lake, the vast Hamilton wealth was being wasted on her senile grandparents and her retarded brother? Had Cavanaugh stumbled upon the truth in spite of himself? Was he right about it having been a "murder for money," even as he was wrong about who'd committed it?

It was enough to drive a person totally crazy, Fielder decided. What on earth had he been doing for the past hour? Concocting a truly preposterous scenario, based on a series of absurdly tenuous assumptions, for which he had absolutely no evidence whatsoever. The more he thought about it, the more he realized that none of it made sense. Here he'd indicted, tried, and convicted Jennifer without so much as confronting her with his suspicions. And what were those suspicions based on, when you came right down to it? That she'd remembered a place as a Dunkin' Donuts, when it was actually some other kind of donut shop? What kind of a slip was that? Would he ever argue such a trivial inconsistency to a jury? Surely they'd laugh him out of the courtroom if he did. Besides, if given half a chance, no doubt Jennifer would be able to come up with a perfectly logical explanation for her mistake, as well as all the rest of the stuff he was imagining.

A numbness spread through Fielder's body. He suddenly felt totally drained, exhausted beyond the point of being able to think anymore. It was time for bed, time for sleep.

Time for escape.

He reached back behind him to push himself up into a standing position. As he did so, his hand slipped an inch or two under the sofa he'd been leaning against, and he felt something. He reached underneath the springs and groped for whatever it was, until he found it and retrieved it. In the firelight, he could make out its shape, but not its color. It was a brush, a woman's hairbrush. No doubt it was Jennifer's, since it had been she who'd slept on his sofa for two nights. He wondered vaguely if she was even aware she'd lost it. Probably not, he decided. Didn't all women have dozens of extra brushes?

Before heading for the bedroom, he placed it on top of the bookcase in the corner.

26

FIELDER'S CHOICE

Fielder awoke to the ringing of his telephone. The numbers on his clock were too fuzzy to read, but he could see that it was light outside. In early February, that meant in had to be seven, seven-thirty, at least. He never slept that late.

He found the receiver, picked it up, and managed to say something approximating "Hello" into it.

"Hey, Matt, Gil Cavanaugh here. Hope I didn't wake you."

"Not a chance," Fielder said. "What time is it?"

"Ten of nine."

"Jesus! What's up?"

"Judge Summerhouse is back," Cavanaugh said. "I'm going over to see him later this morning. Wanted to know if you'd like to go with me."

Where, Fielder wondered, had this sudden burst of ethics come from? He considered the offer briefly before saying, "No, I think you may have a better chance without me." Which was true: Fielder's presence would only serve to add a confrontational aspect to the meeting, and make it less likely that the judge would go along with the disposition Fielder had proposed. Better for the two cronies to put their heads together and see if there was some way they could live with it without losing face.

"You sure?" Cavanaugh asked.

"I'm sure," Fielder told him. "Tell him I've given you permission to do it on an ex parte basis." A bit of lawyer-speak never hurt. Why say something in English, after all, when plain everyday Latin would suffice?

"Okay, Matt. I'll call you later, let you know how it went. Unless you're able to hear the judge's reaction from there, that is."

A touch of humor from the home team. Then again, Cavanaugh had the advantage of being awake.

Fielder set down the phone and looked at his watch. It really was almost nine o'clock. He tried to remember what time it had been when he'd finally gone to bed last night. Three? Four? What was it that had kept him up so late?

The answer came to him, and with it, the absurdity of it all. He'd stayed up concocting fantastic scenarios pointing to Jonathan's innocence. And of all the people in the world he might have picked to pin the crime on, he'd managed to come up with Jennifer—surely the unlikeliest candidate of all, the very individual who'd been trying her hardest to help Jonathan, and who'd already been largely responsible for saving him from the death penalty. And what was it that had set Fielder's fantasy in motion? A mistake about how long a stupid donut place had been in operation! That's what.

He wondered what Freud might have had to say about such fanciful thinking. Was Fielder so threatened over the prospect of getting involved in a lasting relationship that he had to turn the object of his desire into an ogre, a quadruple murderer, at that? Wasn't that a wee bit drastic, perhaps, even for someone whose idea of paradise was to live like a hermit in the woods?

He spent the better part of an hour puttering around in his cabin, accomplishing nothing. He tried to read, but found he couldn't concentrate. Every few minutes he'd catch himself stealing a glance at his watch, wondering why the phone hadn't rung yet. When was it Cavanaugh had said he was meeting with the judge? Later this morning? That could mean anytime before one, Fielder knew. Hell, to a lawyer, that could be four o'clock in the afternoon.

Fielder put on a jacket and walked outside. It was still on the warm side, probably right around freezing. He knew he should take advantage of the midwinter thaw and split some wood, burn off a little of his nervous energy. But for some reason, he felt the need to get away from home, to put a little distance between himself and his cabin. He walked over to his Suzuki. It was salt-streaked and splattered with mud, and the windshield was an opaque gray, except where the wipers had cleared twin semicircles of transparency. Say what you might, the little car had gotten him through winter so far. He stepped closer and gave it an affectionate pat on the fender. He couldn't see through the driver's-side window, but he knew the keys would be in the ignition, where they belonged.

It had taken him a full six months to learn to leave them there. When he'd first moved up to the Adirondacks, not only would he remove them, he'd also lock the doors each time he left the car, a New York City habit that—though he knew it was ridiculous—he seemed powerless to break. Over time, he'd forced himself to lock it up only at the end of the day, before going to bed. Then, one night, he left it unlocked, though entirely by mistake. In the morning, miraculously, the car was still there. Gradually, Fielder had managed to become bolder, leaving the keys first under the floormat, next in the ashtray, and finally right in the ignition itself. Eventually, he got to the point where he was able to do so overnight—but not without worrying if he wasn't being overly reckless. Surely he'd wake up one morning to discover he'd been victimized by some kid who'd wandered up from the South Bronx in search of a set of wheels to take for a joyride! It was only much later—when it had become truly second nature to go to bed with his keys purposefully left in the ignition, with his cabin door unlocked by choice and not inadvertence, and his mind nevertheless free of fears—that Fielder could say he'd finally shaken the city mentality and arrived in the woods for good.

The engine started on the first try.

Coming out of the driveway, he turned right and headed toward Big Moose Lake. He picked up Route 28 at Eagle Bay, and took it as far as Blue Mountain Lake, where he headed north on Route 30. He had no particular destination in mind, he told himself. It just felt good being out on the road. He made believe he was simply a passenger along for the ride, that it was the Sidekick that was in charge of deciding where they were headed, much the way a trusty dowsing rod might lead a well-digger in search of water.

But he knew better. As each mile passed, and as each turn came up, he knew where they were going.

As BEFORE, EVERYTHING was still, just as he'd known it would be. There was no sound of man in the air, and no evidence of him in sight. He was the only one there. There were tracks on the path leading downhill, but they were the tracks of deer, of rabbit, and of wild turkey. In the shelter of the trees, the snow was white and untouched.

And all around him, silence.

As he neared the water's edge, he wondered if he'd be rewarded, as he had been last time, by the sight of the lake in its smooth, unbroken flatness. He found himself hoping that it might be so. He desperately needed to see it again that way, and no different. For some reason, it took on an importance he couldn't quite understand, and certainly couldn't have begun to explain, had he been called upon to do so. He just needed to see it again as it had been before.

But as he reached the spot where the trees ended and the bank dropped off, he realized that he was to be disappointed. Things had changed. Covering the ice was a layer of snow—beautiful enough in its whiteness, but broken here and there by the crisscross of track lines laid down by earlier visitors, four-legged and two-legged alike.

The breathtaking, perfect flatness had been reduced to a thing of the past.

Gone.

*   *   *

CAVANAUGH'S CALL CAME at one-thirty. Fielder picked up on the third ring, his heart pounding as though he was awaiting the return of a jury filing back into the courtroom to announce its verdict.

"It's a go," the DA said. "I gotta tell you, Matt, it took some doing. But Summerhouse'll go along with us, as long as we do it quickly, before public sentiment shifts again. Like, tomorrow. You there, Matt?"

"I'm here."

"You should be *thrilled*."

And so he should have been.

FIELDER SAT ACROSS from Jonathan Hamilton once again. Once again, they were separated by the Plexiglas partition. Once again they spoke through telephones. This time, they were alone. Jennifer was nowhere in sight. She was back in New Hampshire with Jonathan's son. Or nephew. Or brother.

Fielder began the conversation by asking Jonathan for the umpteenth time if he knew whether or not he'd caused the deaths of his grandparents. For the umpteenth time, Jonathan answered him by saying he didn't know. Fielder had expected as much; at the same time, he had to ask the question.

He told Jonathan that the time had come for them to make their decision. "We've worked it out so you can leave here and go to a hospital," he said. "They'll want to keep you two years, maybe a little more. After that, they'll let you go home."

Wherever "home" might be, by that time.

"If you don't want to do that, then we have to take a chance. If we're real lucky, you could go home much sooner. If we're unlucky, you could end up staying in a place like this forever."

Jonathan held the phone pressed to his ear for a long time, as though waiting for more words, more help, more clues. When finally he spoke, it was into the mouthpiece.

But even as his lips moved, his eyes remained riveted on Fielder's.

"I don't w-want to stay here forever," is what he said.

THAT NIGHT, FIELDER took up his familiar spot on the floor in front of the woodburning stove. He leaned back against the front of his sofa, watched the flames dance against the darkness, and wondered what on earth it was he was supposed to do.

One thing he knew for sure. They didn't teach you stuff like this in law school.

Not even in Death School.

The thing was, when it came right down to it, he really knew no more than his client did. He couldn't say for sure if Jonathan was guilty of murdering his grandparents in cold blood, wasn't responsible because he'd been asleep when he killed them, or was totally innocent of everything.

Not that there wasn't a way to find out, he knew.

All it would take would be a blood sample from Jennifer, to submit for testing. If her DNA wasn't the same as that of the seventh hair—the one that didn't quite match Jonathan's—then Fielder would know that all of the previous night's ravings were nothing but the product of his overworked imagination.

On the other hand, if it *was* the same, that was a different story altogether. Then he'd have to confront her about everything.

Confront her, and accuse her.

Of course, there was the little matter of obtaining a blood sample. Just how was he supposed to go about doing that? Perhaps when they were lying in bed one night, in the midst of making passionate love, he could turn to her and say, "Oh, by the way, I think you just might be a quadruple murderer. Might I trouble you for a blood sample?"

But then again, could he *not* do it?

Didn't he owe his client that much?

Could he go ahead and plead someone guilty to a crime he might not have committed?

One way of answering that question was to say, Of course he could—lawyers did it all the time, and rightly so. Some clients lied to you so much that you reached the point where you couldn't tell if they were guilty or not. That didn't mean you forbade them from accepting a good plea bargain when one came along. Other clients turned out to have been so drunk or stoned at the time, that they often didn't know what they'd done. There were even rare instances where defendants' memories had become impaired by injury or illness, resulting in cases of amnesia. In such situations, the law permitted guilty pleas, even where defendants were unable to honestly acknowledge their guilt in open court.

But those were only the legal rules. There had to be more to it than that.

Suppose Fielder could truly establish that it was Jennifer, and not Jonathan, who'd committed the crimes? Fielder himself would emerge as a hero. Jonathan would be released, free to go home. Cleared of any wrongdoing, he'd also be permitted to inherit the Hamilton fortune.

But what was left for Jonathan back at Flat Lake? His parents were dead, and now his grandparents, too. Would he live with the Armbrusts? They were old, and hardly the sort of nurturing company Jonathan needed. And what would he do with millions of dollars? All he ever asked for was to be fed and sheltered and kept warm. Money was something he didn't even understand, let alone need.

And Jennifer? She'd be arrested and prosecuted, not only for the stabbing deaths of her grandparents, but possibly for the arson deaths of her parents as well. There was enough there to send her away for life four times over. Maybe worse. Juries tend to take a dim view of those who try to pin their crimes on others.

As for Troy, he'd become—what was the expression they used?—a "ward of the state," that was it.

So whereas Jonathan's guilty plea might bring some closure to the long line of tragedies that had plagued the Hamilton family, his exoneration would trigger a whole new chapter, more bizarre and more sensational by far than any before it. With Jennifer as the target.

Was that what Jonathan wanted?

But even if he didn't owe it to Jonathan to turn the tables on Jennifer, didn't he perhaps owe it to the public? The answer was an unqualified yes, he decided quickly—*if* he believed that not only had she killed, but was likely to do it once again. But he *didn't* believe that. How *could* he believe that? He loved Jennifer. Two days ago, he'd been ready to spend the rest of his life with her.

And, if he was satisfied that she *wasn't* going to do anything like it again, was he nonetheless duty-bound to try to uncover what had really happened? Wasn't that what the process was supposed to be, after all, a search for the truth?

But surely that was the job of others. Wasn't Fielder, who still loved her even as he suspected her, the very last person on the face of the earth who should now have to turn on her and accuse her?

Life was often a matter of conflicts, he knew, of choices between unpleasant alternatives. You were expected to step up, pay your money, and take your chances; that was all there was to it. You were never supposed to look back. Regrets were for suckers.

But this was different. This wasn't just your ordinary, everyday, garden-variety conflict. This was a choice that comes along maybe once in a lifetime.

And the phrase that came back to Matt Fielder wasn't one out of the fine print of *Black's Law Dictionary*. It wasn't some wise Latin maxim borrowed from Caesar's time, or some bit of lawyerspeak designed to confuse and impress the common folk. It wasn't something solemnly intoned by the likes of Oliver Wendell Holmes or Learned Hand or Benjamin Cardozo.

None of that.

Instead, it came drifting across the years from a Saturday afternoon in summer, long, long ago. It came from the memory of a makeshift ballfield, adjacent to a dirt parking lot. It came damp with sweat, streaked with grass stains, and coated with infield dust. It came in a nasal Lower East Side voice, from a kid named Whitey Ryan. And it came in two words.

Fielder's choice.

What was the lesson he was supposed to have taken away with him that day? With the game safely in hand, and the ball bouncing your way, what was it you were supposed to do?

EVEN AS THE *ball comes your way, out of the corner of your eye you can see the runner breaking from second and beginning to dig for third—something he's got no business doing. You've got a play on him, you know. You can wheel around and fire to third, try and cut him down before he can slide in under the tag. A good throw nails him by two steps. Or you can play it safe, go for the sure out at first, just thirty feet away.*

This time it's not Goober Wilson's glove the ball's in; it's yours. The runner heading to third presents a tempting target. He never should have gone for it. He doesn't deserve to make it.

But when it comes right down to it, he doesn't matter. What you need to do right now is to fight the impulse to grandstand, to avoid going for too much. It isn't about whether or not the runner deserves to make it to third safely. And it surely isn't your job to punish him.

You're supposed to take care of business. You're supposed to respect momentum. *You're supposed to remember that if you don't, it can shift once again, in a heartbeat. And you can end up blowing the whole ball game.*

He knew he ought to forget about this crazy business of Jennifer and Dunkin' Donuts, of the two photographs and the seventh hair. *Leave well enough alone,* he told himself. *Get Jonathan his two-year deal, and be done with it.* Because that's what it had all come down to, this *Fielder's choice* of his: being smart enough to go for the safe play, the sure thing.

But even as he knew all that, Matt Fielder also knew that there was no way on earth he was going to be able to do it. Not any more than Goober Wilson had been able to do it some thirty years earlier. The thing was, try as you might, there's just no way on earth you can play it safe, not with that runner streaking for third, daring you to go for him.

You scoop the ball up. You pivot. You cock your arm. And you put every last ounce of whatever you've got into that throw to third. And you hope for the best.

There's simply no other way to play the game.

HE LIFTED HIMSELF up from the floor. He placed a half log of oak on the fire before shutting the doors of the stove for the night and plunging the cabin into darkness. Needing some light so he could straighten up the room, he walked over to a bookcase in the corner, where he flicked on the switch of an old table lamp. An unfamiliar object next to it caught his eye: a pink, plastic object. For a second, its presence there confused him; he couldn't think of anything pink he owned. Not him, a macho child of the fifties.

But then he remembered. It was Jennifer's hairbrush. The one he'd found under his sofa, just the night before.

He picked it up. White clumps of bristles were set into the pink plastic in neat rows. Idly, he counted them off. There were four rows across, and eleven clumps of bristles to each row. Forty-four clumps in all. His own age, 44. Was there, he wondered, some sort of special significance in that?

Then something else caught his eye, something between the rows. He squinted to try to make it out. It was a hair, a single hair. Gently, he unsnaked it from the bristles. It came away easily enough. Holding it up to the light, he could see it was long, blonde, and straight. One end came to a point. The other end seemed to have something attached—a root it was.

A follicle.

He looked about the room, and spotted a small glass

bottle on the windowsill, one of the ones he'd picked up for collecting samples of his well-water for potability testing. Each bottle was sterile inside, and sealed around the top with plastic.

He twisted the top until the plastic seal broke, and the cap came off. Carefully, he dropped the hair into the bottle and replaced the cap.

Back in college, Fielder and some buddies had gone down to the Village one night to check out a standup comedian who was said to be headed places. He was a thin, balding, nerd of a man, with glasses that kept slipping down his long nose, and a kind of whiny, apologetic way of speaking. He told this story about how he'd been walking along in the city one day, when he'd noticed something small lying on the sidewalk. He'd bent down and had realized it was a bullet, a single live round of ammunition. Afraid of leaving it there, he'd picked it up and dropped it into his shirt pocket, and promptly forgot about it. Months later, he was out walking again, when his attention was caught by one of the city's certified crazies, a religious fanatic of a woman who was shouting at other pedestrians at the top of her lungs. She took one look at him and, gathering all her strength, hurled her Bible directly at him. Her aim was good, and the Bible would have struck him right over the heart, and no doubt killed him on the spot, had not the bullet saved his life.

The man's name was Woody Allen.

Fielder thought of that story now, a story that prompted him to take the bottle and drop it into the pocket of his old flannel shirt. The next-to-last thing he did that night, before going to bed, was toss the shirt into the bottom of his closet. The last thing he did was to pray that he was wrong. That the time would never come when he'd have to reach inside that pocket again.

HE CALLED HER first thing in the morning. He'd spent half the night trying to figure out a way to ask her the things he needed to know, without coming right out and accusing her. He spent the other half knowing there *was* no other way.

"Matthew!" She sounded glad to hear his voice.

He had no idea where to begin.

"What's the matter?" she asked.

"What's the matter," he repeated. "What's the matter is, I don't think Jonathan killed your grandparents."

"That's *good*, isn't it?"

"No," he said. "That's not good."

"Why not?"

"Because I think maybe *you* killed them."

There was the briefest pause before she said, "Me?"

"Yes," he said. "You."

Then—nothing but silence on the other end of the line. *Tell me I'm crazy,* Fielder pleaded silently. *Tell me I'm on drugs. Tell me I'm out of my fucking mind. Tell me something, anything.*

But there was only silence. And then a click.

THE DRIVE TO Nashua took him four and a half hours. He thought not having slept might be a problem, but it turned out not to be. He felt as though he was back in college, having pulled an all-nighter before a final exam, downing No-Doz with black coffee, operating on adrenaline, running on fumes. His hands cramped from gripping the steering wheel so tightly. His eyes ached from watching mile after mile of white line slide underneath him. He knew he must have stopped for gas along the way, but afterward he couldn't recall when or where that might have been.

It was a little after one by the time he pulled into Nightingale Court. The police were already there; a sheriff's department car was parked directly in front of number 14. They had a woman with them, a nervous gray-haired woman who described herself as a social worker trained in crisis intervention. They were waiting for the boy, they explained. Waiting for him to come home from school, so they could tell him there'd been a terrible car accident, and that his mother wouldn't be coming home.

"You his next of kin?" asked one of the deputies. He had a round face and couldn't have been much more than twenty, Fielder figured.

"Yes." Fielder nodded. "I guess I am."

THE LETTER WOULDN'T arrive for three full days. Mail travels slowly between places like Nashua, New Hampshire, and Big Moose, New York. But even before he opened it, Matt Fielder knew what it would say. It would say how much she loved him, and how sorry she was. It would tell him it had been no accident. It would ask him to look after Troy.

And it would set Jonathan free.

27

SUMMER

IN THE HEART of the Adirondacks, winter eventually gave way to spring once again, and spring to summer. The snows melted at last, the trees grew heavy with leaves, and the air was filled each afternoon with the rich scent of dry pine needles baking in the sun.

Troy Walker finally found the father he'd never had, and Matt Fielder the son he hadn't quite expected. And as things turned out, the cabin was plenty big for two. It didn't take Troy long to become handy splitting wood, caulking logs, and working on the new barn.

Jonathan Hamilton was taken in by Bass McClure and Bass's wife, Betsy. When asked about the arrangement, all Bass will say is, "I always did like that boy." Early most mornings, Bass and Jonathan can be spotted fishing in one of Ottawa County's many lakes or streams.

Gil Cavanaugh was reelected for yet another term as Ottawa County District Attorney, receiving 72 percent of the vote.

Arthur Summerhouse retired from the bench.

Kevin Doyle, Mitch Dinnerstein, Laura Held, and the rest of their team at the Capital Defender's Office continue to fight the good fight, and have so far kept the wolf at the door.

Flat Lake is as beautiful as ever.

*   *   *

THERE WOULD COME a day when Matt Fielder would have occasion to pull an old flannel shirt out of the bottom of his closet and put it back on, unwashed. Men who live in cabins without women tend to do things like that. No crazy religious fanatic would suddenly appear and hurl a Bible toward his heart. Instead, at some point Fielder would idly touch his hand to his chest, or reach into his pocket, or simply become aware of something in there. Then would he rediscover the bottle that he'd placed there months ago. He'd step outside with it, out into the sunlight. There he'd open it up and invert it, tapping it ever so gently, until a single blonde hair would tumble out and land on the open palm of his hand. He'd stare at it for a long moment, taking in its length, its blonde color, and its perfect, undamaged follicle.

Then a warm breeze, gusting out of the south, would lift it up, carry it off, and drop it soundlessly among the pine needles.

From the acclaimed author of *Flat Lake in Winter*
comes a gripping legal drama that's
"just like Grisham."*

FELONY MURDER

Joseph T. Klempner

A small-time lawyer in private practice, Dean Abernathy has a big case on his hands. His homeless client has confessed to killing the police commissioner, claiming it was an accident. But Dean thinks there's more to this case than anyone's admitting. And with the help of a gutsy single mom, he's about to discover that behind the notorious blue wall of police silence stands a conspiracy so menacing, that the deeper he gets into it, the more he realizes he'll be lucky to get out alive...

"A book you can't put down...A winner."
—Edwin Torres, State Supreme Court Justice and author of *Carlito's Way*

"[A] tautly woven legal drama."
—*Booklist*

*Kirkus Reviews

**AVAILABLE WHEREVER BOOKS ARE SOLD
FROM ST. MARTIN'S PAPERBACKS**

FM 2/00